SINEWS OF WAR:
THE COMPLETE ADVENTURES
OF THE MAJOR, VOLUME 4

SINEWS OF WAR
The Complete
Adventures of the

Major

VOLUME 4

BY

L. PATRICK GREENE

INTRODUCTION BY

ED HULSE

ILLUSTRATED BY

WILLIAM M. ALLISON

ALTUS
PRESS

2022

TABLE OF CONTENTS

INTRODUCTION
BY ED HULSE

THIS FOURTH Altus Press volume of L. Patrick Greene's "Major" adventures reprints eight novelettes from the 1925–26 period and finds the series having hit its stride. A number of previous installments have been excellent, but with this group of stories Greene achieves a level of quality that will be sustained, with little variance, throughout the remainder of the series. By this time the Major and his loyal servant, Jim the Hottentot, have made Doubleday's *Short Stories* their permanent home, although scattered exploits will also appear in a British periodical, *The 20-Story Magazine,* until early 1933.

At this point Greene has perfected a storytelling approach frequently attempted by other pulp writers of long-running series, but seldom carried off with the skill and consistency he brings to the Major saga. Once or twice a year he will devise an elaborate plot continuity in which a lengthy adventure unfolds over the course of six or eight novelettes. Each is complete in itself and can be enjoyed as a standalone series entry, but a narrative thread established in the first will be woven through subsequent installments. The sequence will draw to a conclusion once Greene has exhausted all the logical subplots.

"A Bloomin' Idol" (originally published in the October 1925 issue of *Short Stories*) opens this particular continuity with the Major and Jim being ambushed in a waterfront dive, fighting their way out with the help of a young, blue-eyed American giant who is mortally wounded in the fray. The dying Yankee explains that while on an expedition "up Killimanjaro way" with his ethnologist uncle John Harding and his cousin Alice, they stumbled onto a secret society of natives identifying themselves with the slogan "Africa for the Africans" and intent on driving all whites from the continent. Prior to their capture, Harding had written a full report documenting the society's existence and makeup, entrusting it to his nephew. The young man escaped with both the report and a hideous wooden idol ("big *ju-ju*," he explains) considered sacred by the society's high priest.

When the American succumbs to his wound, the Major vows to complete his mission, beginning a long trek north to the fabled "Mountains of the Moon," where the secret society—comprising natives from the Zulu, Swazi, Basuto, Mashona, and Matabele tribes, among others—is head-quartered preparatory to beginning their campaign. First he tries enlisting the aid of British authorities, but they pooh-pooh the notion of rival tribes joining forces to expel colonial occupiers. So the Major and Jim are left to rescue the Hardings and quash the rebellion themselves.

The notion of a vast native conspiracy led by a mystery man in a legendarily remote African region is, of course, pure pulp. It even predates pulp, if you take H. Rider Haggard's fanciful fiction into consideration. But this adventure of the Major, like all the others, is informed by its author's real-life experiences.

As I explained in my Introduction to the first volume of this reprint series, English-born Lewis Patrick Montague "Pat" Greene was barely 18 years old when, craving adventure, he traveled to Africa in 1909 and roamed around the southern part of the continent. When his money ran out in Rhodesia, Greene became a mounted policeman. In this capacity he had ample opportunity to educate himself in the customs and characteristics not only of the indigenous peoples but also of the European colonial administrators who much too often exploited them. He maintained particular contempt for the Portuguese, later portraying them in the Major stories as corrupt, duplicitous, and none too bright.

After several years Greene's career in public service came to an abrupt halt when he sustained a serious injury in a sunstroke-induced fall from his mount. Following several months in hospital he was declared medically unfit for further duty and returned to England with an honorable discharge. He sailed to the United States in 1913 and settled in New York City, where over the next four years he held several legitimate if unfulfilling jobs—timekeeper, stockbroker, insurance agent—before turning to fiction writing.

Greene's first published story, based in Africa and reflecting his substantial experience there, was "The Snakes of Zari," which appeared in the February 3, 1918, issue of *Adventure,* the all-fiction pulp then just entering its peak period. The magazine's editor, Arthur Sullivant Hoffman, was partial to writers with first-hand knowledge of exotic locations and peoples, and this talented newcomer filled the bill. In a brief autobiographical sketch written for *Adventure's* "Camp-Fire" department, Greene explained: "Dealing almost entirely with natives, I learned to speak their language and came to admire them. They taught me many things [about life in sub-Saharan Africa] that were good for a youngster to know."

His series about Aubrey St. John Major (occasionally called Aubrey St. John) began in *Adventure's* November 3, 1919, number with "No Evidence," a 6,500-word short story. Although the yarn's English protagonist affected a "silly ass" persona reminiscent of P.G. Wodehouse's Bertie Wooster, he shortly revealed himself as a capable adventurer whose activities as an I.D.B. (Illicit Diamond Buyer, a genus common to South Africa) placed him on the wrong side of Her Majesty's law. As the series progressed, Greene allowed the Major to evolve into a lovable rogue *a la* Leslie Charteris's The Saint—technically still a crook, but one who did the Crown a service by preying on much worse crooks and helping British authorities with the natives.

Pat Greene's tales of African intrigue bristled with authenticity, from the scrupulously accurate descriptions of real places (along with the region's flora and fauna) to the frequent use of such common native terms as *kraal* (enclosed native village or encampment), *assegai* (native spear with long iron blade), *sjambok* (whip made from rhinoceros hide), and *skoff* (Boer word meaning food). This commitment to realism, very much appreciated by avid followers of the series, naturally extended to the "Mountains of the Moon" continuity reprinted in this book.

The cycle's first sequence takes place in Mozambique's port city of Beira, which Greene describes as "a town of tin-roofed shanties, every other one a bar and every bar an infamous den of iniquity." Nestled on a channel of the Indian Ocean between Madagascar and Mozambique, Beira was established in 1890 by the territory's Portuguese colonizers. Within a fairly short period of time it supplanted Sofala as Mozambique's main port and served as headquarters for the *Companhia de Mocambique,* a trading company chartered by Portuguese royalty and initially

financed with capital obtained from multi-national finan-
ciers.

The *Companhia* showed little interest in developing
Beira beyond its role as a facilitator of commerce. Law
enforcement was perfunctory at best, with officials always
happy to look the other way when malefactors greased
their palms. Corruption ran rampant; consequently, the
port became a rendezvous for human detritus. Greene
summed it up thusly in "A Bloomin' Idol," the first install-
ment in this cycle: "At Beira congregated the moral scum
of the world; men and women who brazenly flaunted their
infamy, who knew no virtue but vice, whose vice was their
only virtue. They lived crimsonly at night and were not
shamed by the light of day."

After obtaining the little red idol, the Major and Jim
proceed slowly north, in search of the Mountains of the
Moon. Based on its evocative name, this legendary range
could easily have been an invention of H. Rider Haggard,
but Greene once again was relying on personal knowledge.
Ancient peoples curious about the source of the Nile River
thought it near the snow-capped mountains stretched
across East Africa, first encountered by a Greek merchant
named Diogenes after traveling 25 days inland from the
coastal emperion of Rhapta. He claimed that natives had
dubbed them the Mountains of the Moon based on the
luminosity of their white-topped peaks.

For centuries, Greek and Roman geographers accepted
this story. Cartographers dutifully produced maps that
placed the range in the region described by Diogenes. By
the 18th century, however, European travelers were doubting the accuracy of his claim and mounting expeditions to
pinpoint the true location. In 1889, explorer and journalist
Henry Morton Stanley—best remembered for locating

missionary David Livingstone in Central Africa—came
upon a mist-shrouded, glacier-capped range that proved
to be the source of at least some of the Nile's waters. These
mountains, spanning the Rwenzori of Uganda and the
Democratic Republic of the Congo, are currently thought
to be those discovered by the Greek merchant. The Major
and his faithful Hottentot servant Jim finally reach the
Mountains of the Moon in "Idols," which brings this
particular continuity to an end.

MENTION SHOULD be made of the relationship between the Major and Jim, which remains prob-
lematic for present-day readers of Greene's fiction. There's
no denying that the characterizations of both men draw,
to at least some extent, upon racial and ethnic stereotypes
common to the era in which these stories were written.
But there's more nuance to them than detractors generally notice. The Major frequently take a paternal attitude
toward Jim, scolding him as one would a child when the
Hottentot gets drunk (as is his wont when in a civilized
setting with too much spare time on his hands), or when
he allows superstition to get the better of him. But such
chiding is never abusive or mean-spirited.

Although unsavory Europeans often use the n-word in
referring to Jim, the Major himself never does unless he's
pretending to be as coarse as his interlocutors. And Greene
never passes up an opportunity to make clear the genuine
brotherly love that binds these two hardened adventurers.
Each saves the other from death countless times, not only
during attacks from human enemies but also during bouts
of jungle fever, encounters with savage beasts, and mishaps
occasioned by more prosaic circumstances. Their loyalty is
unquestionable and unshakable: any white man who takes
a sjambok to Jim can count on swift in-kind retribution

from the Major. And any foe who harms Jim's *baas* can expect a "reckoning"—occasionally a lethal one—at the Hottentot's hands.

It should also be remembered that Jim is the Major's *servant*, not his *slave*—a distinction Greene constantly makes clear to readers. Unlike native bearers utilized by other white adventurers as little more than pack animals, Jim is a combination of valet, cook, and guide. He takes enormous pride in contributing to the fastidious appearance of his *baas*, and the Major has great respect for the Hottentot's skills along these lines. All in all, their relationship is far more complex than might be apparent from the cursory reading of a story or two.

And now, without further ado, let's embark on a journey to the Dark Continent's Mountains of the Moon....

A BLOOMIN' IDOL

BEIRA WAS—MAYBE still is—a place of mango swamps, of black evil smelling mud when the tide was out, of flies and flying dust, of fever and all the feverish sins of Africa. It was a town of tin roofed shanties, every other one a bar and every bar an infamous den of iniquity. At Beira congregated the moral scum of the world; men and women who brazenly flaunted their infamy, who knew no virtue but vice, whose vice was their only virtue. They lived crimsonly at night and were not shamed by the light of day.

The only honest people in the town were the Portuguese officials and even some of them, having learned their jobs under the expert supervision of the officials at Lourenço Marquez, the Territory's other port, were always agreeably accommodating. The customs officials, in exchange for a little ointment to salve their itching palms, would cheerfully pass in goods without going through the formality of examining them; and no man, provided he had sufficient money, needed to fear imprisonment, no matter how great his crime. It was far easier to impose fines! Besides, it saved the government needless expense in the way of prisons and food for the prisoners. On the face of it, the government should have made money out of the criminal tendencies of Beira's population; but the officials, so great was their efficiency, dispensed with book-keeping and the fines were generally swallowed up in that eloquent item, "Out of pocket expenses."

It was a wonderful system and helped to cheapen the cost of living—and dying. Especially of dying, for a fine of fifty pounds earned a murderer his pardon; his official pardon, that is, for generally some one of the murdered man's friends had to pay a fine a few days later.

"Sink of the Indian Ocean," that was Beira; an unclean sink, presided over by slatternly scullery maids who cared not what filth cluttered it up as long as they could grab an occasional tidbit.

And if Beira was a sink, One-eyed Louis' place was the cesspool into which it drained.

Although the hour was early, his dive this afternoon was crowded with men and women from the four quarters of the globe. The clamor of their voices made of the place a modern Babel. All languages were spoken, but only one god was worshipped—and that, Mammon; only one creed was followed—and that, vice. Every shade of color was represented, from pure white to darkest ebony; from the yellow of China to the red of a self-styled North American Indian. And, seated in a sunless corner, laughing softly, drinking Beira's morning pick-me-up—a little soda and a lot of absinthe—was a woman in whose veins flowed the mixed blood of white, yellow and black.

She was almost beautiful—evil often is—in an exotic, bizarre way, yet men avoided her, seemed to be blind to the insolently provocative invitation of her eyes. One-eyed Louis had his own peculiar way of remonstrating with men who ventured to make eyes at his woman!

And One-eyed Louis, the proprietor of Beira's cesspool, was seated on a dais just behind the piano. From there he

could see all that was going on; there was very little that missed his shifty black eye. He was a heavy set, oily skinned brute of doubtful ancestry. His long, black hair, parted in the middle, was slicked down with some strongly perfumed grease. His black velveteen trousers were supported at the waist by a flaming red cummerbund. His left eye was covered by a red shade.

A volley of shots suddenly sounded, muffled slightly by distance and the thick walls of the room. More shots followed, nearer, accompanied by fierce yells.

One-eyed Louis stroked the back of his neck with long, white fingers, letting them rest finally on the haft of a knife which he carried in a sheath between his shoulder blades. But except for this and the fact that the consumptive-looking individual, who was drumming a barbaric dance tune on the battered piano, struck a wrong note, causing the dancers to curse him vilely, the habitués of the place appeared deaf to the sounds outside. Shots meant nothing to them; they were better able to appreciate the thrust of a knife in the dark.

More shots, the sound of running feet outside and then, after a signal had been rapped—*toc, toc-toc, toc*—the door opened and two men entered.

Louis looked at them inquiringly, scowled as they shook their heads in negation and then drummed impatiently on the table top with his long, sinewy fingers.

The two men made their way to a vacant table, greeting acquaintances, muttering insults to enemies, and, sitting down, called loudly for absinthe. Two scantily attired girls joined them; the man at the piano played with increased vigor, the dancers exhibited wilder abandon and then stopped to applaud the bestial exhibition of a drunken little Cockney fireman and his half-caste partner.

Again the signal knock at the door and a man entered. He was very fat and looked ludicrous in the ornate uniform of the local police. He carried a tiny sword in his right hand; in his left, a smoking revolver.

As he stood there, peering about the dim, smoke filled room, the sunlight streamed past him, seeming to stir up the filth of the place as clear water does when poured into a stagnant pool.

One-eyed Louis stood up and bowed courteously. "To what do I owe the pleasure of this visit, senhor," he asked in his suave, oily voice. There was a slight impediment in his speech. Men who did not know him were inclined to laugh—once. Afterward they knew him too well to mistake the lisp for softness. "You are looking for someone, yes? A most dangerous criminal, undoubtedly, for you to enter my humble place so heavily armed."

"*Si, Senhor* Louis," the policeman answered. "I look for two most dangerous men. I thought they came this way. You have not seen them?"

Louis shrugged his shoulders and spread his hands in a gesture of denial.

"Ah, no, senhor. None but ladies and gentlemen of surpassing honor come to my poor place. Honest workers, all of them. As you see, some of them even now are leaving me to go to their places of business."

As he spoke a number of men and women, not too sure of their standing with Louis, and, therefore, doubtful of the protection he would give them, sidled covertly past the policeman, gained the open street and hastened swiftly away.

"Honest workers, all of them," Louis repeated sharply as the policeman barred the way to a vicious looking half caste.

"Truly, senhor," the policeman said abjectly and hastily stood on one side to let the woman pass. "It was only that I thought I recognized an old friend."

"And you were mistaken?"

"Si, senhor."

"Then come inside and shut the door before the cursed sunlight makes this room as hot as hell outside."

The policeman stepped outside, looked up and down the street, fired his revolver into the air, then, entering the room, slammed the door behind him.

"What cursed fools you police are," Louis said vindictively, "as if by such showing you would persuade people you are honest."

"But we are honest, senhor," the policeman said, grinning. He sheathed his sword, returned his revolver to its holster and then joined the two men who had first entered. He sat with his back to Louis, facing the woman.

"Por Dios!" one of the men swore. "Louis is right. You are a fool Luigi. Are you tired of life that you make eyes at the 'Yellow Rose'?"

"Did he see?" the policeman asked in alarmed tones and hurriedly changed his seat, glancing covertly toward Louis.

The woman laughed—a shrill, but not unmusical laugh.

"What does he not see?" the other asked sententiously. "Besides, even if he were totally blind, Luigi, that woman is not for a fool like you."

"You will call me fool once too often, Carlos," the policeman said threateningly.

"Bah! Then I, Miguel, will also call you a fool," the second of the two men said roughly. "We planned things well, Carlos and I, and then you must need interfere. Why did you, fool?" Miguel twisted the waxed ends of his mustache fiercely upward.

"Then you got nothing?" the policeman asked anxiously.

"Nothing! You came too soon."

"If I had waited longer it might have been too late—for you," the policeman said suggestively. "He was very strong."

"Bah! There was no danger. We were two to his one. Besides, why waste breath? You are a fool. Because of you we failed. Louis will not be pleased with you when he hears why we failed."

The policeman sighed with relief. "Then you have not told him yet?"

"No. But—"

"Then you must not tell him. There will be no need. Listen. All is not lost; I have arranged so that things will be easier. He is coming here."

"Here!"

Miguel and Carlos exchanged triumphant glances.

"Si, here. I told him, before I gave chase to you, that you were sure to come to this place. He said that as soon as he had gathered together his possessions which you had scattered all over the room, he would come here: he was anxious, he said, to discover why you took such an interest in him."

"He will learn," Miguel said softly and rising, crossed over to where Louis was sitting, whispered in his ears, nodded understanding of that man's low toned orders and returned to his seat. He scowled fiercely at Luigi who was making ardent love to one of the girls.

Becoming conscious of the other's threatening glances, the policeman pushed the girl away from him and beckoned to another who was sitting alone at a nearby table. She swiftly joined him and presently the six of them were drinking with an outward show of comradeship.

"For the matter of that," the policeman said suddenly, "I, too, would like to know why we are to take such an interest in this man. He has no money; I am sure of that."

Carlos nodded thoughtfully. "It is the only thing I have against Louis," he said irritably. "We, too, would like to know why we should take such pains with this man. He has a little wooden image Louis wants. But why? If Louis were not so secretive—"

"Ah!" the policeman breathed softly. "Maybe it is an idol stolen from some witch doctor up country. I have heard of idols with diamonds of the finest water for eyes. Maybe— *Por Dios!* I will ask Louis about it. It's not just that we should not know more. Working in the dark, how do we know that he shares fairly with us? Yes. I, myself, will ask the one-eyed—"

"And what will you ask me?"

Luigi looked up with a start into the sneering face of Louis who had come up quietly and stood there, scratching the back of his neck. "Nothing, senhor," the policeman stammered, his eyes fixed apprehensively on Louis' hand— the one that was so near to the haft of the knife.

"Then what is it that troubles you?"

"Nothing, senhor. Nothing, except—" he looked to the others for support but they studiously avoided his gaze—"nothing except that we wish that you would trust us more fully."

Louis laughed sardonically. "And does this fat pig speak for you others? You, Carlos? And you, Miguel?"

"No, Senhor Louis," Miguel growled and fiercely eyed the policeman. "It is the fool's own wind. We are in no way interested in his bellyaching."

"I think you lie, Miguel," Louis said softly. "I think there are a lot of things you would like to know. But no matter. So you wish that I would trust you more, eh, Luigi? I trusted a man once and, in consequence, pigs like you are enabled to call me 'One-eyed Louis.' That was a big price to pay—an eye for a trust. But I learned my lesson. I do not trust anyone now; I do not wish to lose my other eye."

The policeman made a gesture of deprecation. "But, senhor," he expostulated, "we are your friends, we trust you fully, we risk our lives in your service. It is only fair, then, that we should know what that service is."

Louis laughed loudly at that. "You trust me," he said, sobering quickly, "because you do not dare *not* to trust me! You obey my orders because now I am *up*. But, if tomorrow I was *down* you would be among the first to thrust a red-hot iron into my other eye."

The others murmured sycophantic denials.

"Yes you would," Louis insisted, silencing them with an imperious wave of his hand. "And because I know that, I drive you hard while I am *up*;—and I do not trust you because I wish to postpone the day that will see me *down*.

"However, for this once I will take you into my confidence; I will tell you why I have such great interest in this man and the thing he carries." He sneered at them as they leaned forward, their eyes gleaming with cupidity. "You will 'get' this man and the thing he carries because I order it. I order it because—*por Dios*—because I, too, obey orders. See?"

He snapped his fingers—*thut, thut-thut, thut*—and then returned with soft, catlike tread to his seat on the dais.

The men at the table were silent, moodily draining their glasses, oblivious to the inane chatter of the girls. "*Sangre del Christo!*" the policeman cursed softly. "I'm afraid sometimes of this unknown one whom Louis serves, and sometimes I think he is only a creation of Louis' brain. And that makes me more afraid of Louis."

"And well it should," Miguel said. "But this unknown one is no figment of Louis' imagination. I have told you— no?—of how the making of that signal of his—*thut, thut-thut, thut*—saved me from being tortured by a lot of niggers. I was up-country at the time, and—"

"Yes. We've heard all that to the point of weariness," the policeman interrupted testily. "And we all know that Louis has never been outside of Beira, hardly outside of this dive of his, and knows nothing of niggers—is actually afraid of them. All that may mean much or nothing. But when Louis tells me that he goes to all this trouble, or that the unknown one goes to all this trouble, for a worthless, carved idol, why then I say 'Pardon, Senhor Louis, but I do not believe you. No.'"

"But you will not tell him that," Miguel sneered. "You are very brave and talk loudly when there is no one to hear. Yet I might be tempted to tell Louis—"

He was interrupted by a loud rapping at the door.

"It is the man," the policeman said in a tense voice. "He must not see me drinking with you; that would arouse his suspicions and then perhaps he would not enter."

"He'll enter, never doubt that," Carlos growled as he and Miguel rose and made their way to the door.

There they took their stand, one on either side, their knives drawn, ready to pounce on the man as soon as he crossed the threshold.

Louis tilted back his chair, his hands clasped behind his head. He seemed to be completely relaxed but his one eye glistened balefully as he focused it fixedly on the doorway. Presently the fingers of his right hand sought and gripped hard the haft of his knife.

"Play on," he commanded harshly as the man at the piano rose hurriedly with the intention of joining the dancers who had huddled together against the wall.

"Play on," Louis repeated, "and you others dance."

Reluctantly the pianist returned to the instrument; his hands shook as he played. The time was ragged. The couples took the floor again, but there was no fire in their dancing now and they carefully avoided the deadline which their imagination drew between the chair on which Louis sat, and the door.

The knocking sounded again; a bashful, hesitating sound as if the knocker lacked confidence.

"Go and sit with Rose," Louis ordered the policeman and bared his teeth in a sardonic grin as Luigi obeyed a thought too eagerly.

"Come in!" he shouted, just as the knocking recommenced.

There was a pause; the door knob rattled, turned slowly. The two men, Carlos and Miguel, crouched low; Louis let his chair come down level and leaned forward slightly, his left hand on his knee, the muscles of his right arm quivering with the tension of his grip on the knife; the policeman and the girl looked toward the door, the girl's lips slightly parted in an expression of cruel anticipation.

The door swung slowly open.

The music stopped with a discordant crash. The pianist and the dancers huddled up against the wall again, ignoring Louis' scowls.

Carlos and Miguel sprang up, their knives flashing in the sunlight which streamed in through the open door—

Then they let their hands fall harmlessly to their sides and turned sheepishly away, muttering obscene phrases, and sat down in sulky silence, glancing apprehensively at Louis.

But Louis did not see them. He was looking at the newcomer who stood there, an expression of hurt surprise on his round, smooth shaven face.

Gradually Louis relaxed; a glint of malicious mirth appeared in his eye. He had set the stage for a tragedy, but the curtain had gone up on a comedy. The tenseness passed and with it Louis' wrathful irritation at plans gone awry.

The one-eyed man laughed uproariously and his laugh was echoed by everyone in the place. It was unkind, mocking laughter. Louis' people had long since lost the art of whole hearted laughter; they laughed with their lips but their eyes were always clouded with the gloom of evil.

"Oh, I say," stammered the man in the doorway, and he polished his monocle with a flimsy white handkerchief. "I hope I don't intrude."

He carefully fixed the monocle in his eye and stared owlishly into the room, peering to the right and left, endeavoring to pierce the thick, smoky haze on either side of the shaft of sunlight which streamed through the open doorway. He finally riveted his attention on Louis whose chair was just beyond the beam of light.

"I don't understand this, really," he continued, drawling the words, making them sound like the dudish inanities of a stage door Johnny. "First murder and sudden death and what not threaten me, and then I am greeted with a lot of silly ass parrotlike cackling. And I don't like it; 'pon my soul I don't. I would have you know that Aubrey St. John—it's pronounced Sinjun, you know, but I spell it S, t period, capital J-o-h-n. Funny, isn't it? But, as I was saying, I am not accustomed to being laughed at—don't *like* it! It makes one feel like a bally ass, what?" He shook a forefinger admonishingly at Louis and the white cambric handkerchief he held in his hand fluttered flirtatiously.

No one answered him. Louis and the others were still laughing derisively. But the woman, Yellow Rose, was looking at him with a shrewd, calculating glance; she could see, or thought she could see, a little beyond the vacuous mask of the stranger's face and vaguely realized that he was not exactly what he appeared.

"I think," he said now, and his air of offended dignity was very mirth provoking; it was as if a drawing room elegant slapped a prize fighter on the wrist and threatened to spoil the shine of his shoes. "I think I will go now. Your manners are bally frightful, not to be tolerated. I mean, you are not gentlemen. I'm sorry. I had important business with a gentleman named—er—One-eyed—queer name, very!—Louis. But—er—under the circumstances my business must wait. And that's very annoying—oh, very. I wanted to get away from this beastly town at once, back to Lourenço Marquez. However, good day to you."

He doffed his white pith helmet, disclosing a well-shaped head; his black hair—it was streaked with gray at the temples, thus giving the lie to his youthful face—was brushed back smoothly in an immaculate pompadour. His forehead was broad, his ears small and set close to his head. His blue eyes, wide spaced, seemed to hold the innocent wonder of a child's.

He took a backward step, almost treading on the bare feet of a squat, ugly Hottentot who was standing close behind him and who now cursed his master's clumsiness in a weird mixture of English, Portuguese and his own tongue, causing the laughter to break out anew.

Overcome with embarrassment, Aubrey St. John called "Good day" again and was about to move away; but when Louis left his chair and walked toward the door St. John returned to the doorway and stood there. Some few of the men in the room then idly noted that the monocled stranger was taller and wider than they had first credited; he was at least six feet, they judged now. The pianist—he had been a doctor with an office in Hawley Street, once— muttered that no man with a square jaw like that could be altogether a fool, and was ready to gamble that there wasn't an ounce of superfluous flesh on him. But no one listened to Doc; he got these silly spells at times. Besides, they had the evidence of their eyes, and they wanted to hear what Louis was saying.

"You pardon, Senhor St. John," Louis' voice was very humble. "Please enter and accept my assurances that you are not the cause of our laughter. The policeman there is such a droll fellow. You will come in—yes?—assured that my place is so very respectable. Does not the policeman make it so?"

The stranger, the Hottentot hard at his heels, advanced hesitatingly into the room, shaking his head doubtfully, looking about him in a manner which indicated that he had not forgotten the men with drawn knives who had greeted his first appearance.

"I will sit here," he said somewhat sulkily and pulled a chair from a nearby table, placing it near the door facing the dais on which Louis had been sitting.

"Sit where you please, senhor," Louis assured him, sneering slightly as the immaculate one dusted the chair seat with his pocket handkerchief and then sat down gingerly, adjusting his close fitting, white duck tunic, pulling his trousers up slightly so that their knife-edge crease would not be spoiled.

"And what will the senhor drink?" Louis asked softly, pulling up a table to a spot several feet away from the other's chair, away from the door. "Absinthe?"

"My word, no," the other said hastily. "I have heard of that beastly stuff. I will have a plain B. and S.—a brandy and soda, you know."

Louis nodded. "I myself will get it for the senhor. But first let me assure you that the reason I delayed so long in speaking to the senhor as he stood there in the doorway was partly because of the mirth caused by that so droll policeman and partly because the Senhor St. John's English is hard to understand and—"

"My English is absobloomin' top hole, dear sir," the other exclaimed indignantly.

Louis assumed a humbly apologetic expression. "Truly, senhor. But I, who was taught my English by scum like that—" he pointed to the Cockney fireman who was convulsing those about him with laughter by a clumsy burlesque of St. John's appearance and speech, using a silver coin for a monocle— "could not be expected to understand the English of the nobility."

The white clad one beamed and waved his hand in a condescending gesture of understanding.

Louis took a deep breath. "Now I will go and get the drinks—on me, of course. What will your nigger drink?"

"My nigger—oh, is that bally bounder in here?" He turned and glared up into the impassive countenance of the Hottentot.

"Get out," he exclaimed angrily. *"Hamba! Vootsac!* Go!"

"It's quite all right that he stays, senhor," Louis put in hastily. "We are all good Christians here. As you see," he smirked, "color means nothing to us. Your Hottentot will not contaminate us."

"That's beastly kind of you, old egg," the other's drawl was provocatively contemptuous now, "but I wasn't thinking of that, really. I was afraid, don't you know, that these good souls might—er—contaminate the Hottentot." He smiled sweetly at Louis, then again ordered the Hottentot to "Get out!"

Grumbling loudly, cursing his master for a white livered son of a hen, the Hottentot slowly obeyed, slamming the door violently behind him.

Louis looked after him thoughtfully, then at this dude of a white man wondering whether the smile which hovered about his lips was one of mockery or nervousness. Finally deciding that it was the latter, Louis shrugged his shoulders and going to the little bar loudly ordered a brandy and soda for the English milord, adding another order in quiet sibilant Portuguese.

At the same moment the pianist returned to his instrument and after a few tentative, mellow sounding chords, played a languorous waltz and the dancers took the floor again, the stranger forgotten.

When Louis returned a few minutes later, balancing a tray loaded with glasses, a bottle of brandy and a siphon of soda, the man who called himself Aubrey St. John was leaning back in his chair, a beatific expression on his face, beating time with a large hunting knife; he was holding it by the blade; occasionally he marked the time by gently beating on the table with the pearl inlaid handle.

Louis scowled when he saw that instead of pulling his chair up to the table, the dude had pulled the table back to the chair which he had moved so that it was close against the wall, close to the door. Sitting there he would be the first to see whoever opened it.

But the monocled one was quite undisturbed by Louis' scowls. It is doubtful if he saw them and yet, when Louis took a glass from the tray and placed it on the table in front of him, St. John let the knife drop from his hand with a quick flip of his wrist. It turned over in the air and stuck quivering in the table, between Louis' outspread fingers.

"*Sangre del Christo!*" Louis swore and looked keenly at the other, then down at the knife and his long, talonlike fingers.

His eyes half closed, softly humming the tune of the dance in a pleasing baritone. St. John groped for his knife, touched Louis' fingers then looked up with a start.

"My word!" he stammered, full of contrition. "I didn't know you were there, old bean. A thousand pardons." Then he looked down at the table and looked with incredulity at the knife between Louis' outspread fingers. "My word!" he exclaimed again. "I might have stuck you. What a bally fool I am. The old chappies are right, what? Children and fools shouldn't play with edged tools. 'Pon my word, no."

He pulled his knife from the table and returned it to its sheath; but where that sheath was, Louis couldn't say;

the other's movements had been too rapid. "I'm deucedly sorry," the monocled one said again and beamed happily into Louis' face.

"It is nothing," Louis said roughly. "I will drink with you if it is permitted. But let us go to the table where the policeman sits. One can see the dancing better there and the girl—" He put his fingers to his lips and kissed them noisily.

"No, thanks, dear lad," the other drawled wearily. "I'm quite comfortable here. With my back against the wall I fear no foe in shining armor clad, if you know what I mean. I'm free from all those cold, steely draughts which cut down a man in his prime, as it were. And, judging from the passionate glances the lady and the policeman are exchanging, it must be frightfully hot at their table!"

Louis cursed under his breath as he glanced in the direction of the table in time to see the flirtatious Rose offer her lips to the overeager policeman. His hand went to the back of his neck, flashed out again. A knife spun across the room, grazed Luigi's cheek and fell with a clatter onto the floor.

The policeman ducked beneath the table. A moment later he peered over the edge with unmistakable fear in his bulging eyes.

Rose picked up the knife and sauntering over to Louis handed it back to him. "It was a poor aim, verry, Louis," she said in a queer lilting voice of mockery.

He returned the knife to its sheath. "I did not try to stick him," he said defensively. "If I had—" he shrugged his shoulders. "You know that I never miss." To the policeman he snarled, "You would be wise to seek some way to make me forget this, Luigi."

The policeman rose, brushed the dust off his flamboyant uniform with pudgy trembling hands and rejoined Carlos and Miguel.

"May I sit wiv you?" the girl looked appealingly at St. John.

He rose, greatly confused, bowed and murmuring, "Charmed, I'm sure," drew up a chair for her and held it while she seated herself. Then he resumed his seat and looked expectantly at Louis who, after a moment's hesitation sat down and poured out a drink.

"I will drink, too, Louis," the girl said. "Go and mix me a veree special one. And you—surely you will not drink this so awful brandy?"

"That is true," Louis said with a show of confusion. "I had forgotten my drink." He rose and went to the bar.

The girl stared hard at the monocled one; there was a hint of madness in the dancing lights of her almond-shaped eyes.

"I like you Mister S-t period, capital J-o-h-n." She spelled out the name mincingly.

"Honored; 'pon my soul, yes." He lifted the glass to his lips. "I drink your health, dear lady." But he had no intention of tasting the beverage; the work of One-eyed Louis was far too crude and apparent.

The woman, eyes alight with interest in him, had no desire to see him dead, either. She suddenly jammed the table forcibly against him, causing him to spill the contents of the glass into the crown of his upturned helmet which he held between his knees. Not a drop of it was spilled on the ground, and that was not altogether due to her maneuver. His hand was very steady.

"Oh my word!" he exclaimed, looking at her reproachfully. "My helmet's ruined."

She shrugged her shoulders. "You should thank me. Have you no kind words to say to me?"

"You are very beautiful," he stammered earnestly. Evidently he was not at ease with women.

She leaned across the table. "Then you would like to kiss me—no?" She pursed her lips.

"Pardon, no!" he said hastily. "The Senhor Louis' knife is keener than the—er—love light in a woman's eye, if you know what I mean."

"Bah! You are so veree careful of your pink and white skin. You are afraid?"

"Of you—yes dear lady. Oh, absolutely—"

Rose shrugged her shoulders scornfully; the yellow-ivory pallor of her face flushed a strange mottled crimson. "You need not be afraid of me, senhor," she said slowly. "I am your friend. You have treated me veree courteously. You made me forget for a little while that I am only the 'Yellow Rose,' the woman of One-eyed Louis."

She rose as Louis came toward them and taking the drink he had mixed her, threw its contents into the monocled one's face; but her aim was poor and the greater part of it slopped into his helmet.

"Blood of Christ! What fool's play is this, Rose?" Louis asked harshly.

"My hat!" the man St. John spluttered, mopping his face with his handkerchief. "My helmet's ruined!" He examined it mournfully, emptying the liquid it contained onto the floor.

"I do not like the senhor," she said coldly, and returning to her table made eyes at the policeman again, sticking out her tongue at him when he remained blind to her blandishments. He had been warned once; that was enough for him!

Louis laughed softly and sat down opposite St. John. "You must forgive Rose," he said. "I suppose she made love to you, and when you did not respond—zipp! She is a hell-cat; sometimes even I am afraid of her. Already I have killed two men because of her and sometime I am very much afraid I shall have to kill Rose. *Si!*—if she doesn't first kill me."

The other shuddered.

"But you were thirsty, senhor! You have already drunk. Permit me to fill your glass again."

"No, thanks, old top. One is sufficient for me in the morning. Two, before noon, would make me talk too much; and nothin's quite so boring as a talkative drunk. What?"

"You lie cleverly, senhor," Louis said coldly; and holding up his hand to silence the other's heated protestations, continued, "You have not had a drink. I saw Rose make you spill it. She told you it was poisoned, eh? The mirror over the bar—she had forgotten that. It was clever of you to spill it into your helmet. I should have suspected if I had seen liquor spilled on the floor. And it was clever of Rose to throw her drink into your helmet; I shall speak to Rose when we are alone—" there was an ugly threat in his quiet voice—"and so give you a chance to empty it onto the ground. Clever, but unnecessarily elaborate. I think I should have suspected something, even if I had not seen."

The other moved restlessly, fingered the collar of his tunic as if it were choking him. "However," continued Louis, "I have learned one thing: You are not such a fool as you look!"

"My word!" blustered the other. "You're most frightfully rude, you know. Let me tell you that I am no fool, neither do I look like one."

Louis smiled. "Suppose we put our cards on the table, senhor," he suggested softly. "You know who I am and *what* I am. How about you?"

"Cards? My calling card, you mean? Oh, I see. I've already told you my name, dear Senhor Louis. My business? What business could a chappy have in a place like this? I—er—pause for a reply."

"And I still wait to hear more about you, senhor. I want to know why you pretend to be a bigger fool than you are; you said you had business with me. Very well, I want to know what that business is; I want to know if that play you made with your knife a little while ago was accident or design; and," he eyed the other keenly, "I'd like to know where you keep your knife!"

"That's rather a lot you want to know, isn't it, old dear? And I'm not quite sure that you ought to have your curiosity satisfied. However, I'll be frank with you, most frank. First of all, then, though my name is really Aubrey St. John, most people call me 'the Major.'" He paused, smiled engagingly at Louis as if expecting that man to make some comment.

But Louis' face was blank. The name meant nothing to him; it only stirred some vague memory away back in his subconsciousness. He had certainly heard something about a man called "the Major" but not enough to register strongly on his brain; the information was crammed away in a brain cell, overwhelmed by fairy tales and the legends of youth. Louis was too self-centered, too concerned in his own affairs, too wrapped up in his crooked life at Beira, to be affected by the doings of men who operated outside his territory. True, occasionally rumors reached him, but they made no stronger impression on him than the outer ripples of circles, made by throwing a stone into a large pool, make upon the shore. And that was a pity for Louis; it weakened his organization, lessened his efficiency as a worker of evil, and caused him sometimes to underestimate the strength of the men who came to his place.

The police of the Orange Free State, of the Transvaal, of Natal, could have told Louis a great deal about this man who called himself the Major. They could have told him that the Major was the cleverest illicit diamond buyer in the country; that he was suspected of a thousand and one things but convicted of none; that his pose of vacuous inanity concealed a swift, eager brain, just as his dandified clothes and slouching posture concealed a powerful body. They could have told him that the Major was an expert horseman, a dead shot—and one of the finest fellows living.

The criminals who swarmed about the diamond fields at Kimberley, and the gold fields at Jo'burg, could have warned Louis that the Major's hand was against all evil; that he seemed to know everything—or what he didn't know, his Hottentot, Jim, did; that anyone who tried to double-cross him was asking for trouble; and that he was a "good sort."

Natives, of all tribes, living in *kraals* which ranged all the way from the Zambezi to the Cape, from Walfisch Bay to Mozambique, could, had they been so minded, have told Louis of the uprightness of this man with the monocle, of his hunting craft, of the stern, understanding justness of his dealings with them.

But Louis knew nothing of this. He correctly judged this man Aubrey St. John to be other than he pretended. Very well! He now knew the man was called "the Major" and the Major was—what? A clever confidence man, a three card monte sharp, most likely. He had the appearance of one; he could probably fool the greenhorns just arrived in the country, but not Louis.

And so the one-eyed man gave no thought to the vague memories which were stirring in his brain and waited for the Major's next move, ready to enter into any villainy that man might suggest provided it promised well for Louis.

"I said that most people called me 'the Major,'" the monocled one said again.

"*Si!* I heard you Senhor Major. What of it?"

The Major looked nonplussed. "What of it?" he repeated indignantly. Then, "Oh!" he said, his jaw muscles sagging.

He took his monocle from his eye and polished it absently. "Well, to continue," he said presently, "to answer all the things you want to know: I have just arrived from Lourenço Marquez. My business there was to deliver a packet of stones to a charming young lady, Miss Lola de Sousa."

Louis started slightly.

"You know the lady?" The Major peered shortsightedly at him.

"Si! Who doesn't know the lady? You fool to deal with her; you should have come to me. I would have given you a better price."

The Major nodded thoughtfully. "But you see," he explained, "it wasn't a matter of buying and selling. Miss Lola gave me the stones at Kimberly—in trust, don't you know?—and I was honor bound to return them to her. True, I was tempted once or twice to clear off with them but," and he shrugged his shoulders, "I'm afraid that would have been very dangerous. Still, I think she might have given me something for my trouble, don't you?"

Louis smiled sardonically. He knew Lola; knew that she had a way of getting men to work for her, of risking great danger, their freedom, their lives, for her; promising them much, giving them nothing.

"But she didn't," the Major continued plaintively, "and so, finding myself penniless, I worked my yaw up here, en route, as it were, for Rhodesia. I hear there are easy pickings up there."

"You do not look penniless," Louis growled.

"Oh," the Major waved his hand airily, "I still have my toilet articles and my—er—nigger is a most clever valet. His name is Jim, you know, and he's quite priceless. You don't know Jim, do you?"

Louis didn't. The police, the crooks, the natives could have told him that the Hottentot was as clever as his *baas* to whom he was devoted.

Louis moved impatiently; he was beginning to feel that he had wasted his time. He looked around the room. The piano player was sitting drowsily on the stool, his hands drooping listlessly on the keys. Most of the men who had been dancing had departed by a rear door; others, with their women, were seated at tables ranged against the walls. Their eyes were heavy with sleep. It was the hour of the midday siesta.

Louis' eye glinted malevolently when he saw that the policeman—his fears for the moment forgotten—had returned to Rose's table and was now resting his head on Rose's shoulder, murmuring endearments into her tiny ears.

Louis swore softly under his breath when Rose, suddenly meeting his eye, made a contemptuous *moué* at him.

He pushed back his chair, preparatory to rising. He was anxious to have a "talk" with Rose—and the fat fool of a policeman!

"And being penniless," he growled to the Major, "it is supposed that you came here thinking that I would stake you? If that was your thought, Senhor Major, you are a bigger fool than you look."

"No," the Major shook his head. "You are quite wrong." He screwed his monocle into his eye and beamed at Louis. It was a disarming smile, bland, innocent. He looked at that moment like a good humored slightly obese priest. "No," he said again, and he drawled the word exaggeratedly. "I really came to ask you why you are so bally interested in a little wooden image thingymagum!"

Louis sprang to his feet, his eye blazing fiercely. His hand went to the back of his neck then dropped empty to his side.

"That's very wise of you," the Major said gently. "Children and fools, you know—but I've already said that. No? And this little friend of mine," he tapped the revolver he had so swiftly drawn from a holster slung under his armpit, "is much more dangerous than a knife.

"And that reminds me. You wanted to know where I kept my little slicer of meat. There!" His left hand moved quickly, fluttered about his tunic, was empty—then suddenly held a knife.

"*Sangre del Christo!*" Louis swore viciously.

"Truly!" said the Major mockingly. "But you will agree—yes?—to keep your filthy paws away from your neck?"

Louis growled. "There is no need for us to quarrel," he said. "This show of arms on your part is foolish. I mean no harm toward you. If I did, you would not be alive now.

"That's better," he added when the Major's knife and revolver had disappeared. "Now we can talk. Why are you interested in the idol?" He snapped his fingers.

"Tut, tut, tut!" exclaimed the Major irritably.

"You said, senhor?" Louis leaned forward, his attitude one of extreme tenseness.

"I said 'Tut, tut!' I mean that I don't like your fingers snapping in my face."

"Bah!" Louis relaxed. "But about the idol, senhor? Why are you interested?"

"I'm not, old lad. Simply curious. I saw two of your cutthroats overhaul a chappy a little while ago; went through his pockets, if you know what I mean. And then that police chappy over there interfered and the cutthroats departed. I followed them an' heard them talk about a bloomin' idol, an' they were worried because they thought you'd be angry because they hadn't got it. That's all."

"But that doesn't explain why you came here?"

"Oh, as to that." The Major waved his hand airily. "I came to see how badly you wanted the bloomin' idol; to inquire how much you would pay for it."

"Then you have it, senhor?" Louis whispered. "You have it with you?"

The Major smiled cryptically. "I think," he said absently, "that the Senhor Louis wants the idol very badly. How much will you give me, Senhor Louis?"

Louis tossed a handful of greasy notes onto the table.

The Major shook his head. "That's not enough I'm afraid."

"Fool!" Louis snapped. "Count the money before you talk like that."

"But the notes are so dirty," the Major expostulated. "Besides, I want to know why you want the idol."

"The senhor would be wise not to poke his nose into things which don't concern him. He would be wise to give me the idol and depart quickly from Beira. Aside from all other considerations, I am not likely to forget that you have made a fool of me. The streets of Beira are very dark, the police are deaf, dumb and blind when I order it, and there are many knives at my service. So give me the idol, take the money and go." Louis held out an eager hand.

The Major laughed. "But you don't think I'd carry the bally thing around with me, surely? Now if you will come with me—"

A loud knock sounded at the door.

The two men Carlos and Miguel again took their stand against the door.

"I hope there will be no—er—killing," the Major said with a meaning gesture.

Louis shrugged his shoulders, hesitated and then ordered the two men away.

They looked at him in surprise. "If it is the man you want," Miguel expostulated, "he is very strong."

"I do not want him," Louis said flatly. "Get out of here." He winked.

They grinned understanding, sheathed their knives and departed, Carlos stopping to whisper to Luigi, the policeman.

The knocking sounded again.

"Come in!" Louis shouted irritably.

The door opened and Jim, the Hottentot, stood swaying drunkenly on the threshold.

He stumbled into the room and close behind him staggered a white man of gigantic proportions. This white man was quite young, little over twenty. His face was covered with freckles, his nose upturned, his eyes a light blue. Undoubtedly he loved fighting for fighting's sake. Not a bully, but a man who loved to compete with great odds.

He and the Hottentot sat down at a table and called loudly for drinks, pounding noisily on the table with clenched fists.

"You should have kept your nigger here," Louis said with a sneer. "He got drunk elsewhere and has made friends with the man you robbed. But perhaps they were already friends; perhaps you are a liar, senhor?"

The Major sighed. "That's Jim's great failing, senhor," he murmured. "He is so bally fond of liquor. I'm afraid it will get him into trouble some day. He—my word! How rude!"

The big man, waving his arms wildly in the air, had almost upset the barmaid who was bringing the drinks he had ordered, sending bottles and glasses crashing to the floor.

He began to sob, bemoaning the spilled liquor.

"I ain't got no friends," he wailed. "First some sneak thieves pinch my god and now the booze is spilled."

Louis sucked in his breath hissingly. Then the monocled one had the idol after all! "I will mix him a drink that will keep him quiet," Louis said. "I will return presently, senhor. Wait for me and we will further discuss this matter."

He rose and stuffing the notes back into his pocket retired to the little room behind the bar where, at his imperious call, Rose presently joined him.

When they returned together almost immediately, the Major looked keenly at the girl. Her eyes were clouded with tears and her face was contorted as if with pain. She gently massaged her throat with her left hand. The wide sleeve of her crimson robe fell back almost to the shoulder and her delicately moulded arm was badly bruised.

The Major whistled softly.

Louis put the drinks he was carrying on the table before the big man and the Hottentot, then returned to the Major, leaving the girl standing by the newcomers.

"The drink and Rose'll keep 'em quiet," Louis said complacently.

But the Major seemed not to hear him, he was watching the group at the other table. Presently the girl sat down on the big man's knees, laughing at his attempt to push her away.

Luigi, the policeman, was also watching, his fat face contorted by a vicious scowl. "Pig!" he screamed as, with a violent shove, the big man sent Rose staggering away from him. "Pig! You shall answer to me for that." He rushed at the big man, thrust viciously at him with his tiny sword.

The big man, strangely sober now, his hand protected by his cloth cap, caught hold of the sword and with a quick twist wrenched it away from Luigi. Then, picking up the little tub of a man, he placed him across his knees and holding him there, kicking, cursing, squirming, spanked him with the flat of the sword.

Instantly the room was in an uproar; men and women crowded around the pair, some of them laughing at the policeman's predicament, others evidently resenting this treatment of one of their number.

The Major and Louis sprang to their feet. "That's enough!" the Major shouted curtly. "Jim! Big fellow! Come along!"

The big man rose, the policeman still in his arms, and made his way slowly toward the door. Jim, walking backward, his eyes sparkling in joyous anticipation of a fight, guarded his back.

"So you were tricking me after all, senhor," Louis murmured. "You know this big man, after all. And he is

not drunk now who, a little while ago, was very drunk."
Aloud he shouted, "Get the fellow!" and dropped quickly
behind an upturned table.

The men who owed their miserable existence to Louis
hesitated a moment and then rushed to the attack.

The big man, turning, flung the policeman at the front
rank of them, knocking them down like ninepins.

The others came on menacingly.

"Hands up!" the Major commanded and swept the room
with his revolver.

A forest of hands shot into the air.

"That's beautiful," the Major drawled.

"Good day to you, senhors."

He backed swiftly toward the door, fumbled behind him
for the handle.

The door suddenly flew open, the weight of men's shoulders behind it, sending him sprawling headlong into the
room, the revolver flying from his grasp. "Good work,"
Louis cried from behind his cover, complimenting the
two men, Carlos and Miguel, who had been responsible.

The crowd milled forward with a sullen roar, and were
upon Jim, the Major and the red-headed stranger before
they had completely recovered their astonishment at the
swift change of fortune.

At such close quarters, hemmed in by their assailants,
the big man and Jim were unable to use their strength to
the best advantage. Jim's weapon was practically useless.
Some of the men they felled, but the fallen ones crawled
up and clung to their legs, hampering their movements.

Their defeat was sure, and they knew it, but they showed
no sign of fear, and the ferocity of their defense did not
lessen. Again and again the thud-thud of their hard knuck-

les on soft, unresisting flesh sounded above the sibilant curses, the half-stifled screams of women and the swishing of knives.

Louis rose to his feet, watching the fight, cheering on his men, directing the attack. Then, glancing to where the Major lay prostrate, he saw that man move, saw him edge slowly toward his revolver.

Swiftly Louis made his way round the outskirts of the milling crowd to a point not two feet away from the Major and to his left. His knife was in his hand, poised ready for the throw. When the Major reached out to grasp the revolver, in that moment of victory, then Louis would act; and he knew that his aim would not miss at that range.

A yell of triumph came from the others as the big man went down. He was up again in a moment, a wiry little Portuguese who flourished a long dagger, clinging to his neck. He reached up, caught hold of the man by the head, stooped and heaved suddenly. The Portuguese shot over the heads of the others, like a stone flung from a catapult, turned somersault in the air and came to the ground with a sickening thud.

The others stared frightenedly at the big man, afraid to move.

"Make for the door," Jim shouted in the vernacular. "I go for my *baas*."

The big man nodded and slowly retreated.

Jim had wrenched a leg off a table and was hitting about him furiously. Men gave way to him. He went forward; slipped, recovered, slipped again and went down.

They passed over him, concentrating their attack now on the redhead.

"Come hon, Doc," yelled the Cockney who had been dancing excitedly on the fringe of the crowd. "It's hup ter hus ter do the w'ite man stuff."

He plunged into the fight, hitting to right and left with the bottles he held in his hands. Doc, the pianist, the one-time Harley Street specialist, forgetting for the moment that he was a poor creature in the pay of One-eyed Louis, followed closely in his wake.

The fury of the attack of the Portuguese lessened. Jim regained his feet and fought his way forward toward his *baas*.

Louis cursed. His hand went back. He could delay no longer.

"*Baas!*" cried Jim.

And then the Major doubled up suddenly and grabbed Louis by the ankles in a viselike grip.

The one-eyed man went down, his head hitting the hard floor with a resounding *whack*. His eye closed; his body went limp.

The Major retrieved his revolver, then rising to his feet, Louis in his arms, fired three shots into the ceiling.

The others looked round, fearing fresh reinforcements had come to the aid of these so fearful fighters. When they saw that the monocled man again had command of the situation—was not Louis his prisoner?—all fight left them. What need to fight now their leader was captured?

They hurriedly got out of the Major's path, leaving the way clear to the door, and made no move when the big man, followed by Doc, Cockney, Jim and the Major—still carrying the limp form of Louis—passed out into the sunlight.

Doc led the way to a tin shanty down by the water front. They went very slowly, breathing hard, smarting from the pain of innumerable small cuts.

As they entered the shanty, ten minutes later, the big man suddenly collapsed onto the rickety cot bed, coughed once—his lips were tinged with blood—then was still.

"He's finished," Doc said after a swift examination, and pointed to a wound—it was hardly more than a slight puncture in appearance—in the man's side.

"You mean he's dead?" the Major asked incredulously.

"Not yet, but quickly. The wonder is he lived so long. He's been bleeding internally." Doc added a long, technical explanation.

The Major nodded thoughtfully. "Will he regain consciousness, do you think, before he passes out?"

Doc shrugged his shoulders. "Possibly. Is he a friend of yours?"

"Never saw him until today."

"Say, cullies," the Cockney fireman put in. "There ain't no use o' me stickin' abart, is there? My bloomin' ship sails tonight. That's 'er." He pointed out of the window to a dingy-looking coaster at her moorings. "I wants ter 'ave a little fun afore sailin' time. I ain't got really drunk yet."

"You're a glutton for punishment, aren't you, old top," the Major said softly. "No. There's nothing you can do. Thanks for taking a hand in the fight. We'd have been swamped."

"You're welcome," the Cockney mumbled hastily. "Don't mention hit. You ain't such a fool as yer look, Percy. Tata!" Licking his lips thirstily, he quickly left the shack.

The big man moaned, opened his eyes and looked wonderingly about him. "That sure was a hell of a scrap," he said. "I feel as weak as a cat." He tried to rise, failed. A hurt look of surprise came into his mild blue eyes. "What's the matter with me?" he asked. "Hurt bad?"

Doc nodded.

The big man looked down and gently fingered the wound in his side.

"And that's what done it, eh? Hell! I've cut myself worse than that shaving, an' it don't hurt half as bad as this scratch on my cheek."

"Suppose you tell us what it's all about," the Major suggested gently. "I know you've got a wooden image Louis wants; you told me that this morning. But why does he want it? And why did you come to Louis' place after I'd promised to handle the matter for you?"

The other grinned sheepishly. "I was a fool there—but I just naturally love a scrap and your Hottentot—he's a good scout, all right, all right—was getting anxious about you. Besides, I wasn't quite sure I could trust you."

He coughed slightly, wiped his mouth with the back of his hand and looked with dull-eyed surprise at the blood which was smeared on it. "I guess you're right," he said softly. "I'm a goner, all righty. So I'll have to talk quick. I'm from the States, see, not that that matters much. We're both white men. I was with my uncle and my sister on an expedition up Killimanjaro way. Unk's a big bug in the ethnological line. Well, we accidentally stumbled onto a big black secret society which has 'Africa for the Africans' for its slogan. Unk wrote a full report of it and sent the report with me downcountry, with the idol, too. That's mixed up in the business, some way. It's big ju-ju. I never quite understood what it was all about—I've got muscle, not brains—but whatever it is, that idol is pretty important; they need it at their mumbojumbo talks. I had a hell of a time getting as far as this. My niggers deserted back there, taking all my trekking outfit, and I had to come on foot. The niggers got my papers, too, and once a band captured me and tried to make me tell 'em where I'd hidden their bloomin' wooden idol. I escaped after a while, but it was sure hell until I did. And then, when those two cutthroats tried to search me, why, I wanted to find out how white men were mixed up in this ju-ju business. I thought it 'ud be something definite to talk about, considering I'd lost Unk's report. But I made a mess of it, didn't I?"

"And where is this idol now?"

"Here!" He touched his tangled mop of red hair. "Say! You'll have to go an' warn the big bugs all about this. Can't waste any time. Unk says it's the biggest thing ever known. He says it'll mean the end of the whites in Africa if it goes through! You'll put it through—and go back an' pick up Unk and Sis. Too bad I lost the papers. But I can tell you a lot—even if I don't understand it. They—oh, hell! I'll tell you in the morning. Right now, I want to sleep."

He closed his eyes wearily. Suddenly he sat erect, his eyes blazing, his fists clenched. "It was a damned good scrap," he said, coughed violently and fell back.

Doc gently wiped the froth from the big man's lips. "He won't fight again," he said softly and then, his little hour over, the Doc lost his bedside manner and the traditions of his caste. He remembered only his fall, the man he had become. He sat dumbly on the foot of the bed, biting his nails and glancing at the unconscious form of One-eyed Louis.

The Major gently searched the pockets of the dead man. They were empty save for a few silver coins. Then he ran his fingers through the man's long, red hair.

His fingers closed presently on a small hard object which was glued and fastened with silk thread to a lock of hair.

He cut it away and examined it closely. It was a wooden image—barely an inch long—a carved caricature. It was of the color of blood, evil looking and hideously ugly.

"My word!" the Major exclaimed softly. "It looks like a West Coast ju-ju. I wonder—" For a long time he sat motionless. The shack was very quiet; weirdly quiet. The Major looked at the dead man; at the abject figure of Doc who sat miserably reviewing his past; at Jim, who squatted on the ground beside the unconscious form of Louis. "My word!" the Major exclaimed again and stooping over Louis, swiftly explored that man's pockets.

In one of them he found a thick, small notebook covered in worn red leather on which a few flecks of gilt still remained.

In silence he thumbed the smudged pages, most of which were indecipherable—mere jottings of dates and abbreviations. Toward the last, however, a frown gathered on the Major's brow. He straightened, his mouth going into a grim line. The big redhead had told the truth; from the diary of One-eyed Louis ample corroboration could be gleaned! No matter whether the native plot actually was of the importance the dead man had assigned to it, the cabal existed—and stretched its roots over more than three thousand miles of coast and jungle!

The Major arose, putting away the notebook. "Do you think he will recover, Doc?" he questioned, motioning at the still inert figure of the dive proprietor.

An odd fierceness shone for an instant in the medico's expression. "Here—in my hands," he replied with slow emphasis, "a fractured skull is a serious ailment! I shall do my best—for all concerned—"

The Major shrugged. Even without Doc's "ministrations" he judged the case of Louis to be hopeless—and was glad therefore. "Then goodby, Doc," he said. "Best of luck, old chappy. Come on, Jim," he added in the vernacular.

The Hottentot sprang to his feet. "Yah, *baas*. Where do you go?"

"Away from this sink of evil called Beira," the Major said as they passed out of the shack. Then, screwing his monocle into his eye, he drawled in English, "I think I know a chappy in Durban—a museum chappy—who knows all about wooden idols. I think I shall have a talk with him. Yes. And now we'll go aboard that ship of Cockney's and see if they'll let us work our passage to Durban. Bai jove, yes. And we'll go aboard at once. I think, yes, I feel it in my bones, that this bloomin' wooden idol, this funny little chappy—" he twisted the idol between his long, well shaped fingers—"is going to cause us a lot of fun."

"Damme yes!" agreed Jim glibly; the Hottentot had not understood a word of what the Major had said; Jim's knowledge of English was essentially parrotlike. "Damme yes. Bloody idol. Funny! Damme no. If I don't see you, s'long, hullo!"

SINEWS OF WAR

SOMEONE THREW a brick into the political waters of South Africa. As a result of the ensuing splash not a few of the big men—including the very biggest—who ran things on the Rand, on the Kimberley diamond fields and in the legislative chambers at the Cape, were obliged to ship on the next Donald Currie boat to England in order that they might air their political linen, which had been dampened by the splash, before the fires of a parliamentary committee. And as so often happens in such cases, following the departure of the big men, hundreds of minor authorities suddenly found themselves out of office, and—this, too, is following precedent—their successors had friends who sought, and found, jobs under them.

The upheaval caused by the throwing of the brick was stupendous, the eddies which followed were far reaching, all embracing. Not even the police were spared. Most especially the police *were not* spared. Experienced officers found themselves demoted overnight, as it were, retired on full pay, half pay or no pay at all. Their posts were filled by sycophantic "time servers" and incompetent upstarts newly arrived with "letters" from England.

Most ironical, but indicative of the wide sweeping changes which followed the brick throwing, was the appointment of an I.D.B. to high political office in Kimberley.

However, all this is simply by the way and is only quoted to explain, among other things, the sudden and prosperous activities of certain gentry residing in and about Kimberley. It explains the increased trafficking in illicit diamond buying, illicit liquor dealing and sundry other illicit forms of trade. It helps to explain the weakness of the "strong arm of the law" and it explains in full why the new chief of police looked blankly at his uniformed assistant, twirled his mustache and said irritably, "The Major? Major *who?*"

The assistant permitted himself to perpetrate a feeble joke. "No, sir, not Major Who. Just Major."

The chief scowled. "I read *Punch* when I want to be amused, Trooper Ashe," he said tartly. "For the rest, I'd have you remember that this is the headquarters of a military organization of which I am the ranking head. Please remember that and comport yourself accordingly."

"Yes, sir. Very good, sir." Trooper Ashe stood rigidly at attention until the other turned to his desk. Then he resumed his slack, lounging posture against the wall.

The chief fussily rustled among the papers on his desk, endeavoring to convey the impression that he was busy with departmental matters. But his eyes always returned to the cheaply printed yellow sheet which was the town's weekly paper, *The Diamond Trader's Star,* commonly known as "the D.T.S.," or, as a certain ribald element of the population would have it, "the D.T.s."

He presently picked up the paper and read a certain trenchant paragraph for, perhaps, the twentieth time that morning.

It said:

Not since the early days of the diamond fields has vice of all sorts been so rampant in our flourishing township.

By their weak and vacillating conduct our spineless police officials actually encourage vice.

The only improvement we can record is the fact that the chief of police's new tunic has an even higher collar than his old one. It may be that it will cut his throat, which like the rest of him is decidedly too fat for true beauty. At any rate it will prevent him from "bleating" so much—and we must be thankful for that. Seriously, however, we take it upon ourselves to warn the C. of P. and his underlings to get on or get out. And believing that they lack the ability to get on, we venture to predict an early return to the old, lawful order of things.

"Damn!" muttered the chief. "What do they want? It isn't my fault that all the thieves in South Africa have flocked to Kimberley. And I can't arrest them all on suspicion."

The chief crumpled the paper into a ball and threw it viciously into the waste paper basket. "Damn!" he said again. Loudly this time.

Ashe came to attention. "You said, sir—?"

The chief turned to him. "You still here?"

The trooper's expression was reproachful. True, he was very thin, but surely he was visible.

"Well! What do you want?" the chief continued.

"It's about this chap, the Major, sir. He's really most persistent. Shall I tell him you'll see him?"

"No!" the chief bellowed.

"Very good, sir." The trooper sighed resignedly and slowly turned the door knob. "But I'm afraid he won't take 'No' for an answer, sir. He—"

"Wait!"

The trooper sighed again, with relief this time, and came back into the room.

"Who is he, Ashe?"

"The Major, sir."

"Yes, I know that, fool. You've already told me his name. I mean what is he? Has he," an anxious note crept into his voice, "a letter of introduction? If so, I'd better see him. Don't want to offend anyone."

"I asked him if he had a letter, sir, but he said he hadn't. He seemed to think that his name was sufficient introduction."

"Well, it isn't. Tell him to go away. Tell him I'm busy. Tell him anything—only go away."

"I told him all that, sir, but he won't go. I was surprised to find him so firm. He's not the type of man in whom one would expect to find firmness."

The chief groaned. "I suppose, then, he's another reform committee of one demanding that I put an instant stop to all the wickedness that's flourishing here."

Ashe shook his head. "No," he said slowly. "I don't think he's that. He's a most astounding person. When he shook my hand I thought he'd break every bone in it, and yet—"

"Oh, he's one of those rough fellows, eh? Probably come to complain that some trooper unjustly arrested him for selling liquor to natives or something like that. Well, he'll get no comfort from me. I've been fooled that way once too often. You send that chap in and I'll let him see that I'm not such a softy, after all."

There were tears in the chief's voice, tears of indignation at the thought of the number of times he had been fooled into accepting the statements of illicit liquor dealers.

"Very good, sir. But he's not that type at all."

The chief exploded violently. "If he's not here to present a letter," he bleated, "isn't a reformer and isn't a criminal come to make a complaint against one of my troopers, then what in hell is he?"

The trooper gaped foolishly. "He's the—the Major, sir," he stammered.

"Oh, get out! Tell him to come in."

Ashe departed precipitately, slamming the door behind him.

The chief, flushing to the top of his bald pate with childish rage, lighted a cigar and biting on it savagely turned back to his desk and pretended to be absorbed in a long, legal looking document.

Presently the door opened and closed again. The chief concentrated even more fiercely on the paper he held in his hand.

Footsteps crossed over to his desk, hesitating, apologetic footsteps.

The chief did not look up, in no way indicated that he was aware of another's presence in the room.

A voice hinted. "Ahem!" and continued as there was no response, "Hope I don't disturb you but, er, I find it rather fatiguing standing. Do you mind if I sit down."

The chief grinned sardonically at the labored, affected drawl, then grunted inarticulately.

A chair scraped along the floor. "Ah, thanks," the voice continued. "That's much better. You did say I might sit, didn't you?"

The chief grunted again but still did not look up.

"Not very chatty, are you, old top? Oh well, never mind me, I know you're busy. Must be with all these I.D.B.s and whatnots buzzin' around. But I'm afraid you've been workin' too hard, and that's bad for one. Gets to a chappy's brain before he knows what's what and all. For instance— Allow me!"

Two hands, their perfectly manicured nails glistened pink and white, reached over from behind the chief's chair and taking the document he was holding from him, turned it around and gave it back to him.

"There," the voice said, and the chair scraped again on the polished floor as the speaker reseated himself, "that's the sort of thing I mean. Comes from overwork. I've seen it before. A laddie I used to know—a bosom friend of mine, if you know what I mean—used to read his papers in the same way before they, er, took him to a nice, restful place. It was a very strange obsession, very strange. A reversion to type, or something like that. I believe he does all his reading now as he hangs by his heels from a trapeze. Sad case, very. And you—"

The chief looked up now. "Damn it, sir," he snapped. "What do you mean by this? What do you mean by it, eh?"

Despite his angry tone the chief was feeling very happy for he saw that his caller was someone he could insult and bully with impunity. He had never before seen such a perfect specimen of a stagestruck Johnny, a monocled dude, a "hawhaw" boy, an incompetent nincompoop. "And what's your business, Momma's Precious Pet?" he continued with a sneer.

"Suppose you call me Major," the monocled one suggested timidly. "It's, er, shorter and easier to say than the other."

"Major, eh? And what's your regiment?"

"Oh, you don't understand, dear sir," the other said hastily. "That's not a military rank. My name's Major. Aubrey St. John Major. Funny you should think I'm a military man, eh, what? But then others have thought that, too. And it always seems so funny to me, because I loathe fighting and all that."

"Funny! You won't find it so funny, let me tell you. First thing you know. I'll have you arrested for masquerading as an officer of the Queen. You—"

He stopped short; he was a little perplexed. He wasn't quite sure whether it was a vacuous or a mocking grin on the other's face. He wasn't quite sure whether the look of admiration in the baby blue eyes was sincere or assumed. Damn it, he swore silently, if the dude was laughing at him, he'd soon have him laughing on the other side of his face.

"Yes," he blustered. "That is a very serious crime. Any magistrate 'ud give you ten years on the breakwater for it. I'm tempted to arrest you without any further delay—" Major looked alarmed, alarm quickly gave way to relief as the chief continued—"but I won't. I'll simply warn you this time. But, mind you," he shook an admonishing forefinger, "I'm being lenient with you solely on account of your youth."

He stopped short once more, again greatly puzzled.

This man, Major, wasn't so young after all! Certainly he was not the callow youth of twenty-odd the chief had at first judged him to be. His black hair, brushed smoothly back from a high forehead, was graying a little at the temples. His clear, fresh complexion was the prize of splendid health, not the gift of tender years.

And so, the chief made a hasty correction, glad of the opportunity to do so. "I'm being lenient with you," he said, "because a man of your enfeebled intellect could not be expected to appreciate the seriousness of the crime of fraudulent representation."

He felt that he was quite safe there. Major looked such a frightful ass, looked like a man who had no thought above the cut of his clothes. From the tip of his head to the toes of his highly polished, brown riding boots Major was all dude, and the gold rimmed monocle he wore in his right eye gave the final, necessary touch to the *tout ensemble*. His face, that seemed as round and as expressionless as his monocle, was set in a vacant, inane, staring smile. The lines of his jaw muscles sagged, giving the lie to the strength of character suggested by the two rows of white, even teeth which showed between his slightly parted lips.

"Really, now," he stammered, "that's—that's most frightfully good of you. Good of you to be lenient with me, I mean. But, of course I'm not such an ass as I look. Oh, rather not."

"I believe you," the chief agreed heartily. "That 'ud be impossible."

"What's that?" Major looked bewildered, hurt. Then he chuckled. "Oh, yes. I see what you mean. Quite! And, I repeat, it's most awfully decent of you to treat me so, er, so glad handedly, in a manner of speaking. I was rather afraid that you'd give me the back of the hand an' the frosty mit, an' all that— Such happy slang these chappies from the prairies of Vermont and points east do have, don't they? I met one the other day—"

"You've gassed enough, haven't you?" the chief snapped. "I'm a busy man. What's your business?"

Looking absolutely squelched, Major fumbled clumsily in the pockets of his well fitting white duck tunic.

"Yes, yes, of course— Stupid of me. Where *did* I put the bally thing?" He turned out the contents of his pockets on the floor and going down on his knees, searched among the weird assortment of rubbish which will find its way into a boy's—and, therefore, a man's—pockets.

"Now where *did* I put it?" he muttered feverishly. And, aloud, "Just a moment, dear lad. Something I want to show you before we talk business. Know you're busy. Must be. Never seen so many I.D.B.s in town since Hector depended entirely on his mother for his sustenance— This Yankee slang is ripping, isn't it?— I must say that I think that beastly rag the D.T.s is most unfair, wouldn't be a bit surprised if the editor were a drinking man— Oh, here's one thing I wanted to show you. Not really what I came about, but I think you ought to see it. Decidedly unfair, I call it."

From an envelope he extracted a newspaper clipping, handed it to the chief and continued his search.

The chief looked casually at the clipping, read the opening sentence. "Not since the early days of the diamond fields has vice of all sorts—" then jumped to his feet, his face purple with wrath, and stood over Major, his fists upraised, one foot drawn back ready to launch a violent kick.

Major looked up, then fell back out of range. "Why— what's the matter?" And when the chief raged, mouthing incoherent curses, pointing with a trembling finger at the offending clipping, Major continued, "It's overwork! First the dear old tubby thing reads his papers upside down and now he's got 'em bad. Frothing at the mouth and what not."

Ostensibly in fear and trepidation he started precipitately toward the door.

"Hi, you! Stop!" the chief called.

Major increased his speed, but did not look 'round until he reached the door.

Then he found that the chief apparently had regained control of himself. He was sitting in his chair, tugging at his waxed mustache, grinding the clipping under his heel.

"You're quite sure you're safe, old top?" Major asked, returning cautiously to continue the search among his little pile of belongings on the floor. "But I'm afraid the fit came on before you had a chance to read the clipping. Never mind, I have read it so many times that I know it by heart. I'll tell you what it said. " 'Not since the early days—'"

But that was as far as he got.

"Stop!" the chief commanded fiercely. "I've read the damned thing until I know it by heart myself."

A light of near intelligence came into Major's eyes. "Oh, I see! And it makes you, er, rather peevish, what? I don't wonder. It's a bally nasty thing to say of a chappy, even if it's true. And, really, you're not so awfully fat, you've only got three chins. And, as a matter of fact, I quite admire that tunic of yours. It sets well across the, er, chest, and the collar helps you to carry a load, doesn't it?" He stroked his chin reflectively.

The chief breathed heavily. Somehow the fun he'd anticipated having with this monocled dude did not seem to be materializing. He was continually being put on the defensive and he had momentary qualms that he was being made the victim of a clever bit of leg pulling. But as he looked now at Major all such fears were dispelled. That man didn't have the brains to conduct a leg pulling campaign, or the brains to carry one out. Some of his inconsequential babbling had hit the mark, just as will the innocent prattling of a child. That was all.

"Did you come here just to show me those clippings?" he asked suavely.

"Oh, no. They were just by the way, as is it were. Of course I never dreamed that you had seen them. Why should I? Must say you show great restraint, oh, quite. Your predecessor, Colonel Ashe—the old fire eater was a great friend of mine—would have lynched the editor by this time. Though, of course, they never printed anything like that about him. And he was really fat."

The chief flushed red again. He was still far from sure of himself and the correctness of his estimation of the dude's character. "Never mind all that," he said gruffly. "Let's get to business, if you have any."

"Oh, I have some, old top, quite important business." Major was feeling in his pockets again in that panicky way men have when they can't find their railway tickets. "Just a minute. Now where did I put the blessed thing? Can't really get on with my story until I've shown it you. It's really the nub of the whole matter. Because of it, I've come to you for the well known sinews of war."

"Sinews of war?" The chief was puzzled.

"Exactly. Wonderful memory you have, old bean. You repeat my exact words. I'll explain in a moment. Now where did I— Oh, what a fool!"

He rose, and going into the outer room returned presently, carefully shutting and bolting the door behind him, holding in his hand a small, wooden image. "There!" he exclaimed triumphantly, as he placed the thing on the desk before the chief. "It was in my helmet all the time, hanging out there. What do you think of that?"

"If you think of going into the toy industry, you'll have to turn out something more pleasant to look at than that. It'ud frighten a kid out of his senses."

"Yes. It is rather hideous, isn't it. But I'm afraid you don't understand, old bean. It's not that at all, not a toy, I assure you. Don't you see what it is?"

The chief looked closely at the image. It represented an enormously fat, naked man supporting his gross belly with his hands. And he noted its thick, pouting lips, its flattened nose, its high collar of necklaces and its succession of bulging chins.

The chief grew red again, as red as the image he held in his hand. "Is it supposed to be a caricature of me?" he bellowed. "Because, if it is—"

"No, no," Major interposed hastily. "Of course not, old thing. Let me tell you all about it, then you'll understand." He drew his chair up close to the chief's.

"It was given to me by a Yankee chappy, a very giant of a Yankee I met in Lourenço Marquez. There was a little brawl at 'One-eyed Louis' place. Never heard of him? Ah, well, he's dead now. His death was one of the little by products, so to speak, of the brawl. The Yankee's death was another. But before he died Yankee gave me that thing," he indicated the idol with a nod of his head, "and told me the story of it. It appears that he and his sister were on an exploration trip with their uncle up North when the uncle, who's a big man in the ethnological line, stumbled on to a big plot among the natives to rise up and wipe out all the whites. And that ugly red idol is the big ju-ju of the men back of the plot. There! What do you think of that?"

"You don't take dope, do you?" the chief asked.

"Eh, what? Oh, I see. You don't believe me. Don't blame you a bit. I didn't believe the Yank's tale, not all of it. However, I took that thing to the curator of the Durban museum and he told me it was unique, oh, quite priceless, and begged me to give it to him. Couldn't afford to pay anything. Not that I was selling, of course—curators are quite poor, aren't they? Brain workers always are, what? Not like you police chappies. However," he continued hurriedly, anticipating and silencing with an apologetic gesture the chief's angry expostulation, "however, the curator said that it was very big ju-ju of the West Coast Leopard Society—*of course* you've heard of that?—said that it showed Egyptian and early Greek influence and what not, and said that the secret of the red dye has, er, died. But that doesn't matter. What does matter is that it, the key to a stupendous plot of the natives to make all Africa black, is in our hands."

The chief laughed and tossed the wooden image from one hand to the other, finally handing it back to Major. "It was probably made in a Birmingham sweat shop and painted by a six-year-old brat, and it means that I've wasted too much time listening to your gabble. Suppose we get down to business."

Major sighed. "I was afraid you'd take that attitude. That's the trouble with you efficient men, you have no imagination. Can't you see that a plot such as I've hinted at is bound to be put on foot sooner or later? Can't you see that there's a guiding hand behind all the native trouble we've been having lately?"

The chief laughed. "If—supposing all you have told me to be true—that's all this gigantic plot means, we don't have to worry."

"I wonder," said Major quietly. The drawl had vanished from his voice now. His face seemed longer, keener, his lips were set in firm lines, and his blue eyes had gray steel lights in them. "Suppose all the little things that have been happening were simply to test the strength of the organization, a little undress rehearsal, as it were. Take for instance the affair the other night, when *all* the natives disappeared from the compounds and did not return until noon of the following day. Do you know where they went to, or why? Does anyone? Have the native police been able to find out? Or, if they found out, have they told?"

The chief moved uneasily, then laughed again. "That's nothing. They just went to a big beer drink, that's all."

"But don't you think it funny that *all* the natives went? Natives of all tribes—Zulus, Swazi, Basuto, Mashona, Matabele and the rest—tribal enemies and yet, for some strange reason, joining together. Oh, no! You can't believe they'd forget tribal distinction like that."

"But I do," the chief said positively. "Working at the mines, being thrown together in the compounds, soon breaks down tribal differences. They become just niggers, that's all."

Major's face registered despair. "I don't think you've ever been in a compound, old top," he said, the drawl returning, the inane, vacuous expression again taking possession of his face. "Ah, well, I was afraid you'd be a doubting Thomas and so," he returned the image to his pocket, "I suppose it's no good talking any further?"

"Talk as much as you like," the chief said airily. "You amuse me."

Major's eyes gleamed. "I didn't come here to amuse you," he snapped.

He rose to his feet, stood erect, and the chief became uncomfortably aware of his splendid physique. And again the chief felt abashed.

"Don't be so hasty," he said soothingly. "If you've got something else to say, say it. You've told a tall story, you know, and you'd be the first to think me a fool if I swallowed it without a little thought."

"That's true," Major said slowly and sat down again.

"There's nothing I can add in the way of proof," he continued. "It may be all lies, but dare you take that risk? The little else I have to tell you is this. The big Yankee told me that his uncle and sister were somewhere in the Mountains of the Moon district. The uncle has all the information. He sent down a full report by the big fellow, but it was stolen from him. And the uncle's ill—fever and a broken leg. That's why he couldn't come down himself, and the girl stayed to take care of him. They are both probably prisoners by this time, if they're alive.

"What I want from you is this: give me the sinews of war—cash, in other words. Give me four men, let me pick them, and I'll outfit and trek North to investigate. Then— What's the matter?"

The chief seemed to be choking. "Nothing," he gasped. "Only your colossal nerve took my breath away."

"That means, I take it," Major said softly, "that you refuse? That I'll have to provide the sinews of war in some other way?"

The chief nodded. He was still too full of laughter for words.

"And you absolutely refuse to help?"

The chief parried the question with another. "Am I the only person you told this yarn to?"

"Oh, no. Of course not."

"And none of them would do anything?"

"No-o. Well, you see, the men who are now sitting in high places don't seem to know much—you've discovered that, no doubt—and they laughed at me, just as you did. And the men who know things and really believe that there's something in this idol business, haven't any authority, no money, no anything. So there you are! I came to you, hoping you'd have some intelligence. But," he shrugged his shoulders and his drawl became even more pronounced, "you were the last on my list of possible backers and I didn't have much hope. That is, er, I mean you are too clever for me. Impossible to throw dirt in your eyes, eh, what? But, honestly now, don't you think the yarn was worth a little loan? I'm absolutely broke, and you've no idea how expensive things are nowadays. A tenner would help no end, or even a fiver or a sovereign—"

The chief's eyes narrowed to piglike slits. "Here," he said and held out a shilling to the Major. "There's the price of a small drink. Now get to hell out of here. I've wasted a whole morning on you."

Major took the shilling and put it in his pocket. "Thanks, old dear," he drawled. "I suppose, in a manner of speaking, that having taken the shilling I'm enrolled in the Queen's service. Ah, well. So be it. And I have to collect the sinews of war myself, eh?"

"That's it. Collect 'em any damned way you please, but not from me."

"Ah, that's kind of you, I'm sure. Well, thanks for seeing me. I've enjoyed our chat immensely. Ta, ta!"

He strolled over to the door, opened it and passed out. The door closed, the chief heard him exchange some bantering remarks with Trooper Ashe—and then silence.

The chief leaned back in his chair, put his feet up on the desk, a handkerchief over his face, and composed himself to sleep.

But almost immediately, it seemed, the door opened again and a thin, cruel faced man entered.

"What the hell do you think you're doing, Tubby?" he lisped slightly. "This isn't a dormitory, is it?"

The chief's chair came down with a crash, he snatched the handkerchief from his face and rising to his feet, grinned sheepishly. "I've had a hard morning," he said glibly. "Been preparing evidence of some difficult cases since sunrise and—"

"Oh, blah!" the other interrupted. Politicians are not overly courteous to the underlings, especially when their underlings have almost come to the end of their period of usefulness. "You can pull that line with the reformers and such like fools, but not with me. I know you. I know you haven't done a day's work since you were appointed to this job.

"Have you seen this week's D.T.s? Yes, I see you have. Well, you fool, aren't you going to do something about it? Or are you just going to sit still and see your resignation thrust upon you?"

"Oh, they can't go as far as that," the chief began confidently.

"No? Don't be too sure about that. And, let me tell you, if you don't do something to earn your salt you needn't look to me for support."

"Well, what can I do?" the chief wailed. "This isn't my kind of job. I didn't want it, I wanted to be in the Customs department at Cape Town. You know that. The pickings 'ud be worth something there. Here, they don't amount to anything."

"That's because you don't know how to get 'em. However—"

"Well, what can I do? It isn't my fault all this illicit diamond and liquor traffic is going on; I don't know anything about it. And I didn't want to come up country anyway. It isn't my fault."

"Then, in God's name, whose fault is it?" the other shouted hoarsely. And added, in a calmer voice, "Oh, I know it's always existed, probably always will, but never so openly as this."

"But what can I do?"

"Arrest the first man you meet on the street, and ten to one you'll have arrested an I.D.B. with his pockets full of diamonds. It's as easy as that. And, after you've made a few arrests, you'll go outside on a tour of inspection. That'll give the 'townies' a chance to miss you and wish you were back again. Understand me?"

"Yes, but—"

"But, hell! There ain't no 'but' to it. They are orders I'm giving you and if you can't obey 'em, all I can say is that it'll be the worse for you. All right, then, that's settled. And sit down, for God's sake. You give me the fidgets, standing there on one leg like a school brat."

The chief subsided into his chair and fumbled nervously with his mustache. It no longer bristled fiercely upward, but curved downward pessimistically.

"That's better. Now tell me: What was the Major doing here?"

"The Major? Oh, that dude Major!" The chief began a spluttering laugh which ended abruptly as the other snapped, "Yes, I said the Major; the blamed monocled dude, if you like. What little game did he pull off?"

"He tried to borrow a tenner but it didn't come off. I gave him a 'bob' and that seemed to satisfy him."

"Just what little game are you trying to pull off with me, Tubby?" the other snarled. "You don't expect me to believe that guff, surely. You gave the Major a shilling, did you? Hell!"

"But it's the truth," the chief said nervously. "That's all he came here for, a loan. And I gave him a bob, as I said."

"And I suppose he just came in and simply said 'Lend me a tenner?' That's all he said, eh?"

"Oh, no, he said a lot more. In fact, I wasted an hour listening to him. Don't know quite why I did; had some idea of having a game with him, making a fool of him, but somehow it didn't come off."

"No, it wouldn't," the thin man said dryly. "Do you mean to say you've never heard of the Major before, never seen him?"

"No. Who is he? God Almighty?"

"Never mind. Go on, what did he talk about?"

"Don't see why you're interested in the ravings of that halfwit," the chief grumbled.

"No, you wouldn't. Can't altogether blame you, either. He's fooled clever men, and you— Oh, go on. What was it all about?"

The chief didn't need any further urging but told, as well as he could remember, the conversation he had had with Major.

"That's all," he concluded. "Hell of a tale to tell, wasn't it. And the damned fool thought I was going to believe him, thought I was going to fall for it."

The other's eyes narrowed. "I wonder just what you have fallen for?" he muttered. "The Major must have had some game up his sleeve. Say," he raised his voice, "you didn't have any papers lying around; secret instructions, codes, or anything like that he might have been after?"

The look of mystification on the chief's face was sufficient denial.

"No. I see you hadn't. Um! Wonder what the fellow was after? Tell me: how big was that idol?"

The chief measured a distance of about five inches with his two hands. "And it had a big fat gut on it," he added.

"Did you examine it closely? Was it hollow inside?"

The chief shook his head wonderingly. "I only just glanced at it. It was damned ugly, that's all I know. What's all this mystery?"

"Listen. That chap, the Major as everybody calls him, is the cleverest I.D.B. living. He's made fools of all the police here and everywhere. Yes, he has. He keeps his brains hidden in ambush behind that dude, silly ass pose of his. And, because he's not like the other I.D.B.s, don't run with women, drink, gamble or anything like that, no one's ever been able to get anything on him. The old crowd of police were always setting traps for him and getting caught in 'em themselves. And everybody likes him so it was next to impossible to frame him. It *was* impossible. Maybe it still is, but we'll see.

"Well, as I say, the police swore by him at the same time they were swearing at him.

"Not so long ago he had a big *indaba* with the Big Man and some of the others at the head of the Syndicate, and as a result they called a truce. It seems that the Major became an I.D.B. as a sort of protest against the I.D.B. laws and when the Big Man promised to try and have 'em repealed, the Major promised to reform and went up north on the Big Man's business. He hasn't been seen in town or anywhere around for months. However, it seems as if the reform didn't take, and now the Big Man's out of the country and out of the game for a time, the Major's gone back to his old tricks.

"Now I'm going to give you a few tips, and if you're wise you'll act on them.

"You were wise to be skeptical about all that talk of nigger plots and the idol being a big ju-ju. That was all a blind—I know the Major's little ways. And, look here," a sudden inspiration had come to him, "suppose you arrested the Major now, and I hadn't had this talk with you, I bet you'd never think of breaking open that bloomin' idol to see if there was a diamond or two in it, would you? Well, I'm betting there is! Oh, he's a crafty devil, all right. He spins a yarn about it, lets you hold it in your hands—and all the time he's building up a nice little hiding place, that you'd never suspect, for any diamonds that come to him in his ordinary course of business. As a matter of fact, I wouldn't mind betting the idol had a diamond in it when he gave it to you to look at. Oh, he's damned clever, all right. Well, now, what you've got to do is arrest the Major. See that you get the goods on him. Get him sent to the Breakwater. You'll find the evidence in that idol of his, I'm betting. That's all. Don't make a fool out of yourself."

With that he turned on his heels and left the room, smiling slyly, determined to investigate the Major's idol before the chief got a chance to. Despite his promotion to political office, the thin man was loath to give up the profitable business of I.D.B.

IT WAS long after sundown that night when the Major left the *dorp* and made his way over the veld to his camp, a bell tent pitched just beyond the township commonage, but the darkness did not seem to bother him.

His step was unhesitating, sure, and his progress was the silent one of a veld, wise man.

Yet, while he was still some distance away and the gleam of the campfire was only a tiny pin prick of light in the surrounding darkness, the Hottentot who was squatting on his haunches by the fire, busily engaged in rubbing a piece of wood with a greasy rag, grinned happily and muttering to himself, "The *baas* comes; all is well," rose, and taking a large stew pot from the fire went with it into the tent. He poured the hot water into a foot bath, and placed a towel, cake of soap and a can of cold water near by. Then, lighting the oil lamp which was in a bracket fastened to the tent pole, he opened one of the steel uniform cases and carefully got out such clothes as his *baas* would need after bathing. Then he returned to the fire and busied himself with preparations for the evening meal.

A horse nickered softly. It was tethered to the wheel of a buckboard, down wind so that the smoke from the fire would keep some of the flying pests of Africa's night away from it. Its coal black coat was flecked with fire tints.

Near to it, turned loose, but hobbled, two mules huddled together, their heads pointing toward the fire, watching the industrious Hottentot.

The horse nickered again, louder. It was an eager note of welcome.

The Hottentot chuckled and said softly, "It is dark, *baas*, but I am not blind. Though you were as silent and as dark as the night's shadows I would still see you."

The Major, who had stopped behind a bush just outside the circle of light cast by the fire, stepped forward. "If the horse had not got my scent, Jim, you would not have known I was near."

Jim, the Hottentot, chuckled. "Say you so, *baas?* Then must you be blind. Is not the lamp lighted in the tent? Enter, and you will find your bath ready. And the food is cooking."

"What food, Jim? Bully again?"

"Nay, *baas.* My *assegai* was faster than a duiker buck. 'Wait for me,' it said, and the buck waited and found death. A guinea fowl—a hen bird, over curious as all women folk are—looked too closely at a snare I had set. And so, guinea fowl for you and buck for me. Buck for you, too, if you wish it."

"No, Jim. The bird is enough. I am not hungry."

The Major entered the tent and undressing quickly, bathed himself in the shallow tub, finally sluicing himself with the can of cold water. That done, he rubbed himself vigorously with a coarse towel, standing at the tent's opening so that some of the fire's warmth could reach him. There was not an ounce of superfluous flesh on him. His development was that of a trained athlete, of a strong man who is also fleet of foot. Every move he made caused the muscles to ripple under his firm white skin.

Thoroughly dry, he dressed himself in the clothes Jim had put out for him and presently he stepped out of the tent, looking as if he were going to a gay party at the Ritz Carlton, instead of dining on the veld alone, and announced that he was ready for skoff.

He sat down at the table which Jim had set close to the fire, the night air being cold, and ate fastidiously of the well cooked meal Jim set before him.

"Take it away, Jim," he said presently, finding it impossible to feign an appetite under the Hottentot's eagle scrutiny.

Jim swiftly obeyed then sat down near his *baas*, his chin resting on his updrawn knees. "The *baas* is not happy?" he said.

The Major sighed. "Far from it, Jim." The Major spoke all the native dialects, had even mastered the "clicking" of the bushmen.

"Then the *baas'* errand today was fruitless?"

"Truly, Jim. The men I used to know have gone, or at least their authority has been taken from them. Those who have taken their places laughed at me."

"*Au-a!* Then they are fools indeed."

"And do you believe the story of the red idol, Jim?" the Major asked suddenly.

"Me, *baas?* I believe what you believe."

The Major nodded. "And I'm not quite sure what I believe, Jim, old top," he drawled. He often spoke English when alone with Jim. And Jim, though his knowledge of English was little more than a parrotlike repetition of words, always responded with one of his queer phrases whether it was apropos or not—generally it wasn't—whenever his *baas* ended a sentence with a rising inflection.

"No, Jim," the Major continued, fishing a monocle from his vest pocket and fixing it in his eye, "I don't know what to believe. Of course, the Yankee's story might be true. And, if it is, something's got to be done about it. No time at all to waste, none at all. One has to nip these roots of rebellion and bloody strife in the bud, as it were. Don't you agree?"

"Golly yes, damme no," Jim said sagely.

"Yes, no—of course. You're such a wise old laddie. But to continue: as no one else believes the story, no one will help and, therefore, whatever is done will have to be done by just the two of us. And that's a tall order. Don't you see?"

"Yah!" Jim nodded violently. "If I don't see you so long hullo."

"Yes, that's just it. It's a long 'hullo'—cry, I should say—from here to the Mountains of the Moon, and the sinews of war are lacking. We must be well supplied if we go on that trek and I don't think we have more than twenty rounds left.

"On the other hand, Yankee's yarn may have been simply the ravings of delirium. But no. I don't think so. And so—Jim?"

"Yah, *baas?*"

"I am like a man lost in the bush, Jim," the Major was speaking in the vernacular now, "and know not which way to turn. I have come to a trail, but know not whether it leads to a *kraal* or whether it is an elephant trail which, should I follow it, will lead nowhere—or to death. In other words, Jim, is the story of the red idol true or should it be spat upon?"

"What does it matter, *baas?* At least if we follow it it will lead us away from the evil of *dorps*. It will give us room to breathe, and a big hut, with all earth for a bed, the sky for a roof and the places of the four winds for walls. We shall live if we follow the trail and, if at the end of the trail is death, we shall have lived. Perchance we will find the story true. Then there will be deeds to be done; deeds which I call for strong men like the two of us. Perchance the story is a lie. But true or false, what does it matter? Let us follow the trail. I have spoken."

"Aye," the Major sighed happily. "You have spoken."

"Then we will trek north, *baas?*"

"As soon as we can get equipment, Jim. As soon as we can get money. There is only one thing to do. We will play the game again."

"Diamonds, *baas?*"

"Aye, diamonds, Jim."

The Hottentot smiled happily and from one of the pockets of the voluminous great coat he wore—it was one of the Major's and save that it fitted him snugly across the chest was far too big for him—produced the piece of wood he had been working on before his *baas'* return.

"Why, what is that, Jim?" The Major went to the tent, and bringing out the idol he had shown to the chief of police, compared it with the one Jim had made. Jim's was obviously a very crude imitation and the stain with which it was dyed lacked the rich, blood-red tint of the other.

"Why, Jim?"

"As you see, *baas,* I have not been idle today. A man came to the camp this afternoon, a white man, calling himself your friend. After a while he talked about the little red idol and, after much talk, offered me great wealth if I would steal it from you—and with it the thing that is inside—and give it to him."

"The thing that is in it?"

"Yah, *Baas.* He would have it that the idol's belly is a hiding place for 'stones.' And, *baas,* this morning the black dog who steals diamonds for him did not keep trust with him. The black one had a big stone hidden in a wound in his leg, so the white man told me. And he thinks, *baas,* this white friend of yours, that you have gotten that stone and have hidden it in that idol of yours. And so, as I have said, he offered me much money if I would steal the idol from you. So, in order to give your friend that which he wants, I made this. When I go to meet him tonight I will sell it to him. That is all."

The Major chuckled softly. "And you think he is to be trusted, Jim? Do you think he'll pay you?"

"I have thought of all that, *baas*. When the time comes, and there is need—you will be on hand."

"But why bother, Jim?"

"Because when men have decided a thing is so, it is best to humor them. Also, I wish to get rid of this. Look, *baas*. The glue has not yet set hard." He pulled the idol he had made in half, separating the back from the front. In the hollow of the stomach was a wad of paper. Unfolding it, Jim exposed a large, uncut, unpolished diamond. A quick scrutiny of it showed the Major, than whom there were few better diamond judges living, that it was practically worthless. Its color was poor and it was crisscrossed with innumerable flaws.

"And so you will give him that, eh, Jim? Clever. But it won't fool him."

"It will, *baas*. Thinking it the stone he lost he will not look at it very closely. Maybe he will send it south tonight."

"And where did you get the stone, Jim?"

"I threw the bones and it came to my hand, *baas*. Nay, truly. The black dog who steals stones for that white man who called himself your friend, came by this way on his way to meet the man and give him the diamonds. I gave him some of the *baas' dop* to drink and then he began to boast of his skill at games of chance. And so I played with him. He was well clad when we started, *baas*. Aye, he was dressed as white men are dressed. He wore only a loin cloth when he departed, and that I suffered him for decency's sake. And so I won that diamond." He held out his hand for the image he had made, put the diamond back in the cavity and stuck the two halves together again. "That diamond—and *this*."

He put his hand up to his head and from the wooly tangle of his hair produced a diamond which he handed to the Major. It was as large as the other, but of finest water.

"Bai Jove!" the Major murmured.

"Is it enough, *baas?* Will it buy food or the guns and for us?"

"It is enough, Jim."

"That is good. I go now to meet the man as I promised. I go to sell him what he wants," he grinned. "Otherwise he might be tempted to try and take it from us by force. The *baas* will come presently?"

"Aye, Jim. But where?"

"To the hut near the old working. You know it?"

The Major nodded, and Jim became one of the night's shadows, vanishing beyond the campfire's glow.

FOR A long time the Major sat motionless before the fire, the diamond resting on one knee, the idol on the other.

The bush about him was full of life, whispering in the darkness. He was subconsciously aware of it all; the stealthy rustlings, the cries of hunters and hunted, the monotonous booming of drums at a distant *kraal.*

The moon rose. The night's shadows shortened, assumed menacing, fantastic shapes.

The Major gave himself up to vague day dreams, pleasantly tired, totally relaxed.

He suddenly awoke to full consciousness, warned by some strange sixth sense of impending danger. Someone was coming. Someone was very near.

He did not move, did not even close his fingers on the diamond and so hide it from view. Yet the discovery of that diamond—of any diamond—on him by the police would mean years of back breaking toil on the Breakwater at Cape Town.

Presently he yawned lazily, stretched, then sat more erect.

He stamped one foot, rubbed the leg as if it were cramped. The diamond fell to the ground, close to the leg of the table. He picked up the idol, patted it thoughtfully, put it in his pocket, then leaned with all his weight on the table, rocking it slightly.

A moment later he rose, knocking the table over.

He cursed aloud at his clumsiness. He stooped to pick the table up again. As he did so, he cleverly pushed the diamond into the hole made by the table leg and with the same motion of his foot trod dirt into the hole, closing it up.

"Hands up, Major!" a voice said curtly.

He straightened swiftly, letting the table fall from his hands.

The fat chief of police advanced slowly from out the cover of bushes.

"And to what do I owe the honor of this visit?" the Major drawled.

"I want to have a look at that idol of yours," said the chief.

"Oh, really? That's bully. Then you think there's something in it, after all?"

"Yes," the chief said dryly. "I think there's something in it."

"I'm afraid you don't mean what I think you mean," the Major said doubtfully. "But may I lower my hands? I'm getting pins and needles in them, if you know what I mean."

"All right. But I'm taking no chances. Watch him, Ashe."

"Yes, sir. Very good, sir."

Trooper Ashe, revolver in hand, looking far from happy, came out of the bushes. He made a gesture of apology to the Major who murmured, "So you've brought good old Ashe with you, eh, Chief?

"Give me your idol," the chief said curtly.

"But why? I'm not under arrest, am I?"

"No, not yet. But I've been warned that you are a clever I.D.B. I didn't know that when you called on me this morning; not so sure of it now. I think you're a damned fool and haven't got the brains to be an I.D.B. However—"

"However? Yes, go on, Chief. This is deucedly interesting."

"However," the chief said heavily, "going on the assumption that you really are clever, it occurred to me that that tale you told me about the idol was all a blind. For instance, having had the idol in my hands as I did this morning, and having heard that story about it, it would never occur to me that it was a hiding place for illicitly purchased diamonds. That is," he amended hastily, "it would not have occurred to me had I not been much cleverer than you suspected."

"I don't quite follow you," the Major said in bewildered tones, "but I suppose you're all right? Nothing the matter with your chief's brain, is there, Ashe?"

Ashe had difficulty in suppressing a chuckle.

"Also," continued the chief, frowning at Ashe, "I have been informed that a large diamond was taken by a native today. So, although I think you are just a damned fool dude, I am going to search you."

The Major sighed. "I'm afraid you're right—and wrong. I'm a fool, because it's better to be a fool and free than to be a clever I.D.B. taking a health cure at the Breakwater. You're wrong, because I'm not going to let you search me. Mistaken wise men have tried to frame me before, you know."

He moved swiftly so that the portly chief shielded him from Ashe's aim. At the same time he drew his own revolver with incredible speed.

"Don't be a fool," the chief said, greatly alarmed. "Who's going to frame you?"

"I don't know, but you're not."

"I had no intention.'Pon my word of honor."

The Major looked at Ashe inquiringly.

"I'll be your witness," that man said bravely.

The Major returned his revolver to its holster. "All right," he said airily. "On with the dance. You'll pardon my suspicions, I know. But one can't afford to take chances. Shall I turn my pockets out, or do you want to do it all yourself?"

"I'm making a damned fool of myself," the chief muttered. Then aloud, "Give me the idol. That's all I want to search."

The Major took it from his pocket and handed it to him.

The chief examined it closely, weighed it in his hand, shook it, scraped it with his knife.

"What are you looking for?" the Major asked. "The Birmingham trade mark?"

"No, I'm looking to see where the thing opens."

"Oh," the Major cried excitedly, "does it open? Show me!"

The chief ignored him, and putting the idol on a rock outcrop struck at it viciously with the axe Jim had left near by.

"Don't do that," the Major said in alarm. "You'll ruin its charming features."

The chief brought down the axe on the idol again and again but made no impression on it.

The chief picked it up and tossed it to the Major. "Take the damned thing," he growled. "I wasted all the morning on you, and half the night. And you're only a damned fool dude, just as I thought. Come on, Ashe."

"Just a minute," the Major pleaded.

"Well?"

"Give me a few rounds of cartridges for my revolver, there's a dear lad. I haven't got a bally one to my name. Look!"

He took out his revolver, broke it and showed it to the chief, every chamber empty.

"Here," said Ashe, and gave the Major his well filled cartridge belt.

"Thanks, old dear," the Major said gratefully. "I'll remember that."

"Come on, Ashe." The chief was impatient. As he spoke he strode quickly off toward the *dorp*. "Good job," he grumbled when Ashe caught him up, "that no one was on hand to report this little affair in the D.T.s. I'd never hear the end of it. Looking for diamonds in a solid image. Bah! And thinking the Major clever—hell! He's just a cadging dude of a remittance man."

"Yes, sir," Ashe agreed dutifully.

FOR FIVE minutes or so after the departure of his visitors the Major sat motionless in his chair, a contented smile on his face. He was sure, now, that he would have little difficulty in negotiating the sale of the diamond without fear of police interference. The chief was convinced that he was a brainless fool.

The Major knew a man in the *dorp* who would give him a price for the stone. Not so much as he could get at the

Cape, or at Lourenço Marquez, but sufficient to purchase a substantial outfit.

He stooped over, picked up a log and threw it on the fire. Before he sat up again he had retrieved and pocketed the diamond.

Suddenly he jumped to his feet, panic stricken. He had forgotten Jim!

He ran swiftly through the bush and ten minutes later came in view of a tumbled down hut built at the end of a long heap of slag.

He walked carefully now, knowing that the ground was pitted with shaft holes. A glimmer of light showed through a crack in the wall of the hut. He crept closer.

He heard a man's voice raised threateningly, heard the snap of a whip, followed by a moan.

The Major's eyes blazed, his mouth set in hard lines, his muscles tensed. He crept closer, peered through a crack in the door and cursed softly.

Jim, the clothes stripped off his back, was suspended by a stout cord, tied to his thumbs and fastened to a beam. His toes just reached the ground. Standing beside him, *sjambok* in hand, was an undersized, half starved looking half caste who looked to a thin cruel faced white man sitting in a rickety chair for orders. On the top of the crate which served as a table was a candle stuck in its own grease. Near it were the two halves of the idol Jim had made, and the worthless diamond.

"Where is the other stone, dog?" the white man snapped, his slight lisp giving the question a ferocious sibilance.

"I do not know," Jim replied sullenly.

"You lie! I have discovered many things since I last saw you. I know the game you played with that dead nigger of mine. But he won't gamble again. He's dead. And you'll die, too, if you do not speak true! Where is the other stone?"

"I do not know. I know nothing. You said you would give me money if I stole my *baas'* idol. There is the idol, where is the reward?"

"Give it to him, Hans," said the white man.

The half caste laughed and raised the *sjambok*, but before it could fall on Jim's naked back the Major fired. The candle went out, plunging the place into darkness, spattering the white man with its grease.

Things happened then with astonishing rapidity.

The Major burst down the rickety door, cut Jim free, and, lighted by the moon rays which poured through the opening administered a white man's justice upon the white and his half caste tool.

In and out his fists went, breaking through the feeble guards of the two men. The half caste quickly threw up the sponge and collapsed groaning in a corner.

"Bind and gag him, Jim," the Major grunted and concentrated his attack on the white man, attacking him so hotly that he had no chance to draw his revolver. "I'll teach you to *sjambok!*" the Major said fiercely, and punctuated each word with a smashing blow which bruised the other's ribs.

The thin man went down before the last one, down and out.

"Bind and gag him, too," the Major ordered.

The Hottentot quickly obeyed. "You were long coming, *baas*," he said reproachfully.

"I was delayed, Jim. Let me see your back."

"It is nothing, *baas*. A little scratch, that is all."

"Turn 'round!"

Jim obeyed and the Major tenderly fingered the ridges left by the cut of the lash. Then he picked up the *sjambok* and lightly flicked the white man on the leg with it, laughing as the other whimpered like a licked cur.

"You don't like it, eh?" he drawled. "I ought to cut the flesh off you. You'd appreciate that, wouldn't you? Why don't you answer?" The lash flicked out again. "Oh, I see. You can't, can you? You're gagged, I forgot. Never mind. I won't thrash you after all. There must be a better way of dealing with you. Let's see: you're a politician of sorts, aren't you? Oh, well!"

The Major turned to Jim. "How much did the white man say he would give you for the idol and the stone?"

"Fifty pounds, *baas.*"

The Major felt in the white man's pockets and brought out a handful of gold coins. "He's only got ten, Jim. Take them, they're yours. This," he picked up the two halves of the idol, "I will keep. Now let us go, Jim. No, wait a minute." He picked up the worthless diamond and put it in the white man's pocket. "That will do it, I think. Now we'll go."

AT NOON the following day, Trooper Ashe received the following note.

Dear Ashe:

If you are wise you will take a trip to the old shack near the deserted working. You'll find there a bally politician who isn't at all the honest man he should be. I rather suspect him of being an I.D.B. At any rate, if I were you, I'd search him thoroughly. Better take two or three men you can trust and whom you know to be honest, as witnesses.

I'm giving you this tip because I used to know your father. And, if you work it cleverly, you may be able to get his old job on the force back for him.

Good luck!

Yours,

The Major.

P.S. Thanks for the revolver cartridges. I told you I'd repay the loan, didn't I?

Just as Ashe finished reading this, the chief of police came out from his inner office. In one hand he held two halves of a crudely made wooden idol, in the other a letter. His face was flushed with wrath. "Here, read this," he said roughly.

Ashe pocketed his own note and read the one the chief handed him. It was in the same handwriting as his own epistle.

Dear Tubbikins:

By the time this reaches you I'll be a long way from your loving embraces. I've just concluded a very satisfactory little deal with a resident of your fair city who collects stones—funny hobby, isn't it?—and we, Jim and I, will be on trek long before sunup. You'll be glad to know, I'm sure, that acting on your advice to collect the sinews of war any way I damned please, I am now very well equipped and am following the trail of the red idol.

Oh, and about that idol. Perhaps the enclosed is the one you ought to have examined? Ah, ha!

Just one other thing: knowing how eager you are to make the dorp a law-abiding town and a credit to your, er, administration, I'd advise you to keep an eye on a certain thin politician. But no doubt you knew that. Probably he, as it were, supplements your salary. Still, knowing what I know and, you will remember, having taken the Queen's shilling I feel it my duty to notify you of any little misdemeanors which come to my attention.

Cheerio, old top.

The Major.

P.S. (I'm awfully fond of P.S.s; they take care of the sins of omission and commission, eh, what?) But to repeat—

P.S. Jim, that's my Hottentot servant you know, is going to occupy all his spare time making wooden idols, they seem so popular. If this little venture of ours falls flat I shall return and enter into the manufacture of the idols on a large scale. They will sell well, I'm sure, and because we used you as a model, as it were, I shall call them "Tubbikins" and pay you a very generous, er, royalty. That's all, I think.

"Hell!" swore the chief as Ashe handed the letter back to him. "What do you make of that? If he thinks he can make a fool of me, the damned monocled dude, he'll soon find— Here, where are you going?"

Ashe was moving toward the door. "I've got to go and investigate a complaint, sir. Case of idol worship on the veld, sir. Very urgent."

"Here, you—" the chief began. But Ashe did not hear him. Ashe was outside in the street, wondering what men he should ask to accompany him to the deserted working.

The chief stared wrathfully at the broken idol he held in his hand.

"Hell!" he exclaimed, and threw it violently away. "The damned monocled dude!" he muttered, and returning to his office composed himself for sleep.

HEADING NORTH

FROM THE south blew a gentle breeze; suddenly, without warning, its force increased, assuming the ferocious velocity of a tornado—driving black storm clouds before it.

The white man looked at the scurrying clouds, laughed challengingly, and bracing his feet against the dash board of the Cape wagon drove the eight mules at mad gallop across the veld, heading for the river's ford a full three miles distant.

"Hold tight, Jim!" he yelled to the native who sat beside him.

The Hottentot's white teeth flashed in answer, and, standing up, the squat, powerfully built black flourished his long whip over the backs of the mules; shouting queer sounding, guttural encouragements at them.

The Cape wagon careened from side to side like a derelict in a heavy sea. The black Arab stallion tethered to the tailboard of the wagon neighed fretfully, continuously, until the white man turned and spoke soothingly; then it ceased to strain at the tethering rope, the wild light went from its eye and it settled down to an easy, machine-like stride, easily keeping pace with the frenzied, topmost speed of the mules.

The clouds dropped lower; the darkness deepened. In the distance flashes of lightning glared and thunder rumbled spasmodically. The air was filled with twigs, leaves, bits of sod and small pebbles which the wind caused to dance before its fury.

The lashings of the wagon's tented cover came undone at the back. The wind howled through the opening, whipping the Hottentot's soft felt hat from his head. The off-leader mule shied as it hurtled past him.

"*Au-a!*" Jim wailed. "It was a new hat, *Baas*. Where will I get another like it?"

The white man made no reply. All his faculties were concentrated on guiding the mules over the broken, uneven ground—swinging them round boulders and the miniature mountains which were anthills.

The wind ceased as suddenly as it had sprung up. The calm which followed was oppressive, breathing was difficult. It was as if all air which supports life had been blown from the earth's surface, leaving it destitute, leaving an abhorrent vacuum; leaving a vacuum which the clouds, in obedience to Nature's immutable law, were dropping quickly to fill. They were so low now that they seemed to press upon the wagon's top; so low that it seemed as if the Hottentot's flailing whip would cut them to ribbons and precipitate the flooding waters they held.

The pace of the mules slackened and their response to the guiding tug of the reins was sluggish; they desired to weave their own path through the enshrouding darkness.

"It is best that we stop, *Baas*," Jim the Hottentot shouted, forgetting that the need to shout had passed with the dropping of the wind—the roar of it was still in his ears.

"I think we can reach the ford and cross before the great dark comes, Jim. I can just see the baobab tree which marks the place."

As he spoke the wagon lurched violently, almost capsizing; the near wheels had dropped into a deep gulley. It took the white man's great skill with the reins, required all his patience and knowledge of mules to avoid the disaster which threatened. For a few sickening seconds the wagon teetered perilously then righted itself and rolled on over comparatively smooth ground.

"Best stop, *Baas*," the Hottentot said again. "You can no longer see the tree."

"True, Jim. But I can see the mules and the ground just before them. We will go on yet."

"*Au-a!* What a man you are, *Baas*," Jim grumbled. "You flee from danger into danger and seek danger by the way. But me, I am frightened."

"Say you so, Jim," the white man murmured absently. He was leaning forward, peering into the darkness. "But you are no child to be frightened at the dark."

"A child is not frightened at the dark, *Baas*," Jim said sententiously, "but at the evil which lives in the dark."

The white man made no reply. The mules' pace had slackened to a walk. Jim climbed over the seat and made his way into the body of the wagon. Locating the hurricane lamp which hung from one of the ribs of the cover, he lighted it and then sat down at the rear of the wagon, his legs dangling over the tailboard, staring in awed silence through the darkness.

Presently a dull roaring noise sounded in the south, a noise like the hissing of a surf on a sandy, gently sloping shore. The roar increased in volume and out of the darkness a faint, wraith-like mist appeared moving rapidly in the tracks of the wagon.

"Hurry, *Baas,*" Jim called, "the rain comes."

The white man's answer alarmed him.

"How many mules am I driving, Jim?"

"The *Baas* is jesting or the darkness has bent him mad," the Hottentot muttered. Then, aloud, "Eight, *Baas.* And you know it, Hurry."

A chuckle calmed his fears.

"I cannot go faster, Jim. I have only two mules; at least I can only see two. And they are fading."

Jim hurried to the front of the wagon. The darkness was now so great that only the sterns of the two wheelers were visible.

"Best stop, *Baas,*" Jim said for the third time.

The white man sighed.

"All right, Jim. But days will pass before we can go on again."

He reined the mules to a standstill.

Quickly the two men got down from the wagon and outspanned the mules—hobbling them and turning them loose. Before their task was done the clouds above them opened, burst like an overfilled balloon, and it rained—not in drops, but in solid sheets of water which bruised the body, chilled them to the very marrow of their bones and turned the sun-parched heat-cracked earth into a slippery sea of mud.

FROM THE south came the message of the drums; from a tiny hill-sheltered *kraal* not many miles from the diamond town of Kimberley, it traveled north; sped to its final destination on the wings of the same wind which marshalled the rain clouds to their devastating attack on the long season's drouth.

From hill top to hill top, from *kraal* to *kraal*, its staccato beat passed on, reverberating among the hills, roaring over the plains. The giant tall elephant grass swayed to its vibrations.

White men hearing the drumming, spoke knowingly of a big beer drink afoot. "Niggers always drum like that if they're planning a big beer drink," they said with a complacent snicker of assurance.

Most natives who heard hid themselves in their huts—frightened, as children are, by something they did not understand. The few who could translate the message of this primitive telegraph, smiled covertly and hoped that no one had seen the blood lust which flashed into their eyes.

At many *kraals* the signal drummers passed on the message, yet had no comprehension of its meaning—the code was unknown to them. But they never thought of breaking the chain of communication and lost no time in relaying the message on; first sounding the African "Are you there? Are you there?" until an answering beat announced that the drummer in the next village—aroused from sleep, perchance, or called from a wedding feast—was at his post, listening in. And then the message would throb out—"*Tum-tum, chi. Chi-tum*—" again and again until the sender heard the bush equivalent of "Message received and understood."

After long hours the message came to the ears of a wizened old man who lived in a cave high up in a kopje overlooking the river's ford. He was sitting at the mouth of the cave, watching the clouds gathering in the south, watching the tiny dust cloud which traveled before the storm, warming himself in the rays of the sun which were so soon to be quenched by driving rain.

As he watched, the dust cloud materialized into a white hooded wagon drawn by eight mules; the dust cloud it created swirled above it and was made to assume fantastic shapes by the suddenly awakened breeze.

The setting sun was engulfed by black cloud masses; the force of the wind increased, howling about the kopje, shrieking through the passages which, leading from the cave, honeycombed the kopje.

It grew cold.

The old man rose stiffly and entering the cave added more fuel to the fire which was burning there, sniffed the acrid fumes with evident enjoyment and then, wrapping his attenuated frame in a magnificent kaross made of leopard skins, he returned to his seat at the cave's opening.

Almost immediately he was conscious of a drum's beat above the fury of the wind; it impinged upon his ears with the force of a thousand spear heads upon a thousand shields.

He leaned forward, inclined his head slightly, and listened. At that moment he was as one numbed of all his senses, only one was performing its proper function. At that moment he was sightless, he could not smell, he could not feel; he sat as one suddenly transmuted to stone. But he could hear; could separate the message of the drum from the voice of the wind.

Presently the old man sprang to his feet, letting the kaross fall from his shoulders to the ground, and stood stark naked at the cave's mouth. A mad fanatical light gleamed in his sunken eyes, decrepit old age seemed to pass from him; at that moment he was the personification of a nation's spirit.

A smother of smoke emerged from the mouth of the cave, caused by a freakish back-draught, enveloping him. It was caught up and tossed into nothingness by the wind. But long before it had entirely passed away the old man had disappeared and a native goatherd who was hurrying his goats back to his *kraal*, venturing, because of his haste, to traverse the path which led before the cave's mouth, shook his head fearfully and mumbled a prayer of supplication to the Great Great. Had he not seen a great wonder-working? Had he not seen Mbike, the Wise One, disappear into nothingness before his eyes?

Fifteen minutes later rounding a spur of the hill, the herd came in sight of his *kraal* which nestled close against the kopje's precipitous side. A party of warriors, armed with *assegais* and shields, hurried out of the opening in the thorn stockade which encircled the *kraal* and took the path leading to the river's ford.

"What's afoot?" the goatherd shouted.

"The Voice has spoken," one answered. "We go to the ford to stop a white man and his black dog from crossing."

The last few words came faintly for the warriors were speeding on their way.

The goatherd nodded importantly.

"I knew it," he muttered. "Did I not see Mbike taken up into the clouds to commune with the Great Ones?"

And he hurried on to the *kraal*, eager to hear what was to be told, eager to tell what he had seen.

MORNING BROKE—A cold, gray, cheerless morning, the sun obscured by weeping clouds. The tented wagon looked strangely forlorn, isolated by a sea of mud. Overnight, desolation had dropped up on the veld, it looked incapable of sustaining life of any sort. But here and there green patches showed where young, tender grass shoots were pushing their way hopefully upward; the leaves of the few stunted trees which dotted the landscape were turning so that they could catch a feast of rain drops on their broad surfaces. Several hundred yards to the east, behind a low spur of the tall, gaunt kopje—the baobab tree which marked the ford was not far from the foot of it—coils of smoke indicated the location of the *kraal* from which came sounds of life—the bleating of goats, a rain bedrabbled rooster's crowing, and the plaintive lowing of cattle.

The black stallion, its ears pricked, stood sniffing at the canvas hood of the wagon, pawing the ground impatiently, scattering showers of mud over the mules which huddled dejectedly together behind him.

Presently, Jim, the Hottentot, crawled from under the wagon's shelter, a measure of oats in his hands. This he emptied into a shallow box and placed it before the stallion, watched the spirited animal daintily commence to feed, and then lighted a fire on a level shelving of rock—using bark and twigs stripped from a near-by tree for fuel.

This making of fire, no matter how heavy had been the rain, or how water soddened the fuel at hand, was one of the many apparent miracles Jim could perform with ease. Civilization has not been a wholly unmixed blessing; the invention of matches, for example, has cost man a great deal more than the mere ability to make fire with flints or fire sticks.

The fire blazing cheerfully, Jim entered the wagon, emerging immediately loaded with cooking utensils and provisions for the morning meal. In a few minutes the appetizing aroma of coffee mingled with the wood smoke and rashers of bacon spluttered merrily in the frying-pan.

A sound of splashing water came from the wagon, followed presently by the full throated purring noise which some athletes make as they vigorously towel themselves. This gave way presently to a lusty, tuneful baritone singing one of the Freebooter Ballads.

Jim listened happily, beating his hands softly together in time to the marching rhythm of the song, then called "O-he!"

The song ended abruptly and a touseled head was thrust through the opening in the canvas hood.

"What is it, Jim?" the white man asked. His cheeks glowed from the drill of the razor and the bite of the ice cold water.

"In a little while skoff will be ready, *Baas*. I go now to the river."

"What for, Jim? Water?" The white man's innocent looking blue eyes sparkled; there was a note of banter in his voice. "Surely there is enough water here without going to the river?"

Jim grinned. The night's heavy rain had found several weak spots in the cover of the wagon and he had been too lazy to move his blankets to a dryer spot.

"I go, *Baas*," he said, with an air of dignified reproach, "to see if we can cross. Also—" it was his turn to banter now—"it is well that we stopped last night when we did. The *Baas* could not see very well; undoubtedly the darkness and the rain covered his eyes. Yet a boy—too young, even, to mind goats—would have steered closer to the ford than the *baas* did." He pointed to the baobab tree. "Had we gone on we should have toppled over the bank and—"

"And made a ford of our own," the white man interrupted. "That is why I came this way, hoping to make you swim. Also—" it was plainly evident that the anger in his voice was only feigned—"I had other things to do beside drive, O impertinent one. I had to calm the fears of a Hottentot dog who was afraid of the dark. If I had a *sjambok* in my hand—"

"You would beat me, eh, *Baas?*" Jim interrupted quickly. "You who saved me from beatings—and worse—how many times?"

He moved the coffee back a little from the fire; turned the bacon and then walked swiftly in the direction of the river. A few minutes later a sudden dip in the billowing veld hid him from sight.

The white man withdrew into the wagon and took up the thread of his interrupted song as he completed his toilet.

When he presently climbed down from the wagon, fully dressed, he was just in time to save the coffee from boiling over and the bacon from charring. Removing them to the seat of the wagon he sat down and broke his fast with that keen enjoyment known only to men whose life is spent in seeking and finding adventure in some one of the world's vast breathing spaces.

When he had finished there was still plenty left for Jim which he placed on some red embers raked from the fire. Returning again to the wagon seat he cheerfully surveyed the dreary expanse of veld.

"I hope Jim finds that we can cross the bally brook," he said aloud, in English. "It'll be most deucedly annoying if we have to potter about here."

The affected drawl in his voice seemed quite appropriate, quite in keeping with the appearance he presented to the casual observer.

A gold-rimmed monocle propped open his right eye. Without it, one judged, the eye would close because the man did not have the energy, was too lethargic, to keep it open without mechanical aid. His black hair, graying slightly at the temples, was brushed back from his high, broad forehead in an immaculate pompadour. His clothes—the khaki colored flannel tunicshirt, the whipcord riding breeches, supported at the waist by a heavy ammunition belt from which hung a revolver and a magnificent hunting knife, the brown poloboots and box spurs were of the exaggerated cut and pattern affected by armchair hunters and explorers. At this moment, one of complete relaxation, his facial expression was one of inane boredom; he looked like a silly ass, and he talked like one. And therefore, following the argument to the logical conclusion arrived at by so many of South Africa's hard cases, he *was* a silly ass.

He fumbled in his pocket and brought out a hideous wooden idol, colored a deep blood red, and toyed with it absently. It was a queer mascot for such a man to carry about him; on the other hand it was just such a mascot the man he affected to be would carry. Think of the sensation it would cause when exhibited at the club? The workmanship of the grotesque thing was perfect; had been carved by a master of the craft. Anatomically it was correct in every detail—from the horns, five eyes, and tribal marks on its receding forehead to the nails on its splayed toes. It was repellent; the leering set of its face and the manner it supported an enormous belly with its hands expressed gross bestiality.

A dude's mascot.

The white man's long, sinewy fingers closed tightly over the idol; steel lights flashed in his blue eyes and every muscle in his body tensed.

He was thinking of the manner in which the idol came into his possession—of a brawl in a low dive in Lourenço Marquez, of the murder of a red-headed giant of an American. All because of this grinning, blood-red idol of wood.

He thought, too, of the strange story the murdered man had told him before he died; of the beginnings of a gigantic plot which had for its aims the supremacy of the black race and the enslaving of the white; of the mysterious secret society to which this idol was a clue; of the red-haired American's invalid uncle who, with his niece, had stumbled on to the secret and were camped—although probably made prisoners or killed now—somewhere in the region of the Mountains of the Moon.

A wild story; one which the white man did not altogether believe, yet professed to believe. In fact, he actually believed it sufficiently to give up his old haunts and the practise of his profession—and men said that the Major was the cleverest I.D.B. that ever succeeded in throwing dust in the eyes of the detectives engaged by the Diamond Mining Syndicate. He believed the American's story to the extent of telling it to prominent South Africans, endeavoring to enlist their support, and, when they laughed at him, ran risks in order to outfit himself properly for the trek north that he might investigate for himself.

After all, in Africa all things are possible.

With an impatient gesture he returned the idol to his pocket and looked out across the veld. When he saw Jim plodding through the sticky mud toward him, coming from the direction of the ford, he relaxed once again and a quizzical expression came into his eyes.

"I wonder what the old heathen 'll say," he muttered. "Some bloomin' cock-an'-bull story, no doubt. The bally blighter doesn't like the idea of this trip at all, been tryin' to put me off it ever since we started. He'll probably say that the river's absolutely impassable, or that there are thousands of crocodiles at the ford, or—

"Do we trek at once, Jim?" he shouted.

The Hottentot raised his head, stared in the direction of the wagon, and increased his pace to a slouching, space destroying run. But he did not answer.

And when he reached the wagon he did not speak but sat down silently beside the fire and ate greedily.

The Major smiled. "Behold, the great one eats," he said softly. "Let no one speak, let no one disturb him. He has done great deeds; his *assegai* is red with the blood of a thousand enemies; his mouth is stuffed with bacon and a white man's coffee—"

Jim, his cheeks bulging with food, looked up reproachfully.

The Major looked very serious. "And what great discovery have you made, great warrior?" he asked with mock gravity.

Jim tried to speak and nearly choked.

"Swallow, warrior," the Major counselled, "then talk."

Jim gulped noisily, cleared his throat with a long swig of coffee. "See if you can swallow the talk I shall make, *Baas*."

"I have eaten, Jim," the Major answered, "but there is room in my belly for many words."

"Well, then, *Baas*, I have been to the river—"

"And found it in high flood so that it is impassable," the Major interrupted. "I knew it."

"It is in flood," Jim said solemnly, "and it is impassable, but it is not the flood which makes it impassable."

The Major crowed with delight.

"You're a dream of a laddie, Jim," he cried in English. "You always run so abso-bloomin'-lutely true to form, don't you know?"

"Me know? Damme yes-no. If I don't see you s'long hullo!" Jim responded breathlessly, almost exhausting his meager stock of English.

"There are crocodiles watching the ford, Jim?" the Major asked in the vernacular. "Yes, of course. There would be crocodiles."

"Yes, *Baas*. There are crocodiles, two score of them, with pointed teeth waiting to eat up any who dare to try the ford."

"Only two score, Jim?" the Major exclaimed in disappointed tones. "Surely your eyes are blinded and you did not count aright. What are two score to a warrior like you? We will eat them up—you and I. Come, let us inspan and trek."

He jumped down from the wagon.

"The *Baas* had best listen to the end of the tale I tell. Men who swallow too hastily have belly aches," Jim said portentously.

The Major sat down on the disselboom of the wagon. "I listen, Jim," he said humbly.

"I went to the river," Jim began again, "first to where it flows near here. It runs between high, rocky banks, *Baas*, and nowhere save at the ford is a crossing possible. And the river is in flood, *Baas*, but not yet have the hill floods come down. And, so, as I have said, the flood would not stop us from crossing. Then I went along the river bank toward the ford, keeping closely under cover—"

"Why, Jim?" the Major interrupted curiously.

"Who shall say, *Baas?* Save that it is always best to remain unseen in a strange country until it is known whether other men who live in that country are friends or—or crocodiles with pointed teeth.

"And, as I have said, *Baas,* I came after a little while to the ford; many spear lengths I crawled like a snake upon my belly. At the ford, *Baas,* I saw two score crocodiles with pointed teeth; aye, and I heard somewhat of their talk."

"I did not know that crocodiles talked, Jim," the Major murmured. "But you were saying?"

"I was saying, *Baas,*" Jim continued gravely, "that two score warriors, armed with *assegais,* guard the ford."

"*Wo-we!*" the Major exclaimed. "The crocodiles became warriors. What then, Jim?"

"A little I heard them talk, *Baas.* All night they have waited at the ford—since before starting of the rain they have waited—in order that they might stop a white man and his black dog from crossing."

The Major knit his brows in puzzled thought.

"But they can mean no harm to us, Jim, else they would have come here in the night instead of waiting."

Jim shrugged his shoulders but ventured no reply.

"How long, think you, before the hill floods come down, Jim?"

"Who knows, *Baas?*" the Hottentot replied with another shrug. "Perhaps not until noon—or tomorrow's noon. Perhaps now. A man might start to cross the river finding the water only knee deep, and be overwhelmed by the flood ere he reached the other side. That you know, *Baas*."

The Major nodded.

"Saddle Satan, Jim. I will ride to the ford and talk with those black ones who lie in wait for us."

"Best not, *Baas*," Jim expostulated in alarm. "It is not wise to talk to men whose tempers are as sharp as the spears they carry. Think, *Baas;* all night they have waited in the cold rain. They are not in the mood for talking."

"Nevertheless, Jim, I shall go and talk with them. Must I saddle Satan myself?"

He walked toward the horse.

Jim sprang to his feet and hurried after him.

"Hasten slowly, *Baas*," he pleaded. *"Au-a!* I know you are not afraid of warriors, but these men spoke of a Voice which ordered them to prevent our crossing the ford. And not even you, *Baas,* can turn a black man's mind against the wonder workings of their witchdoctors."

"I shall go, Jim," the Major said again, "and arrange for our crossing. If we cannot cross here—and we cannot remain here—maybe they will tell me of another ford."

Reaching into the wagon he brought out Satan's bridle and saddle. Jim took them from him and silently put them on the horse. As he was tightening the girths the low murmur of the river changed suddenly into a loud, sullen roar.

He straightened himself, grinning contentedly.

"With, or without, the warriors' permission, *Baas*," he said, "we cannot cross now. The floods are down. And look, *Baas,* here come the warriors."

He pointed in the direction of the ford where a party of warriors suddenly appeared on the skyline, mounting the steep bank leading from the river's ford. They were coming now toward the wagon at a slow, stiff-legged gait.

"The water has got into their bones, *Baas*," Jim said with a chuckle.

The Major keenly eyed the oncoming warriors; there was something ominous about their silent advance. The Major was reminded somewhat of the tactics of a cat playing with a mouse.

"What does it mean, Jim? Is it this?"

As he spoke, the Major took the red idol from his pocket. The Hottentot looked at it with an expression of disgust and awe commingling.

"Undoubtedly it is that, *Baas*," he muttered. "It is an evil thing. Give it to them, or throw it away, and let us trek south again."

The Major laughed softly.

"How often, Jim, have you turned aside from following the spoor because the path was beset with thorns? And what joy in living if one treads only a path well-trodden by the feet of men?"

"*Tchat!*" Jim exclaimed and glanced swiftly at the warriors. They were still a good hundred yards away, their pace still slower.

"Hide that thing, *Baas*," he said. "If they must have one, give them this."

This was one of two clumsy imitations of the Major's idol which Jim had carved during the long hours of uneventful trekking. He had colored it with red paint filched from a kaffir store.

The Major took it and gave the original to Jim.

"Hide it," he said.

"If I were to throw it into the river, *Baas*—" Jim began.

"I said hide it, not lose it," the Major interrupted sternly. "Now unsaddle Satan. The warriors are close at hand, but you can not, will not see them. Neither shall I. Wait until I speak."

He climbed up into the wagon and seated himself on the driver's seat, facing the west, his back to the warriors. On his knee he placed the idol Jim had carved and looked at it steadily.

The warriors, there were forty of them, swarmed about the wagon now. Some of them were warming themselves at the fire, squatting on their haunches, blowing at the red embers; others stood sullenly about, eyeing the wagon, the horse and mules, Jim and the white man, with ill concealed curiosity. But their bearing was infinitely more hostile than curious; they bore themselves like men with chips upon their shoulders and, undoubtedly, they would have welcomed an excuse—no matter how trivial—to color their spear heads with the blood of the Major and Jim, the Hottentot.

Minutes passed.

The Major did not move. Jim, busily grooming the mule, cleverly avoided meeting the stares of the warriors; apparently he was unaware of their presence.

One of them ventured close to the stallion's hind quarters and, not understanding the warning of the twitching ears and thrusting underlip, was guilty of a much greater folly. He pricked the blooded animal's flanks with the point of his *assegai.*

An outraged squeal, the flashing of hoofs and their thudding impact on the warrior's chest followed with lightning swiftness. The warrior went backward, down, rolled ever and over. By some strange chance no bones were broken, his skin, even, was not cut, and the man scrambled hastily to his feet, more distressed by the mocking laughter of his comrades than the pain of the kick.

He shouted threats and abuse at the men who laughed at him; but they only laughed the louder until he, too, was impelled to laugh with them.

Laughter—and death—come very easily to Africa's black children.

Gradually the laughter subsided, ceased entirely save for a half-smothered chuckle from the man who had been kicked. Last to see the joke he was the last to relinquish it.

Presently all was quiet again. The warriors huddled together now, looking at each other uneasily. Evidently they were greatly puzzled by the attitude of the white man and the black dog, his servant. Doubts arose in their minds. Were the strangers flesh and blood—or figments of their imagination? Or were they, themselves, spirits—invisible, noiseless, without form or substance? How else explain the white man's conduct? All this time he had not moved or given any sign to indicate that he was aware of their presence. Even the laughter had not moved him.

He turned now and looked full at them, through them— apparently not seeing them.

"Jim," he said, "put more wood on the fire."

"Yah, *Baas*," the Hottentot replied and moved swiftly to obey the order. Looking straight before him, Jim passed through a knot of warriors, guiding his feet so cleverly that he did not even brush against one of the intruders. One deliberately got in his path, menaced him with upraised *assegai*. Jim did not falter nor turn aside; he would have trodden on the warrior's naked toes had not the man jumped aside with a frightened yelp.

The other warriors shivered. Here and there a man slyly pinched himself, appearing relieved at the ensuing pain.

Having replenished the fire, Jim returned to the horse, passing again through the warriors.

They whispered together.

"At least the horse is no spirit," exclaimed the man who had been kicked.

There were subdued titterings at that and then one of the men—the captain of the party—was pushed to the front and propelled, by men who saw that their path of retreat was clear, toward the Major.

A few yards from the wagon they halted, their *assegais* a mere nail's thickness from the buttocks of their chosen spokesman.

"*Sauka bona, umlungu!* Good morning, white man," he stammered.

There was no answer. The white man did not look at him.

The leader turned appealingly to his followers; they motioned to him to speak again. He tried to retreat, to back away, but the *assegais* barred his way, pricked his flesh, drew blood.

"Good morning, Chief," he gasped humbly, desperately.

The Major turned then, a smile of greeting on his face. "Good morning, my father. Good morning, all you people."

"*Au-a!*" they all cried in happy relief. "Greetings, Chief."

They greeted and received greeting from Jim who, squatting on his haunches at the front of the wagon, grinned in happy confidence at his *baas*. Big beads of sweat rolled down the Hottentot's face; they were not the result of his labor over the horse, but of the severe mental strain he had been under. He had known the temper of the warriors, knew that the game his *baas* played with them was a dangerous game, knew that a very little thing would have been the signal for his death, and his *baas'* death.

But his *baas'* knowledge of the black folk was as great as his own; his *baas'* ability to use that knowledge was infinitely greater. So the danger was past now. The Major's ruse had succeeded. The warriors were mentally disarmed; they had greeted him as they would a great chief. For the present the Major's word was law.

"What is your name?" the Major asked abruptly.

"Kawiti," the spokesman answered. "I am the son of M'Jamba who is headman of the *Kraal* of the Voice yonder."

He jerked his thumb in the direction of the kopje.

"And M'Jamba sent you and these others to welcome me to his *kraal?*"

"Yes, Chief," Kawiti stammered, abashed.

"You lie!" the Major cried. "Or, if you speak truly, where are the gifts M'Jamba sent to me as is the custom? Yet it may be that M'Jamba is very poor and—"

"There is no richer headman in this district than M'Jamba," Kawiti interrupted proudly.

"Then you lied," the Major countered swiftly. "Now what is the truth of it? Let me think." He beat his forehead with his clenched fist. *"Au-a!* I have it. Last night a Voice"—the warriors trembled visibly—"spoke to you, ordering you to watch the ford against my coming. Well? Why are you not at the ford?"

"Wo-we! You know all things, Chief," Kawiti said in awed tones. "Then know you not that the need to watch the ford has passed? But a little while ago the hill floods came down and no man can cross; nor will cross for many days to come."

"And had I tried to cross before the flood waters made the river rise, what then?"

"Then we should have spoken to you and, if you had not listened, the water would have run red with your blood."

"And of yours," the Major said absently.

"Maybe, Chief. But you would not have crossed. As the Voice orders, so we, its servants, perform."

"And what now?" the Major questioned.

"Now we come to escort you to the *kraal* where you will stay until—" Kawiti hesitated.

"Until the river goes down," the Major prompted.

"Until," Kawiti corrected, "the Voice gives us further orders concerning you."

"And if I chose not to come with you to your father's *kraal?* What then?"

"You would still come, Lord," Kawiti said firmly. "You are only two; we are two score."

The Major hesitated a moment, then, "Inspan, Jim. We trek for the *kraal* of M'Jamba," he said.

As he spoke he waved his hand imperiously, knocking the red idol from his knee to the ground.

Kawiti stooped quickly and picked it up; looked at it with idle curiosity and returned it to the Major.

"Aye," the Major said thoughtfully, "we will stay for awhile at the *Kraal* of the Voice. Concerning many things I am as a little child wandering in the dark."

A WEEK passed slowly.

The Major and Jim were housed in two guest huts, fed well, and their animals given every care. To the Major was given the freedom of the *kraal* save that he was not permitted to go into the council place.

With M'Jamba, the fat, pleasure-loving old headman, the Major was on the best of terms and the people of the *kraal* reflected their headman's attitude.

In all respects he was treated as an honored guest yet, when he spoke of continuing his journey, he realized that M'Jamba's polite protestations, his urgent entreaty to honor the *kraal* still longer with his presence, were but the velvet scabbards hiding the force by which his departure would have been prevented had he insisted on leaving.

Wisely, he never allowed matters to reach that climax. Actually, had he been so minded, the Major had little doubt of his ability to get away unharmed. Armed with revolver and rifle, choosing his time, he could have left; but that way would have meant bloodshed, would have cost him the respect of these people. And that was not the Major's way. He was a man, and a man does not trample upon children who seek to bar his way.

Jim, the philosopher, was quite content to remain at the *kraal.*

"Here, *Baas*," he would say, "we are dry and warm at night; there is plenty of food and the beer is good. Until the rains abate somewhat we are better here."

But even Jim's philosophy was shaken when, desiring to set snares for klipspringers on the kopje which overshadowed the *kraal,* he found his way barred at the gate in the stockade by a party of warriors who ordered him to return to his hut. His contentment vanished now that knowledge that he was a prisoner had been so rudely thrust upon him.

"It is all that red idol's doings, *Baas*," he complained. "Give it to them and let us go."

The Major shook his head.

"I do not think that these people know anything about the red idol, Jim. And how can I give it to them seeing that I gave it to you to hide?"

"Then I will give it to them."

"No! That you must not do."

"Au-a, *Baas!* I am afraid. This is a place of witchcraft; they call it the *Kraal* of the Voice. I am afraid."

"Afraid of a voice, Jim? A voice is only the wind," the Major scoffed. "There is no cause for fear. You should be content. Here we are dry and warm, there is plenty of food and the beer is good."

The Major chuckled at Jim's gloomy face, was silent for a little while. When he spoke again it was in English.

"It's bally funny, Jim, come to think of it. Can't get a word out of these Johnnies. Even old M'Jamba, now—and, my word, how the old blighter can talk—won't tell me about the things I want to know. He shuts up tighter than the well-known clam whenever I talk about the Voice and the reason for keeping us here. As a matter of fact, I believe the old bounder is in mortal terror of the Voice—whatever that is. He's afraid it'll tell him to do something he doesn't want to do. He's bossed by a Voice and a witchdoctor who never seems to appear. And, you know, Jim," the Major let his monocle fall from his eye into the palm of his hand and polished it absently, "I'm beginning to think that when we've discovered the witchdoctor, we'll have discovered everything. What do you think, Jim?"

"Me?" Jim exclaimed. "Godame yes. Think what you say. No?"

The Major nodded.

"Exactly, Jim. And so—Jim?"

"Yah, *Baas?*"

"You have heard of the witchdoctor, M'Bike?" the Major was talking in the vernacular now.

"Yah, *Baas*. They talk much of him—with their hands over their mouths. He can turn himself into a baboon, he is a great rain maker, he is the mouthpiece of the spirits."

"And have you heard where this wise one lives?"

"Aye, *Baas*. In a cave high up in the kopje overlooking the ford."

The Major nodded.

"So they told me. From his cave M'Bike can undoubtedly see the trails leading to the ford for many miles to the north and south. Even if the drums were silent he would know of strangers approaching before they knew down here at the *kraal*."

"Undoubtedly, *Baas*," Jim agreed with a grin. "That is no little part of his wisdom."

"I shall talk with this M'Bike, Jim."

Jim shrugged his shoulders resignedly.

"It is folly to thrust a hand into a lion's mouth, but if the *Baas* says he will see M'Bike, he will."

"Yes," the Major continued thoughtfully, ignoring Jim's comment. "Tomorrow, during the great darkness which heralds the dawn, I shall go to the place of M'Bike."

"The guards will stop you," Jim said hopefully.

"The guards sleep at that hour, or at least they shut their eyes, fearing to see spirits."

"But what shall I tell them when they ask for you in the morning, *Baas?*"

"Say the spirits have taken me, say—say anything. What matter?"

LATE IN the afternoon of that same day the witch-doctor, M'Bike, came to the *kraal*. With him was a man in whose veins flowed the blood of white and black; a man whom the Major instantly recognized—having heard much of him and nothing good—as a vicious half-caste named Maritz. His Boer father had endowed him with a splendid, bull-like physique and low, animal cunning; from his black mother he had gained a great understanding of her people. But whatever good qualities he may have had had been destroyed by the bitterness of his life. The offspring of two races, he was despised by both, a tragic outcast. In time he came to hate those who despised him and applied his strength and craft to deeds of evil. And so men who before had despised him, come to hate and fear him. And on hate and fear he flourished.

He leered now at the Major as he passed by with M'Bike.

"Ach sis, ma-an!" he said. "I will come and talk with you presentlee."

M'Jamba, rubbing the sleep from his eyes, hurried out to greet his exalted visitor.

"Tonight," the witchdoctor began, disdaining any preamble, "you and your people will gather at the council place." His voice was high pitched, nasal, and had a lilting lisp in it. "Last night I saw a vision and it was made known to me that the Voice wished to speak to the people of the *kraal.* See that you are there and that your ears are open."

"We will be there, O Great One," M'Jamba said meekly, "and our ears will be open. Is the white stranger and his black dog to listen to the voice?"

M'Bike glanced contemptuously at the Major who was standing nearby.

"Aye, let him listen. You guard him well?"

"Well, Great One."

"Yet offer him no hurt, no indignity?"

"As the Voice ordered, so we have performed."

"That is good. So continue until the Voice speaks again concerning him."

He pointed then to Maritz.

"You know this one," he said to M'Jamba. "He is my friend. He comes and goes as he will."

"He is no friend of mine, or of my people," M'Jamba grumbled. "The maidens fear him and—"

"That is sufficient," M'Bike interrupted imperiously. "I have said that he is my friend. But," he turned sharply on Maritz who was grinning evilly, "my friendship can be recalled as easily as it was given. Therefore tread warily and give no cause for offence to the maidens who live here."

Maritz bowed his head in humble submission.

"I go now," said M'Bike and stalked swiftly away.

M'Jamba glared truculently at Maritz, held out his hands in a helpless gesture to the Major, then, shaking his head doubtfully, reentered his hut.

Maritz turned to the Major with a harsh laugh.

"The headman would kill me if he dared."

"I don't see why he doesn't," the Major replied suavely. "It's always best to kill a snake."

"Allehmahtig!" Maritz roared. "For that, Englisher, I will—"

He advanced threateningly, his big clenched fists raised high above his head. He seemed to tower head and shoulders above the Major.

He stopped suddenly. The Major had yawned and stretched himself lazily; the monocle had disappeared and so had the inane expression on his face. His eyes were a cold, steel gray; his mouth indicated a resolute firmness.

Also, he was no longer dwarfed by the half-caste; actually he was a fraction of an inch taller. He was slimmer, but his slimness was evidence of perfect physical condition.

"Yes?" he said questioningly.

Maritz laughed ingratiatingly.

"We must not quarrel, we two," he said. "It is not wise for two white men to fight where black ones can see."

"We can go into one of the guest huts," the Major said evenly. "Some men hold that there is no disgrace in a white man thrashing a black." He swayed lightly on his feet, but the expected rush did not materialize.

Maritz laughed again, choosing to ignore the insult.

"Ach Gott! I am no fool and you are no fool—yet, for a little while I thought you were one. But now I see that you are veree clever because you make men think you are soft and a fool. So you catch them off guard and—yes, you are clever. I am chilled to the bone by this cursed rain and cold. Let us go in the warm and talk. But wait—your name? Ah, I have it. They call you 'the Major,' no? I have beard of you. And me, 'Nigger Maritz.' You have heard of me? Yes?"

"Yes," the Major said shortly, hesitated a moment and then led the way to his hut.

Entering, Maritz sat down close to the red embers of the fire, facing the doorway. The Major, standing up, leaned against the wall, his hands in his pockets.

"Why are you here, Mister Major?" Maritz began abruptly. "Here there are no diamonds."

"I am here because they will not let me go," the Major answered slowly.

Maritz considered this for a moment. "Ah, of course. But why do you travel this way. The police? Maybe they are after you?"

The Major nodded and Maritz rubbed his hands together.

"Yes, I see. It is a pity. You have brains. You should do bigger things than cheating the Syndicate out of diamonds."

"Such as?"

"O-ah! There are many things. Come in with me and I will—"

The Major's eyes narrowed and Maritz smoothly passed on to something else.

"So you do not know why they keep you here, eh?"

"No, unless it is this."

The Major pulled from his right hand pocket and held out for the other's inspection the idol Jim had made.

"Are you playing the fool with me, Mister Major?" Maritz asked as he handed the idol back to the Major. "What has that oogly thing got to do with it?"

"Who knows? But I happened to see the original of this little fellow. A curio collector in Durban had it; he'd just bought it from a Portuguese half-caste who appeared to be frightened out of his wits by it. He said it was the emblem—if you know what I mean?—of a secret society which is plotting to rule Africa. Of course that's all bosh; at least I thought it was then. Anyway, it was a good yarn and it struck me—you see what a big belly it has—that if it were hollow it'd be a good place to hide 'stones.' So I had Jim—my servant, you know—carve one like it. He made it in two pieces, so they could be glued together, with the belly hollow. No one would ever think of looking for stones there, would they? Specially not after hearing my little yarn about the secret society. Jolly smart, eh? Why, a detective in Kimberley had the little red cuss in his hands when he was on the trail of stolen diamonds; two big ones they were.

They'd just about fill the insides of this little chappy. But of course the detective never thought of examining him very closely. Why should he? So he gave him back to me—just as you did! But something made him suspicious—perhaps Jim got drunk and talked; he does, you know—and the detective came looking for me again. But I had flown; dear me, yes. I was on my way north."

A light of greed came into Maritz's eyes. His fingers opened and closed convulsively.

"Ach!" he murmured. "You are veree clever. So the policeman held it in his hands, and I held it in mine. Let me see it again."

The Major laughed and put the idol back in his pocket.

"Not bloomin' likely," he said.

Maritz scowled, keeping his temper with an effort.

"You do not trust me?" he questioned. "If you knew me better—"

"I know you well; that is why I do not trust you," the Major said and his hand dropped carelessly on to the butt of his revolver.

"Why do you think M'Jamba keeps you here because of the idol?" Maritz asked. "Do you think they care about diamonds?"

"No; not that at all, my dear chap. I thought, you see, that they might have discovered in some uncanny way that I had it and think it's the real idol. Why then, if the story about it is true—well, don't you see?"

"It's true, all right," Maritz said heavily. "M'Bike is a member of the society; so am I. Well, M'Bike got word by drum talk that you, and your nigger were to be stopped. And so you were stopped. See?"

"Amusin', very. Go on."

"M'Bike doesn't know anything about the red idol yet, but he will know as soon as a messenger comes. Maybe that messenger'll come tonight. You won't live very long after that. So—give the idol to me now, just as it is, and I'll take it to M'Bike and explain everything. You'll be free to go, then, by morning."

He held out his hand, scowling as the Major laughed derisively.

"It won't do at all, 'Ritzy, old dear. Quite a weak effort on your part, if I may say so. Supposin' your story to be true—about the society and all that—what power have you over M'Bike? I mean—if he would accept your explanation, why wouldn't he accept mine?"

"Accept yours? Don't be a *verdoemte* fool. How can you go to talk to him? They won't let you leave the *kraal*."

The Major's face fell.

"I'd forgotten that."

"So you'll let me do it for you. No? You see, Mister Major," Maritz lowered his voice to a hoarse whisper, "M'Bike does everything I tell him. He thinks I'm a member of the society for the same reason he is. *Tchat!* As if I care who rules this land—nigger or white. No matter; I've done a lot for M'Bike. I found the cave in the kopje there; the ancients used to work gold from it, I think. There are galleries running back into the hill and— Never mind that. I put M'Bike up to a lot of tricks which make these superstitious niggers think he is a worker of big magic. And in return for it M'Bike does what I tell him.

"Listen; just to prove I'm telling no lies. Eighty miles or so east of here there's a white settler and his wife and daughter. His name is Johnson. The niggers call him N'dhlovu. Almighty! He's as strong as an elephant; haven't I felt the weight of his fist? He beat me with a *sjambok* before all his niggers; and they laughed and threw filth at me. And all because I dared to look at his white-faced daughter."

Maritz's eyes contracted to pin points; he muttered a jumble of threats in the vernacular. At that moment he was all native; an evil blood lust had full control of him.

"Yes?" the Major questioned softly.

"As soon as I was freed I rode here," Maritz continued, "and talked with M'Bike, gave him a message from the society." He laughed harshly. "He believed it—the fool—and so tonight the Voice will talk and in two days the warriors of this *kraal* will leave for the place of Johnson and wipe him out. He and all that he has will be destroyed. And my hands will be clean. None can point the finger of guilt at me."

"You forgot me," the Major commented mildly.

"You! Don't you understand yet? Unless you see eye to eye with me, you will die also. And if you lived and told all that I have told you, who would believe you? What proof have you?"

"If I thought it any good to kill you—" the Major said and drew his revolver a little way from its holster.

Maritz did not flinch, laughed at the threat.

"It would do no good," he boasted. "Also—see how well I know you—you can not kill a man in cold blood."

The Major's hand dropped from his revolver.

"I do not kill you," he said in a hollow voice, "because it has suddenly come to me that the time of your death is at hand but that I am not the instrument."

Maritz shivered. He was not entirely free from the superstitious fears of his mother's people.

"Why talk of death?" he said and swallowed hard. "Tell me: Have I not proved my power over M'Bike? And I proved my cleverness? He sends out these warriors of M'Jamba, thinking to further the work of the society, little thinking that I use him for my revenge."

"Well?"

"Well!" Maritz repeated sarcastically. "Suppose that I whisper into M'Bike's ear that you are a spy? *Au-a!* We talk too much. Give me the idol and I will arrange for you to be set free. If you do not give it, then I will take it."

"If you can take, why beg?"

"Because there is no time to waste; because any moment further word may come to M'Bike concerning you and the opportunity be lost."

"But not my opportunity. When they find that the idol I carry is only a copy—they will set me free."

"You think so?" Maritz sneered. "And what can you do to make M'Bike believe that the thing is not the real one? And I shall not be silent."

"I still think you are bluffing, 'Ritzy. If you are in such a hurry and can take what you want, why don't you take it now?"

"Don't be a fool, ma-an. We are much of a size, we two. You can draw your gun and shoot as quickly—perhaps quicker than I. If I go out and call warriors to help me they will not listen; I have no power over them except through M'Bike and to reach M'Bike is not always possible. Not until tomorrow can I talk with him and then he would have to give word to M'Jamba through the Voice. And so, because I am clever I do not take risks. Therefore I bargain with you, Mister Major. Give me the diamonds—"

"Diamonds?" the Major echoed blankly.

"The red idol, then, Mister Major. The red idol with a belly fat enough to hold two large stones."

"No!" the Major said decidedly. "I won't give it to you now. But I'll tell you what, 'Ritzy. Give me until noon tomorrow and if M'Bike hasn't sent word to let me go free by that time I'll give you the idol."

"And all that it contains?"

The Major appeared confused.

"You're deuced clever, 'Ritzy. Can't put anything over on you. All right—I promise. I'll give you the idol and all that it now contains."

"Don't try any tricks, Mister Major," he warned as he walked toward the door of the hut.

"I won't," the Major said fervently.

A COCK crowed—anticipating by two full hours the break of day; hens clucked sleepily; a dog barked, then yapped shrilly as its master kicked it; the oxen in the cattle *kraal* lowed protestingly.

Then all was silent again.

A dark shadow crawled slowly over the ground, entered a hut and there, in the fire glow, took form and substance.

"It is time, *Baas*," whispered Jim, the Hottentot, and shook the Major into wakefulness.

The white man dressed quickly, every faculty on the alert. When he was fully dressed, revolver in holster, heavy cartridge belt about his waist, he went to the door of the hut and peered into the darkness, listening attentively.

"It is well, Jim," he said quietly as he came back to the fire, sitting down and spreading his hands to its warmth. "In a little while I will go. First tell me what the Voice said to the people of the *kraal*."

"Au-a, *Baas*. I was glad you were not there. You would have said things that would have caused our death—of that I am sure. The Voice ordered the warriors of M'Jamba to go to the place of a white man and wipe him out. The Voice said that he, and his people, were enemies of the Great Spirits."

"And how liked M'Jamba and the people this command, Jim?"

"Not well, I think, *Baas*. But they will obey—not daring to disobey. In two days they set out."

"From whence sounded the Voice, Jim?"

"There is a clump of thorn bush growing out from the kopje just beyond the reach of a tall man. The Voice seemed to speak from behind those bushes."

"And you were not afraid of the Voice, Jim?"

The Hottentot chuckled softly:

"The voice, *Baas*, was the voice like that of a very old man who had an impediment in his speech."

"Such as a lisp, Jim?"

"*Au-a!* You heard, *Baas?* You were there after all?"

"I was not there, Jim. I went to sleep as I said I would. But I have heard that voice before."

Jim nodded.

"Was the man Maritz at the council place, Jim?"

"Yah, *Baas*. He was drinking much with the young men—making them drunk. He was drunk also, but only his legs. His head, I think, was not drunk."

The Major rose to his feet.

"I go now, Jim," he said. "When men ask for me in the morning, say that baboons came and carried me away. Say that one of the baboons talked—with a lisp. Be sure the man Maritz hears of it. And when Maritz leaves the *kraal*, follow him if you can. I think that no one will say you nay; the warriors will be busy elsewhere, preparing for their trek. Now I go."

"I will come with you, *Baas,* as far as the stockade."

Noiselessly they left the hut and made their way slowly through a darkness intensified by a thick, mist-like rain.

A dog sniffed at Jim's ankles, commenced a low, threatening growl, and then was still. Jim had stooped quickly and his hands were very powerful.

A fire gleamed dimly through the darkness. It was straight ahead of them. As they neared they saw the guard of the opening in the stockade squatting about the fire, blankets draped over their shoulders, talking excitedly about the forthcoming raid on the place of the white man.

The Major halted abruptly. The warriors were all facing toward the opening in the stockade and to reach that opening he would have to cross a bar of fire light.

"Wait, *Baas,*" Jim whispered. "I will make them hide their eyes."

The Major was suddenly conscious that Jim had left him. He went forward slowly, very slowly, until he came almost within the radius of the fire light. And there he halted again, the opening in the stockade barely six feet distant.

To the right and behind the guards suddenly sounded a loud rustling noise as if some wild beasts were trying to break through the stockade; the barking of a dog ape followed.

As one man the warriors covered their faces with their blankets fearing that M'Bike the Wise One was about to work a great wonder working, fearing to see—and so die—a manifestation of the spirits.

The Major sped forward, passed through the gate and was swallowed up by the night before the warriors dared to uncover and question each other in awed tones.

DAWN CAME swiftly, gray clouds evaporating before a yellow molten sun. Shafts of light penetrated into the cave of M'Bike, smothering the pale flames of the fire.

The witchdoctor sat erect, stretching himself, wincing with the stiffness of old age. He rubbed his rheumy eyes and then crawled on hands and knees closer to the fire. And there he sat, his kaross draped about him, blinking stupidly at the flames, shivering like a mangy cur. At this, his moment of awakening, M'Bike was only a decrepit old man-an object of pity rather than fear.

The light in the cave grew stronger and, suddenly, M'Bike was conscious that some one was sitting opposite him.

"Au-a!" he exclaimed fearfully. "What make you here, white man? Do you mean to kill me? Take care—"his voice quavered—"I am not unprotected. The spirits—"

The Major laughed mockingly.

"I am not to be frightened by talk of spirits," he said. "Neither have I come to kill you. I come only to talk. But sit closer to the fire—old bones are cold bones."

M'Bike splashed water from a nearby gourd into his face. He gasped at the coldness of it, but when he again looked at the Major his eyes were brighter. He looked keenly at the Major and nodded approval.

"I think you are a man," he said. "And I think, at least I have been told, that you are a friend of us black ones. Speak then; you will not lie."

"And you will not?"

"What need?"

"Listen. I will tell you what I know. You dream of the days when your people were all powerful, when the white men were unknown. And you work for the return of those days, forgetting that the evil of those days was greater than the present evil, forgetting that blood ran freely where now all is peace."

"And what good is peace, white man?" M'Bike said sharply. "Our men are becoming weaklings. White men are everywhere and father men like Maritz. Wo-we! Better that the blood of my people be spilled than it should be so diluted."

"True," the Major agreed sadly. "The white men are greatly to blame in many things. Still, some day you people may again be supreme in this land, but never if fools like you disobey the orders of the drums."

"I have never disobeyed, white man," said M'Bike.

"Say you so," the Major said sharply. "Then whence come the orders?"

"I do not know." M'Bike peered at the Major with trouble filled eyes. "Sometimes from the north, sometimes from the south, sometimes—"

He paused irresolutely.

"And sometimes the man Maritz whispers in your ears," the Major prompted.

"True. We work together. He is wise, and if the beer be good, what matter the color of the pot?"

"And are you so sure the beer is good? So sure that the man Maritz works for the good of your people? Think well of the many things he has told you to do. In what way have your people been helped? Always his word is 'Kill.' How does that help?"

"The enemies of the Spirits must be killed," M'Bike muttered.

"Tchat! And have the drums ever bidden you kill?" The Major added in English, "I'll be done if they have."

"No," M'Bike said uncertainly. "I have wondered at that."

The Major's eyes gleamed.

"Then think of the things Maritz has ordered. Who has gained but Maritz? *Au-a!* He uses you for his own ends."

"If I thought that," M'Bike began and rocked back and forth, pulling at his fingers making the joints crack. "Yet," he continued presently, "he has assisted me in many ways."

"I know," the Major interrupted wearily. "He showed you this cave, he showed you the passage which ends near the council place. He taught you how to play you were the Voice of the Spirits; he taught you many tricks whereby you can throw dust in the eyes of the people."

"You know too much, white man," M'Bike said wrathfully.

"But I have told no one—yet," the Major said softly.

"Nor will not?" M'Bike implored, seeing his power slipping from him, fearing still more the laughter of the people of the *kraal.*

"Nor will not—unless you fail to see your folly."

"I am in the dark; I can not see. But my ears are open. Speak."

The Major sighed with relief.

"Then listen again. The drums ordered you to stop me— and it was done. Yet you do not know why that order came. Have you heard of this?"

He took out the red image and handed it to M'Bike.

The old man blinked uncertainly, turned it over and over, then clutched it tightly to his bony chest.

"I have heard of it; it is strong magic."

"And that is all you know?"

"All."

The Major was disappointed. He had hoped to discover more about the red idol.

"By chance," he said slowly, feeling his way with care, "that thing came into my hands. You were bidden to stop me because men seek it—the men whose orders come to you by the drums. Soon they will come here and ask for it. I give it now to you that the honor of returning it may be yours. But, heed this, now. I told the man Maritz that that thing was only an imitation, that it was hollow and had two diamonds hidden in its belly. He asked for it, begged for it, bargained with me, promised to free me, to make you let me go, if I would give it to him.

"In a little while, I think, he will come here. The Hottentot, who is my servant, will have told him that you carried me off in the night. He will ask for the idol—listen to him—sift out his lies—watch him. And then judge how great has been your folly to obey the behests of such a man. Now bind me that we may play the game properly."

Muttering to himself M'Bike rose and bound the Major hand and foot, following the Major's instructions so that though the white man appeared to be tightly bound he could readily free himself.

Then M'Bike sat down again, staring fixedly at the idol as if hoping that it would come to life and assure him that he was pursuing the right course.

The cave grew lighter. M'Bike did not move, did not speak, did not take his eyes from the idol. The Major watched him anxiously.

The ringing sound of nailed boots on solid rock sounded just outside the cave, a grotesque shadow was thrown on the floor.

M'Bike covered the idol with his kaross.

A moment later Maritz entered the cave and looked doubtfully at the witchdoctor, then at the Major. Seeing that the latter was bound he burst into laughter.

"Ach sis, ma-an?" he shouted gleefully. "Did I not tell you there was danger in waiting."

He turned his back on the white man and squatted on his haunches close to M'Bike.

"How comes the white man here—and bound?" he asked.

"Because the Voice so ordered it."

"Why? Do not talk to me of the Voice."

"In the night the drums spoke," M'Bike said smoothly, "and I obeyed their orders."

"I did not hear the drums," Maritz said suspiciously.

"Doubtless you were asleep. I never sleep."

Maritz laughed.

"And said the drums anything about an idol?"

"Aye—they told me to take it from him."

"Good." Maritz rubbed his hands together. "It was for that I came here. You are to give it to me."

He held out his hands.

"The drums did not say that," M'Bike objected.

"Fool. How can the drums tell everything. I order you, that is enough. Give me."

The witchdoctor fumbled nervously with his kaross then, greatly reluctant, handed the idol over to Maritz.

"Almighty!" Maritz shouted in English as he jumped to his feet. "You are clever, Mister Major, but I am cleverer. In the belly you said, yes?"

He looked carefully at the idol, then, craftily at the Major.

"It may be that you have played a trick on me," he continued. "Maybe you took the stones out after I left you yesterday. I will see now. If they have gone—you will pray for death a thousand times before you die."

He squatted down again, put the idol on the floor and taking out a large knife stabbed at the idol with its stout blade, endeavoring to split it open.

"It is well glued together," the Major said and chuckled.

M'Bike, seeing in the half-caste's action an act of great sacrilege, jumped to his feet and with hoarse cries of rage rushed at Maritz, clawing at him with talon-like fingers.

Cursing, the half-caste rose and with a wide sweep of his powerful arms sent M'Bike-hurtling from him. M'Bike rushed back to the attack, deaf to Maritz's threats and expostulations, grappling with him, clinging to him with his arms and skinny legs.

"Old fool!" Maritz roared. "Let go, let go."

He brought the haft of his knife down on the old man's head with stunning force and M'Bike dropped senseless to the ground just as the Major rushed to his assistance.

Maritz turned and grappled with him, caught hold of the Major's wrists. They stood thus for a moment, glaring wildly at each other. Then Maritz's eyes dropped and the Major laughed softly.

"You slim devil!" Maritz cursed and then, exerting all his force, endeavored to bend the Major's arms, attempted to break them.

The Major's knees bent, as he felt as if he would collapse under the strain. Beads of sweat stood out on his forehead. But he laughed merrily.

Maritz looked at him with astonishment, relaxed for a moment his awful strain. When he tried to exert it again he found that he had lost his advantage. The Major had succeeded in forcing his hands lower, thus getting a better leverage.

Maritz loosed his hold on the Major's left hand intending to concentrate all his strength on the right. As he did so the Major swung hard for his stomach. Maritz doubled up, but held on grimly. Suddenly he gave ground, pulling the Major off his balance and at the same time kicked him viciously below the knee.

The Major stumbled and fell headlong on top of M'Bike, nauseated by the pain.

Swearing triumphantly Maritz dropped on top of him, the knife flashed in his hand.

Before he could drive it home, the Major turned over on his back and caught hold of Maritz's wrist, staying the blow. They struggled furiously, rolling over and over, Maritz attempting to strike his knife home, the Major exerting all his strength to prevent it.

The Major was on his back now, Maritz stooping astride him. One of Maritz's hands was closing about the Major's windpipe; the other, the one holding the knife, was descending slowly, implacably, despite the Major's frenzied efforts to ward it off.

Black spots floated before the Major's eyes—the pressure on his wind-pipe increased—the light seemed to grow very dim—the cave, Maritz, everything material seemed to be dissolving. He felt consciousness slipping from him.

He laughed, a harsh croaking laugh, and relaxed suddenly.

Maritz was thrown off his balance, almost pitched forward on his face; the knife dropped from his hand as he strained to recover himself.

And at that moment the Major suddenly shifted his grip, holding on to the sleeves of Maritz's thick shirt, and he doubled up his legs, planting his feet in the half-caste's belly. Then with a jerk he straightened his legs, pulling forward at the same time.

Maritz went flying through the air, floundering grotesquely, landing on his head with a dull crack.

His legs twitched, he tried to draw his feet up under him, tried to rise, groaned and slumped forward again.

The Major rose to his feet and stood swaying uncertainly; fingering his bruised throat, breathing painfully; tugging ineffectively at the revolver in his holster.

He peered about the cave, feeling that he was alone in the world—meteors flashed past him at incredible speed. He ducked to avoid them; one was heading straight for him. He closed his eyes.

When he opened them again he saw M'Bike the witch-doctor bending over Maritz. A knife flashed in the old man's hands.

"You have made a mock of me," M'Bike screamed, "dog that you are!"

The knife dropped downward. When it rose again it was stained with red. M'Bike struck again and again.

Like a man in a dream the Major stumbled forward.

"You mustn't do that really, old fellow," he mumbled in English.

The witchdoctor looked up and laughed harshly.

"He is dead now, white man," he said contentedly. "This dog who has shamed me, who lied to me, who caused me to bid my people do evil things—he is dead. Four times he marred the idol with his knife—see?" He held out the idol, pointing to the marks Maritz had made. "Four times the knife drank his blood. Truly, the idol is avenged; and I, also, am avenged. He is dead and my folly is a thing of the past. I see with a clear eye now, thanks to you, white man."

He rose to his feet and taking the Major by the arm led him to the cave's opening and made him sit in the sun. From a small gourd he took a handful of spicy smelling ointment and with this he skillfully massaged the Major's throat.

"All my wisdom does not consist of tricks," he chuckled.

"It is good, M'Bike," the Major said presently. "And now what?"

"A little while ago," M'Bike said slowly, "it came to me that it would be well to kill you; you know too much, white man. Then a wiser voice spoke to me. You have shown that you are my friend and the friend of all black ones. You have pointed out evil and helped to rectify it. Therefore I make a bargain with you: For my part I promise to let you go free if you will promise to keep secret the things you know concerning me."

"You do not promise enough, M'Bike," the Major answered.

"What else, then?" M'Bike asked.

"You must promise not to send the people of M'Jamba on any errands of death; you must excuse them from the task you put upon them only yesterday."

"But of course," M'Bike assented promptly. "The orders of death came from Maritz. He is now dead—there will be no more such orders."

"It is agreed then," the Major said slowly.

M'Bike rose to his feet.

"Where go you?" the Major asked.

"I go to speak to the people of the *kraal;* as the Voice. I go to give them orders concerning you; to go to recall the order that was given yesternight. Come with me, if you will, and listen."

"There is no need for you to go," the Major said slowly.

M'Bike looked at him sharply.

"No?"

"No. This morning, before you awoke, I crept down the passageway which leads through the hill. To the opening that is close to the *Kraal's* council place I came. And there I saw M'Jamba and certain of the old men talking together. They were greatly worried, I think, concerning the order to kill the Voice had given them.

"And so I comforted them. Unseen, I spoke to them. They thought I was the Voice. I told them there was to be no more killing. I said—and mark this well M'Bike—that if at any future time the Voice spoke of killing then they would know that that was an evil voice and not the Voice of the Spirits. Such a voice they were to disobey; if they heard such a voice they were to come to the cave of M'Bike and there search for what they would find. Also, I said that the white man and his Hottentot servant were free to go when they would."

M'Bike's eyes blazed wrathfully; expressions of anger, chagrin and admiration struggled for mastery.

Presently he smiled.

"Au-a," he said softly. "You are all wise; you could not lose."

He flung his skin kaross about the Major's shoulders.

"Take it," he said, "You are worthy of it; it is worthy of you. I am only a child, lacking complete understanding." He buried his face in his hands.

"But your heart is right, your feet are now set upon the right path!" the Major said gravely. He rose, thoughtfully stroking the magnificent kaross. A moment he stood there, looking down pitifully at the old man.

Then he stooped and placed the kaross on the ground beside M'Bike.

A moment later he had left the cave and was striding quickly down the hill toward the *kraal.*

IT WAS high noon. All the people of the *kraal* were at the ford to see the crossing of the white man and the Hottentot, his servant. The flood waters had passed and though the river was high, it was fordable.

The sorrow M'Jamba's people felt at the departure of this white man who had so quickly won a place in their affections, was more than counterbalanced by their joy at the removal of the shadow under which they had formerly lived. Assured that their young men would never again be sent out to kill, relieved of the fear of retribution, they could spend the days in feasting and dancing; in marriage and the giving of marriage. Their crops would prosper, their herd increase. Freed of the shadow they could—as children of the sun should—live for the day's pleasures with no thought of the morrow.

The ford crossed, the young men who had acted as pilots liberally rewarded, the Major shouted last farewells to the people on the other side, waved to a tiny black speck sitting outside a cave high up in the kopje, then climbed up into the driver's seat of the tented wagon and gathered up the reins in his powerful hands.

"Ah, there!" shouted Jim the Hottentot and cracked his long whip.

The mules broke into a canter.

The Major brought them round in a sweeping arc and a moment later the wagon hit the trail heading north.

"We are well rid of that place, *Baas,*" said Jim. "Had the Voice not spoken this morning not even your wisdom, I think, could have saved us. The man Maritz hated us and—"

"The man Maritz is dead, Jim," the Major said absently. "And I was the voice which spoke this morning."

"Au-a!" murmured Jim. "I should have known. Great is my *Baas* and I—I am his servant."

TRUTH *IS* MIGHTY

AFTER A night of darkness, of a hell infested darkness, the sun rose. Gray swirls of mist still blanketed the veld and shrouded the jagged peaks of the barren kopjes. And the fog-like vapor thinned visibly; it no longer had an icy, numbing penetration; it had been changed almost instantly by the alchemy of the African sun into a steaming fever mist. Green and gold lizards darted in unceasing energy amongst the rocks, passing perilously near to an adder which was doing its best to resemble a dead, harmless twig. A secretary bird swooped down suddenly upon the snake, flew aloft with the squirming thing, dropped it amongst the rocks and then flew down to its repast.

The sun rose higher, the mist completely disappeared.

Black forms which had looked like rocks were pitilessly exposed by the sun for what they really were—the horribly bloated carcasses of ten mules. Flies buzzed ghoulishly about them.

In the electric-blue of the sky a dark speck appeared. It swooped earthward, opening out its wings when but a few feet from the earth. It landed awkwardly, perching on a near-by, brilliantly flowered tree, croaking hoarsely.

Other specks appeared, earthward swooping specks. Presently the tree was fruited by Africa's hideous, bald-

headed, feathered scavengers. The branches sagged with the load of them. The tree had become a thing of desolation, of death.

The eyes of the birds, red-rimmed and bleared, seemed to be filled with contemptuous indifference as they watched the restless, impatient trotting up and down of four hyenas. Occasionally, as if in response to the fretful titterings of the beasts, one of the birds croaked dismally. "Wait!" it seemed to say. "We can wait! All die—we wait! Wait!"

The clean *crack* of a high powered rifle broke the stillness. One of the hyenas dropped; the others closed upon it—tugging, snapping, snarling. There was a sound of bones being crunched between steel trap-like jaws.

Two vultures flew down from the tree and tore tentatively at the flesh of one of the mules. Another shot and one of them toppled slowly over with a grotesque fluttering of its wings. The other flew back to the tree and was greeted by harsh croaking chorus of derision.

"Wait! All die—we wait!"

A large stone, shrewdly aimed, hurtled through the branches of the tree. It was followed by another, and another.

Some of the birds fluttered upward, croaking a discordant protest. Presently they settled again and when another stone whizzed by them merely followed the example of their more courageous companions—turned ponderously so that they faced the direction from which the missiles came and, their obscenely naked heads sunk deep into the hollow between their hunched-up wings, stared with a basilisk rigidity of purpose at the thrower of those missiles.

They could afford to be patient. They were experienced; they knew. Soon this strange creature who walked on two legs, yet could not fly, would have to depart—or die—and then the feasting would begin.

Some such thought as this must have come to the man for, with an expressive shrug of his shoulders—it indicated repugnance and a "what's the use?" spirit of despair—he turned his back resolutely upon the tree and its unclean fruit and busied himself with selecting and gathering together certain of the provisions which strewed the ground in frightful confusion.

Near by were the charred remains of what had been, but yesternight, a large canvas-topped trek-wagon.

The man worked quickly though moodily, and presently the stores were stacked in a more or less orderly array. The perishable food stuff in one heap; fire arms and ammunition—there was a regular arsenal of them—in another; steel, ant-proof uniform cases made yet another heap, and a fourth was composed of all the odds and ends—spare wagon parts, tools and so forth—which an experienced traveler always includes in his equipment.

The man sat down on one of the uniform cases and nodded absently.

"It's a deuce of a mess," he muttered. Then he looked at the wound on his left forearm. It was a little more than a slight abrasion of the skin, but it had an angry, puckering centre. "Don't think there is any danger now," he went on. "Jim must have sucked out all the poison last night. Still—"

He pressed the wound hard, causing the blood to flow, then from his pocket he took a small case which contained a lancet and a vial holding crystals of permanganate of potash. He lanced the wound and then rubbed into it some of the crystals.

"Just to be on the safe side," he muttered as if somebody had accused him of being over cautious. "Of course there's no danger, I know that. But if it hadn't been for Jim—I'd be as dead as the bally mules. Poor devils! Wonder what poison those chappies used on their beastly arrows? Wonder what put it into their heads to attack us? Wonder—"

A steely light came into his mild-looking blue eyes as he lived over again the night's horrors: The sudden attack on his camp by a number of naked, wild-yelling bushmen; the setting fire to the wagon; the stampede of the mules and their screams as the poison began to take effect.

And then the withdrawal of the bushmen. It had been as sudden as their onslaught—that was an even greater cause for wonder. The camp had been practically at their mercy; in the darkness the white man's aim was uncertain—not that he would have aimed to kill anyway—and they had surrounded him. He had stood with Jim full in the light of the burning wagon. Yet, after that first flight of arrows they had disappeared.

What was the cause of it all? Not revenge. He was respected and admired by all natives with whom he came in contact. Not loot—they had not touched anything. Not fear, surely. He shrugged his shoulders; it is hard to say what actuates the deeds of the youngest of all Africa's black children—the bush pygmies. But most certainly fear was not the explanation of their sudden retreat.

The white man rose to his feet and stretched his arms wearily above his head. He was very tired. Despite his superb physical condition the strain of the night's long watch—after the first attack he had stood on guard until the rising of the sun—had left its mark upon him.

Gray ashes clung to his touselled hair; his face was daubed with sooty streaks; his clothes were grimy and ragged—most of the holes having charred edges, offering mute testimony to his attempts to subdue the wagon fire and, that failing, the perilous task of saving the wagon's contents.

He looked at his well-shaped, powerful hands; then reflectively rubbed his chin.

"Think I'll have a bathe and shave and change," he murmured. "Ought to be able to think better then—must look like a tramp. Wonder where that blighter Jim has got to?"

He opened one of the uniform cases and from it took a very elaborate toilet case.

He stooped over it, apparently examining the things it contained with minute care. He took out one of the razors—there were seven of them—and tried its keenness on a hair which he yanked from his head. Then he commenced to strop it slowly and deliberately, on the palm of his hand. The expression in his eyes was that of a man whose whole faculties are concentrated on listening.

Presently he put the razor back in the case and sat down again on the uniform case. He leaned forward, his elbows resting on his knees, his chin supported on the palms of his hands, and gazed fixedly on the ground before him. Deep lines of puzzled thought corrugated his brow.

He reached out absently for his toilet case and took from it a small mirror:

"By Jove, yes," he said aloud, "I really must shave! But it's such a bore. Wish I could remember."

He patted the ground impatiently with his foot. Evidently the thing he wished to remember was of great importance, for he entirely ignored his desire to shave and, gazing moodily into the mirror, searched laboriously into the deepest recesses of his brain. The blazing sun, last night's disaster, the hyenas and vultures at their feasting— everything seemed to be forgotten, had ceased to exist. He breathed, occasionally a hand moved; save for that he might have been a graven image, or his splendid, muscular frame a mere shell which housed a gigantic brain pondering on hidden mysteries.

The hand which held the mirror moved nervously, erratically. The mirror caught the slanting rays of the morning sun, reflecting them back in a dazzlingly white blob of light. That blob danced to the right and to the left, high and low.

Presently at the moment the man seemed to be still more deeply engrossed with his thoughts—it focused on a patch of bush some forty feet to the right and a little to the rear of the thinker.

A slight sound came from behind that bush, a furtive, shuffling noise—and then silence.

The blob of light passed on, danced long-legged over the veld, finally disappearing as the mirror was replaced in the case.

The white man chuckled softly—then frowned.

"If it wasn't Jim—" he mused, "and it wasn't—who the deuce was it? And why? Oh well—I'll wait a little while. Perhaps Mister Watcher Behind-a-bush will return."

His head drooped dejectedly.

Five, ten minutes passed and then came the pattering sounds of horse's hoofs. A little later a horseman rode cut of the bush and reined to a halt at the edge of the clearing almost directly opposite.

The newcomer, a stockily built man with a jet black beard, cast a swift appraising glance at the ruins of the camp and then, masking his smirk of satisfaction with a well simulated look of deep concern, said smoothly, "Looks as if you'd run into a patch of bad luck, stranger."

The other looked up with a start of surprise; his hand moved fumblingly toward his revolver. Then he laughed and rising exclaimed, "My word, old top! How you startled me! A patch of bad luck, you say! Well, rather! My goodness, yes."

The horseman sneered slightly at the affected drawl.

"What happened?" he asked. "Judging by that—" he indicated the vultures and hyenas which were now feasting gluttonishly on the bodies of the mules—"I should say that your beasts went down with East Coast fever—or something."

"It was something," the other said sadly. "Undoubtedly something. East Coast fever wouldn't account for the wagon being set on fire, would it?"

"Come to think of it, it wouldn't," the horseman agreed.

"Clever of you to see that," the other murmured. "Very! I'm afraid my poor beasts died of bushman fever, if you know what I mean?"

The other's eyes narrowed.

"No, I don't," he said flatly and taking a cake of tobacco from his pocket, bit off a big chunk. "Have a chew?"

The other recoiled a pace.

"No, thanks, old dear. Stomach can't stand it. Makes me beastly sick."

"Yep, it would. Suppose cigarettes are more in your line. Thought so. But what's this bushman fever your beasts died of? It's a new one on me."

"I'm afraid I was a little vague," the other murmured, puffing lazily on a cigarette he had extracted from a heavy silver case. "What I meant to infer was that a party of bushmen—merry little devils, aren't they?—visited me last night and inoculated my mules. I suppose they set fire to my wagon so that they could see to do their work properly."

"I suppose you think you're being funny," the horseman said heavily.

"Oh no, not at all. At least I don't mean to be. Truth is, I mean to say, that I'm so deucedly upset that I don't quite know what I'm saying. You will understand just how upset I am when I tell you that those merry little devils nearly inoculated me." He pointed to the wound on his forearm.

"Inoculated you. What with?"

"Death, dear laddie. You understood that, surely. Death. They fired nasty little poison arrows—"

"I reckon I'd better be going," the horseman said shortly and tightened his grip on his reins. "I was going to see if I could help you in any way—you looked to be in a bad fix here. But, seeing as you're only a ruddy fool, what's the use? And, besides, I do a lot of trading with the little people, they look on me as their friend, and I'm damned if I'm going to offend them by helping you."

"Why, what do you mean," the other asked in alarm. "You're surely not going to desert me? Really, I'm awfully sorry, I can't help talking like a bally fool. I mean, that's the only way I know how to talk. I am such a bally ass. But you mustn't go, positively not. They-they might come back again."

"If they do, it's because you've done something to offend them, I bet you deserve all you've got. I know the little people, I do. They're peaceful little blighters. They wouldn't go for a man unless he'd played them a mean trick."

He rode off a few paces, coming to a halt at the other's agonized cry.

"Please wait, dear sir!"

"Well?" he asked coldly.

"Can't we—er—put matters on a business basis? I mean here's me and all my equipment—and there's the mules entombed, so to speak, in the bellies of vultures and hyenas and my wagon's gone up in smoke. Well? Can't you help me to get my stuff to the nearest settlement?"

"And do you think I can pack it all on my horse?" the blackbearded man said sarcastically.

"No—" confusedly—"of course not, Never thought of that. Still, you might—er—ride hot foot to the settlement and have a wagon sent out here."

"There's only one wagon there—and that belongs to me."

"Of course I'd pay you the usual transport rate."

The horseman looked shrewdly at the piles of stores and licked his lips greedily.

"My rates'll be high," he grunted. "You ain't in a position to bargain, mister. You're like a ship what's signalled she's out of control and wanting a tow. After I've deducted my salvage fees, mister, there won't be a hell of a lot left for you."

The other sighed.

"At least you'll leave me my personal wearing apparel, I hope, and so forth. I wouldn't insist on that—I mean I'd kiss my hand farewell to all this stuff and be content with getting out of this mess alive; only what's the good of life if one hasn't decent clothes to wear?"

"You agree to my terms, then?"

"Oh quite, dear lad. Even if you haven't stated them."

The horseman nodded with grim satisfaction.

"I'll go on to the settlement now," he said. "I'll be back with the wagon shortly after noon. See you later."

"No! Wait a little later. I don't like being left alone. Wait at least until Jim returns."

"Jim? Who's Jim?" the horseman asked suspiciously.

"Why Jim's the whitest man I ever knew. I rather fancy he saved my life by sucking the poison out of this wound. And this morning before sun-up, he went out there somewhere on the trail of two mules and my horse. He thought they might have escaped the attentions of the bushmen. So stay a little while, there's a good fellow. I want you to meet Jim; everybody ought to know Jim. He's a Hottentot—"

"A nigger, eh? Thought you said he was a white man?"

"I did. Well?"

"Well? Hell, I say. You're a nigger lover, eh?"

"In a sense, I suppose you might say that. But you'll stay? Oh, good. Have a cigarette? No? Have another chew, then. As I've said, I don't chew myself but I have no real objections to other people chewing."

The horseman dismounted.

"Don't your jaw ever get tired?" he growled.

"I don't understand? Oh, you mean I talk a lot. Yes; I've always been told that's a failing of mine. But there are so many silent people in the world! And I've always thought that if everyone spoke freely and truthfully a lot of misery would be avoided."

The horseman groaned.

"And here I am talking to you as if you were a lifelong bosom friend," the other continued gayly. "And we don't even know each other's names. Mine's St. John—Aubrey St. John. But I'm generally known as 'the Major.' Don't know why. I'm not a military man—simply loathe fire-arms."

"Well, you've got plenty of them; that don't look as if you were very afraid of them."

The man who was generally known as "the Major" laid a forefinger along his nose and winked expressively.

"Just swank, dear lad; just swank and—er—a way of self protection. For instance—take this revolver I'm wearing. Suppose now I meet a big strong bully of a fellow. Well, he doesn't bully me. Do you know why? Because he sees this revolver and knows that, strong as he is, he can't stop a bullet. And so he leaves me alone. He doesn't know that I wouldn't fire at him. And I wouldn't—unless I was greatly provoked. But your name, dear lad?"

"Name's Bird—Pete Bird—and I ain't as soft as that sounds."

"Why no, of course not!" the Major exclaimed. "And I should imagine—judging by your business dealings with me—that you're feathering your nest very well, eh, what?"

"Man's got to live, Aubrey," Bird growled. "An' I'm taking a big risk—helping a man who the little people have got it in for."

"Of course, Petey. I understand. A man can't live by risk alone, can he? Now let me see—what was it I wanted to ask you? I was trying to remember something before you came on the scene; something quite important. Oh, I know. What day of the week is it?"

"Tuesday."

The Major looked infinitely relieved.

"Oh, thanks! Now I can shave."

He turned to his toilet case, took out of it the mirror, soap and brush, and the razor with Tuesday engraved upon its handle.

"Forgot to light a fire this morning," he murmured. "Have to use cold water. Oh, well—"

He filled his shaving mug from a canvas water bag and commenced to lather himself.

"Do you believe in second sight, Petey, old horse?" he asked presently, blowing the creamy foam away from his lips.

Pete Bird—he was busily estimating the value of the Major's equipment—started violently.

"What do you mean, Aubrey?"

"Only—it's very hard to explain—just before you arrived on the scene I had a very strong presentment that some one was hastening to my rescue. No—let me be quite truthful—I felt that some one was watching me, playing the part, as it were, of a guardian angel. Funny, don't you think?"

As he spoke the Major moved the mirror, apparently adjusting it in order to get a clearer reflection of his face. By some queer chance it focused the rays of the sun full into Bird's face, dazzling him.

"Blast you!" he roared, rubbing his eyes with his knuckles. "What are you trying to do—blind me?"

The Major turned round quickly, a look of deep concern on his face.

"I'm frightfully sorry, old top," he exclaimed. "Really"

"Oh, shut your jaw—go on and shave. That ought to keep you quiet."

The Major turned back to the mirror and for a while the only sound—-apart from the croaking of the vultures and the snarling of the hyenas—was the clean, crisp scrape of the razor.

Pete Bird looked at him uncertainly, wondering if the man was quite the fool he looked and acted, came to the conclusion that he was and smirked maliciously.

He drew his revolver and fired at the hyenas, laughing boisterously as the Major turned round with a startled cry of fear.

"Just getting rid of a few *schelm*," he claimed.

The Major looked at him indignantly.

"You should be more careful," he exclaimed hotly. "You nearly made me cut myself."

Pete laughed again and juggled skillfully with the revolver.

"Oh, I say!" the Major exclaimed admiringly, his resentment forgotten. "That's awfully clever. I must try it." And before Pete could object he had drawn his revolver and was clumsily attempting to imitate Pete's trick. "It's not loaded," he said reassuringly as Pete started to take cover.

Almost before the words were out of his mouth the revolver went off and Pete's hat was whipped off his head by the speeding bullet.

"You fool!" Pete screamed.

"Oh, I say," the Major stammered as he stooped to pick up the revolver which had fallen from his apparently nerveless fingers. "I'm no end sorry. My goodness— had it been loaded I might have killed you." He retrieved Pete's hat for him and stared incredulously at the jagged holes in its crown. " 'Pon my soul—it was loaded!"

He hastily returned the revolver to its holster.

"I can't begin to tell you," he went on abjectly, "how fearfully sorry—"

"Oh! Go on and shave," Pete said disgustedly.

The Major turned back to the mirror, relathered himself, and once again the whistling scrape of the razor was heard.

"Aubrey?" Pete said presently.

"Yes, old thing?" the Major replied absently. Looking into the mirror he could see that Pete was standing just behind him, looking over his shoulder into the mirror. He felt something pressing against the small of his back and knew that it was the muzzle of Pete's revolver.

"Yes, old thing?" he repeated.

"You are not such a fool as you look, are you?"

"I'm afraid I am," the Major sighed. "And I do hope your nerves are steady. If anything was to alarm you and make you contract your finger, why—"

Pete grinned.

"You'd be blown to hell," he finished. "But my nerves is all right, Aubrey, only I've got a quick temper and anger 'ud make me contract my finger too. So you'd better not get me mad."

"I won't," the Major promised fervently. "At least I'll try hard not to. But it will be difficult. I might say some apparently innocent thing and find that I'd stepped on one of your pet mental corns, so to speak."

"That'll be all right, Aubrey. Only I'll just warn you that I hate liars worse than poison. Now go on and shave that pretty face of yours and I'll ask you a few questions."

The Major dipped his brush in the soapy water and lathered himself once again.

"And now Mister Aubrey St. John—what's generally known as 'the Major'—just what's your little game up this part of the country?"

"If I tell him the truth," the Major murmured, rounding his firm, well-shaped chin, "he won't believe me. And I can't tell a lie—so what's a poor chappy to do?"

"I don't like being kept waitin' for an answer," Pete growled. "That's another thing that makes me mad."

"Hold your trigger finger, ducky," the Major exclaimed hastily. "I'll tell you—only it's a long story. It begins in Lourenço Marquez—"

"You tell me just the plain facts," Pete Bird growled. "I'll supply all the fixings meself—I've got an imagination, all right."

"You have? Well, that's a useful thing to have. I say, take care! You're poking that bally thing through my back. Yes! Yes! I was just going to tell you—in the fewest possible words. Well!" He drew a long breath. "Red headed Yank in Lourenço Marquez said his uncle and sister were held prisoners by leaders of secret native society up in Mountains of Moon—asked me to go up and rescue them—said society plotting to overthrow the white rule in Africa—died before he could tell me any more."

"What did he die of?" Pete interjected.

"A knife between his ribs," the Major replied tersely.

"All right; go on."

The Major continued in melodramatic voice.

"So I'm on my way to the Mountains of the Moon, just like a knight of old, to rescue a lady and her aged avuncular relation from the clutches of the benighted heathen. And that's that!"

"And that's a hell of a yarn, Aubrey," Pete said skeptically. "Now for the truth."

"But that is the truth, dear lad," the Major protested. "Of course, as a side line, I hope to confound the plot of the plotters, if you get my meaning."

"And, supposing your yarn to be true, are you fool enough to think you could do it all alone?"

"Not exactly alone—I didn't say that, did I? Jim's with me, and aided by strategy and tactics, we ought to be able to pull it off. And I forgot to mention—" He paused to lather his face for the fourth time, swearing loudly when a flake of soap got into his eye; but, though that eye was screwed up tightly and he rubbed it frantically with the back of his hand, the other eye stared unblinkingly into the mirror— "and I forgot to mention," he repeated, "that the Yank gave me a red idol which he said was the symbol of the society."

"A red idol," Pete said after a long pause. "Oh, go on! You've got a better imagination than what I have."

"But it's true," the Major insisted. "And, my word, if you'd known all I've been through just because of that idol you wouldn't be so ready to laugh. Why, do you know—" he lowered his voice—"I'm half inclined to believe that the affair last night was all because of the idol."

Pete snorted, but there was a look of satisfaction on his face, the look of a man who has found out what he wanted to know. He hesitated a moment, half inclined to leave the dude fool to his own resources; he would have done so only he harbored a suspicion that the man was laughing at him. And Pete was somewhat of a bully; consequently he was determined to make the Major squirm before he left.

"I don't believe your tale," he growled, "and I'm getting mad." He forced his revolver still harder against the Major's spine, making that man squirm. "Stand still," he continued harshly, "and don't talk. It's my turn. And you talk of strategy and tactics! Hell! Don't help you now. Didn't help you any last night, eh?"

"No!" the Major agreed mournfully. "But the bush-men didn't play fair. How was I to know they were on the war-path?"

"A man who travels in this country ought to be always ready for things like that," Pete said heavily. "He ought to reckon everything and everybody his enemy."

"Again I'm afraid you're right. Still—strategy and tactics are awfully good allies, if you know what I mean. For instance—"

He broke off with a loud yell of, "There's a snake!"

At the same moment he flung the soapy water in his shaving mug over his shoulder into Pete's face, leaped suddenly to the right, drawing his revolver as he did so.

"There you see," he said with an air of breathless triumph, "that quite proves my point, doesn't it?" He stepped forward quickly and retrieved the revolver which Pete had dropped in his instinctive attempts to ease his eyes from the smart of the soapy water.

He offered it to Pete with an elaborate bow.

"You nearly blinded me, you fool!" Pete growled as he took back his weapon, his red, inflamed eyes blinking piggishly. "Can't you take a joke?"

"Why yes, of course. Were you joking? I thought you were quite prepared to blow me to—er—hell. But you do see what I mean, don't you? About my having proved my point. First of all my yell caused you to somewhat relax your guard—you actually stepped back a pace and took away the revolver from the middle of my back. Before you could regain control of yourself, the soapy water put you out completely. But why go further? Dear old strategy and tactics were completely justified. Oh, rather."

Pete, muttering something about, "wasting time on a damned fool dude," sulkily mounted his horse.

"I'll be here with the wagon about noon," he announced savagely. "And my price has gone up because of your smart Alec tricks. Yah! Suppose you think you're funny."

He spurred quickly away.

The Major laughed softly.

"And now for a cold sponge down and a change. Hope Jim'll have returned."

FIFTEEN MINUTES later the Major was seated in a canvas deck chair which had escaped the fire, waiting patiently for the return of Jim.

If Pete Bird could have seen him now as he lolled back, blowing intricate smoke rings, a look of inane boredom on his face, Pete would have derided himself for having doubted the correctness of his first estimation of the Major's abilities. Real men, bush wise men, did not, in Pete's world, dress and look, and talk like dude fools. Men—according to Pete's ideas—who earned their living and lived because they knew the ways of the veld and all of its creatures—did not wear such idiotic, sight-obscuring ornaments as monocles!

As for the Major's clothes! Pete had seen such garments on a tailor's dummy in the window of an outfitter's shop in Jo'burg—and seeing had laughed: White drill riding breeches, white tunic coat—flaring slightly at the hips—white pith helmet with an elaborate green puggaree, highly polished, brown polo boots to which were fitted tiny, gold-plated spurs. All that looked very pretty on a tailor's dummy, or on the hero of a musical comedy; but a man couldn't wear such an outfit on the veld!

Truly, it was to laugh! Men—the men of Pete's acquaintance—were satisfied with a pair of khaki slacks, patched maybe with a piece of sacking—a gray flannel shirt and a pair of ammunition boots.

But then Pete had never seen a man like the Major before and, consequently, in certain particulars his education was lacking—sadly lacking.

Seeing the Major now, noting the vacuous, almost inane grin on his full moon of a face, and the glossy black hair brushed back in an immaculate pompadour, Pete would have at once thought of the tailor's dummy, would have been quite sure that the Major's ruse of throwing soapy water in his face was just a fool's luck, and would have been encouraged to greater impertinences.

In so doing, he would only have been following a well-established precedent. Many men, on first acquaintance with the Major, had laughed at him, dubbing him a soft fool of a monocled dude, and had set snares with the intent of conveying the Major's ostensible wealth from his pockets to theirs.

And then— Oh, well! Experience is a good school—but it's a hard one and damned expensive.

The Major rose from his chair presently, evidently worried by the non-appearance of Jim. After a little while he chuckled softly, reminiscently, and drawing his revolver juggled with it in a manner which would have caused Pete to stare in incredulous wonder.

Three times the revolver spat flame, at the very moment, it seemed, when it was in the process of being tossed from one hand to the other. Three vultures dropped, making a dessert, as it were, for their fellows' feasting.

The Major chuckled again, the revolver was returned to its holster and he sat down. He was completely relaxed now.

Minutes passed. The sun grew hotter; the air was filled with the lazy drone of insects; a hot breeze blew and dust devils gyrated madly. There was a crashing noise in the bush behind the Major, but he did not turn his head.

A horse whinnied softly; a mule brayed discordantly; a deep, resonant voice called, "O-he, *Baas!*"

At that the Major turned and grinned at the Hottentot who, mounted on a coal black, Arab stallion, was riding slowly toward him. A mule followed.

"Only one, Jim?" the Major asked in the vernacular.

"Only one, *Baas*," the Hottentot replied. "An arrow stuck the other one."

"But Satan is unhurt, Jim?"

"Aye, *Baas*." Jim laughed lugubriously as he slid stiffly to the ground. "But almost I could wish that an arrow had stuck him. He would not listen to my voice and carried me through thick thorn scrub. Look at my clothes, *Baas!*" He ruefully indicated the rents in his clothing.

Jim almost looked as ludicrous as most natives do when they ape the dress of white men. True, his tunic fitted snugly across his chest—there was not a quarter of an inch difference in the chest measurements of Jim and his *Baas*—but the sleeves were far too short—Jim's arms were abnormally long and muscular—and the riding breeches were shapeless monstrosities which hung in concertina-like folds from his waist to his enormous feet.

"Where did you find him, Jim?" The Major had risen and was running a practised hand inquiringly down the stallion's withers.

Jim gestured vaguely behind him.

"Back there, *Baas.* They were both grazing, heading this way."

"It was foolish to ride him without saddle or bridle, Jim," the Major commented mildly.

"Maybe, *Baas,* but I was in a hurry. I heard shots—"

"A hyena and a vulture or two died—that's all, Jim." The Hottentot nodded.

"Yah! I knew that the *baas* was dealing with *schelms.* I desired to be on hand to aid him."

"And you saw nothing of the little people, Jim?"

"No, *Baas.* No man sees them unless they wish to be seen. But—" he added grimly—"I think they saw me. I could feel their eyes watching me. Has the *baas* found a reason for their manner of dealing with us last night?"

"None, Jim."

The Hottentot looked disappointed; he was not accustomed to seeing his *baas* at fault.

"If the *baas* is blind now," he said consolingly, "sight will come later. But, truly it is easier to follow the spoor of a snake than to understand the workings of the little people. They leave no spoor, they cast no shadows—yet think of this, *Baas.* They could have killed us last night—yet did not. Why? Have you thought of that?"

"Yah, Jim. I have thought of that but found no answer."

Jim grunted and then, stooping very nearly double, closely scrutinized the ground about the camp.

Presently he turned to his *baas,* walking with a pompous gait, smiling confidently.

"The ground hereabouts is well marked with spoor; a man whose eyes are open, as mine are open, can read much."

"Yes, Jim?" prompted the Major and smiled boyishly. He knew Jim so well. He knew the Hottentot was about to pretend the possession of an almost supernatural knowledge. Jim was like that; at times he delighted to play a trick on his *baas*, professing to have been told some great secret by the spirit of a dead chief, quite overlooking the fact that the actual manner in which he had gained his knowledge was quite as wonderful as the spirit messages he claimed at times to receive. It was this delight in the playing of games which was one of the strong bonds between the two men—the white man and the black. During the long years they had been together—nominally master and servant; actually, close comrades—they had kept their youth. They could joke, had joked, though faced with death.

"Yah, *Baas*," Jim said solemnly. "I have looked, I have examined the spoor. My eyes were open but I could see nothing. Then I opened my ears and a Voice of the Great Spirits spoke to me. *Au-a!* The *baas* has hidden things from me!"

"Yes, Jim?"

"Truly, *Baas!*" Jim spat. "A white man has been here and spoke to the *baas*. A white man with a black beard; a white man riding a boney horse. An evil man, *Baas!* You would do well not to trust him. His thoughts are evil—everything he does is evil. But he is somewhat of a fool. *Au-a!* Truly he is a fool for he threatened the *baas* with death!"

"And did not the Voice of the Spirits tell you what the white man said to me, Jim?" the Major asked earnestly.

Jim shook his head.

"No, *Baas!* I could not hear, and if I had heard I could not have understood—"

He paused, confused, grinning sheepishly.

"As always," he continued, "the *baas* knows. I was hiding behind the rocks yonder. I saw it all. I laughed when the *baas* threw the water in the black bearded man's face. Before that I was frightened. The *baas* was very near death, I think."

"I think not, Jim," the Major contradicted mildly. "I think he only tried to frighten me. But why did you hide and watch?"

"Because, *Baas*, I saw him first ride up to this place and watch you from behind the cover of the bush yonder—"

"I knew he was there, Jim," the Major said quietly.

Jim nodded.

"Of course! The *baas* is not blind. Still, as I say, having seen the white man spy on you and then go back to his horse and ride up to the camp as if he had but newly come that way I decided to hasten slowly."

"After he had gone, you were long in coming, Jim."

"Yah, *Baas*. I wanted to think; I wanted to find the answer to a question which troubled me."

"What was the question, Jim?"

"I wanted to know why this white man should hold speech with one of the little people. Aye; I saw him do that."

The Major started. "And did you find the answer to the question, Jim?"

"Yah, *Baas*," Jim said complacently.

"And it is?"

"That the little men are his servants; they attacked us last night because he ordered it."

"And why did he order it, Jim?"

"Because of the red idol, *Baas*."

The Major looked very serious.

In English he drawled, " 'Pon my soul, I believe the bloomin' old heathen's right! Yes; I rather fancy you're right, Jim."

"Gorblessmi, no-yes. Me right! Absolut'y top-ole!" The rest of Jim's English—it was equally incoherent—would have done credit to an intelligent parrot reared in the fo'c's'le of a hell-ship.

The Major took out his monocle and polished it absently.

"Yes, Jim," he said in the vernacular. "I think you're right. And so, when the black-bearded man returns with a wagon to take me and all this to the settlement, you and Satan, and the mule will not be here. You will be a long way from here. You will go to Jamba's *kraal* and there await me."

"No, *Baas,*" Jim pleaded. "If there is a game to play, let me play with you."

"That is the part you will play, Jim. Unless you do that—there can be no play."

"But the *baas* will be careful?"

"I am always careful, Jim."

Jim grinned.

"*Au-a!* Of me you are careful, of Satan you are careful; of that glass thing which keeps your eye from sleeping you are very careful—but of your life? No."

The Major waved his hands.

"I had forgotten to say," he continued hastily, "that you will take with you the little red idol. You have it still?"

Jim nodded.

"Where is it?"

"You told me to keep it safe in a place where no one can find it but myself. I obeyed, *Baas.*"

"You have not combed Satan's tail for many days, Jim?" the Major commented casually.

Jim chuckled.

"Are your eyes never closed, *Baas?* You know then where it is?"

When the Major assented briefly, Jim continued.

"It is as much as a man's life is worth to go close to the hind quarters of Satan, *Baas.* That is, if the man is a stranger. And even me he does not like to touch his tail. I have to talk to him softly first."

AN HOUR later, about the same time that Jim, the Hottentot, set off on his solitary trek to the *kraal* of Jamba, Pete Bird was giving a highly colored account of his encounter with the Major to a fat, oily individual known as "Parson."

"Sure—he's a fool all right, Parson," Pete concluded. "He won't dare open his mouth at all if you handle him right; and we can hold on to as much as we want to. If you like, I'll handle the whole business myself. I hate the dude and I'd like to see his face when he finds out that he ain't got a thing left. Let me handle it, Parson, won't you?"

Parson placed the tips of his fat fingers together, pursed his lips thoughtfully and shook his head slowly.

"I'm afraid, Pete," he said in a whining, sing-song voice, "that you made a fool of yourself. Don't you know who the Major is? Haven't you even heard of him?"

"I know all I want to know about him. He's a dude, fool and—"

"He's the cleverest I.D.B. in the country," Parson interrupted suavely. "He's a wonderful horseman, a crack shot, knows the niggers better than they do themselves—and he's far from a fool. Yes, Pete; He's so far from being a fool that I wouldn't be exaggerating if I said that he was one of the cleverest men in the country."

Pete Bird laughed. "We ain't a-talking about the same Major," he said.

The Parson sighed softly.

"There's only one Major in the world," he said. "He's unique. Although he's a crook according to the laws of the Diamond Mining Syndicate, he's absolutely on the level."

Pete sneered.

"To hear you talk a chap 'ud think you was that way too, Parson."

The Parson assumed a smug, pious expression.

"We should all strive for higher things," he murmured. Then he laughed softly and continued jeeringly, "And all the time you thought you were having a game with the Major, he was having a game with you."

"That's as may be," Pete said hotly. "Just the same, the Major's cleverness didn't save his camp from being rushed by the little people, and—"

"You forget that I planned the raid, just as I did the others," the Parson interrupted softly. "And I didn't say that the Major was the cleverest man in the country—but one of the cleverest. There are five men in the country I could name. We are in a class by ourselves. We— But go on. You were saying?"

"I was saying that he'd have to pay high for transporting his stuff here—damned high. He threw his shaving water in my face."

The Parson leaned forward, grinning maliciously.

"You hadn't told me about that."

"And I ain't going to. It was just a damned fool dude's trick. Oh, well!" Pete laughed exultantly. "You're a funny cove, Parson. I don't know what your game is—I don't care. All I know is that I've made a lot of money since you've been here. And when I think of the way you got hold on the little people, pretending you're in high with the big witch doctors, and all that jabber about a red idol—why, when I think of that I near bust myself laughing."

"You don't want to laugh too loud," the Parson said in a mild voice of reproof. "And I wouldn't talk at all about the red idol. It's dangerous."

"But the game's safe enough, ain't it?" Pete expostulated. "You said it was, Parson."

"Oh, yes! The game's safe enough. But you forget me. I've told you to keep your mouth shut—" He took out a big clasp knife and opened it and industriously set about sharpening his pencil.

Pete quailed. According to rumor that knife was accustomed to far less peaceful tasks.

"I never talk outside, Parson," Pete said hastily.

"Better not, much better not, Pete." The Parson slowly closed his clasp knife. "Now you'd better be on your way to get the Major's stuff. And for this once, Pete, we won't charge anything at all for bringing the stuff in."

"What?" Pete almost screamed. "And why not?"

"At least," the Parson amended, "we won't charge anything until I've found out whether he's going to be a good friend of mine or not. And now, my dear brother, it's time for you to start on your errand of mercy. Be very kind to the Major. Remember that it is sometimes possible to catch a mackerel by baiting with sprat."

A cunning light of comprehension came into Pete's eyes.

"I'm beginning to see," he murmured. "You mean—?"

"Oh, get out!" the Parson exclaimed wrathfully. "Damn it! My pencil's broken again."

He opened his knife—and Pete got out.

PETE BIRD yawned audibly.

"You two gab like old women," he said disgustedly. "I'm going outside."

"I was going to suggest that, Pete," the Parson said equably. "And don't hang around too near the door or window. I don't like eavesdroppers. Understand?"

Apparently Pete did understand for he flushed an angry red, choked back an insulting speech, muttered something about "being ordered about like a bloody nigger in my own store," then went out and slammed the door violently behind him.

The Parson laughed and poured himself another drink. There was silence for a while. The two men watched each other covertly. Apparently, now that Pete had gone, they had exhausted their conversational abilities.

Presently the Major drawled, "Topping place old Pete has here. Doesn't look a bit like a kaffir store hut. Clean, comfortable chairs and what not. Why, Pete's quite a voluptuary."

The Parson smiled.

"You should have seen the way he lived before I came here. Dirty? My dear man! If cleanliness is next to Godliness, Pete wasn't far removed from hell. I'll give you my word! All this—" with a wave of his pudgy hands he indicated the large, spotlessly clean hut—"is mine."

"I must say you've done well. And I must say, too, that I'm no end grateful to you for the way you made Pete lower his price for carting in my stuff and supplying me with another wagon and team of mules. Yes; I'm no end grateful."

Again there was an interval of silence. It was broken this time by the Parson.

"Look here, Major," he said heavily. "I suggest that we two throw in our hands."

"I don't understand, old bean."

"You do; I know you and you know me."

"Oh, yes; I've heard of you. Nothing very pleasant, though," the Major drawled. "Yes; I know you, and you know me. Well?"

"Let's put our cards down on the table—face up. We're both too clever to lie."

"That's a nice thought. But I'm still in the dark, old top. For instance, what in the world is there to lie about?"

The Parson gestured impatiently.

"We've been indulging in airy persiflage long enough. I'm a blunt man and I want you to come to the point."

The Major chuckled softly.

"Will have your little joke, won't you. There's no point to bluntness, dear lad."

The Parson smilingly ignored the interruption.

"I know you're a smart devil, Major. I know you hide a brain under that dude pose of yours. I know you and you know me. So—let's get down to business."

"All right. Fire away, laddie."

"What are you doing up this way?"

The Major shook a reproving finger.

"Ah; that's not fair. You want me to expose my cards while you hold yours close to your—er—manly bosom. That won't do at all, dear man. Besides, you know why I'm up here. Surely Pete told you."

"And that yarn's true?"

"Oh, surely!"

The Parson looked at him shrewdly, then nodded.

"But not the whole truth?"

"Oh, surely."

"Ah! I'm afraid you don't trust me. And so—"he breathed deeply—"I'll tell you about myself."

"That will be interesting," the Major drawled. "I'd like awfully to know just what hold you have over the little people that'll make them attack a white man's camp.

The Parson started.

"That's a score to me," the Major said happily.

"How did you know I had a hold over them?" the Parson demanded.

"A little bird told me."

"Pete Bird?" the Parson questioned wrathfully.

"To be quite truthful—no. At least, not in so many words. But he's not very brainy, you know. He's so ready to talk and he gives information when he doesn't suspect that he's being pumped."

The Parson mumbled threats toward Pete. "What's the use of beating about the bush," he then exclaimed with a show of candor. "Here's what I know; I stumbled on to the fact that there's a powerful secret society with headquarters somewhere up in the Mountains of the Moon district. They're plotting something—don't know what, don't care. All I know is that they're damned powerful. A nigger servant I had—he's dead now—"the Parson grinned cruelly—"was one of their agents. I learned something about their pass words from him. Never mind how. And I learned, too, that their big ju-ju had been stolen.

"Know what that ju-ju is, Major?"

"Not the faintest."

"You do—and you've got it. It's a red idol."

"Oh!"

"Yes. Anyway, knowing what I know, I came up here and started operations; I wanted to find out a great deal more. See? And I've been collecting information, a bit here and a bit there. But nothing that really counts. And then you appear on the scene, with the red idol and—" he waved his hands—"there you are."

"Oh, absolutely," the Major murmured. "But just what's this business of having men's camps raided and burned and all that?"

The Parson sniggered.

"The first time I did it was just to test the pass words I had to see if they really gave me authority over the little people. They did. The little people are not long on brains. And then—why I went into the game regularly. Pete has cleared up quite a sum on the business. Of course the police have been up here trying to catch the raiders, but a fat chance they've got of trapping the little people."

"You're clever—very clever. But suppose the little people kill a white man?"

"Accidents do happen sometimes," the Parson said casually.

The Major nodded.

"True! I nearly met with one myself. Well, go on."

"I've heard the story you told Pete; about you setting out to rescue a white man and his niece; and trying to outplot the plotters. And that's bosh!"

"But it's true!" the Major quietly insisted.

"Bosh!" the Parson said again. "You've got information about this society I haven't got. You've discovered that there's big money to be picked up by a clever man—and you're after it. And you've got the red idol."

"Yes, I've got that. At least Jim has it."

"And where's Jim?"

The Major glanced toward the window, noting the position of the moon. White rays poured through the window, paling the yellow candle flame.

"Jim ought to be at Jamba's *kraal* by now," he said.

The Parson accepted this statement after a moment's thought.

"Let's join forces, Major, and we'll work this thing out together."

"Splendid!" The Major breathed deeply. "I'm so glad you believe my story, Parson; gladder still of your offer of help. I've taken the matter up with so many people—police officials and what not—but they all laughed at me. And it's a big thing—a serious thing. Let's call Pete in and see if he'll help us."

The Parson scowled.

"We don't need him—he's a fool. And, besides, why split the money three ways?"

The Major sighed wearily.

"I'm afraid you're on the wrong tack, Parson. There's no payment involved except, maybe, death."

"You insist, then, on sticking to that damned fool yarn of yours?" the Parson questioned harshly.

"It's true," the Major replied simply.

"You fool!" the Parson said. "Let's have this straight once and for all. One way or the other I'm going to get to the bottom of this business, I'm going to get hold of the key to it all—the red idol—and I'm going to clean up big. You see, I'm being frank with you. I can afford to be. You can't get away from here without my sayso. You've no equipment—Pete'll hold back what he's sold you—and a word of mine to the policeman stationed here'll see you held for I.D.B. Now then; are you coming in with me on equal shares or not?"

"I'm afraid not, Parson dear," the Major drawled, as he took out his monocle and polished it. His eyes glittered strangely, the set of his mouth was stern. "You could be of no help to me and—because my story is true—I can be of no help to you. And so, it seems that we will be bitter enemies, and all that. Frightfully melodramatic, isn't it? I'm going outside now, if you don't mind. I feel a little faint. I've never been in the company of a—er—white kaffir, before."

"You poor fool!" Following a jerking movement of the Parson's hand, a flash of light whizzed over the Major's shoulder, stuck into the wooden frame of the window and hung there, quivering.

The Major pulled the knife out and handed it back to the infuriated Parson.

"I'm glad I ducked," he said mildly; his monocle gleamed mockingly in his eye. "Oh, well. I suppose I'll see you again some time."

He backed to the door, watching the knife the Parson was balancing on the palm of his hand.

A moment later he had passed outside, closing the door behind him. As he did so, Pete Bird scuttled around the corner of the hut, heading for the stable.

The Major evinced no sign of having seen him and when, a few minutes later, Pete rode swiftly away from the place, heading straight across the moonlit veld for Jamba's *kraal,* he only chuckled softly.

He sat down on a wooden settle and leaned back against the mud wall of the hut.

"I only hope," he mused, "that Jim hasn't drunk too much beer."

OVER AN hour passed; the Major did not move. He was appreciating to the full the night's beauty.

The door of the hut opened and the Parson came out.

"I was a fool to lose my temper, Major," he said apologetically. "After tonight we'll be against each other, but that's no reason why we should act like spoiled brats now. Let's talk. I'm as lonely as hell—"

"Sit down, old man," the Major said heartily, but his hand fondled the butt of his revolver.

The Parson came slowly over to the settle, licking down the paper of the cigarette he had just rolled.

He seated himself, lighted his cigarette and for awhile the two men smoked in silence.

Presently they talked; exchanging reminiscences of the diamond diggings and the lights of Paris; of hunting and music—

The Parson threw away the stub of his cigarette, accepted one of the Major's, lighted it and continued the discussion of Wagnerian music.

He whistled—very tunefully—one of the themes from "Tristram" in order to prove an obscure point he wished to make. The cigarette burned down to his fingers, scorching them.

"Hell!" he swore.

The Major started. His hand closed again on his revolver. He had almost forgotten the present in a flood of memories.

He offered his case to the Parson.

"Yours are too mild for me," that man said with a laugh. "I'll roll one of my own."

He continued the interrupted tune as he got out tobacco bag and paper.

"Now here," he said presently, turning to the Major, the cigarette up to his lips ready to lick down the paper, "is where the theme changes. Listen!"

The Major turned slightly toward him and at that moment the Parson blew into the cigarette paper. A cloud of black pepper went into the Major's eyes, blinding him; the haft of the Parson's heavy clasp knife crashed down on his head.

WHEN THE Major recovered consciousness, he was lying on a bunk in one of the sleeping huts, bound hand and foot. He grinned sheepishly; chagrined at the manner in which the Parson had tricked him.

"Deuced clever—just the same," he murmured. "And now what?"

His head throbbed; his eyes pained him fearfully; his cheeks burned—they were streaked with tears and blackened by pepper grains. Some one came into the hut—heavy-footed, slow, ponderous.

"So you've come to your senses, *hein?*" a deep voice boomed. *"Ach!* What fools you Englishers are to drink so much."

The Major's vision cleared somewhat. He saw that the newcomer was a mounted policeman; a slow-witted, good-natured Dutchman.

"Why am I bound? Where's the Parson?"

The policeman chuckled.

"You're bound so that you can't hurt yourself. The Parson? He's gone with Pete to bring in your things. You should be thankful to them—they're very kind."

"Yes. They're very kind," the Major said dryly. "But cut me free, now—I am quite all right."

The Dutchman shook his head.

"No; that I will not do. The drink madness may come on again. The Parson warned me of that. You were very violent, the Parson said. You would have killed him if Pete hadn't first hit you on the head."

"Listen," the Major began earnestly. "You must loose me. I—"

The policeman gave a little grunt of pleasure.

"So-a! You speak the *taal,* eh? It is good to meet an Englisher who can talk a man's talk. You would say?"

And the Major told him of all the things which had happened.

The policeman considered it.

"Yah," he said slowly. "The Parson said you would rave of things like that. Men coming out of the D.T.s always talk so. And so-a!—I am no fool."

"I tell you that I am speaking truth," the Major insisted. "Cut loose my bonds—I can do nothing to harm you. You are big and strong—I am still weak. The Parson's blow has taken all strength from me."

The Major looked very sickly in the moonlight.

The Dutchman nodded thoughtfully. He was confident that he could manage the Major. He was armed, the Major was not—and the Major spoke the *taal* as one to the language born. And so—

He stooped over and cut the ropes.

The Major stretched himself.

"That's better," he said. "Now I can trek."

He moved toward the door.

"Where? And how?" the policeman asked, interposing his big bulk, his revolver aimed at the Major's stomach.

"To the *kraal* of Jamba—riding in the Wagon and driving the mules I bought from Pete."

The policeman chuckled.

"It is all as the Parson said it would be. It is the drink fever. You bought no wagon or mules—there are none here at the store now."

"Then I will borrow a horse, a mule—anything. I must get to Jamba's *kraal.*"

"You do not leave here—no," the policeman said stolidly. "You have a reputation. You are the Major, yes? *Ach!* The Parson told me about you. You stay here until they return with your things. Then I will search your things and if I find diamonds I will take you under arrest to Kimberley."

"If you do not believe me—come with me to Jamba's *kraal.* I will help you to catch the men who set the little people on to raiding the camps of white men," the Major said desperately.

The policeman's eyes glinted angrily.

"Do not try me too far." His voice was harsh. "Because you speak the *taal* so well, I released you. More I will not do. You must wait here with me until the Parson returns."

The Major shrugged his shoulders and turning back to the bed sat despondently on the edge of it.

He was forced to admire the Parson's cleverness. That man had covered himself at every step. The story he had told the policeman was the sort of story that credulous man would be most likely to believe and, at the same time, it answered any story the Major might offer in denial. The Parson had made sure of the Major being kept out of the way until he had secured the red idol, and the Major had no doubt but that the policeman would discover diamonds—planted there by the Parson—in his kit. And the end of that would be a long trip to Kimberley and a still longer trip to the breakwater at Cape Town. He had been a thorn in the flesh of the Diamond Mining Syndicate too long to expect mercy from them, or to deceive himself with the hope that they would believe his story.

Meanwhile, the men who plotted in the remote Mountains of the Moon to overthrow the white rule in Africa, could go their way entirely unmolested; and the Parson, possessed of the red idol, would be able to further his own selfish designs. And Jim!

What was happening to Jim? What could he do against the diabolical cleverness of the Parson?

The Major groaned. So he'd had the D.T.s, had he? He groaned again—laughed softly—muttered vague curses—laughed again—broke off into snatches of song.

The policeman moved uneasily, edged slowly toward the Major—revolver in one hand, a pair of handcuffs in the other. He reproached himself for having released the Englisher; he was going mad again; the devil had entered him. The policeman was afraid—he was ignorantly superstitious. The very thing which had made him the ideal man for the Parson's purpose, now counted against him.

The Major sprang to his feet—his eyes, red and inflamed, had a mad glint to them; his face was horribly contorted. He shrank back, cowering against the wall, his hands outstretched before him as if to ward off some threatened evil.

"Look! Look!" he screamed. "It has pink eyes. It has pink eyes! It is a devil. It is spitting fire. It will burn me up—burn me up, up—up and down, this is the way to London town. Ha! Ha!"

He laughed wildly. Then in a wheedling voice, "Pretty pussy, then, diddums."

He went down on hands and knees, crawling toward the policeman, talking about a green cat with crimson eyes.

The policeman drew a deep breath, endeavoring to conquer the feeling of terror which possessed him. Suddenly, determining to act before the Major could rise to his feet again he stooped over and struck at the Major's head with the barrel of his revolver.

But the Major, hoping for just such a move, dodged the blow. He dropped back into a sitting position and at the same moment caught the policeman's wrist in a grip of steel. Then, throwing himself backward, he pulled the policeman entirely off his balance so that he fell heavily to the ground.

Before the big man could recover the Major had jumped to his feet, had wrested the handcuffs and revolver from him, and had handcuffed him to the center pole of the hut. That done, laughing at the policeman's bellows of rage, the Major ran from the hut, mounted the policeman's horse and galloped swiftly across the veld.

WHEN PETE BIRD—determined to gain possession of the idol and so be in a position to bargain with the Parson—came to the *kraal* of Jamba, he found the men of the place seated about a fire, drinking and listening to the tales of Jim, the Hottentot.

He called Jim to him.

Muttering something to the men, Jim rose to his feet and staggered to where Pete awaited him.

"Your *baas* sent me to get the red idol," Pete said. "Give it to me."

"What idol, white man?" Jim asked innocently.

Pete flicked Jim's legs with a *sjambok*.

"Do not try to bandy words with me. Get me the idol. Quick!"

He raised his *sjambok* again.

"Yah, white man. I will tell you where it is," Jim said hurriedly. "But," he added with a cunning leer, "if the *baas* sent you for it, he doubtless told you where it is."

Pete nodded.

"I know—but you will get it."

"Come with me, then, *Baas*."

Jim led the way to where the Major's horse was tethered.

He untied Satan, the spirited animal plunged and kicked playfully, and brought it up to Pete.

"The idol is there," he said.

Pete swore angrily, "You jest with me, dog."

"Nay. The idol is there. It is hidden in the horse's tail."

Pete laughed.

"Then get it, dog."

Jim dropped to his knees.

"I dare not. That horse is a devil. He does not like me— he does not like any black dogs."

"Get it," Pete, ordered.

Jim rose to his feet and trembling ran his hand along Satan's back. The horse squealed, reared and struck out viciously. It did not like the prick of the thorn concealed in Jim's hand.

"You see," Jim exclaimed in fear. "He will kill me. It is a white man's horse. You could do anything with him. But me—"

Pete swore again.

"Hold his head. I will search his tail. But if I find nothing there—" The swishing of the *sjambok* through the air complete his threat.

"I have not lied. The idol is there."

Pete came closer to Satan—came too close, too carelessly. With a squeal of rage the horse lashed out with its hind feet; they thudded into Pete's chest, bowling him over. Still squealing the horse broke from Jim's grasp, leaped the thorn stockade and vanished.

Jim shook his head mournfully. "I pricked him too hard," he muttered.

Aided by several of the men of the *kraal* he carried Pete—that man was unconscious; several ribs were broken—into one of the huts and left him to the care of the women.

"You will give witness that the thing was not my fault," Jim asked the men.

"Truly, Hottentot," the headman answered. "Now tell us more of that *baas* of yours."

"Nay, I must go and look for the horse."

"What need?" Jamba urged. "He will not go far. In the morning we will find him; we will all go to look for him. Now sit—the night is young, there are stories to tell and beer to drink. Sit."

And Jim sat; the beer was very good.

THE BEER pots were empty; the fire burned low; one by one the men had gone to their huts. Jim alone, sat by the fire—dozing.

Someone touched him on the shoulder.

He opened his eyes and saw a white man standing beside him. Behind the white man were a number of the little people. He staggered to his feet.

"Give me the red idol," the white man said harshly.

Jim blinked. "It has gone," he said thickly.

"Where?"

"Who knows?"

"Answer," The little men closed in on Jim.

"Another white man came," Jim said dully. "He wanted the idol. It was hidden in the tail of the *baas'* horse. The white man tried to take it and the horse ran away—first kicking the man."

"You lie," the Parson said curtly. "Where is this white man?"

Jim gestured toward one of the huts.

"Watch him closely," the Parson said to the little men in their clicking tongue. He entered the hut Jim had indicated. His voice was heard raised in anger. Presently he emerged again. His face was white with rage.

"You are a liar," he said to Jim. "You tricked that other white man—he is a fool. You do not trick me. Where is the idol?"

"Where the horse is."

At an order the little men bound Jim and staked him out on the ground.

"Where is the idol?" the Parson asked.

"I have told you," Jim answered.

The Parson drew his knife, opened it—then closed it, smiling cruelly.

"There is plenty of time," he said. "Now I am tired and would sleep. In the morning I will deal with you. In the light of the sun I will be able to see the pain in your eyes when I light a fire on your belly. You will remember, I think, where the idol is."

As the Major neared the *kraal*—it was shortly after the arrival of the Parson—he saw his horse, Satan, standing in the shadows. He rode up to him, was greeted with a soft *nicker* of pleasure, and quickly transferred the bridle and saddle from the horse he had been riding to the black stallion.

Released, the policeman's horse moved slowly back along the trail.

Before mounting Satan, the Major ran his hand gently along his back, combed the long tangled tail with his fingers. They closed upon a small object, cunningly concealed. He cut it loose and held it in the palm of his hand. It was a wooden idol, about two inches long. A hideous thing—it was symbolical of all that is beastly in a black man's soul.

The Major sighed, put the thing in his pocket, mounted and rode on.

He dismounted in a thicket not a hundred yards from the *kraal* and went forward on foot, keeping cleverly to the cover of the ground hollows. His wagon and mules—the wagon and mules he had bought from Pete—stood just beyond the *kraal*. The Parson had driven it over. In all probability, the Major thought, his equipment was still loaded on it.

Finding a weak place in the thorn stockade he leaped over and made his way to where the Parson held Jim captive. Taking shelter behind a hut, he heard the Parson's threatening promise of the evil the morrow would bring Jim.

For a moment he was tempted to essay a rescue then— but a second thought decided him against it. The chances of failure were too great. There was the Parson's knife and revolver! More to be feared, even, was the poison which tipped the bushmen's arrows.

And Pete? Where was he? Unseen, he was a menace. He might appear at any moment. From this hut—or that.

The Major retired cautiously, reproaching himself for having been responsible for Jim's predicament. He leaped over the stockade and landed on top of a bushman who, left on guard outside the stockade, had come to investigate a suspicious noise.

The two rolled over and over, the Major's hand closing the little man's mouth so that he could not shout an alarm.

Presently the bushman's struggles ceased, the Major was far too strong for him.

"If you make a sound you will die," the Major said. "Understand?" He had no difficulty with the *clicks*.

The little man nodded.

Taking him by the wrist the Major lead him to where Satan calmly awaited him.

"Here we can talk—but softly," the Major said. "You will lead me to your people; I want to talk to them."

The little man shook his head.

"I will not. It is only by hiding that my people remain free."

"And yet that white man—" he nodded toward the *kraal*—"comes and goes as he pleases. You are his slaves?"

"Not so, white man. We are slaves of no man. But that white man is the servant of the red idol. Therefore we obey him."

The Major nodded. He silently considered his next step. He wanted the help of the bushmen; he knew that he would never locate their abode unless this one showed it to him.

"And if it were proved that he is no true servant of the red idol?"

"Then he would die."

"What is this red idol?"

"I do not know, white man. Save—" he hesitated—"save it is a thing our wizards have told us to obey."

The Major nodded again and taking out the idol balanced it on the palm of his hand.

The dwarfed native stared at it, bulge-eyed.

"You will take me to your people," the Major said.

"Aye," the other agreed fearfully. "Follow me."

WITH THE rising of the sun a party of little people came to the *kraal* of Jamba. In their midst walked the Major, closely guarded. Two men, greatly fearing, led the black horse.

They passed unhindered into the *kraal* and came to the place where Jim was staked out on the ground.

The Parson was heaping some twigs on the Hottentot's chest, describing, almost gleefully, the biting burning pain the native would feel as soon as the twigs were lighted.

Clustered about the Parson was his body guard of little people, and beyond—looking on incuriously—the people of Jamba.

The Parson jumped to his feet as the Major and the bushmen neared.

"So you escaped from the policeman, eh, Major?" he shouted. "I was afraid you'd be too clever for him. But you couldn't escape my little people, I see. And they brought you to me just in time. Yes. Just in time to save this dear, black brother of yours from a foretaste of hell."

The Major made no reply. There was a mocking light in his eyes. His guard forced him forward, nearer to the Parson.

"Where's that idol, Major?" Pete demanded.

"In my pocket," the Major said and pressed forward. His guard had commingled with the Parson's men. They were jabbering excitedly.

The Parson caught a word here and there. His face blanched. His hand reached for his revolver.

One of the bushmen behind the Major loosed an arrow from his puny bow at the Parson. It stuck in that man's thick riding breeches, hung there a moment and then dropped to the ground.

"Whew!" the Parson muttered, realizing how close death had come to him. But, for the moment, he did not perceive that that arrow was meant for him. He thought it had been aimed at the Major.

The noisy clamor of the little people was suddenly stilled. The Parson looked at the Major and gasped in dismay.

He saw that the Major, monocle gleaming in his eye, was standing before him unbound, covering him with his revolver. The little people—all of them—were looking angrily at him, menacing him with their arrows.

The Parson appealed to them, commanded, pleaded.

They completely ignored him. By their attitude they made it known to him that his hold over them no longer existed. He realized, suddenly, that the Major meant more to them than he had ever done. For him they only had intense hate.

The little people are like that; they only know two emotions.

"You'll save me from them, Major?" he stammered. "You can't turn a white man over to them."

The Major laughed softly.

"The theme changes again, Parson dear," he drawled.

Then, to the little people, "Bind him."

It was swiftly done—even more swiftly the Major released Jim.

"Where is the other white man, Jim?" he asked.

The Hottentot told him, with many chuckles, of Pete's plight. The Major went into the hut and interviewed Pete; told him of many things that were good for his soul if not very comforting to his bruised body.

"I'm going to send you back to the store with the Parson," he concluded. "The little people will see that he does not try to play any tricks. And, if you take my tip, you'll tell your story to the policeman before the Parson has a chance to tell his. And I'd tell the truth, the whole truth and nothing but the truth, if I were you. It's the only chance you'll have of saving your skin—by turning Queen's evidence, I mean. Serious crime, you know, this encouraging natives to raid the camps of white men. Yes; you'd better tell the truth. The little people will back you up, but, of course, the Parson won't. He'll blame everything on you. You know that. That's why I'll arrange it so that you can tell your story first. Well—ta-ta!"

The Major went outside again and mounted his horse.

"You're not going to leave me like this?" the Parson shouted in a frenzy of fear. "They'll stick me with their poisoned arrows—and it's a hellish way to die."

"Of course," the Major said smoothly, "accidents will happen—your own words, I believe—and I can't be blamed for that. Think of the poor devils who've died because you unloosed the little people on them. Yes; I suppose it would be a painful way to die. I'm quite sure of it. You see—I heard my mules die last night. So many things have happened since then—haven't they?

"Oh, well! I don't think it matters what happens to you. I don't really care whether the little people let you go free or not. You're quite harmless now—in this district at least. But cheer up! I'll give orders you're not to be harmed. Listen:"

To the little people he said, speaking slowly in a loud voice so that the Parson could follow him, "And now I go from you—on the way to the Mountains of the Moon, there to do what I am called upon to do. When I have gone, some of you will carry the sick white man who is in that hut to his place at the store. And there you will tell the policeman the truth of all the things this man has ordered you to do.

"When the sun is overhead, the rest of you will take this man—" he gestured to the Parson—"to the store. And you will tell the truth of things. That is all. It is understood?"

"Aye, it is understood," they answered.

The Major turned again to the Parson.

"I'm sending Pete ahead of you," he said, "because the dear fellow has a desire to turn Queen's evidence. He is, to be exact, going to tell all of your operations and so forth. He's doing this, he says, because you kicked him in the ribs when you saw him last night, and because you've always cheated him out of his share of the takings.

"And when thieves fall out— Oh, well. No need for me to point a moral, is there? You can supply your own. And you won't be given a chance to talk with Petey so I think he'll carry through with his revenge.

"That's all, except— Of course you won't believe me when I tell you that the reason I gave for following up this idol affair is the real one? You won't? I'm sorry about that. Sorry, because I hate to have you think that I'm in the same class as yourself."

He waved to the little people, turned his horse and rode slowly out of the *kraal*. Jim, grinning happily, shouting to Jamba, "What did I tell you? Is he not a man? And I—I am his servant," followed quickly after him.

BUSH SHADOWS

OVERHEAD, THE African sun blazed fiercely; here and there the dazzling blue of the sky was flecked with wisps of clouds which looked like puffs of steam generated by the sun's intense heat. Above the trees heat waves danced and the ape folk resting in the topmost branches gazed in puzzled wonder at the grotesque distortion of a distant range of rugged kopjes.

Beneath the trees—down in the swampy ground which fostered their gigantic growth and nourished the enormous parasitic creepers by which their life was fated to be choked—the sun's rays could not penetrate and the light was similar to the yellow, murky gloom which presages a violent thunderstorm.

It was a place of hideous reptilian creatures; of trees which grew to unbelievable heights; of stunted, thorn-armored trees from whose gnarled branches trailed a gray, fungous growth which caught at the faces of travelers with a leprous touch of uncleanliness.

It was a place of gray, menacing shadows; a place of twilight gloom while the sun was yet high—a place of Stygian darkness when the sun had set.

Through the gloom trekked some thirty men, following the lead of an undersized Mashona, dressed in a ragged shirt of red flannel, who found a path through apparently impassable barriers of thorn and tangled creepers.

The men, their hands raised to steady the heavy loads they carried upon their heads, marched in silence; but their lips moved continually as they voicelessly repeated charms to ward off the evil spirits whose abode this was.

Sweat, tinged with blood from the thorn scratches which scored their flesh, dripped from their almost naked bodies; they were besmeared with the gray-green mud of the place; they all looked hungry, tired and greatly frightened. Their eyes bulged in their sockets as they fearfully scanned the bush to the right and the left of them.

Occasionally they turned to regard the squat, powerfully built Hottentot who brought up the rear of the line, and seemed to find some comfort from the sight of the ponderous, muzzle-loading elephant gun he carried.

At such times, whenever one of the natives turned to look at him, the Hottentot grinned and made gestures of confident assurance; he thumbed his broad nose and spat noisily to express his contempt for any lurking spirits. Once he commenced a ribald song, but when the thin line of men halted and expressed their distaste of his bravado by a series of reproachful *"Tchs!"* he closed his thick lips closely together, waved his hand to signify that he would sing no more and marched on in silence. After all, it is not wise to try the spirits too much! It was still more important, the Hottentot knew, that the nerves of the carriers should have no strain put upon them.

After a time the red-shirted guide came out on to a large clearing in the center of which was a peculiarly shaped rock formation. At a first, casual glance it looked like a group of crocodiles basking in the sun.

Squatting on his haunches, the guide watched the others file slowly before him with dull, apathetic eyes. One by one they deposited their burdens on the ground, stretched wearily and then sat down facing their headman.

Lastly the Hottentot emerged from the jungle.

"*Tchat!* Lazy ones!" he stormed. "Are you baboons that you sit so lazily in the sun? When we have come to the place appointed, then you can rest. To your feet, M'Bumvana,* before I—"

"Softly, softly, Hottentot," M'Bumvana replied. "We go no farther. This is the place. This is the Place of Crocodiles." He pointed to the rock in the center of the clearing.

The Hottentot looked swiftly toward it, nodded and stretched himself luxuriously. A button flew off the tight fitting tunic he wore as he expanded his mighty chest.

"You have done well, M'Bumvana," he said condescendingly. "You have done well—for a Mashona."

"Yah. I have done well," M'Bumvana agreed with a complacent smirk. "Yet it was nothing. Once, long ago, when I was only an unmarried youth—that was before you were born, Hottentot—I came to this place. The two score years which have passed since that time have not dimmed

---

* The little red one.

my memory. Still, as you say, I have done well. Will your white man, the man you call your *baas,* do as well?"

"I have always heard," the Hottentot's tone was heavy with sarcasm, "that the lion is a better hunter than a hyena."

He sat down, his back against the stump of a tree, his legs outstretched before him, his gun resting across his thighs.

M'Bumvana chuckled softly.

"Meaning that I am a hyena?" he remarked casually.

The Hottentot did not answer. He was listening intently to the multitude of bush noises which surrounded them—the drone of countless insects, the rustling of leaves, the *whirr* of wings, aimless chatter of monkeys and the soughing noise made by a host of tiny feet floundering in heavy mud. From this chaos of sound—and a white man would have heard nothing; to his untrained ears the individual noises would have been merged into a brooding silence—the Hottentot was endeavoring to distinguish some alien note, some clue to the whereabouts of the white man—his *baas*—who had trekked on ahead of them, and who was to meet them at this place.

Loud snores close at hand disturbed his concentration.

"Pigs!" he exclaimed in disgust and he scowled threateningly at the carriers.

Nearly all of them were fast asleep, their fears and hunger for the time forgotten, their chins resting on their updrawn knees. Those still awake gazed vacantly at the Hottentot as if wondering at the cause of his anger, smiled simperingly; then they, too, closed their eyes and presently they slept.

"Pigs!" the Hottentot exclaimed again.

M'Bumvana chuckled, admonishingly.

"They are tired, Hottentot. Tired, hungry and afraid. Therefore they sleep."

"We also are tired, hungry and afraid. But we do not sleep."

"We are men!" M'Bumvana explained with simple dignity.

The Hottentot looked at him and smiled.

"Yah! For all that you are a Mashona and no bigger than a dog ape, you are a man," he said.

M'Bumvana helped himself to a large pinch of snuff, sneezed, and then asked incredulously:

"But you are not afraid, Hottentot?"

"For myself—no. For these sleeping fools—yes. If my *baas* does not come before tomorrow's sunrise they will trek back to their *kraals*, leaving their loads behind them. And, because I will not be there to guard them with my gun, they will die on the way."

"They will not go. I, M'Bumvana, their headman, will order them to stay."

"They will be deaf to your voice. Their fear of the spirits and of the bush pygmies, is greater than their fear of you. They will die by the way, but that is no matter; baboons and Mashonas are plentiful. But because there will be no one to carry the loads, my *baas* will not be able to trek on to the north as he had planned. And that is bad."

M'Bumvana sighed.

"You speak true word, Hottentot. If the white man does not come back, they will go. He alone can hold them. Almost they turned back today—you know it?"

"Aye. I know it." The Hottentot smiled grimly as he recalled the heated protests the carriers had made that morning before breaking up camp and trekking still farther into the mysterious, fever and spirit infested jungle. Only the most cunning diplomacy, mixed with hard words and harder blows, had forced them to take the trail onward.

"But if they go," M'Bumvana resumed encouragingly, "what matter? We two remain, so all will be well."

"And we two, alone, you think," the Hottentot said scathingly, "can carry all that?" He pointed to the pack loads.

"I had forgotten the loads," M'Bumvana admitted.

"It is no matter. Undoubtedly my *baas* will be here before today's sun goes down. And if he comes not—a way will be found. You are a man, M'Bumvana."

"A man—and somewhat of a fool!" The little headman sighed lugubriously.

"And wherefore?"

"Wherefore? Listen to the folly of it. Ten days ago a white man, riding a coal black devil of a horse, came to my *kraal.* With him, driving eight mules harnessed to a cape cart, was an ugly grinning ape of a Hottentot. The white man had speech with me. *Wo-we!* He treated me as if I were a great chief, yet never permitted me to forget that he was a still greater one."

"My *baas* is a man," the Hottentot murmured. "There is none other like him."

M'Bumvana nodded.

"A man, yes; and a man with a voice to charm. His horse, the mules, the cape cart, he would leave at my *kraal,* he said. That was easy, that was soon agreed to. But that was not all! He wanted a guide to take him by the quickest path through the jungle; he wanted men to carry his provisions. Because of the magic he exerted upon us—and it was not all in his voice—I said that I would be his guide and did not bargain for a reward."

"The reward will be most just," the Hottentot promised.

M'Bumvana waved his hand, dismissing the matter as a thing of no consequence.

"Of course—that is understood," he said. "So I came with him to guide the way through the bush. I left my *kraal,* the peace of my huts, the beer my wives had newly brewed. And with me came twenty-eight of my young men, carrying the white man's loads, daring the vengeance of the spirits and the poisoned arrows of the Archers, the bush pygmies. Truly I am a fool."

"It is no folly to enter the service of my *baas.* It is a thing to boast of to your children's children."

"Maybe!" M'Bumvana clapped his hands softly together; his eyes glistened. "He is a man. His talk is as straight as the line of his back; his strength is beyond that of any two of my strongest people; his eyes are open to all things. And, Hottentot? Is it because he is constantly washing that his skin is white and not black like ours?"

The Hottentot grinned. "Wash, Mashona, and become a white man!"

"I have washed before now, Hottentot, and my skin itched because of the washing and I could not sleep! Does your *baas'* skin always itch?"

"It would itch if he did not wash and the fat you smear upon yourself, M'Bumvana, would not help him."

The little headman sighed.

"A strange race these whites! And that glass thing your *baas* wears in his eye. At first I thought he could take his eye out. What do you call that?"

"A 'mon'kle.'" The Hottentot gave a weird pronunciation of the English word.

"Mon'kle," M'Bumvana repeated. "It is a great charm. But I think the charm is in the wearer and not of the thing itself."

There was silence for a little while.

Some of the sleepers stirred restlessly and one man started up in the panicky fear born of nightmare, grinned sheepishly then composed himself to sleep again.

From a sun bathed spot, the clearing was gradually becoming a place of creeping shadows; grotesque shadows cast by the fringing tops of the trees.

Mosquitoes commenced to *ping* savagely; monstrosities, flying blindly, bumped into the faces of the men with violent impact; tsetse flies, their bite like a jab from a white hot needle, feasted greedily.

M'Bumvana rose stiffly to his feet and shivered as if with cold. His red flannel shirt clung to his attenuated form as if it were soaking wet; sweat drops hung from the end of his broad nose, others rolled down and gathered on the tip of his straggling wisp of a beard.

The Hottentot looked up inquiringly.

"Shall we gather wood for a fire, Hottentot?" the little headman asked him.

"Aye," the other agreed absently. "It grows cold."

He scrambled to his feet and for the space of ten or fifteen minutes the two men occupied themselves collecting a pile of wood. But neither ventured into the jungle, or far away from the sleeping porters, and the Hottentot never relaxed his hold on his cumbersome firearm.

When at last they had a fire burning brightly, they sat down close beside it and sighed like men who have come safely through great perils.

"When the sun sinks in jungle-land," said M'Bumvana, "it is good to have a fire."

The Hottentot said:

"Truly! It grows cold."

They huddled closely together.

But it was not the fear of chills which had actuated them. The heat was even more oppressive than it had been at high noon.

"We are two fools," grumbled the Hottentot. "Evil spirits cannot harm us. There are no evil spirits save the fears that are in our own minds. My *baas* has told me that many times, and he is all-wise; neither does he lie."

"I have crossed many rivers I knew contained no crocodiles," M'Bumvana said sententiously, "but never yet have I crossed a river without first beating on its surface a spear's throw beyond the place where I intended to make my crossing. Here there may be no evil spirits, but if there are, the fire is lighted."

The Hottentot was still unappeased.

"My *baas* will laugh at me," he muttered, and he spat into the fire as if, by so doing, he could extinguish that material evidence of his fears.

Again there was silence and the two men stared morosely into the heart of the flickering flames, finding there visions of ill omen.

On the far side of the clearing a bushman, looking like a hobgoblin of the jungle, flitted noiselessly to and fro. He paused presently, and stared at the strangers; he fitted an arrow to his bow—its barb was tipped with deadly poison—

Somewhere, deeper in the jungle, a guinea fowl *clucked*. At the first metallic note the pygmy disappeared, swiftly, noiselessly.

The Hottentot shivered and muttered uneasily:

"I felt as if the death spirit came very near us then."

"I, too, was cold," M'Bumvana agreed and threw more wood on the fire, softly voicing a charm as he watched the fountain of sparks which spurted up, floating like fireflies, and then vanished.

"Tell me," he continued presently, "more about your *baas*. Tell me about the things you and he have done together."

"As well ask me to count the drops which fall during a great rain. We have been together many years and only the nights have been given to sleep. North, south, east and west this land knows us— 'the Major' and his Hottentot dog, Jim."

"Trading?" M'Bumvana questioned.

"Trading, hunting, acquiring wealth and losing it. We have played the diamond game at Kimberley—robbing the robbers!" The Hottentot laughed. "But mostly, it now seems to me, we have left our own trails and traveled through thorn scrub and over waterless deserts, in order to set the feet of other people upon their right trail."

"And was it for that purpose, you think, that your *baas* left us two suns ago?"

"Undoubtedly." Jim, the Hottentot, was very positive.

"But it was the spoor of a jungle ghost he followed," M'Bumvana objected dubiously. "A gray, evil shadow. We all saw it—and it was in no sense human. Think you then that your *baas* has gone to give aid to the spirits?"

"Undoubtedly," the Hottentot said again and did not consider it necessary to point out to M'Bumvana that the gray apparition which had so greatly alarmed them two days ago had left a well defined, human spoor behind it.

"Maybe the spirits will keep your *baas?*" the little headman said.

"Maybe." Jim agreed sadly. He thought of the many ways in which death could come to his *baas*—from an Archer's poisoned arrow, from fever, grim starvation, the fangs of a snake—

"I should have followed him," Jim, the Hottentot, murmured uneasily. Then aloud, "No harm will come to him. He knows all things. Before sundown he will come to this place, and as he said, he will bring food for us all."

"It will be good to taste meat again," M'Bumvana said hopefully. Then continued, "And if and when he comes, where then does the trail we follow lead?"

"Wherever the wind blows," the Hottentot answered evasively.

"And if no wind blows?"

"To the Mountains of the Moon. We follow the trail of a little red idol."

"*Au-a!* I have heard of *that* and of the men whose charm it is. Is your *baas* a friend of those men?"

"Nay. He goes to rescue from them a white man and a white girl. He goes to put an end to their evil plotting."

"And are the white ones friends of your *baas?*"

"He does not know them. By chance he received word—"

"And he gains no reward?"

"There is no reward—that is my *baas'* way."

"*Tchat!* Many days of hard trekking are between us and the Mountains of the Moon. In my youth I visited them, and the path is beset with perils. *Au-a!* He will meet death!"

"That is a game he plays, what need for further words?"

"None. He is a fool, and you are a fool, Hottentot. I, too, must be a fool for I go with you."

"You are a man, M'Bumvana," the Hottentot exclaimed admiringly.

"And a fool," the little headman insisted mournfully.

"Without doubt." The Hottentot laughed. "I have heard say that the Great Spirit made baboons and Mashonas on the same day. In his haste, however, he gave the Mashonas power to speak and on the baboons he placed tails."

M'Bumvana chuckled.

"This is a new tale I now hear, Hottentot. Are you a maker of legends?"

They were silent for a little while.

The shadows lengthened, deepened; the tree tops were splashed with the blood-red tints of the setting sun; the outcropping of rock more closely resembled the river scavengers; by some queer chance of lighting they seemed to be of a sudden endowed with life and for a fleeting second appeared to move menacingly in the direction of the fire.

"But they are only rocks," Jim, the Hottentot, breathed aloud.

M'Bumvana relaxed with a sigh.

There was a heavy crashing noise in the jungle thickets, a loud, bellowing roar followed and then a buffalo bull came out into the clearing, the sun gleaming on the wide, sweeping spread of his horns.

His vindictive little eyes glinted red; his sleek hide appeared as black as ebony as he stood there, pawing the ground in angry indecision, his outstretched nostrils working to catch the scent of the fire and the two who sat beside it. There was something fiercely implacable about him; he personified the relentless, bovine cruelty which is some part of Africa.

"Your firestick, Hottentot," M'Bumvana whispered excitedly. "Shoot him before he catches our scent and charges. If, then, you kill him, we can all eat. If you miss him—we die."

"Still!" the other commanded fiercely. "There is no wind; he cannot scent us, he cannot see us. Maybe he will go away. But whether he goes or stays—I cannot shoot him. He and his people are tabu to me and my people!"

Not for an unlimited supply of the beer he loved too well would the Hottentot have admitted that his gun was useless or that he had no ammunition. He would have cheerfully faced death rather than confess to a Mashona that he was afraid of guns.

"He does not know he is tabu to you," the little headman wailed, "and you are not tabu to him. He is going to charge." He pulled a blazing brand from the fire. "Maybe," he added grimly, "he will be ready to forget us when he feels this searing his flesh."

"It is well thought of," the Hottentot agreed, as he, too, took a burning log from the fire. "My tabu says nothing about killing a buffalo any way other than shooting—that I must not do. We will roast our meat, Mashona."

The two men rose warily to their feet and edged slowly round the fire so that it was between them and the buffalo, an animal whose vindictive cunning and obstinate bravery cause it to be ranked by experienced hunters as the most dangerous of Big Game.

The bull bellowed once, challengingly.

Not one of the sleepers stirred. If the bellow penetrated their consciousness at all it served only to add a semblance of reality to their dreams of their home *kraal;* dreams of fat oxen grazing contentedly on the sweet grass of the high veld.

"They are fools," the Hottentot muttered contemptuously. "Well, let them sleep. We two can handle this noisy one. It is best, I think, that we carry the fight to him. What do you say, headman? Maybe he will turn and run when he sees that we have no fear."

"As you say Hottentot. But if he sees at all, he knows that I tremble with fear. I wish that *baas* of yours would come, or, at least, that you would forget that tabu of yours!"

"It is a strong tabu—it cannot be broken. Come!"

The two advanced slowly, swinging their brands in wide circles, sending showers of sparks flying in all directions. The Hottentot still clutched his gun, strangely finding moral support in the possession of a thing he feared above all things.

The buffalo bull lowered its head, evidently puzzled by their maneuvers. He was on the point of turning to seek the safe shelter of the bush when a sportive breeze played with the ragged ends of M'Bumvana's red shirt, causing it to flap about his thin legs.

It was a very little thing, that breeze; it died away as suddenly as it had sprung up. But it was responsible for the bull's decision to charge.

With head held low, tail stiffly perpendicular, he came on at an unbelievable speed.

M'Bumvana threw his brand at the beast, hitting him on the shoulders, then turned and ran. The bull wheeled swiftly and gave chase, paying no attention to the Hottentot or to the brand he threw at it.

Back and forth the little man dodged with great agility, but he was too panic stricken to think of the comparative safety which the jungle growth beyond the clearing would give him. And the Hottentot, who was following closely on the buffalo's heels, gave no thought to that either.

Presently, with a courage born of despair, for his wind was leaving him, M'Bumvana turned to face his pursuer and shouted shrill curses.

The effect on the buffalo was surprising. It came to a dead standstill; its jaws moved as if it were peacefully chewing the cud. But when M'Bumvana moved, it savagely began to paw the ground again.

"Still!" the Hottentot shouted. "Stand still." But the caution was too late. The massive beast began to move ponderously toward the red-shirted manikin who barred his way.

M'Bumvana turned to run again but stubbed his toes on a half buried rock and fell headlong. There was something devilishly human, then, about the way in which the buffalo advanced toward his fallen foe. His head swung to and fro—a little nearer and the puny man would be impaled upon the curving horns. M'Bumvana tried to contract himself into a still smaller object.

Then a crisp report echoed through the jungle, followed by another. The buffalo lurched to its knees, bellowed once and toppled slowly over.

Then silence. And then, pandemonium!

The sleepers, awakened by the alien noise of the reports, jumped to their feet, yelling with fear. But fear immediately gave way to acclaims of joy when they saw the dead beast and thought of the good red meat on which they could feast.

They hailed the Hottentot as a mighty hunter.

M'Bumvana, rising slowly to his feet, cried, "It is well that you forgot the tabu, Hottentot!"

For a moment Jim was puzzled, then, understanding that they credited him with the killing of the buffalo, he strutted proudly to and fro, basking in their effusive praise.

His mood changing, he pushed aside the excited men who were muttering charms over the carcass preparatory to disemboweling and skinning it, and bade them stand back.

"You will wait," he cried, "until my *baas* comes."

They obeyed, slowly, sulkily.

"Your *baas*," one muttered. "He will never come. The spirits, or the Archers, have taken him."

"By the bull I have killed," Jim swore, "he will be here presently. Now make camp."

More to humor him—was he not a mighty hunter?—than because they believed the white man was near, or because they acknowledged Jim's authority over them, the carriers ran to their packs.

In a very little while, they had been well drilled, a camp was created out of chaos; a camp which centered about a small bell tent in which was a folding cot. The bed had been made with clean white sheets; silk, monogrammed pyjamas were placed on the pillow, a small collapsible table, a deck chair and two steel uniform cases put in place.

The cook boys of the outfit were busily preparing food for the carrier's evening meal—corn mush to balance the red meat—while others were storing the provisions neatly upon a piece of sailcloth, covering them all with a water-proof sheet. Still others were erecting small grass shelters. Each one had a task to perform; there was no aimless running to and fro, no duplication, nothing overlooked.

The Hottentot and M'Bumvana, seated on the dead buffalo, watched the busy scene with eagle eyes, shouting some caustic comments whenever they saw a man idling.

"Maybe it is all to no purpose, Hottentot," the headman said slowly. "Maybe your *baas* will not come."

"He will," Jim replied flatly. "He said he would meet us here and have food—good red meat—for us. My *baas* always makes good his promises. Here," he drummed his heels on the buffalo's body, "is the meat."

"But you shot the bull," M'Bumvana expostulated.

"What matter? My *baas* only said there would be meat. He did not say who would kill it. He keeps his word. Listen!"

Jim made a megaphone of his hands. "O-he, *Baas!*" he shouted.

The bush echoed his words; other than that there was no answer.

Jim called again—then listened intently.

"O-he, Jim," a voice came from the jungle. It was very faint; little more than the indistinct murmur among the palm fronds when a gentle breeze blows.

The Hottentot sighed relievedly, then chuckled to hide the sigh.

"My *baas* keeps his word," he said again.

M'Bumvana looked at him suspiciously and muttered some scathing doubts under his breath. His ears were not so keen as Jim's.

Presently they heard a voice behind them.

"Greetings to you all," it said in the vernacular.

"*Baas!*" the Hottentot cried happily as he turned to face the newcomer. "Greetings!" M'Bumvana shouted.

"Greetings!" The carriers added their welcome. "We have been like lost children without you, but now we can eat."

"Presently!" the white man replied and laughed merrily.

He was tall, actually taller than he at first appeared. The slouching pose he affected detracted somewhat from his height. Save for a pair of badly scratched and bemired polo boots, a battered, once-white helmet, and a ragged shirt draped about his loins he was naked. In his right hand he carried a rifle at the trail; a cartridge belt was slung about his shoulders; in his left hand he carried a bunch of dirty clothes.

His skin was startlingly white against the dark background of the jungle. When he moved, his splendid muscles rippled smoothly and there was something suggestive of a lion's grace and strength about him. A two days' beard blurred the strong lines of his face. When he took off his helmet a lock of his touseled hair—it looked as if it had just been shampooed—fell down over his forehead. He looked very young then—years younger than the graying patches of his temples indicated. He looked as young as the spirit which shone in his eyes.

"We are hungry for meat, *inkosi,*" the Mashonas shouted. "Give the word and let us feast on this buffalo the Hottentot killed."

"Presently," the white man said again. "But first you must wash, my children. You are dirty. The filth of the jungle is upon you. Over there—" he pointed back in the direction from which he had come—"not more than two spear throws distant, there is a large pool. Go and wash now, before the sun sets. Afterward you shall eat. But be careful, there are crocodiles in that pool."

They trooped off noisily—the Hottentot and M'Bumvana with them. Now that their white man had returned to them, they no longer feared the jungle spirits and in a few moments they were splashing noisily in the pool, indulging in good natured, if rough, horseplay, giving not one second's thoughts to the crocodiles which watched them with cold, basilisk eyes.

WHEN THEY returned again to the camp, uncomfortably clean, the sun had set and darkness was close at hand.

The white man, clean shaven, his hair brushed back in an immaculate pompadour, a monocle gleaming in his right eye, dressed in a spotless suit of white duck, was sitting in his deck chair just outside his tent.

They lined up before him and silently awaited his orders. They were given in a quiet, well modulated voice and shortly the place was a hive of activity.

The buffalo was quickly and expertly skinned. A steak was cut off for the white man and then huge hunks of meat were distributed amongst the natives, Jim and M'Bumvana keeping close watch to see that no man got more than his share. Several natives were told off to cut the meat that remained into long strips—that would later be made into biltong.

The preliminary work over, the natives sat down to their feasting, bolting huge lumps of almost raw food with the avidity of half starved wolves. Only Jim ate sparingly; long association with the Major had taught him the folly of overloading the stomach, had taught him the value of moderation.

His own appetite satisfied, Jim waited on his *baas* and then, squatting on his haunches near by, assumed an attitude of eager expectancy.

The Major leaned back in his chair. He chuckled softly as he glanced at the overstuffed carriers who lolled dangerously close to the fire.

"They'll all come to me for *muti* in the morning, Jim," he said.

"Yah, *Baas*." Jim's teeth flashed white in an answering smile. "And it is not nice medicine you'll give them—I know!" He made a wry grimace, then continued.

"It was well you came when you did, *Baas*."

"Why? What need?" the Major asked banteringly. "They had you to protect them. You are a mighty hunter; you provide meat for them. What need, then, of me?"

"*Au-a, Baas!*" Jim said reproachfully. "You know I did not kill the buffalo; you killed it. But I thought it no harm to let these Mashona dogs think that I had killed it. All Mashonas are fools, but M'Bumvana, he is a man."

The Major nodded.

"I nearly came too late. The buffalo ran too fast for me."

Jim clapped his hands softly together.

"I might have known. You drove the bull to this place, intending to kill it here."

"And was it not well thought of," the Major asked triumphantly. "By so doing I save the labor of having the meat brought to this place. It was a good stalk save at the end, when as I have said, he went too fast for me."

"But how did you do it, *Baas?*"

"Six Archers helped me, Jim."

"*Wo-we!* Where can my *baas* go and not find friends?" Jim murmured softly. Then, aloud, "And after you had shot the buffalo, why did you not then show yourself?"

"I heard a certain Hottentot—Jim, they call him—boasting of his prowess. I did not wish to dim the light which shone upon him. Also, I was very dirty and went to the pool and bathed."

"*Wo-we!*" Jim's eyes sparkled. "I wish I had been with you to help you stalk the bull. But again I say, it is well that you have returned. The Mashonas, save only M'Bumvana, are cowardly dogs. They are afraid of shadows. Tomorrow they will try to depart for their own place. It may be that you can hold them."

"And if I fail, Jim?"

"It will be hard trekking for us, alone, without carriers, but we can do it. It will be death for them."

"Therefore they must not go, Jim."

Jim nodded agreement.

"They will want to know about the shadow the *baas* followed. They—"

"Meaning that Jim, the Hottentot, would like to hear about it now," the Major interrupted.

Jim grinned.

"The *baas* always knows!"

"About the shadow I know—nothing."

"*Au-a!* Nothing, *Baas?*"

"Nothing. The shadow knew the bush well and was a cunning traveler. Save for the time when it showed itself to us back there and I followed to take up its spoor, I have never seen it. And so I know nothing. Nothing, except—"

"Except, *Baas?*" Jim prompted eagerly.

"Except that the shadow was a white man playing the part of an evil spirit."

"But you said you did not see him, *Baas*. Then how—?"

"I did not say that I was blind to his spoor. He wore shoes, Jim.

"The Archers," he added, "are afraid of him. They swore that he was a ghost, one of the 'Wicked Dead.' Apart from that, they knew nothing."

"All pygmy folk are liars," Jim remarked succinctly.

"Without doubt." The Major rose, yawning widely. "And so, Jim, knowing nothing, being tired, I am going to bed."

"And tomorrow, *Baas?*"

"Tomorrow we trek with the rising of the sun, Jim."

"Do we follow the spoor of the white man who is a shadow, or do we follow the trail of the little red idol which leads to the Mountains of the Moon?"

"It may be that both paths lead to the same *kraal,* Jim. But," he shrugged his shoulders, "of what avail to wrap oneself up warm tonight as a protection against tomorrow's cold? What wise man at night eats the morrow's breakfast? Sleep well, Jim."

He entered his tent, undressed, and a few minutes later was sleeping peacefully. Jim, the Hottentot did not move. He sat with his hands clasped about his ankles, his chin resting on his knees, staring fixedly before him.

"At least," he muttered, "if a wise man knew that the morrow would be cold, he would take precaution tonight to collect a good store of kindling; if he knew that he could not eat tomorrow, he would feast well today."

And then, some of the men about the fire bursting into noisy song, he rose and joined the others.

"My *baas* sleeps," he said. "Why then do you hyenas howl so loudly?"

The singing ceased suddenly; conversation was limited to soft, liquid whispers. The night aged; constellations rose and set; the fire flames died down, the darkness deepened.

One by one the carriers, heavy with food, crawled to their grass shelters and slept heavily. Jim and M'Bumvana talked together for a little while, then they, too, slept.

The night passed swiftly. From the jungle pool the hoarse bellowing of crocodiles occasionally sounded. At one period there was a heavy rustling noise in the bush. A monstrous, loathsome shadow emerged into the clearing and dragged itself slowly across the ground to the carcass of the buffalo. Its jaws opened in a stupendous yawn, and closed on a thigh bone of the buffalo. Then it started to back steadily, inch by inch, dragging the carcass with it.

Again there was a heavy rustling noise in the bush, then a violent splashing and bellowing from the pool as if the monsters who dwelt there were quarreling over the partition of the food.

Then silence again.

The false dawn glowed in the eastern sky. With its passing, another shadow crawled on all fours across the clearing. It busied itself about the crocodile rocks.

The real dawn came swiftly.

With the first gray streak of light, one of the Mashonas awoke and, impelled by gluttonish desires, rose stealthily, intending to cut off a hunk of meat and eat it before his comrades awoke. Almost immediately his eyes were attracted to the crocodile rocks and stared in petrified fear at the grotesque form crouching there.

He tried to give an alarm but, though his lips moved no sound came from them.

And then the *Thing* rose to its feet and gestured menacingly at the Mashona, who, in an agony of superstitious fear dropped full length on the ground and buried his face in his hands.

When he dared to look up again the *Thing* had gone and the gray of early dawn had given place to a blaze of vivid color.

"*Wo-we!*" he wailed loudly. "My time has come to die. I have seen the death spirit."

The sun shot up above the horizon and the camp awoke.

The men crowded about the fear-stricken man, questioning him excitedly.

But save that he moaned repeatedly, "I have seen the death spirit," they could get no word from him.

The Major hastily donned a few clothes and ran out to join them. His appearance had a calming affect on the native.

"What ails you, Kawiti?" he asked.

"I have seen the death spirit," the man replied stolidly. His tone and attitude was that of a man who resigns himself to an unkind fate. "He was all white; I could see his bones through his flesh; he had horns upon his head."

"Where did you see him?" the Major asked curtly.

"There—by the crocodile rocks."

"He is not there now, you were dreaming! You ate too much red meat."

"He was there," the man insisted stolidly. "He vanished before my eyes. With the coming of day he went. That is his custom."

The natives stared at the Crocodile Rocks, but not a man of them moved. It was as if they were held riveted to the ground by an electric current, a current of superstitious fear.

Then one pointed a shaking finger.

"Look, *inkosi*. The spirit left charms there to warn us away."

On that part of the rock outcrop which formed the "jaws" of the crocodile were a number of objects—a heap of stones; a broken twig; a bunch of hen feathers tied together by a piece of bark fiber and a piece broken out of a small calabash.

The Major walked over to the rocks and examined the thing's left there by the spirits. The bunch of feathers he put into his pockets, the piece of calabash he also put carefully away.

Then he returned to the natives who edged away from him, looking at him with an expression of admiration mingled with dread. Had he not dared to handle the charms? Was he not, therefore, a doomed man?

"It is nothing," he said lightly. "There is no cause for fear. You are men. You are not to be frightened by a man who apes the part of a spirit."

"Did you find the footprints of a man, *inkosi?*" M'Bumvana asked cautiously.

"No," the Major admitted, "but—"

"There is no 'but,'" Kawiti interrupted forcefully. "The spirits do not leave footprints. And it was a spirit. I saw—I am not blind. A warning has been given us. I go no farther. Today I return to my *kraal.*"

"We go with you," the other carriers shouted.

Then one cried, "The buffalo! It is not here! The spirit took it for himself."

They turned as one man to where they had left the remains of the beast. Jim, the Hottentot, ran to the place, examined the ground closely all about and then burst into a peal of laughter.

"Come and see," he shouted. "Come and see the footprints of the spirit of the dead."

They ran to him, exclaiming in wonder when he pointed out to them the spoor of a crocodile. But their fear was increased.

"It is known," they said, "that the death spirit can change himself into a crocodile. We want no further proof."

And nothing the Major could say—there were few white men who understood the black children of Africa as well as he—could persuade them otherwise. Even M'Bumvana was greatly shaken although he professed to have nothing but scorn for the foolish fears of his people.

"It is a sign," Kawiti cried again. "We must go back or we die."

"You speak foolishly," the Major said curtly.

"Foolish or no, I go no farther. Today I return to my own place."

"And we go with him," the others cried. "It was folly for us to come with you into the jungle, white man. Mashonas were made for the kopjes of the high veld and to them we return."

The Major looked at Jim, then at M'Bumvana.

"They are fools!" said the Hottentot.

And the headman, "They are only children."

"Children or fools, no matter," the carriers shouted. "This is sure—we go no farther. Today we return."

The Major was too well-versed in their psychology to attempt now to sway them from their purpose. Such a course, he well knew, might stampede them into attacking him.

"It is wise to pay heed to the charms and advice of spirits," he said smoothly. "Therefore—because it may have been the death spirit Kawiti saw—I make a bargain with you. If you return now you gain nothing, you lose everything—your names and the right to be called men. Also, you may meet your death."

"Better to die than to offend the spirits," one muttered.

"Truly, but listen now to me. If I go back with you my purpose is defeated; you know that I desire to get to the Mountains of the Moon with all speed. Also, if you return—whether I go with you or not—my purpose is defeated for I need you to carry the packs. Rest here then for three days whilst the Hottentot, M'Bumvana and I endeavor to catch this evil spirit, this terrifier of little children. If, at the end of three days, we do not return or if, when we return we cannot show you that the evil spirit you fear is a vain shadow and no real spirit, then you shall return to your *kraal* taking with you all the things of mine. They shall be yours. What say you?"

The men whispered together and then Kawiti—whom they had appointed their spokesman—said, "How can we wait here without food, *inkosi?*"

"There is plenty of food—and you know it."

"We are tired of corn mush."

"There are many tins of meat; eat what you will."

"*Au-a, baba!*" they chorused happily.

"And I hope you all get ptomaine poisoning," the Major muttered grimly in English. Aloud, he asked, "Then it is agreed?"

"There is still the matter of the spirits," Kawiti objected.

The Major waved his hands.

"As to that, the Hottentot shall make you a charm that will protect you."

"And M'Bumvana must stay with us," Kawiti concluded stolidly.

"I will not," the little headman cried wrathfully. "You are like foolish hens. You cluck triumphantly when a man finds food for your bellies; but if, for one moment, a passing cloud hides the glory of the sun, you run screeching to your roosts. I go with the *inkosi*. You—" he spat contemptuously—"can die for all of me."

The Hottentot looked at his *baas* as if to say, "Said I not this Mashona was a man?"

The Major nodded and then turned to M'Bumvana.

"They are right. You are their headman. You must stay."

"Au-a, inkosi!" he exclaimed in sorrowful reproach. "I am no woman to be left behind when there is work to be done."

"I will leave Jim's gun with you," the Major promised. "Does that restore your manhood?"

The little man's proudly beaming face was answer enough.

"You hear, chicken hearts," he cried. "I stay with you and I carry the gun with which the Hottentot killed the buffalo."

They were not one whit affected by his scorn.

"Order the Hottentot to make the charm," they demanded, "and we will wait here until three suns have risen and set. On the sun's fourth rising, and you are not here, we return to the *kraal*."

"Make a powerful charm, Jim," the Major said solemnly, and with that he returned to his tent and prepared for the journey ahead.

As he dressed he heard snatches of Jim's elaborate charm making and, looking through the tent fly, he could see the Hottentot capering about the clearing, followed at a respectful distance by the Mashonas who clapped their hands softly together in token of their awe-stricken admiration.

The Major chuckled softly. Jim's charm making was evidently proving a great success. The actual words of the charm included practically the whole of Jim's English vocabulary.

"My word yes," it ran. "Gorblessmi. Golly damme no. If I don't see you, s'long hullo!"

The Hottentot managed to get a splendid rhythm into the words and, together with his catlike leaps, his dramatic gestures and wild flashing eyes, made the ceremony very impressive.

HALF AN hour later the Major, dressed in stout khaki riding breeches and thin coat, a gray flannel shirt, polo boots—now highly polished—and white pith helmet, started off on his quest. His revolver he carried in a holster slung under his arm-pit.

Jim, naked save for a scanty loin cloth, carrying a small pack and four or five *assegais,* walked close behind his *baas.*

The Mashonas watched their departure in silence. Even M'Bumvana was too engrossed with the old muzzle-loading gun to do more than wave a casual good-by.

"They will not weep if we never return, *Baas,*" Jim commented as they paused at the pool to fill their water bottles.

The Major nodded absently. He was sitting on a rock, looking keenly at the two ju-jus he had taken from the rock.

"What is the meaning you read there?" Jim asked.

His *baas* handed him the bunch of feathers.

"Who tied that knot which holds the feathers together, Jim?"

"A child or a white man," the Hottentot answered promptly.

"A white man, surely," the Major said. He held out his hand for the feathers and when Jim had given them he put them in his pocket.

"And the other thing, *Baas?*"

"It will have no meaning to you, I think. Nevertheless—"

He gave Jim the piece of calabash.

"No, *Baas,*" he said, with a puzzled shake of his head. "It has no meaning for me. What do the scratches on the thing mean?"

He pointed to a crude series of drawings which had apparently been scratched on the thing with a thorn, or, maybe, a knife. Thus:

"I think, Jim—" the Major said slowly. "But no. I do not know yet. I think; but until I am sure my lips are closed."

Jim nodded agreement. "That is often wisest, *Baas.* Sometimes when a man says a thing is so before he is sure, he comes to believe that this is so and neglects to seek further. And so, what now, *Baas?*"

"The spirit is a man, Jim, a white man. Therefore he must have left a spoor here in the soft ground. Let us look for it."

They cast about in wide circles, scrutinizing the ground with eyes that missed nothing.

Presently Jim gave a cry of triumph and pointed to footprints—booted footprints—in the mirey soil. They pointed north.

"Shall I fetch the Mashonas?" Jim asked eagerly. "When they see the footprints they will know that the thing they fear is no spirit and will trek with us."

The Major considered this for a moment.

"No, Jim," he finally decided. "The spoor alone would not be sufficient. Besides, this is, I think, a white man's game. Therefore, alone we will follow the spoor."

The Hottentot hesitated no longer. Like a hunting dog, keen on the scent, he followed the spoor at a fast pace and the Major, effortlessly, with the silent ease of a born bushman, followed close on his heels.

ALL THROUGH the long day they followed the spoor; at times it led them through dense thickets of thorn and tangled creepers, at times across acres of quivering bog.

It was a hard day, a day of hopes and disappointments. Several times Jim lost the spoor despite his uncanny skill and ability to read a whole jungle comedy—or tragedy— from a rust colored stain on a broad, bruised leaf.

They were obsessed at such times with the premonition that the man they followed was hiding close by, laughing at them.

Then night came and they were forced to halt.

"We are beaten, *Baas*," Jim exclaimed mournfully as they broke the long day's fast beside a blazing fire.

The Major shook his head.

"No, Jim. We will unravel this puzzle. If not tomorrow, then the next day or the next—"

"We have food for tomorrow," Jim interrupted sarcastically. "After that, we starve."

"The jungle is full of food, Jim."

"And poison, *Baas*."

The Major laughed.

"You are such a pessimistic blighter, Jim," he drawled in English. Then, in the vernacular, he added earnestly, "We must go on, Jim. To go back now means that we would be delayed two score days or more before we could take the trail again for the Mountains of the Moon. To go back means failure—it may mean death."

"Death, *Baas? Au-a!* Save that death is always around the next bend in the trail I do not see that going back brings it any closer to us."

"The Archers are in the bush all around us, Jim. They may be watching us—now. If one of their poisoned arrows pricked us we—"

"Pouf!" exclaimed Jim, indicating the coming of death and the passing of the soul.

"And I promised to show the Archers that this spirit they fear is no spirit."

"A foolish promise, *Baas.*"

"As I see it now, a very foolish promise. But it was made. It was given in return for their promise that they would not attack us. And if we go back now, thus acknowledging failure—"

"Pouf!" said Jim again.

"Exactly," agreed the Major. "Now sleep. Tomorrow we trek as soon as there is light to show us the spoor."

"There will be no light," Jim said miserably and then, obediently, turned over on his side and slept.

But the Major sat for long hours endeavoring to find answers to the questions which were troubling him, but the more he endeavored to reason things out logically the deeper was the mental mire in which he found himself embogged.

He groped absently in his breast pocket and taking out his monocle, fixed it in his eye.

"Of course," he muttered in English, drawling the words affectedly, looking, now, like an effete dandy, "he may be a madman, or a white kaffir, or a half caste. 'Pon my soul, he might be most anything. He may be a top-hole spirit. But I fancy not. Spirits don't wear hob-nailed shoes."

He took the broken piece of calabash from his pocket and traced the scratched designs on it with well-shaped, strong fingers.

"By Jove!" he resumed. "If I could only decipher these things. Now, what the deuce is——?"

He closed his eyes and concentrating strongly, cast everything present from his mind; and presently a long disused memory cell opened and the mind pictures it contained flooded his brain. He was in Northern Nigeria. He—

There was a stealthy rustling in the branches overhead, a pungent animal smell.

Jim awoke swiftly.

"*Baas!*" he cried.

The Major opened his eyes.

"I nearly had it, Jim," he said reproachfully. "And now it's gone."

The Hottentot pointed up into the branch above his head.

Two orbs of yellow fire glared balefully at them. They descended lower. Jim stirred the fire with the haft of an *assegai*. A tongue of flame shot up, picking out the form of a magnificent leopard.

"Shoot, *Baas*. Shoot before it leaps." He bunched his *assegais* together and going down on one knee held the hafts firmly on the ground, the blades sticking upward.

"It is afraid of the fire, Jim, it will not hurt us. I do not want to kill—it is very beautiful."

"It is death, *Baas*."

The flames died down; the leopard crouched, its body stiffened.

The Major drew his revolver with lightning speed and fired, anticipating the leopard's leap by a mere fraction of time. The heavy bullet crashed through the animal's skull, but before death came to it its splendid muscles acted on the order of its brain. It leaped out from the branch but, in midair, all life went from it and, from the highest point of the arch, it dropped to the ground with a dull, lifeless thud, falling just short of Jim's barricade of spears.

"Yah!" the Hottentot exclaimed derisively. "It will not hurt us, and it is very beautiful."

SUNRISE NEXT morning brought them to the banks of a river.

And there they lost the spoor completely for the ground all about was hard, impressionless rock.

"Now we must return, *Baas,*" Jim said happily.

"No. Not yet. First I am going to shave."

"What a man!" Jim exclaimed as he handed the Major his toilet articles. And while the Major shaved the Hottentot pegged out the leopard skin and scraped it industriously with a sharp-edged stone.

"I feel much better now, Jim," the Major said fifteen minutes later as he returned from the river where he had been to wash.

"Yah, *Baas?*" Jim grunted, not looking up from his task.

"Yah, Jim. I have washed the film of blindness from my eyes. Now I can see."

"And is there anything to see, *Baas,* save jungle and rocks, river and sky?"

The Major chuckled.

"If you stand on this rock, Jim, and look across the river, above the tops of the jungle trees, you, too, may see something."

Jim looked suspiciously at the Major.

"I will climb the rock," he grumbled, "and look where you tell me to look. But first I say that I know you are playing a game with me. I know there is nothing to see."

He climbed up on to the rock and looked in the direction indicated by the Major's pointing finger. And there he saw a faint wisp of smoke floating wraithlike against the white haze of the sky. The Major's finger traveled slowly downward and then Jim saw a blob of twinkling light and knew it to be the tin roof of some white man's homestead.

"*Au-a, Baas!*" he exclaimed in tones of deep reproach. "I was blind not to have seen that before."

He swiftly packed up the skin and the Major's kit.

"Come *Baas*," he said. "Once we have crossed the river I think we will pick up the spoor of the spirit. I think it will lead us to the house of the white man."

"Maybe," the Major replied absently, "maybe it will end there."

The river crossed—it was so shallow that at no point did it reach to their knees—they wasted no time looking for spoor but headed straight through the bush in the direction of the tin-roofed building.

After a while they came onto a broad trail which they followed at a fast pace.

Yet, even so—African distances are very deceptive—it was nearly high noon when Jim halted abruptly and held up his hand in a caution for silence.

For a moment there was absolute quiet—the uncanny quiet of the African jungle which is really no quiet at all, but a furtive symphony of sound.

And then a woman's voice, a full, rich contralto, flooded the jungle. The affect was strangely weird. It brought home civilization, into the heart of the savage jungle.

It was a simple ballad the woman sang; the words were trite. Then the song ended abruptly, was lost in a rush of choking sobs.

"Oh, I say," the Major muttered. He tiptoed back along the trail, and Jim looked at him in amazement.

When he had gone about fifty paces the Major stopped and, singing loudly, marched noisily forward again.

Almost immediately they came out on to a small clearing in the center of which was a well-constructed bungalow with a galvanized tin roof. On the porch steps sat a woman, holding a rifle across her knees.

Jim, shrugging his shoulders, sat down on the ground and commenced to work on his leopard skin.

As the Major doffed his helmet and stood waiting uncertainly, apparently at a loss for words, the woman rose to her feet and covered him with her rifle.

She held herself with the graceful ease which comes from the possession of perfect health. Her flaxen hair, it was cropped short, curled about her well shaped head, making her look almost boyish, but the scanty dress she wore revealed the lines of a mature woman. Save that her eyes were inflamed, and the corners of her mouth drooped despondently, she was very beautiful.

The Major advanced slowly.

"You have nothing to fear, dear lady," he assured her. "My name's Aubrey St. John, but my friends—" he smiled hopefully—"call me Major."

"And what do you want here, Mister Aubrey St. John?"

He halted, nonplussed.

"Well, as to that—really, I don't know. I wanted a lot of things—but now, I'm dashed if I know. The sight of you, dear lady. I—" He fished his monocle out of his pocket and fixed it in his eye.

"I'm quite overcome," he continued glibly. "First that there should be a white man's habitation in this benighted spot; secondly that there should be a white woman living here; and thirdly—pardon my sermonizing—instead of receiving the right hand of fellowship which one white expects from another in this back of the beyond, it's a case of the frosty eye, the back of my hand, and here's your hat, Good-by! What!!"

The corners of her mouth twitched ever so slightly, her eyes sparkled. The next moment she was dour and forbidding again; she seemed to be listening, to be expecting the arrival of some one she feared.

"If you're wise," she said in a low voice, "you'll go away from here—quick!"

"But really!" he expostulated and walked slowly toward her.

"Stop!" she ordered crisply, and her finger toyed with the trigger of her rifle.

The Major stopped, realizing that she had reached a pitch of hysteria which had broken down her self control. Pushed a little bit further and her finger would contract on the trigger.

He put his hands above his head ordering Jim, who had risen to his feet and was furtively fingering his *assegais,* to do the same.

"You will obey the orders which come from my lips, Hottentot," the woman interposed sharply.

"Ah, you speak the vernacular," the Major observed.

"That is my one accomplishment," she replied bitterly. "I set myself the task of learning many dialects. I thought the mental exercise would help me to forget the jungle loneliness, forget the brazen yellow of the sun and the black shadows into which one can walk, shadows which can swallow one up. Instead, the knowledge I have makes the jungle realer, the sun hotter, the shadows more oppressive. God! What wouldn't I give for a gray, cloudy sky and a shadowless day!"

She closed her eyes and swayed slightly. With a cat-like leap the Major reached her side and took the rifle from her unresisting hands.

"There, there!" he said soothingly and stood there abashed, wondering what he could do to put an end to her dry, racking sobs.

"Be careful, *Baas*," Jim warned with the sophistication of a four times married man. "A gun in a woman's hands is less dangerous than her tears!"

The Major turned on him angrily, but before he could speak the woman—stung by the Hottentot's epigram into a semblance of self-control—demanded, "Give me my rifle."

The Major handed it to her without comment.

"Now go," she ordered. "Please, please go!"

He looked at her wonderingly, knowing that she was in trouble, knowing that she needed help, cursing the bashfulness which made him inarticulate in a woman's presence.

Her eyes refused to meet his; they stared at the blank wall of the jungle beyond him. He saw fear come into them. Then she spoke again; the harsh note had returned to her voice; her eyes glittered.

"Put up your hands," she rasped. "And you, Hottentot, throw down your *assegais,* then come and take your *baas'* revolver from him and give it to me."

Raising his hands above his head the Major half turned and whistled softly as his eyes fell on a grotesque shadow which was projected out on to the clearing, commencing at the path which led from the place.

He heard footsteps; the shadow moved, became two shadows, and then two men stepped into view.

One was a black-mustached, sinister looking individual. He was tall and of powerful build but his strength—the Major judged—had been sapped by excesses. His pasty complexion and the baggy pouches beneath his eyes told that.

The other, fair haired and slender, was evidently the girl's brother. But where her chin was firm, full of character, his was weak; his eyes were furtive; he had allowed himself to slump physically and morally. He studiously avoided looking at his sister.

Both men covered the Major with their revolvers.

"Who's your dude friend, Grace? What does he want?"

The girl's laugh was not a happy one.

"I'm glad you came, Standish! I'll leave him to your tender mercy. He's beyond me."

She ran into the house and slammed the door behind her.

"Oh, I say," the Major exclaimed foolishly. "This is absolutely beastly. Can't I take my hands down now? They ache most frightfully."

"You keep 'em up," the man Standish said with an oath. "Watch him close, Tom. He may not be such a fool as he looks."

First disarming the Major and Jim he made them stand back to back. Then, taking a long *reim* from a nail driven into one of the porch posts, he bound them together, their hands by their sides.

"There, my beauties," he leered. "Now we can talk."

"I demand to know the meaning of this outrage," the Major stammered.

Standish laughed.

"You're not in a position to demand, are you?"

"Do you mind if I go in, Standish?" the fair haired man asked in a weary monotone, speaking as if he were not quite sure of the pronunciation of the words. "You can handle this man without my help, and I'm dead tired."

"You'll stay here with me," Standish replied roughly. "I may want to question the nigger—and how can I do that without your help. Besides, that sister of yours might think I'm plotting something with this chap if you leave us alone."

Tom Johnson shrugged his shoulder and then, squatting on his haunches native fashion, rested his head on his knees and drowsed.

The Major closed his eyes to hide the look of triumph which gleamed for a moment in them.

"Well, what brought you here?" Standish demanded.

"My feet, kind sir, she answered blushingly," the Major drawled.

"Don't be funny," Standish snarled. "Answer my question." He jabbed his revolver into the Major's ribs.

"Ouch! Don't do that. You nearly made me drop my monocle and I haven't another with me. All right, all right, dear chap. Don't be so bally touchy. I'll tell you. You see, I am on my way north to rescue a beautiful damsel—at least

I hope she's beautiful—and her aged uncle who have been captured by the Red Idol Society. Never heard of them?" He looked keenly at Standish. "No I see you haven't. Well, as I was saying, back there my carriers got the wind up because they swore they were being haunted by a spirit. They wouldn't come on and so I had to come on alone. I mean to say that I promised to show them that there are no such things as spirits roaming about the jungle. So we followed the spoor, and then we lost it at the river, and we lost ourselves. Frightful feeling, what? Luckily Jim—that's my Hottentot you tied to my back—saw the roof of this bungalow and we came on here looking for hospitality. And we got it—I don't think."

"You are a liar!"

The Major rolled his eyes upward in a mock pious expression.

"It's the truth, the whole truth and nothing but the truth! S'elp me! I can tell a much better story if you'll let me lie."

Standish's rage was almost funny.

He turned to Johnson.

"Find out the nigger's story, Tom," he snapped.

That man wearily opened his eyes and spoke to the Hottentot, speaking the vernacular with a surprising fluency.

He translated Jim's reply, word for word, for the benefit of Standish. Save for one or two minor points the two stories tallied exactly.

"You've learned your nigger to say that by heart," Standish growled to the Major and threatened that man with his clenched fist. He recoiled before the steel cold glare of the Major's eyes, then laughed to cover his confusion.

"All right," he said. "We'll let you wait until the morning. I'll feel in a better mood for questioning then." He raised his voice, calling, "Sixpence, Tikkey, Situta, come here."

Three stoutly built natives came running in response. By their scarification and the fact that their incisor teeth were filed to sharp points, the Major knew them to be members of a cannibal tribe.

"Tell the boys to take these two to my store hut," Standish said to Johnson. "Tell them to stand guard at the door."

"Oh, I say," the Major bleated feebly as Johnson repeated the order to the boys—he spoke to the cannibals with the same fluency and command of idioms as he had spoken to Jim.

Not without difficulty the three picked up Major and Jim and staggered away with them into the bush.

"I say, let me go, let me go," the Major cried. "These brutes will eat me. They will—"

His voice trailed away into silence.

Standish rubbed his hands gleefully together.

"And now," he said with a malicious chuckle, "we'll go and have a talk with your sister."

He walked swiftly toward the house, whistling discordantly.

Tom Johnson gazed after him; there was a half mad light in his eyes.

"The swine!" he muttered, and spat out a string of lurid, wholly untranslatable native curses, then rose to his feet and followed slowly.

THAT NIGHT drums sounded at some distant jungle village, inviting all within hearing to a beer drink and dance.

The three natives appointed to guard Jim and the Major muttered together resentfully as they clapped their hands in time to the beat of the drums.

"Let us go," said Tikkey.

"But of the white man and his black dog; the word was given that we were to watch them."

"They are safe bound, they cannot move," Tikkey insisted.

"At least let us wait until the black white man has gone to his hut and shut himself in as is his custom," Sixpence advised.

"He is in his hut now," Tikkey answered. "See, fools! The light comes through the cracks in the door."

The others demurred no longer but rose and vanished with Tikkey into the jungle.

In the hut all was silent for a little while.

"They have gone, *Baas*," Jim whispered finally.

The Major chuckled. "I thought the drums would call them. And now to get free."

"That should not be hard, *Baas*. I have a sharp stone in my hand. I was scraping the leopard skin with it. And the *reim* is new."

Actually the hide rope was slack about the two men— at least it did not cut into their flesh. Being new, it had stretched and, besides, at the time Standish bound them, both men had expanded their chests and flexed their muscles and had strained apart from each other so that when they relaxed there was a noticeable lessening in the tightness of the coils.

They both strained again now, then the Major suddenly relaxed and Jim, with a little cry of triumph, found that he could slip a hand through one of the coils.

"Still now, *Baas*," he said and began to saw with his stone.

An hour later they were free, rubbing their cramped arms and legs.

"And now what, *Baas*?" Jim asked.

"Now we will pay a visit to the hut of the black white man."

It was close to the store hut in which they had been imprisoned and they made their way cautiously to the window. It was a crude affair; no more than a slit in the mud wall.

The Major looked in and saw the man Standish sitting in a deck chair, shaping a crude image from a lump of wet clay. A hurricane lantern hanging from a nail in the center pole cast a queer half-moon shadow over the upper part of his face, bringing out in strong relief the cruel lines of his thin lips.

Occasionally he fingered the revolver which was on the table before him as if its touch gave him confidence. Apparently satisfied with his modeling, Standish placed the grotesque figure he had made on a shelf just above his bed, opposite the window. There were five other images there already.

He walked over to the door and tried it. Satisfied that it was securely locked, he made ready for bed.

He examined his revolver and put it under his pillow, then, kicking off his boots, kissing his fingers to the row of grinning clay figures, he turned out the light.

The Major heard the bed creak, then silence.

"I want to get into the hut, Jim. Listen!" he swiftly outlined a plan of action.

Jim nodded approval and ran back to the store hut, returning presently with a knobkerry and a small bundle of dry thatch from the roof of the store hut. He gave the thatch to the Major—but said nothing of the knobkerry—and then went to his post by the door.

The Major rolled the thatch into a compact ball, lighted it and gave the flames a chance to get a good hold.

When it was blazing sufficiently to satisfy him he tossed it through the window so that it fell on Standish's bed. At the same moment Jim charged with all his might at the door.

They could hear Standish yell blasphemous threats, heard him jump out of bed. The fire ball had set fire to his bedding and he was too rattled to think of anything but extinguishing the flames.

Jim put his massive shoulder to the door again. It creaked badly, there was a splintering sound, but the door held fast. The Major now joined Jim and together they charged the door.

It went down with a loud crash and then, too late, Standish thought of and retrieved his revolver.

Before he could bring it to bear on them, Jim—the Major had fallen full length with the door's collapse—rushed at him and struck him on the head with the knob-kerry.

Standish went down like a poleaxed bullock.

"I said nothing about killing, Jim," the Major said in stern reproach as he dragged Standish away from the flames.

"He is not dead, *Baas*," Jim replied cheerfully. "I did not hit him very hard. Besides, he had a gun; we were unarmed."

"No," the Major said with a sigh of relief. "He is not dead. But I wanted to talk with him and you have closed his mouth for a time."

He helped Jim extinguish the flames—actually they had made very little headway—then lighted the lamp and examined Standish more carefully. Save for a bruise on the temple the man was apparently unharmed. Fortunately for him Jim's blow had been a glancing one.

"I could not see very well in the dark," Jim said by way of excuse. "And now what, *Baas?*"

"I suppose— Oh, bind and gag him well, Jim."

While Jim carried out his instructions, the Major pocketed the clay images and then searched among the debris for Standish's revolver.

Finding it, he slipped it into his holster.

"Ready, Jim?"

"Yah, *Baas.*"

"Then now we will go and talk with the woman and the other man."

"Do we throw more fire balls?" Jim asked with a grin.

"We do not! And you will leave your knobkerry behind."

"Au-a, Baas!" Jim expostulated. "I will be very gentle."

The Major chuckled softly and, leaving the hut, led the way up to the bungalow. As he neared, he heard the girl's voice raised in tearful reproaches and pleadings; the man answering in sulky tones.

Leaving Jim to keep guard the Major climbed confidently up the porch steps and beat a rapid tattoo on the door with the butt of his revolver.

"Come in!" the man shouted.

The Major smiled. Evidently, they thought he was Standish.

He flung open the door.

"You!" the girl gasped in astonishment. "You!" she said again, and there was a note of relief in her voice.

The man jumped to his feet, then slumped back in his chair, his jaw sagging foolishly.

The Major shut the door behind him.

He was surprised at his reception. He had rather expected that they would try to get the drop on him. Instead of which, his appearance was, apparently, a relief to them both.

He glanced swiftly round the room. The girl had put her personality into it; it lived. The only garish note about it was the collection of curios cluttering a deal table to the right of the door. A West African ju-ju was given the place of honor.

The Major grinned at it; it revived old memories; it supplied him with the clue which he had nearly got when the leopard had arrived on the scene.

"May I sit down?" he asked. "Thanks!"

"How did you get free?" the girl asked.

"Jim cut the rope—and there you are. Very simple. And then we paid a call on Mr.—er—Standish. He was quite stunned by our boisterous overtures of friendship. Oh, quite.

"And now," the dancing light left his eyes; they changed from blue to the color of hard, cold steel, "suppose you tell me all the things I don't know?"

"Suppose you tell us what you do know," the girl countered.

"Well," the Major said slowly, "that your brother is the spirit that has been haunting the jungle and putting the wind up all and sundry. I know that he is gradually forgetting that he is a white man. I imagine that you are both afraid of Standish because he has a hold over one of you. That's all."

"That is a lot," the girl replied in a low voice. "How did you know Tom was the Death Spirit?"

"Does it matter how I know? But that helped," he nodded to the ebony ju-ju, "and this." He took the broken piece of calabash from his pockets. "That ju-ju's from Nigeria, I imagine; I take it that your brother has been there. And these—" he pointed to the scratchings on the calabash—"are the signs of the Egbo society. Unless I'm mistaken they are warnings of great peril ahead—capture, torture, death."

Tom Johnson looked at the Major with a show of interest.

"And so," continued the Major, "I put two and two together; the markings of the calabash, the fact that your brother knows the West Coast; the fact that your brother squats on his haunches and sleeps like a native, that he speaks the vernacular fluently, and—Oh, there were many things which pointed to him being the spirit I was after.

"Now suppose you tell me the rest," he suggested gently. "It may help you to clear the shadows."

"You are not a detective?"

"Oh, rather not."

"But of course you wouldn't admit it if you were," she mused.

"Go on, tell him, Grace. I'm sick of all this. He's right. I'm nearly a white kaffir and, and, I'm sane now. The way I feel now, I'd rather spend the rest of my life in prison than carry on like this. So tell him; tell him before it's too late. Tomorrow I may be off again and—"

His eyes glistened strangely; his face twitched.

The girl patted his arm and with an effort he regained control of himself.

"I'll tell him," he said quietly.

"It started six years ago—in Nigeria," he began in his deadly monotone. "I was an assistant overseer on a teak mill. One night—we had been drinking—I quarreled with my chief and shot him. And then, still crazy with drink and fear, I helped myself to all the pay gold in the Company's safe and escaped into the bush.

"For three years I did not see a white man; I lived with the natives, like a native. I joined an Egbo lodge; they made me a big ju-ju man. I— There is nothing of their evil that I do not know.

"Gradually I worked my way east and south, avoiding white men, begging my way from village to village—killing, eating, lying, thieving.

"North of here I met Standish. He was on a prospecting trip. His natives had left him and he was stranded. He asked me to join him. I was nearly naked, I was dirty, I had forgotten, almost, my mother's tongue. I had nothing. The gold I stole went very quickly; some I smelted and poured over a ju-ju in an Egbo house.

"We became partners. We were to share everything equally. I told him all about myself. *Tchat!* What a fool I was!

"He encouraged me to keep up the native traits I had acquired—as if I needed encouraging! I am more comfortable in a loin cloth than trousers. Standish knows nothing about natives himself. He is afraid of them. He treats them as if they were dogs. He said the natives would give me information they wouldn't give a white man. He was right there. Only—only I *am* a white man. A native told me of this place. He said we would find diamonds. He laughed harshly. Three years I've been here, but, save for a few splints and stones Standish calls off-color, my labor's been all for nothing."

"Would you know a diamond in the rough if you saw one?" the Major interrupted.

Johnson shrugged his shoulders.

"I suppose so. But I don't do any of the sorting. Standish is the mining expert. I do the dirty work, and look after the natives, and keep other white men from coming this way."

"Is that the only reason you play the part of the spirit and crawl through the jungle like a native?"

"No," Johnson admitted sullenly. "I do it because I like the thrill of it. The jungle lures me; I feel that I'm a part of it—"

His voice trailed off into silence, a film seemed to fall over his eyes.

The Major looked at the girl.

"And where do you come in, dear miss?"

"Tom managed to get word to me and I came out here to be with him; to help him get back. I brought him the happy news that the man he thought he had killed was still alive, had only been creased by the shot. We planned to work together and make enough money to make resti-tution. When we could do that, Tom was to go back and face the music. That was three years ago, and we are farther from our goal now than we were at the beginning. I have had to watch Tom sink lower and lower; to realize that the jungle call is growing stronger on him every day; to wonder each time he goes out if he will ever come back."

"And if you had money? You would go back tomorrow?"

"God, yes!" the man wailed.

The Major turned to the girl again.

"Why did you try to persuade me to go away?"

"Partly because I was afraid you were a detective—and Tom must not go back until he can repay what he stole—and partly to save you; chiefly to save you, I think."

"From what, dear lady?"

She hesitated a moment, then, "Standish is a little mad sometimes, I think. He goes into most frightful outbreaks of temper if anyone goes near his hut while he's away. And when he's there, and you go in, he watches you all the time like a cat watches a mouse. And I think he killed an old prospector who happened by this way."

The Major nodded. "And if he's not getting any diamonds, don't you think it strange that he should be so suspicious of every one who comes here. For the matter of that, why does he hang on here?"

"Yes, I've thought of that. I've accused him of tricking us, but Tom wouldn't back me up. He was afraid Standish would denounce him to the authorities."

"Give the devil his due, Grace," her brother said. "He's playing square about the claim. We've been getting just enough stones—off-color stones, Standish calls them—to keep us going. That's all. If he wanted to play a crooked game, what's to stop him from denouncing me now. Then he wouldn't have to bother about us."

The Major smiled.

"I suppose you do some mining?" he suggested.

"I do all the heavy work," Johnson insisted. "That's the only thing that's saved me from going native altogether. I do the heavy work—Standish won't have a boy on the claim; Tikkey, his cook boy, is the only one he trusts—and he attends to the washing and sorting tables."

"And Standish is afraid of natives you say? He can't speak the vernacular? Well! There are two reasons why he won't denounce you until he's worked the claim out."

They both sat up at that.

"You have discovered something," the girl asked sharply.

"Maybe. I don't know yet. But before I go any further, I want you—" he turned to the man—"to go back with me tomorrow—you and your sister. That will be one stage of your journey back to rehabilitation. You promise?"

"Without money?" he demurred feebly.

"Yes, if need be," the girl cried, "without money. We'll work our way. We should have done that long ago. You'll promise, Tom."

"Yes, Grace," he said, meeting her eyes with an effort, "I promise."

"And," continued the Major lightly, "because your giddy play acting has put the wind up my carriers and sundry little Archers, you will, for the last time play that you are the Death Spirit and give me the pleasure of unmasking you before them. I have to insist on this. Otherwise my carriers desert me. I mean, if I can't prove to them that evil spirits only exist in their silly imaginations—why, they're going to leave me."

"I'll do it," the man said heavily. "But you'll keep close by me all the time, won't you? I don't trust myself when I have my bush things on."

The girl clapped her hands together.

"That's top hole," the Major exclaimed. "That means that tomorrow—or the next day, another—I can trek for the Mountains of the Moon. I'll tell you about that tomorrow, Johnson. You may be able to help.

"And now, tell me—have you seen these before?"

He pulled five clay idols out of his pocket and set them on the table.

Tom Johnson grinned.

"They're Standish's work. He tries to copy my ju-ju because I told him once that it 'ud keep natives from molesting me. He's not much of a craftsman, is he?"

"Good enough," the Major said drily. "Look!"

He hammered one of the images with the butt of his revolver.

It crumbled into fragments. He picked up a large piece and handed it to the girl.

"That," he said triumphantly, "is a diamond. And so is this, and this, and this! And the other idols contain more."

While the girl and her brother were exclaiming joyfully over the discovery, the door opened slowly and Standish, revolver in hand, entered. His eyes were bleared, his hand shook.

Just behind him was the native, Tikkey, grinning like a gargoyle.

"You devil!" Standish roared. "Give me back my diamonds!"

He fired.

The Major dropped to the ground and turned, drawing as he did so; Tom Johnson sprang forward, ready to fight it out with Standish with his bare fists; but the girl was quickest of the three.

She whipped a revolver out from a holster strapped to a table leg and fired, the report of her shot almost coinciding with Standish's.

The Major's shot echoed hers and the big, ebony ju-ju on the table—at which he had aimed—fell with a crash to the floor. Standish reeled, turned half-way round and dropped limply to the ground.

With a loud howl, Tikkey departed hurriedly.

The three were very quiet, experiencing many emotions as they looked down at the dead man.

Jim appeared in the doorway, breathing hard. He grinned when he saw that his *baas* was unhurt.

"They fooled me," he gasped. "I heard a noise at the back and while I had gone to look—they entered. *Au-a!* What a fool I am. To think they should play such a baby's trick on me!"

He looked down at Standish.

"You hit him harder than I did with my knobkerry, *Baas*," he muttered.

The Major turned to the girl.

"That was a ripping shot of yours, dear miss."

"It was a bad shot," she said sadly. "It is a bad beginning for the new life. To kill a man—"

"But your shot did not hit him," the Major exclaimed hurriedly. "This is where your bullet went."

He picked up the splintered ju-ju. "And that's why I said it was a good shot. It's symbolical, if you know what I mean. It means that the jungle power is broken, eh, Johnson? It means that in future shadows will be simply a haven of retreat from the rays of the sun.

"And we start back tomorrow."

He held out his hand.

"We start back tomorrow," Johnson said stoutly as he took the Major's hand in a firm grip.

The girl's eyes were brimming with happy tears.

"How can I ever thank you?" she murmured.

"By going to bed, dear old thing," the Major replied, bowing low. "We start at sunrise tomorrow. I have delayed too long on the road."

AN ACHING AFFAIR

"I THINK, Jim," drawled the Major, "that we will outspan under the shade of yonder tree."

Jim, the Hottentot, grinned widely and made play with his whip.

"I said, Jim," the Major repeated in the vernacular, "that we will outspan here."

The long lash of Jim's whip flicked over the backs of the six mules which were harnessed to the light, canvas-topped trek wagon.

The mules increased their pace to a canter, to a frenzied gallop.

The Major chuckled softly and, leaning forward in the saddle, patted the arched neck of his coal-black stallion.

"After him, Satan," he whispered, and gave the spirited animal its head.

As if some switch controlling its great energy had suddenly been turned on full, the horse reared, wheeled sharply and plunged into its fastest speed.

The Major laughed happily as the wagon swiftly came back to him. Then he reined in slightly and rode for a while behind the wagon.

The dust spurned up by the fast revolving wheels formed a reddish coating on his immaculate white twill riding

breeches and silken shirt; it turned his horse's coat to the color of dirty dun. The monocle in the Major's eye no longer gleamed as it caught the rays of the sinking sun; the dust had fogged it. He took it out and put it carefully into his tunic pocket.

His clean-shaven, strong-jawed face wrinkled in thought. Presently a mischievous light twinkled in his eyes, and when the pace of the wagon slackened somewhat by reason of the trail taking a sharp, upward slope, he leaped lightly from his horse and clambered over the wagon's backboard and through the opening in the tented cover. Crouching down on the floor, he cautiously covered himself with a pile of blankets.

All this he did without awakening suspicion in the mind of the Hottentot; all Jim's faculties were concentrated on his driving.

The horse, freed from the burden of its rider's two hundred pounds of bone and sinew, missing its master's powerful, restraining guidance, galloped ahead of the wagon, its nostrils dilated, head high in the air, leaping and bounding gracefully as the iron stirrups thumped against his ribs.

"Argh, there!" Jim shouted.

The pace of the mules slackened, but not quick enough for the Hottentot who, putting the whip aside, took hold of the reins and hauled powerfully on them. And Jim had a gorilla's strength in his long arms and barrel-like chest.

In response to his pull on the reins, the mules came to a halt so suddenly that the two wheelers went down and slid a little way on their haunches.

Jim jumped down from the wagon and looked back along the trail.

"O-he, *Baas!*" he called.

There was no answer.

The horse, which had come to a halt with the stopping of the mules and was now standing just behind the Hottentot, whinnied softly.

Jim turned quickly and, catching hold of the reins, examined the animal carefully.

"There is no mark on it," he muttered, his anxiety somewhat lessened. "I thought at first a lion—but, *auha!* Even had there been a lion, what matter? The *baas* has killed many of the yellow curs."

Jim took off his old, battered felt hat and scratched his woolly pate in puzzled indecision.

"O-he, *Baas!*" he called again, and listened.

When there was no response to the call which rocketed across the sweeping veld, he led the horse to the rear of the wagon and tethered it there. Then, climbing up into the driver's seat, he swung the mules round and headed slowly back along the trail.

"O-he, *Baas!*" he cried again and again and listened anxiously for a reply.

Save for the horse, the mules and himself, there seemed to be no living thing in that vast, undulating green sea of bush.

A few minutes later he came to the place where he had first lashed the mules into their maddened gallop and, climbing down from the wagon, closely scrutinized the ground round about.

While he was so engaged the Major climbed out from under the cover of blankets and made his way to the driver's seat, a triumphant grin on his face.

"Have you lost something of great value, Jim?" he asked suddenly in the vernacular.

The Hottentot looked up, an expression of intense relief on his homely, good-natured face. Then, laughing inwardly at the way he had been fooled, he looked studiously on the ground again.

"Nay, *Baas*," he growled in well-simulated anger. "I have lost nothing; but you have—it is for that I seek."

"And what have I lost, O wise one?" the Major asked banteringly.

"The knowledge that you are a man, *Baas*. That was a boy's trick you played on me."

The Major threw up his hand in the gesture of a fencer acknowledging a hit.

"You were deaf, Jim."

"The *baas* means?"

"I said that there, under that tree—" he pointed to a thickly leafed baobab—"was a good place to outspan. And you did not hear but drove on as if evil spirits pursued you."

Jim shrugged his broad shoulders.

"I like not the place, *Baas*."

"But it is a good place, Jim," the Major insisted as he scrutinized the ground about him with eyes that missed nothing.

"Nevertheless, I do not like it," Jim repeated doggedly. "The white man's *dorp* of Jonesburg is but short trek away. If we hasten, we will be there before the night's darkness overtakes us."

The Major chuckled.

"*Wo-we!* Is that what drives you, Jim? You are anxious to get to that place because you think that there you will find men who will sell you the white man's *puza*. How many times have I told you that the white man's drink is poison to you?"

"I have lost count of the times, *Baas,*" Jim answered with a sheepish grin. "But you are wrong; that is not the reason I wish to trek on. I like not this place, I say. Why—I cannot say why. Maybe the Spirits have warned me against it."

"You mean," the Major replied curtly, "that the spirit which is contained in a bottle calls you on. Now, I like this place, so let us outspan and make camp before the sun sets."

Jim sighed resignedly and without further protest swiftly unhitched and turned the mules out to graze. That done, he lighted a fire and, first washing himself with fastidious care, commenced cooking operations for the evening meal.

Meanwhile the Major, having attended to the horse, erected his bell tent, set up his camp bed, unloaded certain provisions from the wagon and then undressed, preparatory to having a warm bath and changing into a suit of clean white duck.

Some men—men who wandered over the veld, prospecting, their outfit consisting of the barest essentials—said that the Major's love of cleanliness amounted to an obsession; that his elaborate outfit labeled him as a nincompoop; that he was a soft, dudish ignoramus who could know nothing of the veld and its mysteries. They laughed at his habit of bathing and changing every night before he sat down to his evening meal, just as they laughed at his monocle, his affected, drawling speech and the vacuous, almost inane, expression of his face.

Others—men who knew him well and counted themselves fortunate to be called his friends—knew that bodily cleanliness was, as far as the Major was concerned, symbolical of the cleanliness which dominated all his doings. He always played the game, no matter what the game might be, for the game's sake. To them he was a well loved, privileged jester; instead of a jester's livery of cap and bells, he wore a pose of perpetual boredom. As his monocle veiled the keen, penetrating light of his eye, so his pose of vacuous inanity masked his keen wit and great physical prowess.

The police of South Africa knew him, liked him, yet never ceased their efforts to arrest him in the act of purchasing illicitly procured diamonds. But they played fair with him; only a few misguided ones had tried to trap him—and they lived to regret it.

Jim brought him a small dipper full of hot water.

"By the time the *baas* has shaved," he said, "the water for the bath will be ready."

"Good lad, Jim," the Major drawled in English and commenced to lather himself.

He whistled loudly as he did so, more as a challenge to Jim than in exuberance of spirits. Actually, he felt uncomfortable. During the many years he and Jim had been together—more like brothers than master and servant; living a life far above creed and racial prejudices—he had learned to respect Jim's premonitions of evil.

"I suppose I ought to have given in to the old blighter and gone on to Jonesburg or camped somewhere else," he muttered as he stropped his razor. "I would now, only—

only I believe the beggar's spoofin' me, paying me back for the trick I played him."

He yanked a coal-black hair—only at the temples was it slightly grayed—from his well-shaped head and tested the sharpness of his razor on it. Satisfied, he began to shave.

"Of course," he continued, but evidently far from assured, "there's nothing to worry about. Lions and so forth—well, they're everywhere, and they wouldn't put the wind up Jim. It can't be that the police are after us. It wouldn't matter if they were. I haven't a 'stone' on me and haven't had one for days. Besides," he laughed softly, "in a sense and for a time, I'm on police duty."

He laughed again, recalling the conversation he had had with the commanding officer of the Kimberley police just before setting out on this hunting expedition.

"If you happen to visit Jonesburg, Major," that man had said, "you might just leave your card with Messrs. Deemper and Van Ness."

"Friends of yours?" the Major had asked.

"Hell, no. They're two of the biggest blackguards unhung."

"Well, I'm that, too, you know," the Major had drawled.

The O.C. had waved his hands.

"But you're different. You're a political offender—not that I wouldn't be most pleased to get the goods on you and send you to the Breakwater for the rest of your natural life. But these two are different. They waylay and rob native laborers returning from the mines; they sell rot-gut booze; they—"

"Well—why don't you arrest them?"

"I can't. Jonesburg is over the border. You know that, Major."

"Yes, I know that," the Major had assented. "Well, then, where do I come in?"

"I thought you might be able to teach them a little lesson, Major. I don't expect you to reform them totally, but—oh, just teach them a little lesson."

"Then I may consider myself—er—unofficially on the force for a while, eh?"

"Without pay," the O.C. had countered swiftly. "Just the same, Major, I wish you'd join up. We need you; I can promise you a commission—"

"Get thee behind me, Satan," the Major had answered with a chortle. "I've other fish to fry. But I'll see what can be done with these laddies you mention."

And that had been that.

"If," he mused now, "they repealed the bally asinine diamond laws and gave me a roving commission, as it were, I'd join the force tomorrow. But they won't; the Syndicate's too damned greedy. Oh, well—"

The Hottentot entered the tent and poured a large kettle of boiling water into a large, tin bath, added cold water, saw that soap and towels were placed close to his *baas'* hand, and, leaving the tent, squatted down nearby, his chin resting upon his up-drawn knees, his hands clasped about his ankles. He stared fixedly at the leaping flames of the vast fire he had built.

The Major quickly finished shaving, divested himself of his few remaining garments, got into the tub and splashed about happily.

When he presently relaxed luxuriously in the lukewarm water he looked like an effete dilettante, or like a silly ass of a stage-door Johnny taking his morning bath in the hope of recovering from last night's headache; he looked like a helpless fool—until one noticed that his apparent paunchiness was really cords of muscle and realized that the whiteness of his skin was the whiteness of health.

He groped about in the water for the soap and, finding it, commenced to lather his hair.

At that moment a colossal gray form came out of the bush and moved ponderously, truculently, toward the tent. Its small, pig-like eyes glinted savagely as they reflected the fire gleam.

"*Wo-we, Baas!*" Jim cried, and jumped to his feet.

"What is it, Jim?" the Major shouted and incautiously opened his eyes.

"Wow!" he yelled then and closed his eyes, rubbed them with the back of his hands in a fruitless endeavor to ease the smarting pain caused by the soap-suds. Tears ran down his cheeks.

And at that moment the gray intruder suddenly launched its massive bulk at the tent. Its temper already strained to the breaking point by the annoying attentions of two young and foolish lions, the rhino—short-sighted at the best of times—thought the tent was an enemy to be demolished. At a twenty-mile-an-hour gait it charged into the tent, tearing through it, upsetting the Major and the bath.

Wheeling suddenly, not ten yards away, the ponderous beast came to a halt. Shreds of the canvas tent flapped coquettishly about its shoulders; a piece from the coat of the Major's gaily-colored pajamas fluttered from its three-foot horn.

The Major's sudden dousing had washed all the soap from his eyes. He retrieved his rifle from the debris. Next he looked for his cartridge belt and, failing to locate it among the disorder caused by the animal's charge, opened one of the ammunition boxes with feverish haste. He snatched a handful of cartridges and hurriedly thrust one in the breech.

"Run, *Baas!*" Jim shouted in a frenzy of fear.

The rhino was charging again and Jim, not realizing that the Major was now armed and ready to deal with the short-sighted beast, was standing directly in its path, menacing it with a flaming log which he had pulled from the fire.

"Down, Jim, down!" the Major yelled, his rifle up to his shoulder.

Swearing strange oaths, mixing the full-flavored curses of the vernacular with parrot-like phrases of English, Jim struck at the rhino's snout with his flaming weapon and then threw himself sideways to the ground.

But quick as he was, the rhino was even quicker. Wheeling with an agility that was surprising in so ungainly a beast, it lumbered into the Hottentot and had made a tentative poke at Jim with its battering-ram of a horn before the Major fired his first shot.

It was a broadside shot and the heavy bullet tore into the beast's lungs. A second and third shot quickly followed, and the rhino suddenly collapsed.

Deep concern on his face, the Major ran up to Jim, who was unconscious and pinned down by the rhino's head. Using his rifle as a lever, the Major managed to drag Jim clear and carefully examined his hurts.

"By Jove," he exclaimed softly. "I think some of his ribs are caved in; lucky, it wasn't worse. I must get him to a doctor."

He picked up the Hottentot and carried him to the place where the tent had stood and placed him down on the bed. Tearing a clean linen sheet into strips, he expertly bandaged Jim and forced a drop of brandy into his mouth.

"I've played the giddy ass today," he muttered as he hurriedly dressed himself. "If Jim wasn't the Jim he is, I'd be a dead ass by now. *Au-a!* He is a great man and I—I am his servant."

The Major was pulling on his riding boots when Jim opened his eyes, blinked hard and attempted to sit up.

"Lie still, worthless one," the Major said in mock sternness.

"The *baas'* skoff will be spoiled," Jim expostulated, yet obeyed the order, a little frightened by the sharp pain in his chest which made breathing difficult.

"I thought he was going to kneel on me, *Baas,*" he said. "And he would have been very heavy. That was a good shot of yours, *Baas.*"

"I am a fool, Jim," the Major began in tones of self-reproach. "If I had listened—"

Jim held up his hand.

"No need to speak of that, *Baas.* In all things the count is to your credit. The little I did just now, that—but, *au-a!* We know, we two. There is no need for further words. Golly damme yes-no. If I don't see you, s'long, hullo,"

The Major smiled.

"Now, rest, Jim; do not move. I will get skoff. After we have eaten and the moon has risen we will trek for Jonesburg. We will have to trek very slow, but we will be there by sunrise."

Jim's teeth gleamed ivory white as he parted his thick lips in an infectious grin.

"Baas?" he said.

"Jah, Jim?"

"I think I was right: this is not a good place to camp."

JONESBURG WAS an almost deserted township of crude tin shacks, tattered tents and native huts. It owed its being to the discovery of a diamond pipe which, Jones, the discoverer, announced, would put Kimberley in the shade.

Some few diamonds were found at Jonesburg; some few still are found there, but the wily Jones was the only man who achieved wealth: and that by selling provisions— mostly liquid—to thirsty miners.

The boom soon broke and most of the miners returned to Kimberley. Of those who remained, some few honestly worked their claims and made a frugal living. But the majority were men of criminal intent who lacked the courage and ability to play their respective games in the more or less well-policed diamond town. In Jonesburg they were under Oom Paul's paternal government and far enough away from his eagle eye to be over particular about their morals.

Occasionally they made raids into the adjoining territory, selling liquor to natives, holding up natives returning from the mines and relieving them of their hard-earned pay, and then retreating over the border and thumbing their noses at the police who were put on their trail. But for the most part they were content to fleece each other or such chance travelers as luck sent their way.

And that is why Deemper and Van Ness scratched their itching palms and smacked their lips in greedy anticipation of a financial feast when they saw a trek wagon coming slowly down the dusty street.

"By yours and by mine," said Van Ness—he was a furtive under-sized Dutchman who had served an apprenticeship to a Jewish I.D.B. in Kimberley and had picked up some of that man's expressions—"he is mine. I saw him first. I will sell him a claim."

"Almighty!" Deemper swore, and taking Van Ness by his coat collar he hurled him forcibly on one side. "He is mine, I tell you, ma-an."

Deemper was a giant of a man, standing well over six foot. He was very fat and very dirty. His long, rust-colored beard was stained with tobacco juice; his small, reddish eyes glinted with a low, animal cunning from under thick bushy eyebrows.

"He is mine," he said again in a deep, roaring voice. "If you interfere I will pinch out your life with my thumb and forefinger. Almighty, yes, I will."

"Why do you talk that way," Van Ness whined. "We're partners, ain't we? What's yours is mine—and," he added swiftly, "what's mine's yours. We've always worked together before. Why then should you be so unfriendly now?"

Deemper growled some inarticulate reply.

"And, look you," Van Ness continued with a greater show of confidence, "always before you have needed my brains to put a deal through."

"Meaning I am a fool, eh?" Deemper said hotly.

"Almighty, no," Van Ness replied soothingly. "You're a *slim* one, Deemper. Everybody knows that. And you're strong— Almighty how strong you are! But supposing this man is a Englisher. You don't know how to deal with a *verdoemte roineck*. Niggers you can handle, and a good Dutch burgher you can handle. But an Englisher—no. And why should you? You do not know them as I know them. Didn't I live from one *nachtmeal* to another with the—"

"Maybe you're right," Deemper growled, somewhat mollified. "So together we will deal with this stranger. But, look you, ma-an if you try any of your *slim* tricks on me—"

He closed his two ham-like hands tightly on his beard, protruded his thick red lips, and somehow managed to convey to Van Ness that he would try no trick if he desired to live.

"Why should I trick you?" Van Ness protested. "A good partner I am to you—not? See how I took you in with me over the diamond game we are playing with the doctor. So partners we will be still, and together we will do business with the stranger."

With heads bent they walked slowly up the dusty road.

As they came abreast of the wagon, the driver pulled up his mules.

"I say, you chappies," he called in an affected drawl, "is there a doctor in this bally burg?"

The two looked up with an air of startled surprise.

"A doctor is it, mister?" said Van Ness. "You're not ill—no?"

"No. But my—er—negro servant is."

Deemper laughed noisily.

"Almighty! What fools you Englisher are? First you hit your niggers; then you take them to a doctor. When I hit a nigger a doctor is no good to him; that I tell you, ma-an."

"I can well believe it," the Major drawled. "But where is the doctor?"

"*Ach!* Let your nigger wait. If he dies, what matter; the country is full of the black swine! Come and have a drink, mister. Let the nigger wait."

"I'm afraid he can't," the Major said absently as he gathered up the reins.

"Of course he can't," Van Ness said hastily, and he scowled meaningly at his partner. "You go on down the street until you come to a red tin house. That's the doctor's. And, mister—"

But, with a drawled, "Thanks, dear lad," the Major had driven on.

"You *verdoemte* fool!" Deemper said scornfully. "Now you have lost the Englisher for us. Slim, you call yourself. Ach sis! Alone I could have done better."

"*Wachtenbije!* Wait a minute, Deemper. Not so fast. He'll stay in the *dorp*, I tell you, until his nigger's better. There is no hurry."

"But some of the others will get him and—"

Van Ness laid his dirty forefinger alongside his nose and winked.

"You leave him to me."

"*Yah!* Leave him to you—and I get nothing! Together we work him—and we split evens." He towered over his little partner threateningly.

"All right!" Van Ness said hastily.

"You go off quick like my father's old elephant gun. Already it has been settled that we are partners, and partners share and share alike, not? And, I tell you, ma-an, we grow rich over this deal. He's rich: six mules and a thoroughbred horse. And his wagon was loaded with trade truck. On my tiptoes I stood and looked in. It'll be all ours!"

REACHING THE doctor's place, Jim was quickly taken care of by the rotund little medico and his gray-eyed, motherly looking wife.

"Nothing broken," Doctor Bainton reported to the Major. "Little sore, of course. Muscles bruised. That's all. Ready to trek in a week at the outside—trek comfortably,

I mean. You'll stay with us, of course you will. Won't he, Mother? Won't take 'No' for an answer."

And when Mrs. Bainton added her voice, seconding her husband's invitation, the Major gratefully accepted their hospitality. A few minutes later he was seated in a comfortable chair listening to the doctor's account of how he had first come to Jonesburg, full of enthusiasm, but had, somehow or other, been caught in the backwash.

"But we'll be able to get away soon," Mrs. Bainton broke in suddenly. "And I'll be so glad. Of course we ought to have left long ago, but Tom got so interested in a claim a miner gave him in payment of his bill. The mining fever had you bad, didn't it, Tom?"

"It did," the doctor admitted. "There's always the thought that the next stroke of the pick'll turn up a big stone. You can't imagine what a fascination it has."

"No, I can't," the Major murmured.

"But," the doctor continued boisterously, "things have taken a turn for the better. We'll be able to get away soon. And I'm glad of it, for Mary's sake. Life hasn't been much fun for her here."

"But I've enjoyed it all with you, Tom," she replied softly, and they smiled happily at each other.

The Major beamed on them.

"Then your—er—claim has turned out trumps, after all?" he suggested. "And diamonds are—er—trumps?"

"No. Far from it. I got a dealer's license yesterday, and this morning I made my first deal. Got some good stones dirt cheap; didn't have to beat the sellers down, either.

"Of course," he continued, "I'm bound to get some illic-itly bought stones, and it's a good job for me that we're in the Transvaal where the Diamond Laws don't exist; actu-ally, I don't need a license to buy stones here, though, of course, having one puts me in a better position to sell again. But about I.D.B.—I don't want to deal with any one who isn't playing straight. I make inquiries, and if I as much as suspect that the stones are stolen, then I don't deal. I can't be fairer than that, can I?"

"Oh, rather not," the Major murmured.

"Just the same," the doctor continued, full of enthusiasm for his subject, "I'm bound to buy from I.D.B.s once in a while. They're such cunning devils and it's so hard to get any proof. Now take the stones I purchased on my first deal: I'm inclined to think now that Mary's right and they are stolen stones. I can't imagine Deemper and Van Ness parting with them so cheaply if they weren't. But I was too excited at the time. It was my first deal and—oh, well, would you like to see them?"

"Oh, rather," the Major exclaimed impulsively.

The doctor took down from a nearby shelf a large jar containing acid and from it extracted nine or ten good sized stones.

He handed them to the Major, who examined them with a great show of interest, contriving to give the impression that he was greatly awed by the wealth he held in his hand. Yet, after the first casual glance, he could have given a minute description of the stones he held, their color, shape, weight and approximate value.

"It's awfully funny," he drawled presently. "One would never think that these dirty yellow things were diamonds. Why—"

"Dirty yellow!" the doctor exclaimed in dismay. "Let me see."

He took the diamonds back and examined them one by one. The happy gleam went out of his eyes; the corners of his mouth sagged.

"We've been bilked, Mary," he groaned. "These things are not worth a tenth what I paid for them. And I thought I was getting them cheap! I've been bilked—"

"But how, Tom?" Mrs. Bainton was incredulous.

"I don't know. The stones I bought were a good color. Look at them now. Oh! What an old fool I am."

"Never mind, Tom," she said soothingly. "Never mind. We—"

The Major coughed.

"Oh, I say! What a deuced shame! But can't you get your money back from the men who sold you these—er—yellow things. Or, if they won't pay you back, prosecute the bally blighters."

"On what grounds?" the doctor asked, as he handed the stones to his wife. "No; I've been done and I'll have to take my medicine quietly. But the worst of it is," he concluded despairingly, "that I daren't do any more dealings. I'm not clever enough. I—"

The Major rose.

"I'm going to see how Jim is," he said in answer to their inquiring looks. "Don't worry too much about this, there's dear people. And I wish—er—look here: I've always wanted to be a diamond dealer. Let me be your partner. That—" he took a wad of notes from his pocket and put them in Mrs. Bainton's hand—"ought to be enough to buy my way in. Now let me have the diamonds. Ah, thanks! I've a jolly good mind to make those two laddies buy them back again, Toodle-oo! Be back anon."

He closed the door softly behind him.

"Why did you take his money, Mary? Of course we can't keep it," the doctor said reproachfully.

"Hush!" she placed her hand over his mouth. "I want to think. I've heard of this monocled gentleman who looks like an utter fool—and isn't."

"But he is, Mary," the doctor said with a wry laugh. "He's an awfully likable chap, but he's a fool; and so am I."

"Hush!" Mrs. Bainton said again.

She covered her face with her hands, endeavoring to untangle some memory from a maze of memories, endeavoring to tap the knowledge contained in some long-disused brain cell.

"Oh, I have it," she cried presently, her eyes shining with a happy confidence. "I know now who this man, who calls himself Aubrey St. John, really is. He's the Major, and—"

LEAVING THE doctor's place, the Major walked slowly up the street. At the Royal Hotel he was hailed as an old friend by Van Ness and Deemper.

"And how's your nigger, Mister St. John?" Van Ness asked, after names had been exchanged and the three were lined up in front of the bar.

"He's in a bad way," the Major said mournfully. "I'm afraid it'll be weeks before I can leave."

"Almighty! Is he so bad? Well, here's to his good health." Deemper winked broadly at his partner.

"How about a little game of cards, mister?" Van Ness suggested.

Mildly protesting that he was "a bally fool, an absolute babe in arms when it came to playin' cards," the Major allowed himself to be shepherded into an inner room and seated at a rickety table.

"We will play poker, not?" Van Ness said as he produced a pack of greasy cards.

"I am quite in your hands, dear lads," the Major drawled. "Any game you say. Only—er—don't you think we should have a limit?"

"What for do we want a limit," Deemper growled. "We're all grown men. *Ach sis!* I shall not be the one to squeal because I lose too much money."

"I meant," the Major amended timidly, "a time limit. I—"

"If we stop at five o'clock, will that do?" Van Ness suggested.

The Major nodded and Deemper shuffled the cards. The Major seemed to be intent on polishing his monocle, and that was well, for Deemper shuffled very awkwardly.

Van Ness caught the cards and Deemper dealt; the game commenced.

It was a weird game, played at times according to rule invented on the spur of the moment by one or others of the partners. The Major lost steadily at first; he practically lost all his cash, then lost two mules to Deemper and two to Van Ness. He wanted to stop playing then, but the other two—Van Ness, fawningly hypocritical; Deemper bellowing threats of bodily injury—would not hear of it, pointing out that a time limit had been agreed upon and to a time limit they would hold.

Finally, with a bad grace, looking like a well-plucked pigeon and exhibiting not a little fear of Deemper's brawny fists, the Major agreed to play on.

But first he clumsily upset a whisky and soda on the table. It ran over the cards, soaking them. He was most abjectly apologetic and then brought a new pack of cards from the bartender. From that time on the character of the game changed. No matter how carefully Van Ness shuffled the cards and Deemper cut them, the Major always got the hand one of the partners had meant for himself. And, as invariably happened when the Major dealt, Van Ness and Deemper, finding themselves with almost unbeatable hands, would bet wildly only to find that the Major had absolutely unbeatable cards.

The money the Major had lost dribbled back across the table; the mules returned to their rightful owner; Van Ness and Deemper were forced to dig down into their pockets.

"By yours and by mine," Van Ness whined after a while, "I don't like this. Me? I stop playing."

"Almighty, yes!" Deemper exclaimed in puzzled tones. "Me also. I do not play no longer, no. It looks like somebody is playing an almighty *slim* game the way the cards are running." He glared truculently at the Major.

"But you must play," the Major expostulated smoothly. "Remember the little—er—time limit. The time's not up yet, you know. And you're gentlemen, surely."

"Who cares about being a gentleman," Van Ness sneered, "when the cards are running this way? No, I tell you, ma-an, I play no more."

"Ah, but you are," the Major said softly.

They looked at him angrily, sneering at his monocle, at the way in which his hair was brushed back in an immaculate pompadour, at the well-kept nails on his long, sinewy fingers.

Then they both frowned thoughtfully and wondered if it was just chance which kept the Major's hands in dangerous proximity to his revolver holster.

"Oh, well," Van Ness said with a shrug of his shoulders, "tomorrow's another day. It's your deal, mister. But you'll have to take my I.O.U.s if I lose any more. I ain't got no more money on me."

"Nor me neither," Deemper said heavily. "For the matter of that, I can't pay you what I have already lost. No."

The Major rose.

"Then perhaps we'd better not play any more. I'll have my revenge some other time, eh?"

"Revenge you'll take, is it?" Van Ness groaned. *"Ach!* And already you have taken everything. But you come down to our office, mister, and we'll give you something to square Deemper's losses."

TEN MINUTES later they came to the "office," a tumbled-down tin shack some distance from the hotel. Van Ness and Deemper entered, asking the Major to wait for them outside.

Presently a queer odor came through the cracks. The Major sniffed experimentally, then nodded, well content.

When the two men came out a few minutes later they found him leaning against the wall, a handkerchief up to his nose, coughing violently.

"What the matter?" Deemper asked suspiciously.

"That frightful—er—stench," the Major gasped faintly. "What is it?"

"I don't smell anything," Van Ness said innocently, and he and Deemper sniffed loudly.

"Oh, well," the Major sighed. "Perhaps your—er—finer sensibilities are blunted, as it were."

"What a ma-an you are," Van Ness said. "You're making a game of us, not? Well, here. That'll pay Deemper's gambling debt, eh?"

He handed the Major a good-sized, light cream colored diamond.

The Major took it and looked at it with idle curiosity.

"It's very—er—pretty," he drawled, "but of course you're having a game with me. I can hardly tender a colored stone as legal tender, you know. What?"

"Ach sis, ma-an!" Deemper bellowed. "Don't you know a diamond when you see one?"

"Oh!" The Major's mild blue eyes opened wide in innocent wonder. "Is it a diamond? Then, of course I can't take it. I'd be arrested for—er—I.D.B. and—"

The other two laughed.

"That should not worry you, mister," Van Ness said with a knowing leer. "This is Oom Paul's country. You can buy as many diamonds as you want and no one will say a word. And, anyway, you ain't buying. We're giving that to you."

"Well, in that case," the Major said slowly as he pocketed the stone, "toodle-oo."

He walked a few paces, stopped, hesitated a moment and then came back to where the others were standing.

"I say," he drawled. "Of course I don't know anything about diamonds, but anyone could see with half an eye that the one you just gave me is very valuable and, really, I don't think I ought to take it in payment of a small gambling debt. Really."

He drew the stone out of his pocket and held it out to Van Ness.

"No, you keep it," that man insisted. "It's worth a lot of money, but we don't mind. Lots more where it came from—eh, Deemper?"

"Almighty, yes."

"Goodness!" the Major exclaimed admiringly. "I wish I had a claim."

The partners exchanged half-veiled, triumphant glances.

"We'll sell you one," Van Ness said promptly. "The one from which that diamond came, I tell you, ma-an, for five hundred pounds."

"You mean that?" the Major asked incredulously. "Oh, upon my soul, if I had the money with me I'd buy the claim now. But I'll tell you what: you show me the claim tomorrow and I'll give you a hundred pounds for an option on it and I'll give you five hundred just as soon as my—er—remittance is forwarded."

"Fair enough," said Van Ness. "Not, Deemper?"

His partner nodded; the big man was slow of speech.

"That's a bargain then, mister," Van Ness continued. "See you tomorrow. S'long."

The Major airily waved his hand and walked quickly away.

"What did I tell you," Van Ness chuckled triumphantly. "Ain't he a *verdoemte* fool of a *roinek?*"

"I'm not sure, ma-an. Not so well did we do at poker."

"Oh, that! We did well until he spilled whisky on our cards. But that's nothing; we've got plenty of time to win all he's got. And think, Deemper: he's going to pay us a hundred for an option—and we'd sell every claim we've got for half that. He's just a fool dude. He—"

"Maybe," Deemper admitted grudgingly. "But I ain't so sure, Van Ness. Me, I know nothing about options or monocled dudes of *roineks*. They—"

AFTER HE had passed out of the two men's sight, the Major took the diamond from his pocket, polished it with a handkerchief and then put it in his mouth. A few minutes later he came to the doctor's place, knocked at the door and, in a response to a shouted "Come in!" he entered.

He found the rubicund little man alone, miserably alone. His wife, he explained, had just gone to take some food to Jim. Then he noticed the bulge in the Major's cheek and his professional interest was aroused.

"What's the matter? Toothache?"

The Major grinned, shook his head and took the diamond out, holding it on the palm of his hand.

"What do you think of that bally thing?" he drawled.

"It's slightly off color, but it's worth a hundred quid at least. Where did you get it?"

"Messrs. Van Ness and Deemper gave it to me."

"Oh!" The doctor pursed his lips thoughtfully. "In that case I'm not sure. I—"

The Major smiled and after dipping the stone into a jar of acid, rubbed it vigorously with a chamois leather.

In a little while the cream tint had vanished from the stone, leaving it a dirty yellow color.

"And now what do you think of it, old top?" the Major asked.

The doctor looked at it closely.

"It's a diamond," he said slowly, "but it's not worth more than two or three pounds. How—"

"Have you got chloride of lime, powdered borax, arsenic and—er—sulphuric ether in your medical stores?"

The doctor nodded, wonderingly.

"And common salt and a blowpipe torch? I think that's what they call the bally thing that makes a hot flame hotter."

Again the doctor nodded.

"All right, then," the Major exclaimed mysteriously. "Let's go into your surgery and I'll show you how to make bad diamonds into good ones."

They adjourned to the doctor's surgery and, after closing the door and making sure that no prying passer-by could overlook his operations through the window, the Major carefully measured out portions of salt, chloride of lime, borax and arsenic.

These ingredients he mixed together thoroughly until they formed a thick, adhesive paste. Into this paste he rolled the yellow diamond, covering it, as it were, with a thin suit of dough.

Then—the doctor having meanwhile lighted the torch—he lifted the coated diamond with a pair of forceps and held it in the hot flame until the transparent carbon, paste and all, was glowing like a deep red golden orb of fire.

At that point he threw the diamond into a big-mouthed bottle containing sulphuric ether.

The ether bubbled furiously; the room was filled with its pungent fumes.

A moment later the Major retrieved the stone. It was quite cold, its color white and its value, apparently, greatly increased.

"There!" exclaimed the Major. "What do you think of that?"

"Why, it looks like a magnificent stone. It's a beauty."

"But not a joy forever," the Major added dryly. "In a couple of hours or so it will be as it was. That is why the fakers carry them in their mouths. The color lasts longer."

"And that is the way the rotters doctored the stones they sold me?" the little man exclaimed indignantly.

"Exactly. It's an old trick and wouldn't work for a moment on an experienced buyer. They've probably bought a large 'parcel' of worthless stones just to palm off on you. And what are you going to do about it?" He smiled expectantly.

"Do? Why I'll doctor them," the little man stammered wrathfully. "When I think of the way I've treated the youngsters of those two—and—oh, never mind. That's another matter. It's a doctor's privilege to serve without pay. But I do hate to be rooked this way. Still, there it is! I'd better resign myself to the inevitable and be prepared to spend my life doctoring natives with Epsom salts and—oh, well! It's damned hard on Mary. Let's go and have a drink!"

"Just a minute, Doctor," the Major said crisply, no trace of a drawl in his voice now. "I'd heard of Deemper and Van Ness before I came here. They're abject rotters—"

"They're that all right," the doctor murmured.

"Well, then: I don't suppose you have any ethical objection to getting your money back from them?"

"None at all," the doctor said positively.

"Good. Here's the situation. Those two angels have already robbed you of a goodly sum and they'll try to rob you of more. They did their best to cheat me at cards; they palmed off a worthless diamond on me, and tomorrow they'll try to sell me a worthless claim. Oh, yes, and they'll try to cheat me at cards again. Of course I can take care of myself. But I want to do better. I want to—er—get back at them. I don't like being thought a fool—even if I am one."

The doctor smiled at that.

"Well, then?" the Major asked quickly.

"We're partners," the doctor said slowly, "and that means, I take it—oh, let's make the beggars sit up and take notice. It may reform them."

"Not a bit of it. But never mind about that. Well, in the first place, our partnership must be kept a secret. I'm going to take a room at the Royal Hotel and you won't see me except when I come down to visit Jim. That'll be sufficient excuse for our getting together occasionally. If anyone ask you, say Jim is in a very bad way and won't be able to trek for weeks. Then I want you to buy all the diamonds those two birds bring you, and if they want to know whether you've placed any yet with the big dealers, say that you're waiting to get a big 'parcel' together, and that then you'll take your stones to Kimberley yourself and'll never come back. That should make 'em a little more eager. Oh, yes— beat 'em down on the price as low as you can. Offer them half what they ask; the chances are they'll accept."

"WELL," SAID Van Ness. "That's that ain't it?"

He beamed triumphantly at his partner, who was dividing a golden pile of sovereigns into two equal parts.

"Yah, that's so," Deemper agreed. "And that's your share, Van Ness." He pushed one of the heaps over to his partner.

Van Ness counted the sovereigns carefully.

"Fifty," he concluded with a sigh of contentment. *"Ach sis!* And so easy we made it. No work and no risk. Ain't he a fool? Just a *verdoemte* fool of a *roinek,* just like I said."

"Maybe," Deemper said doubtfully. "But I'm not so sure. He may be a *slim* one. This paper he made us sign? What is it all about?"

He peered suspiciously at the paper which was on the dirty table before him.

Van Ness laughed.

"Almighty! What a man you are, yet. A contract the English dude draws up, thinking he's a business man. I know all about contracts. He can't throw dirt in my eyes with his contracts. Didn't I work in Kimberley for a year as partner to Moses Goodman? *Ach!* There was a *slim* one, yes. But what worry do you make over this?"

"I was thinking," Deemper replied, his brows wrinkled with the effort of thought, "about what it says about giving him the right to work the claim even before he's paid us the rest of the money; and it also gives him the right to keep any stones he finds."

"And what of it?" Van Ness asked.

"Suppose," Deemper breathed heavily, "suppose he finds diamonds. You would not laugh then, I think. No."

For a few minutes Van Ness looked worried. Then he laughed loudly.

"Don't be a fool, Deemper. There ain't no diamonds in the claim for the dude to find. You know that. And listen. The doctor told me to drop in and see him. He wants to buy some more stones."

Deemper brightened at that.

"Why didn't you say so before? We will some fine ones get ready for him. Then we'll go and watch the dude dig for diamonds. Almighty! That will be funny."

A little later a pungent odor came through the cracks of the shack, and presently the two men emerged, red in the face, their cheeks bulging as if they had toothache.

The afternoon sun was very hot when Van Ness and Deemper came to the claim where the Major was prospecting.

The Major was dressed in spotless white flannels; a monocle gleamed in his eye; on his head was a white pith helmet, on his hands a pair of cotton gloves. His tools were a cause for laughter. He had no pick, and his spade, shovel and rake were little larger than those sold in sets to lady gardeners. Beside him was a canvas deck chair with a large sunshade attached to it.

The two men made their way to a deserted hut and from there watched the Major unobserved, with difficulty refraining from loud, shouts of laughter.

The Major would first make one or two futile attacks on the sun-baked day soil with his spade, then, sitting down in his chair, used the hoe. Finally, having succeeded in breaking off a crumble or two, he raked the loose earth toward him and crumpled it slowly between his fingers. Finding nothing, he would rise wearily to his feet again, shaking his head mournfully.

Van Ness soon got tired of watching and, closing his eyes, nodded sleepily.

But Deemper did not miss a move the Major made. Presently he saw the dude pick something up out of the dust and hold it to the light. He saw the Major caper excitedly and then, suddenly sobering, put the something in his pocket and turn to his digging with renewed vigor.

Deemper's face blackened. What he had feared had come to pass. For all Van Ness' cleverness, the monocled dude of a *roinek* had got the best of the bargain. He had found a diamond and—

"Come on, ma-an," he said and shook Van Ness roughly by the collar, "Let's get out of here."

He left the hut, half dragging his partner with him.

"I wonder what's got into him," Van Ness pondered, and he looked suspiciously toward the Major. But that man was sitting down in his chair again, apparently exhausted by his manual labors.

THAT NIGHT the moon was at the full. Consequently Deemper experienced no difficulty in finding his way to the diamond claim. He carried a pick in his hands. He looked behind him frequently, but never at the right moment to see Van Ness, who was stealthily following.

Reaching the claim, he removed his coat, but before he could get to work with his pick the Major confronted him; the moonlight glinted on the barrel of the revolver he held in his hand.

Van Ness, who was just on the point of rushing up to accuse his partner of duplicity, managed to creep into the hut unobserved, thanking his stars he had not made his presence known.

"Almighty!" Deemper growled. "You startled me, ma-an. And what are you pointing that little 'popper' at me for?"

"Really, you know," the Major drawled. "I think it's my turn to ask questions. Just what are you doing here, dear laddie? Going to dig a grave?"

"Well, it's this way," Deemper began hesitatingly. "My old *frau* says to me the other day, 'Piet, ma-an, to keep your money in the house with all these *skellums* about, not safe is. Why don't you dig a hole and bury it on one of your claims.' And so I did, mister; the old *frau*, she is wise. And in my hurry to do you a good turn today by selling you this claim, I forgot all about the money I'd hid until the *frau* just asked me about it. And so I came here quick to get it. But now I've told you, of what use to hurry? You're a gentleman, not? You'll let me dig for it tomorrow. So, good night, mister."

Deemper sighed with relief; he prided himself that he had told a convincing story.

"Wait!" He stopped short at the crisp command. "You stay here and dig," the Major continued. "Yours is a very touching story, very. I can't think of letting you go back to your lady emptyhanded. Why, the shock might kill her. So—dig!"

His revolver clicked ominously, and Deemper, after first considering closing with the Major, dug.

"It ain't here, mister," he gasped presently. "I was lying to you and you're too *slim* to be fooled that way. *Ach sis,* yes!"

"You flatter me," the Major drawled as he seated himself in the deck chair. "All right, now let's have the truth."

Deemper drew a deep breath.

"Almighty, yes," he exclaimed with a show of frankness. "I will tell you the truth. I don't want to go through with the deal we made today. Alone I would not have made it. But that Van Ness! *Ach!* He is a *slim* one. But I'm a honest man. Listen: the claim's no good. You won't find no diamonds on it. A splinter or two you may find, but that is all. No, the claim is no good; it ain't worth the hundred you paid for the option. And because I'm an honest burgher, I want to deal honestly with you. Listen, Englisher, I'll give you back your hundred and we'll tear up the option."

"But I'm quite content with the bargain I made, dear old top," the Major replied suavely. "I like the claim and I'm quite sure I shall decide to take advantage of my option. You know, I find the exercise so beneficial."

Deemper's mutterings lost themselves in the jungle of his beard.

"You said?" the Major queried.

"I'll give you two hundred pounds for the option."

The Major shook his head.

"You talk instead of working, dear man. That's bad. So dig, laddie."

The revolver clicked again.

"Almighty! Listen," Deemper gasped desperately. "It was not here I hid my gold, but over there." He pointed to the far edge of the claim.

"All right. Go there and dig."

Deemper went, swung his pick a few times and then fled in great haste.

The Major chuckled softly.

"I say, mister."

He looked up and saw Van Ness standing before him.

"What surprises the night has in store for one," he murmured. "What is it, dear lad? Are you also looking for buried treasure?"

"By yours and by mine, no," Van Ness said positively. "I'm a straightforward business man. I don't do sneak work like Deemper. Out in the open, that's me. Deemper—he doesn't know anything about business. But me, I worked in Kimberley for a year and—but never mind that. I followed that sneak out here and hid in the hut. I heard all you said. So-a! Though I don't know what it's all about or why, I'll double Deemper's offer. I'll give you four hundred pounds for the claim. That's fair, ain't it? By yours and by mine, that's all I'll offer; not a penny more. What do you say, mister?"

"Why, good night, Van Ness, dear," the Major drawled. "I'm so tired and I'm not—by yours and mine, I'm not—selling!"

DURING THE next seven days the Major hardly ever left the claim and, when he did so, a burly Irishman stood guard over it for him.

Van Ness and Deemper—they were still partners and, apparently, friends—kept a close watch over him but learned little.

On the eighth day—the Hottentot having completely recovered—the Major ordered Jim to inspan. After he had loaded onto the wagon the new tent his *baas* had purchased and sundry new provisions, Jim set out on the road leading north.

The Major escorted him a little way along the road, then returned to the doctor's. After a short interview with the

little man the Major mounted Satan and rode to the office
of Messrs. Van Ness and Deemper.

He looked a victim of chronic toothache; both his cheeks
were badly swollen.

He dismounted outside the shack and fumbled for a few
moments with his saddle girth. When he turned to enter
the office his cheeks had returned to their normal state,
and his tunic pocket bulged with diamonds.

"Mornin' gentlemen!" he said blithely.

They looked at him sullenly.

"Come to talk business?" Van Ness asked.

"Absolutely. I'm sick of mining. It's beastly hard work."

"Then you're not going to take up the option?"

"Oh, rather. But I'd rather sell it."

"What's your price?" The two men spoke as one.

"Five thousand pounds!"

"Almighty!" they both screamed. "Why, it ain't worth a
penny."

"Oh tut, tut-tut!" the Major remonstrated. "That will
never do. Why only nine days ago you both assured me it
was very rich. And—" he smiled—"let me assure you that
I found it very wealthy; all that you said it was, in fact. I've
only scratched the surface, as it were, yet—lo and behold!"

He emptied the diamonds from his pocket on to the
table.

The two partners stared stupidly at the stones, then
angrily at each other.

"Of course they're not a good color—whatever that may
mean," continued the Major. "But they are diamonds, aren't
they? And—"

The others were still speechless.

"Oh, well, if you're not interested," the Major said huffily and returned the stones to his pocket. "I thought you'd rejoice with me, what? Instead, you seem to be green with the well known envy. Really, I'm ashamed of you. Well, I must go now. I'm trekking north. Jim's already on his way. He's made a most marvelous recovery. Toodle-oo! I'll send you the five hundred in time to close the deal. Beastly good of you to let me have the claim so cheap. There was a time when I almost suspected that you were trying to swindle me. But of course you wouldn't do anything like that. No. Oh, one other thing. Mike Sullivan—he's a broth of a lad—is going to work the claim for me, so it would be wise for you to keep away, eh? Mike might not understand if you tried to do any digging for buried treasure on my claim. He's a hasty tempered johnny. Very! Well, once more, toodle-oo!"

He had almost passed out of the hut before the partners managed to struggle back from the stupor into which the sight of the diamonds had thrown them, diamonds which they supposed to have been taken from the claim they had sold as worthless.

"Wait!" Van Ness implored.

The Major turned and looked at them inquiringly.

"Is five thousand your lowest figure, mister?" Van Ness stammered.

"Absolutely. And a low figure it is. Why, Mike Sullivan said he'd give me ten thousand if I'd give him three or four months to collect the cash. But I'm in a hurry and—"

He glanced keenly at the two men; they were conversing in low, excited whispers.

"Mister," Van Ness said presently. "Throw in the diamonds, and we'll pay your price."

"All right," the Major said with a shrug of his shoulders.

He emptied the diamonds out on to the table again.

"We ain't got the money here," Van Ness said. "But at Kimberley, at the bank—"

"I'm afraid I must go," the Major interrupted sadly and made as if to gather up the stones again.

"*Ach sis!* What a ma-an!" Van Ness wailed. "I was going to say that a check would be no good to you—you going north. You wait a minute and Deemper, here, will get you the cash."

"Almighty, no! I will not get it," Deemper said flatly. "Not alone with the *roinek* will I leave you, Van Ness. You would try to cheat me out of my share; I do not trust you. You will get the money."

Van Ness was about to expostulate heatedly but, seeing that the Major was showing signs of impatience, he hurriedly left the hut. He returned five minutes or so later, carrying a large carpetbag. From it he took two packets of dirty notes which he handed to the Major.

"There's five thousand there," he said.

"Thanks," the Major drawled and swiftly counted the notes, nine hundred in one, four thousand in the other. "Actually you're a hundred short. But never mind. Here's the option agreement—" he tossed a long envelope on to the table—"and that concludes the business, I hope. Yes? Good! I'm in a fearful hurry or I'd ask you to have a drink and, maybe, a game of poker. But I don't want Jim to get too far ahead. I might get lost. Farewell, laddies."

A few seconds later he was riding down the dusty street on his way to say goodby to the Baintons and to give the little doctor his share of the profits of their brief partnership; it was a distorted division, but doctors are worthy of their hire and the four thousand pounds would go a long way toward establishing the doctor in a better and more hopeful community.

"WELL," SAID Van Ness.

"Well?" snarled Deemper.

"Look here," Van Ness said placatingly. "I ain't going to quarrel. Say it was my fault we had to pay five thousand for the claim that was ours by right; say it was my fault that we sold the option for a hundred pounds and gave the *roinek* dude the right to keep the diamonds he found. I don't care. I don't even say it was your fault, too. We're partners, not? But if you ain't satisfied, I'll give you my I.O.U. for the twenty-five hundred you had to pay. What's twenty-five hundred to me when I think what I'm going to make out of claim. Why—"

"You give me the I.O.U. and I'll forget the fool you've been," Deemper said, restored again to good humor.

"I'll give it to you now," Van Ness exclaimed grandly. "Where's paper? Here, this'll do."

He opened the envelope the Major had left, intending to write his I.O.U. on the back of the agreement.

A note dropped out.

Picking it up, Van Ness glanced at it, gasped and read the note again, his eyes rolling fearfully.

Then he gasped and threw the letter across the table to Deemper. Then, picking up one of the diamonds, he dipped it in an acid and rubbed it on the lapel of his coat.

Wonderingly, Deemper picked up the letter and read:

Dear lads,

I feel an urge to preach a little story to you and, by yours and mine—that's a lovely curse, Van Ness—I'm going to. It's this, dear hearts: what's yours is yours, and what's mine, is mine. In other words, one should keep one's hands from picking and stealing. Oh, quite. Therefore it was wrong of you to have sold fake stones to the doctor; wicked to sell a worthless claim to a dude fool who didn't know what was what, and absolute folly to try and cheat that same fool at cards.

And now I must remind you that if you cast your bread upon the waters—in a manner of speaking—it will return to you after many days, and with interest.

So. The claim is yours again. You were quite right about it; it is absolutely worthless. And on the table before you—are they?—are the stones you sold the doctor. But I faked them better than you did; that is why I asked so much more for them.

As I write, I am fervently praying that you won't have enough sense to test the stones before I close my deal with you. If you do, of course you'll never read this letter. But I don't think you'll be a bit suspicious. Why should you be? Who's going to play such a simple trick on such wide-awake fellows as you two?

I wish I could see your faces turn green as the stones turn yellow. I ache with laughing at the very thought of it. Still, one can't have everything.

> *Yours achingly,*
> *The Major.*

Deemper groaned, too stunned for the moment to visit his wrath upon his puny partner.

"Ach sis! Look now at that."

Van Ness held out the diamond he had been working on. It was a dirty yellow, comparatively worthless.

"The *verdoemte* swine!" growled Deemper.

"The dirty, damned crook!" whined Van Ness.

IDOLS

THE FLAMES of the campfire died down; only a bed of ashes remained and their glow did little more than pick out in red highlights the features of the solitary watcher by the fire, making him look as if he were wearing a grotesque mask; giving him the appearance of a good natured gargoyle.

He sat very close to the fire, his naked feet almost in the embers, and draped about his shoulders he wore several thick, woolen blankets. Even so, he shivered, and his teeth chattered together as the cold wind howled through the tops of the stunted trees. It was sub-tropical Africa, but that wind was born among the snow clad peaks of the Mountains of the Moon.

To the right and left of the watcher, perilously close to the fire, huddling together for warmth, were the figures of men; men who had been overcome by the coma-like sleep of physical exhaustion. They had trekked until they could trek no farther, and then, dropping to the ground, had not moved again—sleeping where they fell. All about them were the loads they had been carrying, loads which had grown lighter with each passing day; loads which had, strangely, seemed heavier with each forward pace. Not one of the packs had been opened, not even the one containing food. Sleep, for once, had been more ardently desired than food.

With a palpable effort the watcher by the fire rose to his feet, letting the blankets fall from his shoulders. He stood there for a moment, stretching, yawning widely. Reflecting the fire glow, his magnificent torso, his overlong, muscular arms, his brawny thighs and calves looked as if they were hewed out of polished bronze.

Stooping, he put more logs on the fire; a shower of sparks leaped up, appearing like a swarm of fire-flies, and were swept up by the wind and emptied into the blackness of the night.

Dense clouds of smoke poured forth from the wood; clouds which momentarily brightened, breaking at length into a fierce flame which illumined the ground.

With an impatient *click,* the watcher picked up his blankets and spread them wide so that their shadow fell athwart the face of a white man who slept on a bed of cut grass some little distance away. He moaned softly in his sleep like an over tired child.

Presently the flames died down again, giving place to fragrant smoke which drove away the few tenacious mosquitoes the cold had not killed.

The watcher looked up at the black mantle of the sky, noting the location of the Southern Cross among the myriads of stars which painted the heavens with an eerie, phosphorescent glow.

"It is time—past time," he muttered in the clicking dialect of a Hottentot. "I will go and wake the *baas.*"

He took a few tentative, almost somnambulistic steps toward where the white man was sleeping.

Then he stopped, hesitated and returned to the fire.

He picked up a water bag and drank greedily; the rest of its contents he poured over his head, shivering as the icy stream trickled down his back and his barrel-like chest.

"Now I have no desire for sleep," he said with a soft chuckle. "I will keep both watches—the *baas* is tired. He has had to carry the burden of the grumblings of these puny fools—" his scornful gesture embraced the sleeping carriers—"set before him. *Ai-e!* And he did more than that! The shame of it! One he carried on his back when the fool's legs could no longer support him. My *baas* should have left that man to die. But, if he had—he would not have been my *baas!*"

He sat down again beside the fire, pulling his blankets about him, staring fixedly at the flames with eyes half veiled by sleep-heavy lids.

His head dropped lower, rested at last on his up-drawn knees; his mouth sagged wide open, his eyes closed.

Time passed.

Jim, the Hottentot, slept.

There were furtive rustlings in the bush beyond the clearing of the camp; faint whispers mingled with the howling of the wind. There was a metallic clatter, instantly silenced, as of steel dropping upon a rock.

A tree hyrax screamed nearby. It was an ominous note; like the strident wailing of a child in a place where one is sure no child could be. It seemed like a blasphemous outcry against the cathedral hush of the bush.

The Hottentot opened his eyes with a start. He grinned self-consciously as he gazed all about him; at the forms of the sleeping men; at the trees beyond the circle of flickering firelight. He listened for some alien noise, a whisper from the blackness of the bush that would indicate the presence of intruders.

Finally, his eyes had seen nothing; his abnormally keen ears had heard nothing, he sighed with relief. Save for himself and the sleepers, the bush was an empty wilderness. There was nothing to fear save—save the blood-congealing cold. He wriggled closer to the fire, pulling his blankets yet closer about him.

There was a noise behind him; first the sharp hissing intake of breath of a man who has plunged his head into cold water, then the soft tread of booted feet.

Jim the Hottentot grinned. He could have distinguished that footfall amongst the tread of a thousand marching men.

The white man, his *baas,* had risen and was standing now behind him.

"Jim—it is past time, long past. You should have called me."

An unseeing listener would have said a native was speaking, so perfectly did the white man pronounce the vernacular.

"I have no need of sleep, *Baas,*" the Hottentot replied. "I will take both watches. The *baas* must sleep. He has trekked far today and the way was very hard."

The white man laughed softly.

"And you—you did not trek! Is that what you would say? You rode on the back of your grandsire, a baboon. For you the way was easy. Yet, I think, but for you your *baas* would have perished in the quicksands; but for you, he—"

"It was nothing," the Hottentot interrupted hastily. "We are men; we do not keep a tally of such things. Even so, the count is in your favor. And, as I have said, what I did today was nothing."

"Truly," the white man murmured. "To risk one's life in order that another may live is always a small thing. But I am a man—not such a man as Jim the Hottentot; there is none like him!—therefore I will keep watch and you will sleep."

He sat down on a pack close to the Hottentot who, knowing that further expostulations were useless, spread his blankets on the ground, rolled himself up in them and prepared for sleep.

"You saw nothing, during your watch, Jim?" the white man asked.

"I saw nothing, I heard nothing, *Baas*. There is nothing to fear and I—" Then sleep caught him in its overpowering ambush and his words trailed off into a raucous snore.

The white man—he was known throughout South Africa, and points north, east and west, as the Major; known as a man who played all games squarely for the games' sake and not for the rewards to be won—smiled wistfully.

"Poor old Jim," he mused, drawling the words affectedly. "He's absolutely played out. Never seen him look so beastly fagged before, and we've been together for five, ten, nearly fifteen years. But no wonder the dear old chap's tired. On top of a hard trek at an altitude which makes one's bally old heart pump overtime, he takes it upon himself to keep my watch as well as his own. The dear old fool."

He rubbed his square, clean shaven chin reflectively; his gray eyes held a half mystic, half wondering light in them.

"Yes," he continued slowly, "it's a brute of a country. Even the carriers, and they're indigent to the soil, in a manner of speaking, are absolutely tuckered out. My word! The things we've been through! That beastly quagmire—miles of it; the jungle; the lava rocks; the cold, the heat; mosquitoes, flies and all manner of unclean, crawling things. The steady uphill grind. And for what?"

He fumbled in his tunic pocket and from it took a small image cut from some iron-hard wood. It was a hideous thing; carved by a master craftsman, it was a startlingly realistic representation of a bestial negro. There was something elemental about it; it suggested the dark soul of darker Africa. Glowing red in the firelight, it looked as if it had been but recently dipped in blood.

The face was that of a West Coast native; the facial and body scarifications indicated its connection with the all powerful Egbo society. Its sinewy, clutching hands, clasped about its enormous belly, seemed indicative of its creator's ambition to subject the whole world to the rule of his people.

The Major closed his fingers upon it with a gesture of disgust.

"And I've been following the trail of the bally thing for months," his thoughts ran on. "Simply because a red-haired Johnny of a Yank told me a wild tale concerning it: of a white girl—his sister—and her uncle held prisoners in the Mountains of the Moon by natives who are plotting to end the white rule in Africa. An incredible story! Oh, absolutely! Yet—" he shook his head—"the Yank was killed because of this grinning image and—"

He was overwhelmed by an avalanche of recollections. His mind's eye was filled with visions of the perilous adventures which had befallen him since he had followed the trail of the red idol, the trail which had brought him to this place—the lower slopes of the Mountains of the Moon.

Faced with such evidence, he could not doubt the existence of a secret society which was insinuating its influence into South African *kraals*.

"And yet—" his voice once again gave utterance to his thoughts—"as far as I can judge, it's not a malevolent influence. Our troubles—mine and Jim's—apart from the natural difficulties of the trail, have been instigated by men who used the society for their own benefit. And one can't judge a society by the black sheep among its members. Might as well say—for example—that all white men wear—er—monocles because I happen to do so. And I wouldn't if it were not for the fact that a monocle makes me look such an innocent chappy. And I suppose I am innocent, if it comes to that. Oh, rather! However, to resume: I fancy my account with the black sheep is settled in full. Actually, the Johnnies at the head of the bloomin' order owe me a rising vote of thanks. I shall point that out to them, if I ever meet them.

"But will I ever meet them? I have my doubts, grave doubts. I'm beginning to believe it's all a myth, quite. Here we are on the threshold of their reputed stronghold, and absolutely not a sign to show which way to turn. There's nothing here; nothing but a howling wilderness; a barren desolation over which snow-capped mountains stand guard. I don't believe there's a human being within sixty miles of us. But, of course, it may be an invisible society."

He chuckled softly.

"But now what to do? Acknowledge it's all a dream? That what Red Head told me was simply a figment of his very vivid imagination, as Jim insists? Or—"

He rose slowly to his feet and paced slowly up and down, endeavoring to marshal his thoughts in some semblance of order. Even such mild exercise affected him; his lungs strained at the rarefied air; his heart pounded with a force that threatened to release it from the confines of his powerful chest.

"We'll leave it to chance," he muttered presently as, stooping over, he placed the red idol on the ground beside Jim. "When he wakes up and sees that, his first reaction will be to throw it in the fire—he thinks it is evil witchcraft. And I think he's right. So, if he does that we will start back tomorrow with the carriers. If, on the other hand, he checks his impulse and brings the idol to me—well, then we'll stay and see the thing through. And, somehow, I'm inclined to think we'll start back."

He sighed as a man will who turns his back on a long sought for goal and resumed his restless pacing to and fro.

He was dressed in a suit of white duck and, as he passed in and out of the circle of light thrown by the fire his appearance was ghost-like or, at least, grotesquely alien to his environment.

He halted presently at the edge of the clearing, silhouetted for a fleeting second against the blackness beyond, by a log which suddenly burst into flame.

Then—darkness encompassed him and he vanished.

There were stealthy rustlings in the undergrowth, the heavy breathing of men struggling under a heavy load.

Again silence. A silence intensified by the screaming of a hyrax.

BEFORE THE sun rose, when the bush was a place of gray, wraith-like shadows and the mountains were shrouded with mist, the carriers awoke as if at a given signal. Silently they rose, took up some of the packs and vanished—heading south.

But Jim, the Hottentot, slept on. What need had he to fear? Was not his *baas,* his baas who could do no wrong, keeping watch?

His hand moved out instinctively toward the fire and his fingers brushed against the red idol, closed on it and gripped it tightly.

THE GIRL and the man shivered together beside the roaring fire which lighted up the deepest recesses of the cave. Occasionally a gust of wind blew in through the cave's opening, fluttering aside the heavy curtain of skins in disdain of man's feeble attempts to block its passage.

It was a cold wind, frost laden, and mocked the heat of the fire. It caused the man and girl to pull their skin coverings still closer about them.

The girl laughed softly.

"If we ever get out of this mess, uncle," she said, "and tell our friends that we nearly froze to death beside a big fire in equatorial Africa, they'll never believe us!"

Her companion nodded. He was a thin, undersized little man. His gray beard had apparently been clumsily trimmed with blunt tools. But despite that and the greasy skins which were his only clothing, he looked like a man of affairs in the civilized world. His head was well-shaped; the big dome of his forehead suggested that he housed a brain stocked with scientific lore; and the eyeglasses he wore—even if they were cracked and in place of the black silk ribbon which in other days secured them, had a piece of knotted string—gave him the precise, intellectual appearance of a college professor.

"If we ever get out of this mess, Alice," he said slowly, "we will have far more astonishing tales to tell the world than one of being frozen. That is not astonishing when one considers the altitude of our—er—prison. But—" he sighed—"I'm afraid our chances of rescue are hopeless and this plan of yours, sheer folly. I should never have brought you on this trip—"

"Ssh, dear!" She placed her firm, shapely hand over his mouth. "You've said that a hundred and one times, and I've interrupted you a hundred and one times, just as I'm doing now. You've nothing to blame yourself for, and if I died tomorrow—I've had an awful lot of fun. Even this experience has been worth while. We haven't been treated so badly, you know. Plenty of food, plenty to drink, exercise—somewhat restricted, I'll admit—and clothes! Latest fashions from the Mountains of the Moon! What more can a girl want!"

She laughed and rubbed her hands up and down the leopard and monkey skins which—with a woman's knack of such things—she had transformed into a barbaric costume.

John Harding, Ph.D., looked proudly at his niece.

"White blood can't be beaten," he murmured.

"Of course not," the girl echoed swiftly. "'Specially not when it is opposed to black. And Mondara's blood is of the blackest. In spite of his college degrees and his show of civilization's culture, he's a savage at heart and is superstitiously afraid of the mysterious men at the head of this movement. And so, I say, my plan will succeed."

Harding moved restlessly.

"I don't altogether approve, Alice. If we fail—we'll only hasten the end. Why not wait; maybe Red managed to win through and is heading a relief expedition. Perhaps this white man, Mondara talks about, is the advance guard of the expedition—"

The girl shook her head decisively.

"No. Red was killed—poor old Red—at Lourenço Marquez. Yes; I believe Mondara about that. He's a liar, I know, but the vindictive gleam in his eyes when he told us about it was too real to be feigned. No; we've got to make a dash for it this morning. It will be easy if Mondara's afraid of his skin as I think he is. We'll make for the camp of this white man and then—" she shrugged her shoulders—"if they come after us—"

"And of course they will," Harding interposed.

"We'll die as whites should," the girl concluded calmly.

She rose, and wrapping her skins closely about her, went to the opening of the cave, holding back the skin curtain.

Two natives, armed with long-bladed spears, stood on guard. They were almost naked, yet seemed indifferent to the bitter cold.

She answered their scowling looks with a smile and stammered a few words in the vernacular. They made no response save to chuckle softly at her ludicrous pronunciation.

She drew herself erect, and braced herself to meet the furious, spasmodic gusts of wind. She looked up at the fading stars; the blackness of night was fast giving way to the somber gray of early morning. But she could see very little, would have seen less had she not known what to look for, and where.

She knew that the cave was one of the many man-made holes in the walls of a crater-like depression—an extinct volcano, her uncle said. She knew that less than two feet from where the guards were standing, the wall dropped a sheer two hundred feet to the bed of the crater, and that crater was a fertile oasis amidst a chaos of barren, snow-crowned heights.

Lightened by the mystical glow of false dawn, she could see far below, the roofs of numberless huts. The light faded, rested for a moment on a huge, grotesque idol just to the left of the cave, then vanished. Clouds of white mist rolled down from the heights above.

The girl shivered, but a light of determination shone in her eyes as she returned to the fire.

The man looked up inquiringly.

"Is it time, Alice?"

"Soon, uncle. The false dawn has gone. I—" she laughed nervously—"I can hardly contain myself."

"You think we'd better go through with it, Alice? It's a gambler's chance at the best. If we lose—we lose every-thing. There'll be no hope for us. We—"

"It's the only way," she said decidedly. "We must make Mondara our prisoner and force him to show us the way out of the crater."

"I know it, Alice. Just the same, I'd like to christen this with the brute's blood."

He flourished a stone-headed club; it was just such a weapon as the first cave dweller might have wielded.

They were silent for a little while.

"Do you think he'll come, Alice?" the man said.

"He always has, uncle. So why shouldn't he this morn-ing, of all mornings? Oh, he'll come, I have no doubt of that, and ask the same beastly question. But—" her eyes glowed—"he won't get quite the same answer."

Her hand opened and closed about the haft of a keen-bladed wooden knife she was holding.

"It will be easy," she continued, talking chiefly to calm her uncle's fears. "He will come in alone, in that insolent way of his. He makes a show of bravery, but he thinks we are unarmed. But this time we'll surprise him. We'll rush him before he has time to draw his revolver or give an alarm. And then, when he's our prisoner, he'll do anything we ask him to once he understands that we'll kill him if he refuses. He's a coward and—"

"And a little mad, I think," her uncle supplemented.

She nodded agreement.

"Yes. That's what makes him so dangerous—and our ultimate success so sure."

Rays of golden light crept into the cave, dulling the fire gleams. The tread of booted feet sounded on the rocks outside. They heard a man's voice singing a ballad of the London music halls.

"He's coming," the girl whispered and moved quickly, taking up a position behind a large boulder near to the cave's entrance.

Professor Harding rose, the stone-headed club gripped tightly in his hand, and tiptoed with exaggerated caution to an angle in the wall of the cave, directly opposite the girl. He was a ludicrous combination of modern savant and prehistoric man.

The footsteps had come to a halt, the song ended. They could hear the newcomer exchanging ribald jokes with the guards. Then sounded the patter of naked feet. The night guards had been dismissed, others had taken their place.

The skin curtain before the opening trembled; a man's voice sounded, forming the English words with precise primness.

"Now I go to talk to the pretty lady," it said.

Long, black fingers appeared at the edge of the screen which bulged slightly, showing the outline of a man's form.

Suddenly the curtain screen was pulled on one side and a man entered, the screen falling into place behind him.

With half suppressed cries of triumph, Alice and her uncle swiftly closed on him. The professor aimed a blow at the intruder with the stone club but, so great was his excitement, missed, the weapon descending with a jarring blow on the man's shoulder, making him lose his balance, sending him headlong to the floor.

Transformed for the moment into a blood lustful savage, the little professor raised his weapon again but, before he could strike, the girl pushed him away.

"Don't," she cried. "Quiet! Don't you see? This is not Mondara. This is a white man."

She knelt down beside the fallen man, cutting the bonds which tied his feet loosely together; taking the gag from his mouth; voicing apologies and hasty explanations.

"It's all right, dear miss," the other said, sitting up with an effort, answering the look of deep concern in her eyes. "I'm quite all right. Quite charmed by the very warm reception you gave me. But what is it all about, if I may ask?"

The little professor, very self-conscious and ashamed of his exhibition of beserk fury, knelt down beside the stranger and gently fingered his shoulder with exploring, understanding fingers.

"Nothing broken," he exclaimed in relief. "But you'll have a most painful bruise. I aimed for your head. I'm glad I missed—"

"So am I," the other interrupted.

"You see," the girl explained breathlessly, "we thought you were Mondara, and—"

"I see—yes. And who is this Mondara you were prepared to greet so lovingly?"

The girl did not answer; instead, she looked helplessly at her uncle.

"I told you it was no use," that man began and finished with a dismal groan.

It had suddenly occurred to them both that their last chance of escape had vanished; that the new captive must be the white man at whose camp they had intended to seek safety. And hard on that realization followed the thought that their jailer undoubtedly knew of their plan to escape.

The girl shrugged her shoulders in a gesture of despair; the wonderful courage and confidence which had supported her during the long months of captivity suddenly left her, and she buried her face in her hands.

Her uncle rose and crossing over to her, patted her comfortingly on the back.

Then, with startling suddenness, the other man commenced to laugh hysterically and to babble an incoherent jumble of English and native words. He bowed his head to the ground, patted the girl's feet and called her strange sounding names.

She drew back with a little cry of fear, thinking that the stranger had gone suddenly mad. She looked to her uncle for an explanation and, when that man winked meaningly at her, she understood vaguely the reason for it all.

A high tittering laugh drew her attention to the entrance to the cave and she turned in time to see a man enter.

He was dressed in a loud plaid suit of thick tweed; the trousers were turned up to display his gaudy socks; his long, light brown shoes were very pointed and he moved with mincing steps. A stiff white collar forced him to hold his weak chin high and the color of his skin in contrast to it looked darker than ebony. His coarse, crinkled hair had been plastered with some strong smelling pomade and his black eyes glittered with malicious mirth.

In his right hand he held a revolver and with it menaced the three.

"And how do you like your new friend?" he asked suavely. "You should be most grateful to me. Knowing how eager you were to seek his company, I caused him to be brought here to you—thus saving you a tiresome journey."

The girl did not answer; her uncle muttered angry curses and the stranger, still babbling foolishly, crept on hands and knees toward the ornately dressed native.

"Back!" that man ordered sharply. "Go back!" His voice ended in a frightened squeak and when the white man still came on, he retreated swiftly and shouted an order to the guards outside.

Two powerful natives immediately entered and, after a short struggle, succeeded in trussing up the white man who was, so evidently, afflicted by the spirits. Because of that they exercised no more force than was absolutely necessary.

Their task done, they again left the cave.

The native laughed affectedly.

"I'm afraid your good uncle hit our friend too hard," he said. "So now—" his eyes glittered—"I must ask you to give to me the club so cleverly manufactured, Professor. Quick! Throw it gently so that it falls at my feet."

Professor Harding hesitated a moment and then threw the weapon with all his force at the man's head.

"That was foolish," the native said icily as he dodged the hurtling weapon. "You will have to pay for that. And now your knife, Alice, dear."

The girl's anger rose at the man's leering familiarity, but she obeyed his order with a pose of meekness.

The native picked it up and examined it with an elaborate show of interest.

"What a foolish waste of time," he said, "to think that you could catch me off my guard! As if I didn't know what you were doing and what your foolish plans were. You must have forgotten, Professor, that walls—even the thick walls of this cave—have ears. And I'm afraid you won't have time to make more weapons. I have at last persuaded the Great Ones to send me out as a missionary. That is funny, is it not? And you will go with me, on my terms, or—"

He passed his finger significantly across his throat.

"We prefer this," Professor Harding said grimly as he imitated the other's gesture.

"It is for you to say," the native looked at Alice.

"I have already given you my answer many times, Mondara. Death is preferable to the shame which—"

"But think," he urged. "Once free of this place I will take you to America, or France or where you will. I have great wealth—diamonds, rubies, gold! I told the Great Ones that wealth—white man's wealth—was necessary if I was to preach the black man's creed. I told them that with wealth I could buy white men, could hasten the day the Great Ones wait for. And that is true, *Au-a!* I know. Have I not lived in the countries of white men? And so the Great Ones have given me freely of their stores. I go from this place the richest man in the world. I—"

"All this is of no interest to us," the girl interrupted coldly. "Talking to you is time wasted. And as for your wealth—we know your end. In a very little while you will be penniless and you will crawl back here—if you dare. But you will not dare confess to the Great Ones that you have been false to their trust."

He was nonplussed for the moment.

"But you underestimate my wealth," he said then. "I do not lie when I say that I will be the richest man in the world—the wealth of Solomon is at my command. Here, in these hills, are the mines—"

He broke off abruptly, looked furtively about him, then repeated, "The wealth of Solomon is at my command."

"But not his wisdom," Professor Harding murmured.

"And what of your mission?" the girl continued, as if she could not grasp the horror of his suggestion. "What of the Great Ones' aim to make all Africa black? What of the part you are to play in order to bring about the fulfillment of their ambition?"

He laughed at that.

"As if I care. The Great Ones are fools. They work and plan for future generations. What are the future generations to me? Nothing—less than nothing. I pretended to side with them in order to gain some of the treasure they have stored up. Possessed of that—I leave Africa and the Great Ones to stew in their own juice."

"Then, besides your other evils, you are a traitor to your people?"

"Have it that way if you please. I shall call myself a prince, as I did at college in England. My royal blood will give me the entrée to houses my wealth alone fails to open. I shall be received everywhere with open arms. White men will fight each other for my friendship and—"

"Yes—you are quite mad," the girl said slowly. "If I could only see the Great Ones and tell them the truth about you—"

He laughed derisively.

"If you could see them, and could speak to them in a language they understand, and tell them what I have told you, my life would not be worth that!" He snapped his fingers. "But you can't see them—and, if you did, you couldn't talk to them. They understand no language but their own. And now: will you reconsider your decision?"

He scowled as she turned her back upon him.

"If you do not come freely, I'll take you by force," he threatened, "and your uncle will die slowly."

"And I would live only long enough to kill you," she replied slowly.

A staccato drum-beat sounded in the valley of the crater.

"I go now," Mondara said. "I will give you until tomorrow. And then, if you haven't decided to fulfill my conditions, I—"

With his threat unfinished he quickly left the place.

The girl went to the cave opening and peering out saw the native disappear down the steep, narrow path, cut out of the side of the rock, which led to the bed of the crater.

Returning to the cave she saw her uncle sitting beside the bound man, whispering excitedly.

Joining them she bent over to unfasten the bonds, telling her uncle to help.

"Has Mondara gone?" the professor asked.

She nodded.

Both the men sighed with relief.

"Then that's all right, dear miss," the bound man said in a normal voice. "No; don't loosen the bonds. The Mondara chappy may return and it's just as well that he should continue to think I'm a little—er—mad."

"But what's to be gained," the girl asked, "by pretending that? And why not let us loose you? With your help, we might be able to overpower the guards and—"

"No, that won't do, dear miss. Any false move just now would hasten our deaths, I think. And whilst there's life there's hope. I played the giddy ass, as it were, because I thought I might get near enough to jump on that poisonous bounder. But he wasn't having any, as you saw. And then I decided to carry on the farce. Don't know why—no doubt there's a good reason waiting to be found."

"At least," the professor said slowly, "you've made yourself a person of some importance in the eyes of the guards. They think you're really mad and, therefore, under the protection of the spirits."

"Ah! That'll no doubt come in useful some time. And now, introductions and what not are in order, I think. You are Professor Harding, and this is your niece, Miss Alice. As for me—I'm Aubrey St. John—generally known as 'the Major.'"

The girl bowed gravely.

"And now," continued the Major, "I think we ought to examine our resources, exchange information, and so forth. And I don't think we ought to waste much time. I am inclined to think that Mr. Mondara will have me transferred to another cell very shortly. Yes; he's much too wise a bird to put all his eggs in one basket, as it were."

The professor nodded agreement.

"Our story is soon told," he said, "and the sum total of our knowledge is very little. With my nephew and niece I came to this district in search of certain scientific data. By accident—actually I fell down the shaft of an ancient mine and broke my leg—I stumbled upon the existence of a secret society which planned to make the black race supreme throughout all Africa; a red idol, a powerful symbol of the society, also came into my possession. Believing at the time that a bloody rebellion was being planned, I sent my nephew down country with the idol and a full report of my discovery.

"The same day he departed my carriers deserted and we were taken prisoners by Mondara and brought to this place. That was months ago. Since then I have discovered—you heard how Mondara talks, a little while ago—that the heads of the society have no thought of overpowering the whites by force, but are concentrating their resources on the educating of their people. I think—"

"May I ask questions?" the Major interrupted. "It will be quicker."

"I'm afraid I'm very vague," the professor apologized, "and your suggestion's a good one."

"Have you seen the heads of the society?"

"No. Except Mondara and the guards, we have seen no one all the time we have been here. No one to talk to, that is. Of course, when we have taken exercise on the narrow ledge outside, we have seen people down in the valley of the crater."

"Have you spoken to the guards?"

"No. They do not speak English, nor do they understand my Swahili."

"They are West Coast natives," the Major explained. "But you have been here months, you say. Surely you have learned their language?"

"No; how could I? They don't talk even to each other in my hearing; they don't attempt to converse with me. I have only spoken to Mondara."

The Major frowned.

"Um! He's a clever blighter. So all you know is what he's seen fit to tell you?"

"Yes," the professor admitted. "But I'm quite sure that he has not lied to us about the society. He lies about his own personal prowess and so forth, of course, but his overweening egotism and his confidence that we cannot give information against him, impells him to speak freely about the society and its endless ramifications. I think, for instance, that we may accept all that he said this morning as substantially true."

"Including the story of Solomon's treasure?"

"Including that."

"That makes my fingers itch," the Major muttered. "And this stone idol Johnny, just outside the cave; do they worship that?"

"I think not," the professor replied slowly. "No; I am sure they do not. It is simply a perpetual reminder of the aims of the society; it personifies the triumph of the black race."

"Um! Funny place to put it. Still, I imagine it can be seen quite plainly from below."

"The little wooden idol I sent down country with my nephew is a facsimile of it," the professor continued.

"And how did that come into your hands?"

"There was a man down at the bottom of the shaft—the one I fell down, you understand. He was on guard there. He tried to kill me. I shot him. He could speak English a little—he told me many things before he died. I took the idol from him afterward. It was a funny experience—"

"And under what conditions does Mondara offer you freedom?"

"My promise to marry him," the girl said evenly.

"Phew! He *is* a little mad, isn't he? He's advanced just that little beyond the savage which makes him very dangerous. But what was your plan of escape which my capture knocked on the head?"

"We were going to attack Mondara, capture him and make him lead us to your camp."

"Then you knew I was in the neighborhood? How?"

"Mondara told us. He has been giving us reports of your progress for the past three weeks. Drum talk, you know. I thought you were the advance guard of a rescue party my nephew, Red, had succeeded in getting together. I had begun to think that Mondara lied to us when he told us that Red had been killed."

"That was no lie," the Major said gravely. "I was with him. He told me about you and I promised him to bring help."

There was silence for a little while.

"But why did you come alone?" the professor asked.

"No one would come with me—the officials laughed at the idea of a secret society and all that. Oh, well! We must put our heads together and think up a way to get out of this."

"Only a miracle can help us," the girl said with a sigh. "Please tell me about my brother."

"He—" the Major began, then began to laugh boisterously as he struggled to free his hands from the ropes which bound them.

The girl started back as if at a blow, but at once Mondara, accompanied by four powerful natives, entered the cave.

"You are clever, very clever, Mister Aubrey St. John Major," he said scoffingly, "but not so clever as Mondara. I left you, thinking you mad. But doubts came and I returned to make sure. So—laugh no more. You are no longer under the protection of the spirits. Instead—you shall be under my protection."

"Splendid!" the Major drawled, but could say no more for in response to Mondara's curt order the four natives came forward and after gagging and blindfolding him picked the Major up and carried him from the cave.

"I think I am very clever, eh, Professor?" Mondara said complacently. "It is very hard to pull the wool over my eyes. You have found that out, I hope. And, if you're wise, you'll use your influence to persuade Miss Alice to—"

"Get out!" snapped the professor and Mondara, first bowing sarcastically, hastened after the men who had taken the Major.

The professor and Alice looked blankly at each other.

"Our last state is worse than the first," the professor said nervously.

"I'm not so sure. I think the Major will find a way."

The professor smiled wearily.

"You're putting your trust in a broken reed, Alice. He has courage and colossal strength—you'd never suspect that at a casual glance—but that's all! I don't believe he has a brain in his head. Besides, even if he had, what could he do? He'll be put in a cave like this with men on guard night and day. He has no weapons, he—"

The girl shook her head.

"You can't shake my confidence, uncle. I'm relying on the Major. Don't know why—call it a woman's intuition. And, uncle, isn't he frightfully handsome?"

THE SUN was hastening upon its westward course; the valley of the crater was a place of purple shadows. As the shadows rose, twilight gloom was everywhere save that one ray of light from the setting sun, shining through a gap in the western wall, focussed on the stone image, accentuating its bestial lines; the red with which it was stained glowed like warm, freshly spilled blood.

The people of the crater were hastening to a clearing directly below the idol. As if at a signal they dropped to their knees, their faces upturned toward the image, and from a thousand throats came their chant of supplication; a prayer that their ambitions might be quickly fulfilled. The rock walls echoed with the mournful cadence, and the volume of sound seemed as if it must fill the whole universe.

The sun sank lower; the shaft of light now only illumined the idol's face. The thick lips seemed to part in an understanding leer.

The chant ended in a wild shout as the light totally vanished, and the people departed to their huts. For them, although the sky above the towering, snow-crowned peaks was still a dazzling blue, night had commenced.

THE MAJOR groaned softly, then, sitting erect with an effort, tore the filthy bandage from his eyes. His clothing hung upon him in shreds, and his back was scored with long, livid weals—the marks of a *sjambok's* lash.

Presently, when his eyes became accustomed to the flickering light of the fire, he rose to his feet, walked unsteadily to the cave opening and peered out. Two natives, gripping *assegais* firmly in their right hands, were kneeling there, their faces turned toward the stone idol which was but a few paces to the right. From below came the sound of a vast multitude chanting.

Cautiously the Major stepped out onto the narrow path. He was possessed with the idea of rushing the kneeling men, obtaining their spears and selling his life as dearly as possible. Suddenly the chanting below ceased; the two men jumped to their feet and turned to face him. They menaced him with their spears and with angry gestures indicated that he should return to the cave.

"I intend no harm," he said plaintively in the language of one of the Gold Coast tribes. "Let me stay a while."

But they only scowled and advanced implacably upon him. When the points of their spears were but a few inches from him, he shrugged his shoulders and reentered the cave.

"This is a deuce of a mess," he muttered as he sat down beside the fire. "I wish Jim, the bally old blighter, were here; things wouldn't be so bad then. Without him, I'm lost. Absolutely!" He sighed. "I wonder what's happened to the dear old chap? Somehow, I don't think they captured him, or the carriers. Yes I am just as sure that Jim and the carriers are alive. I should say that the people who run this little affair are not exactly bloodthirsty. If we could only eliminate the Mondara chappie, I'd be willing to gamble that I could get us all out of the mess as easy as wink."

He rose to his feet and paced slowly up and down.

"Yes," he continued. "Mondara must be eliminated and there's very little time in which to do it. Of course, if he's telling the truth, he leaves here in two days' time. But first, I think, he will eliminate us—and that's not so good. And he plans to take Miss Alice by force if she won't go willingly. And she won't, of course. So there are two good reasons why Mr. Mondara must not go—or why we should go first. Yes; I think that would be best. But there are a lot of obstacles in the way—a frightful lot. And I want to see this reputed Solomon's treasure and—" his voice sharpened—"I want to teach Mondara that it is not wise to *sjambok* a white man.

"He's cunning. He had me carried for miles an' miles. Then he *sjamboked* me, then more traveling—blindfolded all the time. And yet here I am now in a cave not a hundred feet from that which imprisons Miss Alice and the professor. Did I say Mondara was cunning? He's not. He's a fool. Trying to make me think that I was miles away from the others when a moment's thought must have shown him that the idol was a dead give away of my location. Oh, well! Even if the other two dear souls are only just the other side of the idol, they might as well be the other side of the world for all the chance I have of getting in touch with them."

The entrance of two native women, escorted by the guards, put an end to his cogitations. One of the women carried a platter heaped high with food, and a large gourd full of water. The other had a pile of faggots for the fire. They placed their burdens on the ground and retired, grinning sheepishly at the Major's fulsome compliments.

"At least," he mused as he sat down to eat, "they don't intend to starve me. This chicken—"

For a time the business of eating fully occupied him.

"And that," he said at length with a sigh of satisfaction, he had been very hungry, "proves my point. We are not meant to be killed. It is undoubtedly the order of the head Johnnies that we are to be well treated."

He shivered.

"Phew! It's getting cold. The sun must have set."

He put a couple of sticks on the fire. Another he held in his hand, balancing it thoughtfully.

"It looks as if Mondara must be killed," he muttered, "and I've used worse weapons than this." He sat staring morosely at the fire, endeavoring to find a way out of the difficulties which embogged him.

Time passed swiftly, but the Major did not move, did not shift his gaze from the fire. Unshaven, his hair in disorder, his clothing dirty and torn, there was little about him to suggest the monocled, immaculate dude which was his well cultivated pose. Only the well trained observer would have been aware of the colossal strength stored in his relaxed frame, of the fighting spirit indicated by his firm, well shaped chin, and of the keen brain which worked behind the mild, vacuous appearing blue eyes.

He rose suddenly and, taking a lighted brand from the fire, explored the walls of his prison cave.

At one point there was a wide crack in the wall. He passed his improvised torch through it and found that it was wide enough and deep enough to admit the length of his arm. Shielding his eyes from the wood smoke which drifted back from his torch, he squinted through the crack.

The rock wall, he judged, was nearly two feet thick and beyond was another cave, or—or a passageway!

"And if it's a cave," he mused as he returned to the fire, "then its opening must be partly concealed by the idol, And if it's a passageway—it may lead to the treasure Mondara was talking about. Better than that, it may lead straight through the mountain and—"

He closed his eyes, realizing that he was too tired to marshal his thoughts properly; and he was too wise to indulge in vague wonderings.

"Tomorrow," he muttered sleepily, "I'll investigate. But now I must relax; there's nothing I can do. There—"

His voice trailed off into silence. His head dropped lower; his chin rested on his up-drawn knees and he slept as a native sleeps, slept with every sense on guard to warn him of the approach of danger.

Time passed.

Then a voice sounded in the cave, a ghostly whisper of a voice, seeming, to emanate from the crack.

"Baas!" it said. *"Baas!"*

THAT SAME morning Jim, the Hottentot, awakened tardily from sleep. Rising to his feet he gazed vacantly first at the swiftly rising sun, then at the dying ashes of the fire and the deserted camp.

"Baas!" he cried, and when the empty echo of his own voice was the only answer, he grinned sheepishly. "Because I have slept overlong," he muttered, "the *baas* plays a game with me." He shook his head doubtfully as he eyed the loads left by the deserting carriers. "I will wait here," he presently decided, "and cook myself food. He will send someone back for these loads."

Then for the first time he was conscious that he was gripping something tightly in his hand. He opened his fingers and looked at the little red idol and his expression of disgust as he suddenly threw the thing from him was almost comical in its intensity.

A cloud of gray ashes leaped upward as the idol dropped into the midst of the smoldering fire.

With a cry the Hottentot ran forward, raked the idol from the fire with his fingers, carefully brushed the ashes from it and secreted it amongst the tangled mop of his hair.

"The *baas* would not like it burnt," he muttered as he walked restlessly up and down, listening intently for any sound which would give him a clue as to the whereabouts of his *baas* and the carriers.

After a while, with a self-condemning grunt of disgust, he examined the ground all about and there read the story of the carriers' departure.

"I am a fool," he grumbled. "I should have known. Wo-we! The sleep spirits must have bound me fast. The carriers—Mashona dogs that they are!—have started back on the long trek to their *kraals. Au-a!* May they die on the way. But I should have remembered, I should not have slept. I should have kept watch with the *baas.* Yesterday they said they would go—and I slept while they departed! But my *baas?* Where is he?"

"I do not see his spoor here," he continued. *"Wo-we!* And all the time I slept."

He scrutinized the ground even more closely, stooping over almost double. Up and down he went, following the Major's restless pacing of the night, until, finally, he came to the spot where darkness had suddenly descended upon the Major.

Little more than a casual glance was sufficient to show him all that had happened and, greatly distressed, he returned to the fire and, squatting down on his haunches, gazed blankly before him. At that moment he wished that death might come to him. Now that his *baas* had gone, his *baas* who could do no wrong, there was nothing to live for. For many years they had played the game together—hunting, exploring, welded together in that bond of sympathy which nature weaves about men—irrespective of color—who are men.

"Wo-we!" Jim moaned.

His *baas* had been captured by followers of the little red idol. They had crept up close whilst he—Jim, the Hottentot—slept. Worse yet—they had probably crept up close during his watch and had bided their time, not moving, doing nothing to betray their presence to the white man when he commenced his watch.

"*Wo-we!*" Jim said again. "And I told the *baas* that there was nothing to fear. Yet I must have slept during my watch. They could not have crept up without the *baas* hearing them. And they were so close that he had no time, even to utter one cry of warning."

Then came a thought which lightened his mood of despair. The little red idol! Probably the *baas* had left that with him as a sign that he was to follow; probably the *baas* had gone off willingly with the followers of the idol. At least they had not raided the camp; they had not been responsible for the carriers' desertion; they had not harmed him. Then, it might be, the Major was still alive.

The Hottentot put some more wood onto the fire, blowing on the embers until the new fuel burst into flame. Then, opening certain of the packs, he methodically cooked himself some food which he ate mechanically. He was storing up vitality for the unknown trek before him.

His hunger satisfied, he took two revolvers and a belt of cartridges from one of the packs and strapped them about him. A long coil of rope he carried about his shoulders. The rest of the packs he arranged in an orderly pile and covered them with branches and armfuls of the long grass which had served as his *baas'* bed, weighting it down with heavy boulders.

Then, from his own little store of things he selected a large hunting knife which he stuck in the cartridge belt, sadly discarded the blankets and set out on the trail.

Picking up the spoor of the unknown abductors, Jim, the Hottentot, followed it at a fast pace. Straight uphill it went, following, as Jim presently perceived, a faintly defined trail. Even so, the trekking was difficult and Jim was frequently forced to call a halt. The trail was so steep in places that he had difficulty in keeping his footing.

It was nearly noon when he came to a large, barren plateau, jutting out from the mountain. There the trail was clearer and he was able to go at a faster pace. An hour later, when he had crossed the plateau, he was faced by a steep, unclimbable wall of rock. In despair he searched the wind polished surface for signs of foothold, but found none; neither could he see any further signs of the trail of the men he followed.

The path—if path it could be called—vanished at a small clump of stunted bushes; at that point his *baas* and the men who had carried him had apparently dissolved into nothingness.

With unflagging energy, Jim cast about in ever widening circles, endeavoring to pick up the spoor again, cheering himself with the memories of other adventures he and his *baas* had shared; adventures which had brought them face to face with death—yet they had always won through.

"And we will be too cunning for death this time," Jim shouted challengingly.

The wind, which howled continually about the plateau with an almost gale-like velocity, snatched the words from his mouth, splitting them up into incoherent syllables, casting them into an abyss of silence. Jim shivered, and vaguely compared himself to a morsel of dirt upon the peak of the world.

He had returned now to the place where he had lost the trail; was standing close to the clump of bushes. Suddenly, with a sheepish grin at his own stupidity, he parted the bushes and uttered a soft cry of triumph. Swiftly uncoiling his rope, he fastened one end securely about a large boulder and, tying a good sized stone to the other end, threw it into the gaping hole the bushes concealed.

Before half the length of the rope snaked into the hole, a rocky clatter told him that the stone had reached bottom and, without further hesitation, he slid down the rope.

The bottom reached, he was challenged by a native who loomed up in the twilight gloom of the place like a creature of the nether world.

"What make you here?" he demanded in the language of the Ekoi, and when Jim gurgled an incoherent reply, repeated the question in a halting Zulu.

When Jim, scratching his head in indecision, still made no reply, the other threatened him with a spear.

"Speak," he demanded.

Jim grinned. He had formulated a plan of action.

"I come on the business of this one," he said and taking the idol from his hair, held it out on the palm of his hand.

The other swiftly examined it, handed it back, and then lighted a torch in the red embers which glowed fitfully in a small brazier.

"The way is before you," he said as he handed the torch to Jim, and sat down beside the brazier having, apparently, no further interest in the matter.

Jim looked at him uneasily. Something warned him that he was not to win through so easily. He edged closer to the sentry, his hand on the hilt of his hunting knife. His eyes had now become accustomed to the yellow light of the torch and he saw that he was in a circular, highroofed cave; shafts led off from it in all directions.

"Which road do I take?" he asked gruffly, and went still closer to the sentry.

The other laughed mockingly.

"If you were sent on That One's business," he said, "the road was made known to you."

"I was not told, or if I was told I have forgotten," Jim said dully. "So show me the road I take. I have the idol."

"Aye, so you have. But that alone is not enough. What is its voice? What word does it give? What word do you give for it? *Au-a!* You have no word. You are a liar. And so—choose your own path. It is all one to me. Only, should you choose the wrong one, death will come very quickly to you. Or, should you by chance choose the right one, the Great Ones will have means of finding whether you are a liar or no."

Jim looked about the place, seeking some clue which would indicate which shaft he should take. But they all looked alike, there were no distinguishing marks. Beads of sweat rolled down the Hottentot's face. He was horribly afraid. Not for himself, but for the safety of his *baas*. If he failed now—

"That is the one I will take," he said with a show of confidence, and pointed to an opening. In order to gain access to it, he would have to pass very close to the sentry.

"You choose well," the other grunted, but Jim detected a note of malicious triumph in the man's voice.

Whistling softly, Jim walked toward it; but as he was about to pass the sentry he drew his knife and leaped upon him.

Over and over they rolled, struggling furiously. The sentry was strong, but Jim was stronger.

"If you kill me," the man gasped, Jim's knife pricking at his throat, "what good will that do you? Let me up and I will tell you the proper road."

"Get up then," Jim panted triumphantly, "and see that you make no sound."

Silently the other obeyed, turning his back to Jim as that man directed, holding his hands out behind him.

Jim cut a length off the rope and tied the man's hands together.

"Now," he said, as he lighted another torch, "show me the road."

"It is that one." The man nodded toward a shaft directly opposite the one Jim had selected.

"So-o? Then you shall go ahead of me and lead me to its end. And remember; I shall be very close behind you, holding the rope which binds you, the point of my knife—it is very sharp—pressed between your shoulder blades. Now, lead on—and play no tricks."

He pricked the other with his knife, urging him on.

"Nay, Hottentot," the man gasped. "I lied. That way is strewn with poison thorns. That way is death."

"*Au-a!*" said Jim. "Then show me the right way."

The other hesitated, then, shrugging his shoulders, "It is that one," he said and walked unhesitatingly toward the shaft directly to the left of the one he had first indicated. "Wait!" Jim said and yanked hard on the rope he held, causing the man to fall over backward.

Quickly Jim tightened his bonds, passing the rope around his feet, so that the sentry was helpless, incapable of moving.

"Now bite on this," he said and thrust a gag between his jaws.

"I will release you when I return—if I return," Jim said as he dragged the man a little distance along one of the shafts.

Then, taking a bundle of torches with him, he went boldly forward.

For what seemed an endless time he followed the winding, tunneled passage, marveling at the ivory smoothness of the walls—as if polished by countless million hands.

"Mostly I'm going toward the direction of the setting sun," Jim muttered. "It may be that this road will take me to the place where the sun buries itself with the coming of night; it may be that this leads to the place of the wicked dead." He shivered at the thought of it. "But at least," he comforted himself, "the man who kept watch was no spirit—but a poor guard."

One by one his stock of torches burned down and out. He had only one left, and that half consumed, when he came to a wide ravine which was spanned by a flimsy rope bridge. The ravine—actually it was a wide crack in the rock caused by some upheaval of nature—extended for an enormous distance.

Far overhead Jim could see a tiny patch of sky.

Dubiously he tested the bridge, then started to cross. It swayed sickeningly to and fro and, when he was but half-way across, he lost hold of his torch.

Almost nauseated by giddiness, he watched the tiny point of flame drop into the darkness below; watched it until it vanished. He listened intently, but no sound came up out of the depths and he visualized it falling for all eternity.

His hold on the ropes stiffened and he clung there, afraid to move. It seemed to him that many seasons came and went before courage returned to him and he moved slowly forward.

When he reached the solid ground again, he crept forward on hands and knees, almost sobbing with relief, yet not daring to stop until he had put several hundred paces between himself and the bottomless horror of the pit. Had he known, there was a store of torches and food hidden in a niche in the wall close by.

Then on again, very slowly, feeling his way cautiously forward, inch by daring inch, endeavoring to make his eyes pierce the darkness.

He lost all thought of time, all awareness of self. He remembered only that his *baas*—the man he worshipped with an almost idolatrous zeal—was somewhere ahead. He was subconsciously aware that the tunnel was sloping upward. His naked feet could feel the steps which had been cut into the rock.

The tunnel suddenly leveled out again and Jim, with a feeling of relief, realized that the darkness was not so intense.

A tongue of flame shot out from the wall ahead. It moved mysteriously to and fro, up and down, then as mysteriously disappeared—seemed to have been swallowed up by the rock.

With a groan of fear Jim dropped to his knees and covered his face with his hands. He was sure that he had seen a manifestation of the spirits. Presently, summoning up courage, though he could not silence the chattering of his teeth, he rose and went on. After a while, and never had his pace been so slow, he came to a place where there was a crack in the left hand wall of the tunnel through which straggled a shaft of light.

Greatly daring, Jim crept up to it and peered through. At first he could distinguish nothing; then he saw his *baas* sitting beside a fire. But his great joy did not destroy his caution.

"*Baas!*" he called softly. Then, when the Major did not move, called in a little louder tone, "O-he, *Baas!*"

He chuckled with delight as his *baas* opened his eyes and stretched himself wearily. He did not call again. He knew that his *baas* had heard, that his pregnant call had penetrated beyond the outerguard of sleep.

Casually the Major rose, put more wood on the fire, glanced toward the opening of the cave—he could see the sentries outside; they were sitting with their backs to him—then went to the crack.

"Jim!" he whispered happily. "Is it really you?"

"Aye, *Baas*. None other. Are you all right, *Baas?* No harm has come to you?"

"I am all right, Jim, save that a *sjambok* scored my back."

"There shall be an accounting for that," Jim said fiercely.

"Softly, softly, Jim," the Major cautioned. "You brought guns?"

"Aye, *Baas*. Two."

Jim passed the revolvers and cartridge belt through the crack with a sigh of relief. Jim did not like firearms. As the Major buckled the weapons about him, under his clothing, he chuckled gleefully. Their possession put escape into his hands.

One of the sentries peered into the cave then, rejoining his companion, announced, "The white man is mad. He stands by the wall laughing to himself! He will give us no trouble. Let us sleep."

"How do I get into that place where you now are, *Baas?*" Jim asked. "Or how do you get out?" He strained at the sides of the crack as if he would rend the rock still farther apart.

"It cannot be done that way, Jim," the Major said. "But we will find a way. There is no great need of haste. Now tell me how you come to this place. But first—are you hungry?"

"What is meat to me now that I know you live, *Baas?*" the Hottentot replied happily. "Yet, nevertheless, I could eat a little."

The Major laughed softly and brought over from the fire the remains of his evening meal which he passed through the crack to Jim. While the Hottentot ate, the Major gave him a full account of his experiences.

"*Au-a!*" exclaimed Jim, the end of the Major's narrative coinciding with the last crumb of food. "And it is all my fault! If I had not slept—"

"There is no fault, Jim. Doubtless if they had not captured me we would now be on our way south again, my mission a failure. As it is— But my voice grows tired. Tell me, then, of your journeyings."

"It is a long trail. And where shall I start?"

"Where is the Red Idol I left beside you?"

Jim grinned.

"I threw it in the fire, *Baas.*"

"Tch!" the Major elicited reprovingly.

"And then I took it out of the fire, unharmed, *Baas.* And it is well I did. It is a powerful charm. It—"

And for a time Jim's deep voice rumbled on, describing in great detail his manifold adventures.

"That is all, *Baas,*" he finally concluded. "And now we will go back the way I came. Let us start now. I like not this place."

"And think you, Jim, that I can squeeze through this crack?"

"I had forgotten that. Then must we stay here until death comes?"

"The way is open for you to return, Jim."

"The way is closed unless you are with me, *Baas*. Such talk is folly," the Hottentot growled.

The Major's eyes glowed.

"Did the carriers take all the packs with them, Jim?" he asked lightly, concealing the emotion he felt at Jim's fresh demonstration of loyalty.

"Nay, *Baas*. Only the ones containing their food."

The Major nodded and rubbed his chin reflectively.

"I'm glad of that," he drawled in English. "I'm beastly dirty and I need a shave. Besides, I feel quite lost without my monocle. That Mondara smashed it to smithereens with his *sjambok*. Ah! I'm afraid he will have to pay for that. Oh, quite. And so, considering that I need so many things, I think the sooner we get out of this place the better. I think, perhaps, if all things go in our favor, we will go tonight. Not a bit of good waiting about. And it should be quite simple—quite. I imagine the passage Jim's in comes out by the stone idol. So—all I have to do is shoot the sentries outside my cave and the sentries outside the professor's and just amble along. But I don't like that idea very much.

"The sentries are quite good sorts, really, and killing them would be such a messy affair. Besides, the reports would give the alarm, and I couldn't shoot the whole bloomin' population of the crater. No! We've got to get away quietly. And I want to take Mister Bloomin' Mondara along with us. He's our only real danger. He's civilized—probably has rifles and revolvers and what not. So he must come along with us yes, for the good of his soul, he must come along. He must be taught a few things. And that's not all 'pon my soul, no! This expedition has cost me a deuce of a lot of money. I must reimburse myself somehow. Don't you think so, Jim?"

"Golly, no-yes, *Baas*. If I don't see you, s'long hullo?" Jim stammered, not understanding a word of what the Major had said, answering the interrogative note in his *baas'* voice.

"I thought you would say that, old top," the Major drawled. Then, in the vernacular, "Now go to the end of the passage and find when it comes out. Also, look for a crack in the wall opposite."

Jim departed returning almost immediately, greatly excited.

"The passage ends less than a spear's throw from here, *Baas*," he reported. "Between the idol's legs is the opening. The light from the fires of the watchers showed me that. And there is a crack in the wall opposite, but it is not so big as this one. It is only a small crack, I could only just see through it. I looked and saw the white woman and the old white man. They were sitting by the fire looking as if death was very close to them."

"It was, Jim, until you came. Death was close to all of us. But you have frightened death away. So now there is no cause for fear. And now what?"

His brows knit in puzzled thought.

"I have no paper, no pencil—nothing by which I can write a message," he muttered. "I'll have to trust it to Jim. I hope they'll have the sense to listen to him. I think they will. At least Miss Alice will. She's splendid. She—" Aloud he said, "Listen, Jim. You must go to the other crack and make the girl or the man come to speak with you. Here, take this—" he passed a thin stick through to Jim—"and wave it to and fro until they see it. Then whisper their names: Missy Alice—Professor—over and over again until they come to the crack. Say their names!"

"Missy Alley! P'fessor," Jim said haltingly.

The Major nodded.

"That will do. Then, Jim, when they have come to the crack you will tell them this:"

And slowly, making Jim repeat sentence after sentence, the Major outlined the first steps of the scheme which would, he hoped, end in escape from the crater.

"Now tell me," he said finally, "just as you are going to tell them, all that I have said. And speak slowly, for their knowledge of the vernacular is not good."

Jim nodded and began:

"I am Jim, I am the Major's right hand; I am his mouth. This is what he says to you: before the rising of the morrow's sun we will all leave this place in safety. But first you, Missy Alley, must play a part. Call now for the man Mondara. If you make much noise, shouting his name, the sentry will send for him. Then, when he comes, this is the meat of what you must say to him:

" 'I have been thinking many things, Mondara. It is better to live, even as your slave, than to die. I am young, I desire to live. I desire much wealth. Much wealth would make me forget, maybe, that your skin is black. So I am almost ready to fulfill your condition and go with you freely. But how can I believe that you are rich? Go, bring me proof, now, that you have all manner of precious stones as you have boasted. If I am satisfied that you do not lie, then, I promise you, I will go forth from this place with you—and that freely.'

"That is what my *baas* says you must say, Missy Alley. And you, P'fessor. My *baas*, the Major, says that you must forbid the girl to do as she says; you must be angry with her.

"Then, after Mondara has departed, I will come again with further word from my *baas*."

Jim looked at the Major.

"Have I the message right?" he asked.

"Quite, Jim. Your words are the echo of mine. Go now and see what you can do."

When Jim had departed on his mission, the Major paced restlessly up and down. Presently he sat down, close to the crack, and endeavored to eject his personality into the other cave, commanding its occupants to listen to the voice of Jim.

Time passed, dragged wearily.

"O-he, *Baas!*"

He roused himself at Jim's excited whisper.

"Well, Jim?" he asked.

"She will do it, *Baas*," the Hottentot said, "Even now she makes ready. At first they would have none of my story. The old man said I was a liar; he said I was one of Mondara's men trying to trap them. But the girl said I was a true man. But first she made me repeat the words the *baas* put into my mouth many times. There, listen, *Baas!* She calls now."

Faintly, muffled by the walls of the cave, the Major heard the girl calling, "Mondara! Mondara!"

He chuckled with satisfaction.

"Keep a close lookout, Jim," he ordered. "He may come by the passage. If he does— You have a knife?"

"Aye; I have a knife, *Baas*," Jim answered grimly.

"Then you will know what to do. Do not kill him, unless that can't be avoided. But do not let him call for aid. Watch now. I go to the opening of my cave to see what is to be seen."

As the Major came to his cave's opening, the girl's voice sounded louder, clearer, "Mondara! Mondara!"

The sentries before her cave were apparently trying to silence her with threats, whilst the men who kept guard over him were grumbling loudly because their sleep had been disturbed.

"Go get Mondara," one of them shouted. "He will silence her."

A noisy altercation followed and then the Major saw one of the guards rise and make his way swiftly down the narrow path leading to the crater below.

After a time—the Major judged a half hour had passed—the guard returned, holding aloft a flaming torch, and behind him was Mondara.

Well satisfied, the Major retreated back into his cave and seated himself abjectly before the fire. Nevertheless, it was only by the exercise of magnificent self-control that he was able to refrain from rushing out and fighting his way to the other cave. He was nervous for the girl's safety; half afraid that she would betray, unwittingly, the existence of Jim.

Someone entered his cave and came slowly toward him. He knew it was Mondara and was half determined to bring matters to an issue there and then. His better judgment, however, ruled otherwise. He must wait a little longer.

"And how is the mad Mr. Aubrey St. John Major?" Mondara drawled mockingly.

The Major sprang to his feet as if greatly alarmed.

"When did you come in?" he gasped. "I must have been asleep. I—" Then the drawl came into his voice again. "I take it that you have come to release me from this hole, eh? Frightfully good of you. But, let me tell you, I shall report your beastly behavior to the authorities."

Mondara's eyes gleamed.

"You are a fool," he said in a contemptuous tone. "I just came to tell you that tomorrow I leave this place and the girl goes with me of her own free will. In less than a month

I shall be on board ship heading for Paris. After that—"
He shrugged his shoulders.

"But you'll take me with you," the Major pleaded. "You
wouldn't leave me here to die in this hole. Why—"

"No; I won't leave you here to die. I shall kill you before
I go."

He turned abruptly on his heel and left the cave.

"Baas!" It was Jim at the crack again. The Major crossed
over quickly.

"Well, Jim?"

"Missy Alley, she says that Mondara has gone to get the
proof of his wealth. In a little while he will return. She now
wants to know what she must do when he comes again."

"Tell her, Jim, that she must make a show of being well
satisfied with what she sees. Tell her to speak soft words to
Mondara. Tell her to make him many soft promises, if need
be. But she must send him away quickly. Tell her to tell him
that she must sleep in order to be ready for the morrow's
trek. Say that to her and then come back here to me."

When Jim returned to report that he had delivered the
message he saw the Major was daubing his hands and arms
and face with the charred end of a piece of wood.

"Is the *baas* mad?" he gasped.

"Nay, Jim. Only, for a little while, I desire to pass as one
of the sentries."

"Then the *baas* is indeed mad. As if the black char from
a piece of burned wood could make him black. *Au-a!* Does
that thicken his lips, change the color of his eyes and hair,
break down the bridge of his nose? What folly. And there
are other things—"

"What I do is enough, Jim. It is only to fool a man whose
eyes are blinded by his own splendor. He will not look at

me closely—until it is too late. Why should he? Suspecting nothing, he will see nothing. Now, Jim, I go to take my stand near to the entrance of this my cave, and you will shout—putting your lips to this crack—'*Monn-akat-chang-obbaw-chang!*'" *

"What is it, *Baas?*" Jim asked wonderingly after he had muttered the words to himself. "A charm?"

"A most powerful charm, Jim. I think it will bring the guards running to see what it is all about. But shout the words loudly and let there be fear in your voice."

"I hear, but I do not understand," Jim muttered and he repeated the words softly to himself as he peered anxiously through the crack.

The Major put more wood on the fire, first dampening it with water from a gourd. The flames died down. Vaguely, through clouds of smoke, Jim saw his *baas* take up a position to the right of the cave's opening. And then he grinned as understanding came to him. His *baas* was holding a revolver in his hand; he was crouching lightly on the balls of his feet; he was ready to strike.

Jim wailed his charm dolorously and repeated the phrase again and yet again. There was fear, loathing and an appeal for help in his voice. Outside, the two guards held a hasty consultation, then—had not Mondara expressly ordered that no harm was to come to the white man, yet?—they rushed into the hut.

The first passed the Major before he could strike, heading for that part of the dimly lit cave from which came the shout of fear. The second man went down like a pole-axed

---

* Monn-akat-chang-obbaw-chang. Literally, Child-feet-not-hands-not; the things without hands or feet. Name given by certain West Coast tribes to snakes—particularly pythons.

bullock as the Major brought down the long barrel of his revolver on his head.

"The snake is here, warrior," the Major said quietly as the other turned at the thud of his companion's fall. "Drop your spear."

The man looked at him with a grotesque air of bewilderment. He was convinced that the white man was in league with the spirits. The voice had sounded from over there, nowhere near where the white man was standing. And there was no one else in the cave. Then the voice must have been that of one of the Spirits. Even so, the warrior was of a mind to try conclusions with the Major; for the moment he feared the Spirits less than he feared the wrath of Mondara.

He shortened his hold on his *assegai* and crept stealthily forward.

"Stand!" the Major ordered sharply and cursed under his breath when the native still came forward.

He knew that the warrior's life was in his hands. He had only to squeeze the trigger of his revolver and the stalwart, menacing form would be lifeless flesh and bone. But, apart from the fact that the Major knew the report would raise an alarm and bring others to the attack—thus ruining his plan of escape—he was averse to killing.

The warrior was very near now, his hand was going slowly back. In a moment, the Major knew, he would rush in to the attack. And then a weird, moaning noise came from the crack. The warrior turned in alarm and at that moment the Major closed in on him.

The struggle that ensued was a very short one. The Major's strength was more than a match for the warrior's— giant of a man though he was—and, besides, the native was defeated already by superstitious fear. In a very little while the Major had him down on the floor of the cave, gagged and bound with the same ropes that, early in the day, had bound him. Rising from his task, he saw that Jim was performing a like task with the other native who was beginning to show signs of returning consciousness.

"And now what, *Baas?*" the Hottentot asked happily. Directly after his cry which had taken the warrior off his guard, he had emerged from the passageway and entered the cave at its entrance.

"Now," said the Major, "we will go outside and play that we are the guards."

A few moments later they were squatting on their haunches beside the fire outside the cave. They were enveloped from head to foot in skin blankets.

Presently there was a sound of booted feet coming up the steep path, and a moment later Mondara came into sight. He had no torch, and in his hands he carried a large tin money box. He walked furtively, continually looking over his shoulder as if afraid of being followed. When he came still nearer and full into the circle of light thrown by the fire, the Major saw that his face was strained, the pupils of his eyes dilated, and that beads of sweat stood out on his forehead.

The Major pulled his skin blanket closer about him. Under its cover he held his revolver, ready for use.

"Dogs!" Mondara said angrily as he neared. "Do you dare to sit in my presence? I—"

He turned suddenly and drawing his revolver aimed at some invisible point in the darkness beyond the fire gleam. So he stood for a moment and then shrugging his shoulders as if in derision at vague half formed fears, he hurried on, rounding the angle made by the Stone Image and vanished from sight.

"I wonder what was the matter with the blighter?" the Major mused. "He acted as if he were afraid of being followed. Shouldn't be at all surprised if he hadn't robbed the treasury, as it were, and is afraid that they are on his trail. Perhaps I should have tackled him then—but no, I think not. On his return, though—"

They waited for a while in a silence so profound that Jim was afraid the beating of his heart must be heard by the inhabitants of all the world. Then, from the cave on the other side of the Stone Image, came a confused murmur of voices. A woman's voice, soft, almost caressing and then the voice of Mondara shrill, blatantly triumphant.

"Good night, Miss Alice," they heard him say. "Tomorrow, then, at sunrise."

The Major and Jim arose to their feet and crept nearer to the Stone Image.

They heard Mondara exchange a crude jest with the guards and then the sound of his footsteps coming toward them.

Suddenly down in the valley of the crater there sounded the deep, menacing boom of drums. Lights flickered about the valley; shrill voices sounded giving orders. The lights massed together, advanced toward the cliff. The next moment Mondara rushed hastily round the Idol directly into the arms of the Major and Jim who were waiting for him.

He was badly frightened and had entirely lost his self-possession.

"Let me go, let me go," he screamed in the vernacular. "They have found me out. Let me go."

He clawed at them with his naked hands. In his terror he had forgotten all about his revolver and the thin veneer of civilization had entirely gone from him. He was now only a puny, badly frightened savage.

"Let me go," he cried again. "They have found it out."

"Found what out?" the Major asked quietly, also in the vernacular, and he shook Mondara much as a terrier shakes a rat.

"I killed the keeper of the treasure," Mondara gasped. "And now the Great Ones have set the avengers on my trail. Let me go before it is too late."

"Hold him, Jim," the Major said tersely and leaving Mondara in the firm grasp of the Hottentot, the Major made his way along the path to the other cave. There he was confronted by the two guards who watched over the cave in which the professor and the girl were imprisoned. They menaced him with their spears but backed at the sight of the revolver in his hands, backed at his order into the cave, their hands held high above their heads. The professor and the girl ran to greet the Major with exclamations of gratitude and wonder. They showered him with questions.

"There is no time for explanations now," he said roughly. "Bind these two Johnnies, Professor, and then we will have to run."

It was quickly done and as quickly they left the cave, hastening back to where Jim and Mondara awaited them. The shouts of the people sounded nearer, the place was illuminated by the gleam of many torches.

"Hurry, hurry," Mondara almost screamed. "In a little while it will be too late."

"Let him go, Jim," the Major ordered, "and see that you keep close to his heels."

As Jim released his hold, Mondara darted through the widespread legs of the Image and was immediately lost to sight in the blackness of the passage beyond.

With a cry of, "Follow swiftly, *Baas,* the path is smooth," the Hottentot hastened after him.

"Follow Jim," the Major said to Alice and the professor. "I will bring up the rear."

The Major was about to follow them when a spear whizzed by his head. The Major fired swiftly at the onrushing warriors, checking them, and then sped hastily through the black depths of the tunnel. Catching up with the professor and Alice, sensing their nearness in the gloom, he urged them to better speed.

Ahead of them was the blackness of the Pit, behind them the warriors, yelling fierce threats, their torches stabbing the darkness with points of yellow light. An *assegai* clattered on the rock just behind the Major.

"You and Alice go on," the professor gasped. "I am all in, let me have a revolver and I'll hold them back."

The Major's answer was to pick up the little man in his arms and with a curt "Carry on," to the girl, they continued their flight. To the professor he gave one of his revolvers and his burden fired at intervals whenever a yelling warrior came to too close quarters. Ahead of them they could hear the shrill piping voice of Mondara; the deep booming voice of Jim, the Hottentot, echoed back strangely in the dim arched passage like the roar of a maddened bull. Behind them sounded the fierce cries of the pursuing warriors, the fumes of powder mixing with the smoke from the torches stung their nostrils.

At last they caught up to Jim, the Hottentot.

"Is Mondara with you?" the Major called.

"Ya, *Baas,*" Jim said grimly. "At first he was very fast but once I had caught up with him the rest was easy. Not once has the point of my knife been farther than a hair's breadth from the great vein in his neck."

Good," the Major said tersely. "Keep it there. And the tin box? Where is that?"

"Mondara carries it," Jim answered.

The pursuers seemed to have slackened their speed and were falling farther behind. Undoubtedly the professor's shooting, erratic though it was, had greatly discouraged them.

"And that is a good thing," said Jim, "for soon we come to the bridge I told you of, and I do not want to hurry over that."

As he spoke Mondara stumbled, and fell to his hands and knees. Jim groped through the darkness after him, but in vain. Crawling several paces on his hands and knees Mondara had evaded him, and then, rising to his feet, ran forward at full speed. His mocking laugh came back to them through the darkness.

"I will get him, *Baas,*" Jim cried and hastened forward. A few minutes later a tiny flame of light appeared ahead of them, and they saw that Mondara, with a lighted torch in his hand, was halfway across the rope bridge. Without any hesitation Jim started to cross, too, making the bridge swing precariously.

"Back," Mondara snarled and aimed his revolver full at the Hottentot, but just as he was about to press the trigger Jim jumped violently up and down. The frantic swaying caused Mondara to drop the tin box in his endeavor to retain his balance. With a cry of rage Mondara fired three shots in rapid succession. Two of the shots went wide, but the third seared Jim's ribs and the shock of it almost caused him to lose his hold. Before Mondara could fire again, the Major's revolver spoke, and Mondara hung limply for a moment to the ropes and then gradually, almost imperceptibly, his stiffened fingers opened and with a wild animal-like scream he dropped into the pit. For a little while they could follow his fall, lightened by the flame of the torch, then it, too, vanished and they were left once again in the darkness.

"Are you all right, Jim?" the Major asked anxiously.

"Ya, *Baas*," Jim replied mournfully. "Only once again I'm at fault. Mondara has escaped me; and he has taken the stones with him."

The Major laughed happily. The potential wealth the tin box had contained meant nothing, less than nothing, when weighed in the balance with the safety of Jim.

"They are coming, Major," the girl warned, and the Major with a startled look over his shoulder saw that the pursuers were very near. He fired rapidly, aiming at the ground before them. He had no desire to kill. The tunnel was filled with the whine of bullets.

"Is the bridge safe, Jim?" he asked.

"Ya, *Baas,* and it is easier to cross it in the dark than with a light. In the dark one cannot see what will happen if a foot goes astray. I'm now on the other side, come quickly."

A few moments later the girl had crossed in safety and the Major, with the professor now on his back, had also made the dangerous crossing.

Almost as soon as the Major's feet had reached the solid ground Jim hacked away at the main ropes supporting the bridge.

"This is quicker, Jim," said the Major and fired point blank at the thick strands. They parted and the bridge dropped uselessly, hanging to its stays on the opposite side.

"Now we can go on at our own pace," the Major announced gaily, and laughed at the infuriated yells of the warriors whose farther progress was halted by the broken bridge.

"Go back to the Great Ones," the Major shouted in the language of the natives. "Tell them their secret is safe with us so long as they refrain from deeds of bloodshed."

"Our quarrel is not with you," a warrior answered, "but with Mondara—the dog! He killed the keeper of the treasure. He—"

"He will work no more evil," the Major answered gravely. "If this pit has a bottom—look for him there. There you will find him and the things he stole."

IT WAS sunrise. Jim the Hottentot squatted by the campfire, cooking the morning meal. From the frying-pan came the pleasing odor of bacon. A coffee pot simmered nearby. Wrapped in blankets not far away the girl and her uncle slept peacefully.

Presently a cheerful whistle sounded beyond the bushes which fringed the camp clearing and the Major appeared. He was clean-shaved and dressed immaculately.

"Do they still sleep, Jim?" he asked.

"Ya, *Baas,* not even the smell of food, wakens them. They must be tired indeed."

"Without doubt," the Major said. "But what of you, you old heathen, are you never tired, are you not tired now?"

"Why should I be, I have done nothing."

The Major laughed.

"No," he drawled in English, "you have done nothing. All you have done is to save my life and the life of Miss Alice and the professor."

Then, in the vernacular, "Jim?"

"Ya, *Baas?*"

"Where is the little red idol?"

Jim fumbled in the tangled mop of his hair and from it took the little wooden image which had first set their feet on the trail which led them to the Mountains of the Moon. He spat in disgust as he held it out to the Major on the palm of his hand, "I do not want it, Jim," the Major said.

"Keep it, it is your reward."

Jim spat again and then threw the idol into the fire.

"So may all evil end, *Baas*," he said with a happy grin.

The Major nodded.

"When did the carriers leave this place?" he asked Jim.

"Yesterday morning, before sunrise, *Baas*. But yesterday morning seems like ten thousand years ago."

"Nevertheless, Jim," the Major responded with a chuckle, "it was only yesterday morning, and, if we hurry, traveling light, we may catch up with them."

"That was in my thoughts, too, *Baas*."

"And, once we have caught up with them," the Major continued, "I can persuade some of them to return here for the rest of the packs."

"When the *baas* persuades, no one can say him nay," Jim said.

"Exactly! After that—the rest will be easy."

"But what is the rest?" Jim asked anxiously.

"We take the Miss Alice and her uncle to a white man's settlement."

"And after that, *Baas?* After that?"

"Why, after that, Jim, we will wander up and down this land, sleeping where the night finds us, eating whatever may fall to our guns, living—"

"Ya, *Baas*," Jim interrupted. "That is living. But we will come no more to this place of cold winds and bottomless pits?"

"No, Jim. Where the wind blows, there we will go."

"And we will play the game, *Baas?*" Jim meant the game of I.D.B.

"Maybe, Jim. Who knows? But, without doubt, we will play whatever game is set before us."

MAJOR METHODS

"**AND WHERE** now, *Baas?*"

"Ask me again, Jim—after we have eaten. Now I can think of nothing but the great hunger which gnaws at my belly."

The Hottentot made the *click* of impatience.

"There was food in plenty back there, *Baas,*" he said and turning his head, gazed back across the rolling veld to where the tin roofs of a white man's dwelling reflected the sun's rays in a dazzling shimmer of white light.

The other—men called him "the Major"—halted his easy stride and looked down at the Hottentot, a whimsical, affectionate expression in his blue eyes.

"If it had not been for one Jim, the Hottentot," he said slowly, "I should be at that place now; eating in comfort and assured of a good night's sleep on a soft bed between linen. I should—"

"*Au-a, Baas,*" Jim expostulated uneasily. "What is the comfort and ease of a mission to us? We are men of the veld. Where the night finds us—there we will find our ease and comfort. Besides—" He paused.

"Go on, Jim," the Major prompted softly, "Besides, you would say?"

Jim swallowed miserably, then continued in an indig-
nant tone.

"The *baas* is a fool. For months we have followed a
dangerous trail; we two against all the evil of Africa. We
have rescued an old white man and his sister's daughter
from the great peril which threatened them and, when talk
is made of recompense the *baas* becomes, of a sudden, deaf.
And so—" He paused again.

"And so," the Major finished for him, "we have less than
nothing. In order to perform a service we have cut a trail, a
wide trail, from the Cape to the Mountains of the Moon
and halfway back again, strewing our possessions along
the way—a horse at this *kraal,* mules at that, a wagon at
yet another; the Little People of the forest make merry
over much of our equipment and the rest is at the bottom
of rivers which had no fords or buried in bogs which have
no bottom. And so now we are beggars, possessing nothing but the clothes upon our backs, a rifle, revolver and
cartridges—" he counted them aloud—"twenty cartridges,
Jim," he concluded and laughed softly.

Jim spat in disgust. "You laugh, *Baas,* but it is a true word
you speak. We are beggars. Yet we might have commanded
great wealth. Life is dear—and the old man was rich. He
was willing to pay the price for the few years of life we
saved to him; for the many years of life we saved to his
niece. We—"

The Major started to retrace his steps.

"Where are you going, *Baas?*" Jim asked in alarm.

"Back to the mission, Jim."

"Wherefore, *Baas?*"

"Because Jim, the Hottentot, is afraid to face the world
unless his pockets are lined with gold and the ease possession of gold brings. And so, we will go back to the mission

and wait there until the old man's messenger returns with gold for us. We will not have very long to wait. Maybe two months, maybe only one. And then we will escort the old man and the girl down to the seaport; maybe we will cross the great water with them. Let us go, then. If we hasten we will be there in time for the noonday meal." He sniffed the air luxuriously. "In my fancy I can scent the food the white girl cooks. Never have I eaten such bread—"

Jim squatted on his haunches with a grunt of dismay.

"I will not return, *Baas*. There is sorrow in bread of a woman's baking. Besides—"

The Major returned to him.

"What is that 'Besides' which trips your tongue, Jim?"

"It is thought of the girl whom we rescued, *Baas. We-we!* She was making of you—my *baas*—an inconsequential thing, making you as feeble as a fallen leaf which obeys the behest of the lightest wind which blows. Further," Jim added brutally, "you were a man when she was only a babe."

"Jim is right," the Major murmured in English, drawling the words affectedly. "It could never have been. Of course she's grateful to me, and all that, and thinks— But I must not even consider what she thinks. She'll return to her own country, wide open spaces, and all that, resume her old life and all this will be just a dream—or a nightmare. Yes. And you were saying, Jim?"

"Yah," continued the Hottentot who had listened attentively to the Major's drawl as if he understood every word, "women—and men, too, for that matter—will always praise the beer they have, no matter how stale it is, if there is none other to be had. But when fresh beer is brewed and all the beer pots are filled, then the stale beer is discarded; it is thrown away and, as it sinks into the ground, it fills the air with a stink of futility."

"Great is Jim, the philosopher," the Major muttered and added sharply, in the vernacular, "I want to know one thing, Jim!"

"And that is, *Baas?*"

"Was it to save me the shame of being discarded—as is stale beer—that you ran amok at the mission? Breaking in to the mission's store hut, drinking the medicine whisky, half killing seven converts, lying about me and making it impossible for me to stay whilst you were free—and I couldn't see you imprisoned, though you deserved great punishment. Was it for my sake that you behaved that way?"

Jim grinned.

"Something like that, *Baas.* I was thirsty, too. And it was nine converts, not seven. They were puny creatures, though, not worthy to be called men. As for the lies I told about you— *Au-a, Baas!* Those who know you, know they were lies. The others, they do not count. And, *Baas,*" his voice softened, "I knew that if your heart was at the mission you would find a way to free me and stay there yourself. But you did not want to stay, and so I was your excuse; my evil doing was the crutch which helped you to limp away."

The Major's face brightened. It was as if he had suddenly found the answer to a question which had been troubling him.

"Bai Jove!" he cried in English. "You're right, you priceless old heathen. I did not want to stay. You're absobloominballylutely right!"

"Golly damme yes, *Baas*. If I don't see you s'long hullo!"

And with that cryptic sentence—it almost exhausted his knowledge of English—Jim sprang to his feet.

"And now," he continued happily in the vernacular, "we will trek."

"But, Jim," the Major was somewhat puzzled, "why did you groan and feign a desire to return to the mission?"

"Because, *Baas*," the Hottentot answered gravely, "it was necessary to free your mind of the doubts which hobbled you. Now the doubts have gone, we can trek swiftly. And," he beat his powerful chest with his clenched fist, "we are men; therefore we are rich. Come!"

He led the way at a fast gait across the veld, heading for the distance-blued hills and the Unknown beyond.

In all the years they had been together—white master and black servant when surrounded by the conventions of civilization; two men, two friends when the veld called them—they had never been so destitute as now. The most abject sundowner carried some sort of pack and, besides, had the lack of pride which enabled him to beg from white settlers and the lack of principle which saw no wrong in stealing from the natives.

But these two were, in addition to their present poverty, burdened with pride and high moral ethics.

Not that Jim was so very moral and it is true that the Major had, on occasions, dealt in stolen diamonds. Still, Jim would never indulge in petty filching—the affair at the mission to the contrary notwithstanding—and the matter of diamonds was the Major's protest against the combine responsible for the Draconian laws regulating the diamond industry. Even the police regarded it more in the light of a political rather than a criminal offence, though that did not influence them to slacken in their efforts to catch the Major in the act, as it were, of his nefarious operations.

However, despite their present poverty and their encumbrances in the way of pride and ethics, Jim had not overstated the case when he said that they were *men* and, therefore, rich.

The Major was young, younger than the gray hairs at his temples suggested. He was old in wisdom, young in his capacity of living. He was good looking in a strikingly masculine way; a masculinity which was not masked to a keen observer by the monocle, the dudish clothes and the silly ass mannerisms which, in more prosperous times, he used to cloak the keen workings of his brain. He was abnormally strong—and knew how to use his strength; there was not an ounce of superfluous flesh on his well knit frame. He could ride, he could shoot—Africa knew few men who were as quick on the draw as he—and the mysteries of the bush-veld were an open book to him.

And, added to all this, he had Jim; Jim, the Hottentot.

As for Jim, the tattered remnants of clothing he wore served only to accentuate the muscular appearance of his squat, ungainly figure. Naked, save for a breech clout or a loin-cloth of leopard skin, Jim became a part of Africa, looked—as in fact he was—a high priest of her dark mysteries. And although the ragged trousers he now wore and the cast off tunic of the Major's—it was too large for him, save across the shoulders—may have misled the uninitiated into thinking Jim a victim of civilization's degradations, actually he was still unspoiled, was still a child of the bush. All his senses were highly developed. His sight was as keen as an eagle's; his hearing abnormally acute; his powers of endurance little short of miraculous. He had besides a sixth sense of direction, and an uncanny instinct which warned him of impending evil.

Added to all this, he had the Major.

And the two of them possessed a strong love for justice and fair play; a well controlled sense of humor and the abounding courage which enabled them to face the things they most feared.

And so they were rich—if poor—and well equipped to wrest wealth, if it was wealth they desired, from the burglar proof safe which is Africa.

They trekked swiftly, silently. Once they passed unobserved through a herd of impala buck; again Jim stalked a duiker ram so cleverly that he was able to kill it with a blow from a knobkerry, thus providing for the evening meal without drawing on the Major's meager store of cartridges.

After that, the carcass of the ram on his shoulders, Jim disdained caution and loudly chanted the savage hunting songs of his people.

Mile dropped behind mile, the hills lost their bluish haze and their jagged peaks showed against the molten sky in a series of grotesque silhouettes.

The sun sank lower; a soft breeze blew fitfully, so gentle a breeze that it failed to disturb the clouds of mosquitoes which had suddenly appeared out of the nothingness and *pinged* about the heads of the two men.

Said Jim, halting suddenly and pointing straight ahead, "There is a *kraal, Baas*. Water is near."

Shading his eyes the Major looked in the direction Jim's pointing finger indicated. For a little while he could see nothing but the hills and miles of rolling veld. Then, as Jim gave him certain bearings, the huts of a native village flashed into his vision with the magical suddenness of a picture thrown upon a screen.

The *kraal* was located at the base of one of the kopjes, on the other side of a deep depression which scarred the veld; and that depression, the Major knew, masked the winding course of a river.

"Tonight we will camp on the river bank, Jim," he said.

"Not at the *kraal, Baas?*" Jim questioned reproachfully.

"Shall we go to the *kraal* as beggars, Jim?"

Jim spat.

"The *baas* has twenty cartridges; he holds twenty lives in his hands. Who then dare call him a beggar?"

The Major laughed.

"If there is a life to buy or sell—let the dealers come to us. We are men of peace, Jim, we will not go to them. Therefore, as I have said, we will camp on this side of the river."

"Au-a, Baas!" Jim exclaimed as one would say, "Of what use arguing with such a man?" Then, shifting the load he was carrying from one shoulder to the other, he continued the trek without further word.

But now his pace had lengthened, was quicker.

The Major chuckled. He knew that Jim was trying to punish him for his stubbornness in deciding to camp this side of the river instead of seeking the hospitality of the *kraal*. He looked toward the goal for which they were heading. Six miles distant, he judged. Then he chuckled again. Jim ought to know better than think to wear him out in such a short trek. Without outward effort he lengthened his stride to keep pace with Jim's.

The Hottentot led a course as straight as if plotted with rule and compass. He turned aside for nothing: thorn bush, broken ground, elephant grass, muddy flats or steep slopes were one to him. He kept doggedly to his line and his pace never slackened. Once, indeed, he quickened it with a grunt of dismay. That was when the Major almost trod on his heels and made a bantering comment on the slow pace Jim was setting.

The sun made low darting shadows of their hastening forms; the breeze brought back to them from the *kraal* ahead the lowing of cattle, the shrill cries of the herders and the drowsy bleating of goats.

Everything seemed suggestive of peace.

And then Africa struck—struck with the sudden vindictiveness which, despite the heavy inoculations of white man's civilization, keeps her still the Dark Continent.

It was very hot, even the breeze brought no relief, and the two men were trekking at a fast gait across a shadeless stretch of veld. But, inexplicably, the Major felt cold; his limbs shook and strength went from him. He snapped off a twig from a mapani bush and bit on it to prevent his teeth from chattering. He dropped behind.

Jim, conscious that the Major was no longer close at his heels, believing that the pace he had set was too much for his *baas,* grinned triumphantly and increased his pace.

The Major kept to the trail with obvious effort; his eyes were glazed and it was only by a stupendous effort of will power that he kept them focussed on a spot between Jim's shoulders.

At times he saw two Jims; the veld heaved under his feet like a heavy sea; the sky whirled about him; the sun multiplied into a thousand flashing, dazzling lights. The skin about his temples felt dry to the point of cracking, his

tongue was swollen, moistureless, he felt as if sharp, burning stakes were thrusting his eyes out from their sockets.

He tried to call out to Jim, croaked harshly and pitched
forward upon his face, crashing upon a fallen tree which—a
victim of ants—dissolved in a cloud of acrid dust.

At the sound Jim turned, a knowing grin on his face,
wondering what trick his *baas* was trying to play upon him.
But when, save for a feeble patting of the ground with his
hands, the Major made no move, Jim's grin gave place to
a look of doubt.

"*Baas!*" he called sharply, then, muttering angry self-ac-
cusations, ran back to find the Major muttering in the
delirium of fever.

THE SUN had set, darkness was close at hand, when
the people of Janva's *kraal* opened the gate in their stockade
to admit a Hottentot and the burden he carried.

This Hottentot, the people of Janva quickly discovered,
had a way with him. He called them many insulting names,
names which would have angered them had it not been
that they were greatly afraid. "For," they reasoned, "unless
this Hottentot has great power, how dare he—one man
alone—so insult us who are many?"

And Jim cursed them in English—queer parrot sounding curses which, not understanding, they mistook for
powerful charms. And having cursed, Jim gave orders,
backing up his orders with a shot from the Major's revolver.
(The shot frightened Jim as much as it did the people of
Janva. His greatest fear was firearms. But the people of
Janva did not know that!)

And so, because Jim was Jim, a swearer of strong oaths
and stronger charms; because he possessed, as he was

careful to point out, the lives of nineteen of them in his hands—they gave him all that he required.

The guest hut was quickly swept out and a bed made of freshly cut reeds over which well tanned skins were spread. Some of the women brewed a nauseating concoction in which quinine bark largely figured; others heated large boulders which they brought into the guest hut and placed in a hole in the ground. Over this hole they put a three legged stool.

And on this stool they sat the Major—Jim having first undressed him—and hung heavy blankets about him, draping them so that they covered him from head to foot, spreading out tentlike.

Then, after Jim had forced his *baas* to drink some of the medicine they had prepared, they threw doctored water on the red-hot stones, enveloping the Major in a cloud of pungent smelling steam.

Half an hour later, almost smothered under a pile of blankets, his head pillowed on a bundle of sweet smelling herbs, the Major tossed uneasily, sweating profusely.

Three times Jim rubbed his *baas* dry, piled fresh blankets about him and made him drink more of the medicine. After that the Major slept soundlessly, dreamlessly.

Whereat Jim heaved a deep sigh of relief and going outside the hut silenced with an imperious gesture the clamor which greeted his appearance. Then, squatting on his haunches, he ate heartily of the food they brought him.

His hunger satisfied, he sat with the headman of the *kraal* and the old men, regaling them with stories of his *baas'* wisdom and colossal wealth.

THREE DAYS passed and with them the fever which had ravaged the Major. Wrapped in a faded red blanket he tottered out of the hut and sat down on a couch Jim had prepared for him. His face was covered with a black stubble of beard, his hair was unkempt and his eyes dull, lusterless.

"With plenty of food, Jim," he said slowly, "I shall be ready to trek in two days. Already strength is coming back to me and my hunger is great."

"You shall eat, *Baas*," Jim said happily. "And in two days, as you say, we shall trek." He knew that the Major had not overestimated the speed of his recovery to normal strength and health. His *baas'* recuperative powers—unweakened by excesses—were great. "And now, *Baas*," he continued, "I go to the river to wash. If there is anything you need whilst I have gone, clap your hands and the women—"

"Where are we, Jim?" the Major interrupted. "And, seeing that we are poor, how have you obtained so much from the people of this *kraal?*"

"We are at the *kraal* on the other side of the river," Jim said with a chuckle, "and as for the rest: I ordered—they obeyed."

"*Wo-we!*" the Major exclaimed. "Great is Jim, the Hottentot. But when a demand is made for payment, I think—"

"When the time comes," Jim said stoutly, "doubtless payment will be at hand. Now I go to the river."

"But I'm naked, Jim," the Major protested. "I can not sit here with only a ragged blanket about me. At least let me have my shoes and my guns and—"

Laughing, Jim went into the hut and brought to his *baas* the things he had asked for.

"Now I feel more of a man," the Major said when he had pulled on his boots, and buckled his cartridge belt and revolver holster about him. The rifle Jim placed on the couch beside him.

"There is still something lacking, old dear," the Major muttered in English. "My tunic, Jim," he added in the vernacular.

When Jim gave it to him he took out of one of the breast pockets a gold rimmed monocle.

"That's toppin'," he drawled as he fixed it in his eye. "S'long, Jim."

"Golly, damme yes, *Baas*," Jim grinned. "If I don't see you, s'long, hullo!"

And with that he picked up the Major's soiled clothing and hurried down to the river.

For a little while the Major looked with interest about the *kraal*, exchanging jokes with the old men and stories of hunting with the younger ones. But, presently, his head nodded, his eyes closed. But the monocle still remained in place, reflecting the ray of sunshine which penetrated the shade Jim had built.

"*Tchct!*" swore Headman Janva in disgust. "How can we steal his guns from him? Two of his eyes are asleep—yes. But that third one. *Au-a!* I have watched it closely. It does not even wink!"

Meanwhile Jim, having succeeded in restoring his *baas'* clothing to a snowy whiteness, spread them out on the bank to dry and sat down, his chin cupped in the palms of his hands, to consider what answer he would give when the headman, Janva, demanded payment for favors given.

He had boasted of his *baas'* wealth, speaking vaguely of oxen and wagon, answering their expressed amazement that a man so wealthy should elect to travel on foot with, "And why did my *baas* come to you afoot? Was it not on my back he came? And am I not more valuable than a team of oxen? Then what need of further words? If my *baas* prefers to ride on my back, it is no concern of yours."

With that piece of casuistry the headman had professed to be content. But now, having boasted, Jim would be called upon to make good the boasts or failing—as he knew he must fail—be driven with jeers from the place. He regretted now that he had been so high handed. Had he appealed to their sense of hospitality they would have given freely all that he had demanded from them by threats. He would have to pay for his bombast; worse still, he knew that in this matter his *baas* would not support him, but would offer sincere apologies for the deception which had been played upon them and promise them payment in the not too distant future.

Jim knew that they would listen to and believe his *baas;* but on his own head would be heaped scorn and ridicule. He squirmed at the thought of it.

"But it will be forgotten," he muttered. "The *baas* is always just."

Faint shouts, a low rumble of wheels and bellowing of oxen aroused him from his reverie.

Looking up he saw a wagon creeping slowly over the veld, making for the river. It was still so far distant that it appeared as little more than a black speck swimming in a cloud of dust.

Jim stared at it wonderingly.

"Sixteen oxen," he muttered, "drawing a heavy wagon. And there is no voortrekker. *Wo-we!* Two white men drive them—two white men riding on horses. *Au-a!* That is strange."

He rose to his feet, intending to return to the *kraal* that his *baas* might be dressed in a manner fit to see and be seen by the strangers.

Then, after a moment's hesitation, he sat down again and waited. After a long hour—the pace of the ox is slow—the wagon came to a halt not fifty yards from the bank of the river.

One of the white men—his eyes glinted savagely from out a thick ambush of eyebrows and tangled beard—rode forward alone.

"Hey, nigger," he shouted across to Jim, "where's the ford?"

Jim stared at him incuriously and shook his head, affecting not to understand. The bearded man swore and turned to his companion.

"Hans," he said, "come and speak to this nigger. He understands not the good *taal*—for all that he looks like a Hottentot."

The man, Hans, rode forward. He was thin and of a puny physique, but his face was evil.

"Where is the ford, dog?" he asked in the vernacular, barely opening his slit of a mouth.

"There!" said Jim, leaping to his feet and pointing to a barely discernible track which led down the bank to the river.

The two men inspected it and, after a hasty consultation, tethered their horses to the rear of the wagon and made ready to cross the river.

The thin man took his place at the head of the span, holding the leading *reim* in his hands, whilst the other took the big driving whip from the wagon and flourished it awkwardly.

"Arh there!" he yelled. "Biffel, Englisher! Appel! Schellum! *Trek jou!*"

The oxen strained at the yokes, the wagon moved slowly forward. Down the steep bank they went, the leaders stumbling, sliding, the wheel oxen bunching up their shoulders and holding back in an attempt to keep the wagon from crashing into them. The white man who led them tripped over a loose boulder and in his endeavor to save himself from falling under the hoofs of the oxen threw himself to one side.

The leading pair of oxen turned to follow him, lost their footing and slid on their sides down to the river bed. The other beasts followed, perforce, in a frightful tangle of confusion. Only the two wheelers, big, black bulls, kept stolidly to their task. But, lacking a directing hand—their driver was expending his energy cursing the others and punishing them with the whip—presently they, too, gave way to the panic which had seized the others. Down the bank they charged at a lumbering trot, the wagon swaying behind them, and came to a halt on the bed of the river, the wagon tilting precariously.

The two white men cursed each other and their oxen.

With wild shouts, and kicks, and vicious cuts from the whip they worked with a frenzied haste to get the oxen in proper alignment. But they only succeeded in making matters worse. The beasts were bewildered, terrified.

Jim had at first watched the scene with contemptuous amusement, but the white man's insane brutality aroused his wrath and he proffered his services; not because he desired to help the white men, but in order to release the terrified beasts from their ordeal.

"Leave them to me," he cried as he waded across the river.

He passed down the line, straightening the tackle, pushing the animals into place, talking to them softly. Gradually their frantic bellowings ceased, the look of fear went from their bloodshot eyes and they stood placidly, chewing the cud.

"Almighty!" swore the bearded one. "Now they shall have it!" and he made a preliminary flourish with the long whip. At its vicious crack the oxen moved uneasily.

"No, *Baas!*" Jim exclaimed and wrested the whip from the white man. And, "Pardon, *Baas,*" he added humbly, "but they will not pull if you hit them so. Leave them to me."

"Yah!" the man called Hans said quickly. "Leave 'em to the nigger, Pete. We'll have the wagon over if we're not careful."

"Ach sis!" Pete growled. "You are soft. I know how to handle cattle—and niggers. I'll flay the skins off them."

He turned away with a scowl at the venomous light in the other's eyes.

"What are their names?" Jim appealed to Hans, and repeated then slowly after the other, inwardly wondering why the white man showed such a scanty knowledge of the ways of their oxen and why neither man seemed quite sure of the names of their beasts.

The names memorized, Jim unyoked all save the two wheelers and led them across the river, talking to them all the time. Returning, he made a great fuss over the two black bulls, whispering in their ears, petting them, praising them extravagantly.

"Biffel! Appel!" he called sharply, suddenly.

The two powerful beasts humped their backs and strained forward. The wagon moved, slowly, very slowly, and righted itself with a jarring bump. The rest was easy. With Jim walking at their side, the two bulls took the wagon across the river and up the steep slope on the other side with a splendid rush.

"Almighty!" said Hans as the rest of the span yoked up, Jim handed him the whip. "That was good work. Here, nigger!"

He tossed Jim a bag of Boer tobacco, then turned aside for a whispered consultation with Pete.

Jim grinned. He guessed what they were discussing. They needed a driver, and where could they find a better driver than Jim? He saw a way now out of all his difficulties. He would bargain shrewdly with these white fools. In return for his services they should give his *baas* accommodation and pay for the hospitality at the *kraal*. In that way, he and his *baas* could leave the *kraal* in triumph.

"You will come with us," Hans said, turning on him suddenly. "We need a driver and will pay you well."

Jim shrugged his shoulders. It was not part of his scheme to be over anxious for the job offered him.

"I already have a *baas*," he said. "He is up at the *kraal*. He is—"

The two men exchanged alarmed glances.

"Keep the nigger here," Hans said after a pause. "I will go up and see what manner of man the nigger's *baas* is. Maybe I can make a deal with him."

He grinned evilly and, mounting his horse, rode up to the *kraal*. Jim picked up the Major's clothes and started after him, but halted at a shout from Pete and the threat of the revolver that man leveled at him.

In a very little while Hans returned, laughing softly.

"His *baas* is a *verdoemte roinek,* he is a white kaffir. He sits with a dirty red blanket about him, a dirty helmet on his head, talking to his women. No; he did not see me. And so-a—we will take his nigger.

"What is your name?" he asked, turning abruptly on the Hottentot.

"Jim, *Baas.*"

"Then, Jim, you are now my nigger. Understand? You drive my oxen."

"But my *baas*—" Jim began, backing slowly away.

"Your *baas*," Hans said with a laugh. "I am your *baas.* Quick now. Trek! We have waited here too long,"

As he spoke he drew his revolver and spurred his horse closer to Jim.

"When my *baas* hears of this," Jim said slowly, "he will demand payment, heavy payment. *Au-a!* And he will collect. He—"

Jim broke off suddenly. The look in Hans' eyes told him that that man was conscienceless and would have no more compunction about shooting him in cold blood than he would a wild dog. And, realizing that nothing he could say or do—now—would have any effect on such a man, Jim surrendered.

"I will drive your oxen, *Baas*," he said and jumped into the wagon.

"*Trek jou!*" he yelled hoarsely and the long lash coiled over the backs of the oxen with a riflelike report.

The wagon moved ponderously forward and the two white men, grinning triumphantly, rode slowly beside it.

"He will need watching for a day or two," said Hans. "One of us must always be on guard—"

"I lose no sleep keeping watch over a nigger," Pete said roughly. "A rope is a good guard!"

They both laughed.

Jim scowled at them, then sought to hide his anxiety by examining his whip.

The stock was well to his liking. Fully fifteen feet long, it was supple, well balanced and the butt of the right thickness for his grip. But the lash!

"Fit only for a Mashona or a Zulu to thief," he grunted contemptuously. He turned and examined the interior of the wagon. It was loaded with wooden boxes on which were piled a motley assortment of brightly colored trade cloths. Jim gave them but a passing glance, but at the sight of a spare whip lash hanging from one of the ribs which supported the wagon's tented cover he chuckled happily. He took it down and ran it through his hands, examining every inch of it.

Fifteen minutes later he had discarded the old lash in favor of the new and, standing up, he gave an exhibition of whip cracking that made the two men grin with renewed pleasure at their luck in finding such an expert driver.

Perhaps it was just as well that they could not see the expression in Jim's eyes as the thirty foot lash, ending in a *voorshlag* not thicker than twine, flew out over the ear of the leaders and then recoiled with two deafening reports.

"A time will come," Jim muttered, "and soon. In a few days my *baas* will take the trail—and the pace of the oxen will be slow, very slow. And then—" His eyes gleamed with triumphant anticipation.

That night at sundown, after the Oxen were outspanned, Jim was ordered to prepare the evening meal. He went about his task with a will and grinned with satisfaction when no notice was taken of the fact that he had baked a much larger quantity of veld bricks than the three of them could possibly eat.

The meal over, the two men helped Jim tether the oxen for the night and then spread eagled him to one of the wagon wheels, lashing him securely to its spokes.

Then the white men sought the comfort of their blankets; in a little while they slept—fitfully, the distant roaring of lions making nightmares of their dreams.

But sleep was a long time coming to Jim; not that the lions bothered him or, especially, his uncomfortable position. He was worrying about his *baas;* wondering how soon that man would take to the trail and the manner of his leaving the *kraal* of Janva. And then, at the remembrance of the clothes he had left behind on the river's bank, Jim groaned aloud.

"Au-a!" he muttered. "I am a fool and a son of fools. My *baas* will have to travel naked—and the season of rains is at hand."

ABOUT THIS time the Major was interviewing Janva, the headman. That weasel-faced individual was wearing the Major's white duck riding breeches and tunic coat; around his head he had wrapped, turban wise, the Major's shirt; one of the sleeves hung down over his face.

"And so," he concluded triumphantly, "I take all that is yours, white man, in payment for that which we have given you."

The Major nodded gravely.

"If it is your custom, Janva, to demand payment for such hospitality which others are glad to give, then all that you have taken of mine can not repay you for your gifts to me. And—pardon! But that which you have about your head—a shirt we call it—should be worn upon the body, and the coat is not worn as you have it. The buttons should be in front."

With a show of confusion Janva made the changes in his costume indicated by the Major's scathing voice.

"Ah! That is better," the white man continued. "But the shirt should go inside the trousers. Yah! So. Now—" he looked with mock admiration at the headman—"now you look like a great chief."

Janva fidgeted. He sensed, for all that the white man's face was so grave, that he was making fun of him.

"In three days the weakness of fever should have left you," he said truculently. "In three days you leave my *kraal.*"

"And you will not send a messenger to the mission for me?"

"Nay; I and my people have no dealings with those soft fools. Further, what proof have I that I will be paid for my messenger's service?"

"My word," the Major began softly.

"Wo-we! Your word! Almost I might be willing to accept it for I think you are not as many white men whose word is of less value than a grain of dust. And yet—listen: your Hottentot told us many stories concerning your wealth and exceeding wisdom. Because of that we obeyed his commands in all things. *Au-a!* He ordered me about as if I were a dog, and I obeyed him, thinking of the reward to come. Yet heed the end of it. Strangers came with a wagon drawn by sixteen oxen and the Hottentot entered their service, discarding you for whom he had professed such great respect."

"Of his own free will he went, you say?" the Major questioned.

"With my own eyes I saw him jump into the wagon," Janva replied. "He went swiftly; therefore, willingly."

"A man runs swiftly if a lion is close at his heels," the Major remarked sententiously. "You would not say such a man ran willingly. However—" he made a lightning play with his revolver—"that is of no matter. But think on this,

Janva: your life and that of many of your young men I hold in my hands. Under the threat of the death this contains I could demand, and take, anything of yours I wished. But that is not my way, neither is it my desire to instruct you in the way of true hospitality. Your greed has so fattened your cheeks that your eyes are closed. So! Tomorrow I shall go out to shoot a buck to pay for the food I will eat tomorrow and the food I will take with me when I leave the following day. And that, together with the clothes you have taken, will repay you in full for the little you have done for me. That is the bargain?"

"Truly, white man. I require no more from you."

The Major nodded.

"And never have I so cheaply repaid hospitality," he muttered, "but the bargain is of your own making. I shall not forget." Then aloud, "Now go! Talking to one whose craft is that of a hyena's, who boasts himself to be a brave warrior because he has captured the empty clothes of a white man, saps my strength. Go—I need sleep."

For a moment Janva hesitated; he was almost of a mind to obey the generous laws of hospitality which prevailed in his tribe. Then he remembered the exclamations of admiration with which his wives had greeted his appearance in the white man's clothing and vanity triumphed over his better impulses.

"Three more days you may stay with us, white man," he said as he rose to his feet.

"I shall be gone in less than two," the Major replied and waved his hand in a gesture of dismissal.

Again Janva hesitated and then, shrugging his shoulders disdainfully, strutted pompously from the hut.

THE FOLLOWING morning, before the rising of the sun, the white men released Jim from the wheel and, refusing the unfortunate man a chance to warm himself before the fire, ordered him to turn the oxen loose that they might feed before commencing the day's trek.

As Jim moved sluggishly to obey the order—every movement a torture by reason of the blood which was flowing slowly back into his cramped limbs, Pete struck him viciously across the back with a *sjambok*, cutting through his thin coat and raising a red, livid welt.

"None of that, you *verdoemte* fool," Hans snarled. "We lost one driver because you couldn't keep your hands off him, and wasted a lot of time on the road we couldn't spare. I don't intend to lose this nigger."

Pete looked as if he were going to make some heated retort but, intimidated by the evil menace in the other man's beady eyes, he choked back the words.

"I can handle niggers and cattle, Hans," he mumbled instead.

"The only way you know how to handle niggers is to kill them," Hans mocked. "That's all right when they're of no more use to you. But until then, Pete, hands off. And as for you handling cattle— Hell! I saw how you handled them at the ford yesterday. A hell of a partner you are. Killing's all you're good for."

"And that's a lot, I tell you, ma-an," Pete protested. "Without killing, where would we be now? Tell me that? *Ach sis!* No, I'll tell you. We'd be sitting down by our wagon, back yonder, our noses filled with the stink of our dead cattle. And we'd be waiting for the police to come by and arrest us. But—" he laughed boisterously—"an old fool of a transport rider comes by and—look you—a dead man has no need of cattle or wagon. And so—"

He broke off suddenly as Jim came and squatted humbly by the fire, spreading his hands to its cheerful blaze.

"Get skoff, nigger," Pete growled and then, slyly, as Jim rose to obey, "Today you understand the *taal*, eh? Yesterday you pretended not to. You think to throw dust in our eyes—but I am too *slick* for you. That you will find."

Half an hour later, while the two men wolfed the food he had prepared for them, Jim announced that he would get the oxen in.

"By the time you have skoffed, *Baas*," he said to Hans, "all will be ready to trek."

Hans nodded.

"See you play no tricks, Jim," he warned. "If you try to run away you will find that this—" he patted his rifle— "runs faster than you."

"Why should I run," Jim expostulated in innocent amazement, "I am your dog."

He strolled away, pretending to nibble at a large *veld brick* inside of which he had baked several thick slices of bacon.

"You keep your hands off that nigger, Pete," Hans ordered, adding, with a vicious leer, "at least until this job is finished. He's forgotten his old *baas*—niggers don't know the meaning of loyalty—and he'll serve us well if we treat him decent."

Despite his apparent willingness for speed, the sun was high above the horizon before Jim had yoked up all the oxen and the trek resumed.

"They do not know me well yet, *Baas*," he concluded his long winded explanation to the cursing complaints of the two men. "They would not come when I called. That Biffel now—"

"Oh, *tula*," Hans said wearily as he raked his horse with his spurs and cantered ahead of the wagon.

At the noonday halt Jim was again instructed to prepare skoff, and once again he disappeared into the bush with a huge portion of food. He carried, also, a water bag which he had discovered in the wagon.

And, once again, there was a delay in starting. True, the beasts came quickly to Jim's call but *yoke-skeyes** will break and it was not Jim's fault that there were no spare ones in the wagon!

"If the *baas* had not tied me last night," he said wistfully, "I should have made spare ones then. Tonight, if the *baas* permits—"

There was hard wood—stink wood—close at hand and only an hour elapsed before Jim had fashioned *skeyes* to replace the broken ones, and the trek was resumed.

THE NEXT day the setting sun was hidden by inky clouds. Later, low-rumblings of thunder sounded in the distance and the night's darkness was split by spasmodic flashes of lightning.

And Jim—they had given him blankets and had permitted him to make a bed beneath the wagon—chuckled and sang happily far into the night as he fashioned spare *yoke-skeyes* with a side-ax; he sang until the monotony of his chant and the *chop-chop* of his ax on the hard wood got on the nerves of the two men and they loudly yelled to him to, "Shut up!"

During the great darkness which presages the dawn, the long threatening storm suddenly broke. The rain descended

---

*   The pieces of wood—about fifteen inches long—which, passed through the yoke, go on each side of the bullocks' necks.

in solid sheets, turning the ground into a quaking quagmire; lightning crackled all about the wagon and the concussion of thunder was almost continuous.

The oxen milled about, lowing in a frenzy of fear.

"Oh-he! Baas Hans! *Baas* Pete!" Jim called frantically as he passed among the oxen, soothing them with his presence. "Come help me. *Au-a!* They will stampede. They are like frightened children. Come quick—they will break their legs in the trek chain!"

He laughed inwardly as the two men hastened to his aid, falling over each other in the darkness, slipping in the ooze, drenched to the skin.

Once, shouting that he was going to get some needed ropes from the wagon he left the men among the frightened beasts. Before he rejoined them he had removed one of the boxes from the wagon—nodding his head sagely at its great weight—and had hidden it behind a bush some distance back along the trail.

Morning broke; the storm had abated but a cold, gray, mistlike rain persisted.

"We will trek now," Pete ordered irritably, his face blue, his teeth chattering.

"If we trek while it yet rains," Jim protested, "the oxen will get yoke sore and then they will not pull. And—"

"We trek, dog," Pete yelled. "We trek now—inspan."

Jim started to obey, but not quick enough to please Pete who struck at him again and again with a *sjambok*.

Jim lurched forward, falling on his face in his frantic endeavors to get away from the stinging cut of the rhinoceros hide whip. Over and over he rolled in the stinking mire until he came to rest under the belly of the big black bull, Biffel.

And there he crouched listening to the violent quarrel which had broken out between the two white men. Suddenly the stormy words and slimey vituperations were punctuated by a crisp report and Pete, clawing blindly at the air, spun 'round then slumped in a lifeless heap to the ground.

Callously Hans turned him over with his foot, looked at the black rimmed hole in the dead man's forehead with a grin of satisfaction and then, putting his revolver back into its holster turned to Jim.

"Inspan," he said, "and we will trek. The big man will not beat you again. For your sake I have killed him."

"Yah, *Baas*. Thank you, *Baas*," Jim exclaimed with an affectation of deep gratitude. But he was not impressed by Hans' statement. He knew that it was not for his sake that Hans had shown himself to be the killer he was. "Nevertheless," Jim continued, making a final appeal for the sake of the oxen, "it is true what I said. If we trek in the rain the beasts will get yoke sore and then they will not pull and—"

"They will pull far enough," Hans interrupted. "A little more than a forenoon's trek distant there is a river and, once across that, their task—and yours—" he smiled coldly—"is finished. So—*trek jou!*"

Jim, realizing that the little man was in no mood for trifling and was, besides, infinitely more dangerous than the big man, Pete, had ever been, lost no time in getting his oxen on the move.

And now Jim exhibited all his cunning and skill in driving a team. With whip and voice he encouraged the beasts to their best efforts. In response, they pulled with a will, moving the heavy wagon with an ease which might have been expected had the wagon been empty, and the ground firm instead of black, clinging mud.

Yet Jim's voice was never raised in angry abuse; his whip—though its riflelike reports sounded continuously about them—never touched the beasts.

They had been trekking about an hour when Jim halted his span and explored the ground ahead. It sloped gently downward, was wide and grassy and the contour of the ground was broken by patches of mapani bush.

"We cannot cross here, *Baas* Hans," Jim reported. "We must go 'round that way."

By an expressive sweep of his arms he indicated a wide detour that would lengthen the journey by one, possibly two, days' trek.

"We cross here," Hans announced impatiently. "Three hours—and the journey will be over. Go ahead."

"The ground is a mire, *Baas* Hans. We will be stuck. But that other way—there is high ground; there we can make good time."

Hans scowled at him and tentatively fingered the butt of his revolver. Jim returned the scowl, his whip held tightly in his strong hands.

"Trek!" Hans spat out the word and pointed straight ahead.

Jim's face clouded as he thought of the hard labor ahead of the oxen. Then his whip cracked and the trek was resumed.

But now the pace was slow, at times the wagon barely moved and, half an hour later, the oxen stopped dead. Within half a minute the wagon had sunk up to its front axles in mud.

Jim turned despairingly to Hans.

"I told you, *Baas*," he said. "Now we will have to dig out and—"

Hans dismounted and floundering through the thick slime to Jim's side took the whip.

"*Trek jou!*" he shouted and thrashed the beasts unmercifully.

They plunged madly, lost their footing, strained forward again and then in an attempt to avoid the sting of the lash and to ease their necks from the pain of yoke sores, the front oxen swung sharply around. The trek chain tightened but the front wheels were so deeply embedded in mud that the *dusselboom* could not come into line with the chain and snapped with a loud report.

"I told you, I told you, *Baas* Hans," Jim cried, capering frenziedly among the oxen. "Now I'll have to make a new one and we will have to camp here all night. Then, in the morning—"

Hans was speechless with rage. He was so near his goal and now, through his own stupid obstinacy—he had the sense to acknowledge that to himself—he would be delayed days; weeks, if the rain persisted.

Suddenly his rage passed and he smiled contentedly. After all, he thought, things were not so bad.

"Never mind another *dusselboom*," he said. "First we will skoff and then I will ride on for men to come and carry the stuff from the wagon."

"And they will carry the wagon, too?" Jim asked naively.

"The wagon is yours, Jim," Hans said with a laugh. "I give it to you."

"Without the oxen, *Baas*," Jim protested, "of what value the wagon?"

"Make skoff," Hans said, and rubbed his hands together. He had no occasion to grumble. He was almost at the end of a long, perilous trek; the promised reward was great and he shared it with no one.

With splinters from the broken *dusselboom* Jim had a fire going, the billy on to boil for coffee and was grilling slices of bacon at the end of a pointed stick.

He looked up suddenly from his task. Two natives, carrying shields and long throwing *assegais*, were advancing toward the wagon.

They greeted Hans with an air of insolent familiarity which, to Jim's surprise, he did not seem to resent.

"You are late, white man," they said as, squatting on their haunches they noisily ate the food Jim was ordered to cook for them.

"The way was long," Hans replied, "yet, if the wagon had not broken, I would have been at the river by the time appointed."

They laughed incredulously.

"Before you got to the river," one said, "your wagon would have sunk out of sight in the mud." He looked about him curiously. "Where is the other white man—the man with a beard?"

"A mosquito bit him—and he died," Hans answered.

They laughed again. "And you have many such mosquitoes for us to release against our enemies?"

"Yah! In there," Hans replied.

"That is good. Chief Sami will be glad. He will reward you well."

There was silence for a little while. "And what brings you here?" Hans asked suddenly.

"To look for you and also to spy out the land ahead. A number of warriors wait at the river—Chief Sami is with them. When his men have the—the mosquitoes which kill, he leads them against the *kraal* of Janva."

"To what end? I did not know that Chief Sami had a quarrel with Janva."

"Nor has he. He desires only to test the merits of the things you bring us and to train some of his warriors in their use. It is only a small force—but if that small number can wipe out Janva—then Chief Sami knows that he can lead a large expedition against his white enemies. *Wo-we!* And he will be assured of victory. He is wise, our white chief. He does not buy an ox in the dark; neither does he risk his chieftainship until assured there is no risk."

Hans nodded understandingly then, rising to his feet, mounted his horse.

"I go to the river to bring the warriors here," he said. "Before they march against Janva they must carry the loads across the river into Chief Sami's country. Guard the wagon until my return."

"And your Hottentot dog? What of him?"

"He is no dog of mine," Hans answered indifferently. "Do with him what you will."

With a wave of his hand he rode off into the gray mist.

For a little while they heard the soughing sound of his horse's feet in the clinging mud—and then, silence.

The two warriors looked at each other meaningly and grinned.

"Come here, Hottentot," one said as he rose to his feet, an *assegai* poised ready for casting.

Jim—he was about thirty feet away from them, casually flicking at a distant mapani bush with his whip—shook his head. He stood listening for a moment, then grinned as the "Go away" cry of a gray lourie sounded from the trees behind him.

"I have work to do, warrior. The oxen must be outspanned," Jim said and half turned as if to commence the task of unyoking the oxen, but his eye did not leave the *assegai* in the warrior's hand. And so, when with a cunning underhand jerk that man sent his weapon hurtling through the air on its errand of death, Jim was ready for it.

Almost at the last possible moment he swayed slightly so that the *assegai* passed between his arm and body. At the same moment he made play with his whip.

The long lash flicked out with the speed and venom of a striking snake and curled about the naked thighs of the warriors, cutting deep into the flesh and jerking one man off his feet. Before he could recover, or the other man get into action with his spear, Jim made the whip play about the bodies of the two so that they howled for mercy.

"Drop your *assegais*," Jim shouted above the cracking of his whip. "Now crawl on your hands and knees, backward, away from them."

Threatening frightful reprisals they obeyed him and Jim followed up, the lash of his whip flicking about them whenever they showed signs of rising to their feet with the intention of rushing him.

When Jim reached the discarded *assegais* he placed his foot on them and waited with a triumphant air.

There was a pause and then from out of a clump of bush a ludicrous figure emerged.

"Very prettily done, Jim," it drawled in English. "In a manner—a very able manner—you have tamed the shrews, eh, what?"

"Golly damn yes, *Baas*," Jim grinned.

The Major strolled slowly forward. He was dressed in a strange garb concocted from a faded red blanket which was smeared from head to foot with the black mud through which he had been crawling. An unkempt beard hid his powerful jaw; his hair fell in untidy locks from under his battered helmet and his once immaculate polo boots looked only fit for a scarecrow. A monocle gleamed in his eye.

Yet the two warriors who were, at first, disposed to laugh at him felt suddenly awed. In the Major they recognized a man among men.

"Tie 'em up and gag 'em, Jim," the Major ordered, "and then we'll put them in the wagon."

When that was done he sat down before the fire, warming himself, and ate the food Jim quickly prepared for him.

"Would the *baas* like some more bread?" Jim asked, grinning happily. Now he and his *baas* were reunited, all difficulties vanished.

"No, Jim," the Major answered in tones of mock disgust. "For two days I have been living on the *veld bricks* you left behind. Hard bread—and water-soaked bread; bread alive with ants and— *Wo-we!* I am sick of bread."

"I hid bacon in the bread, *Baas*. And there was no other food I could leave. And the water, *Baas?* Did you find that? And the box? And the man who was killed?"

"Yah, Jim. I found them all."

"And the *baas* is quite strong?" Jim looked anxiously at the Major. "He came sooner than I suspected. Not until tomorrow did I expect to see him—though I knew he was here before he gave the call of the 'Go-away' bird."

"I am quite strong, Jim," the Major said gravely, "and I came in time. Tomorrow would have been too late."

Jim nodded.

"Maybe, *Baas*. Yet I did what I could to delay them. Listen!"

He dramatically recounted all that had befallen during the trek.

Jim chuckled softly as he concluded, but the Major's face was stern as he inspected Jim's whip-seared back.

"The man, Pete, has already paid for that, *Baas,*" Jim protested. "Yet he was only a temper mad fool. With him, alone, I could have dealt. It is the other man who is all evil. Him, I feared. So shall we go, *Baas,* before it is too late. You shall ride the horse of the man who is dead and I, holding a stirrup strap, will run by your side. Come—"

He moved impatiently as the Major shook his head.

"No, Jim! There is work to be done."

"What a man!" Jim exclaimed. "What work, *Baas?*"

"First tell me what passed between those two warriors and the man Hans. I could not hear—I dared not come any closer."

Jim gave a quick resumé of their conversation.

"And what, think you, Jim," the Major asked when he was finished, "was in that box you hid in the bush for me to find? What in these other boxes?"

"They spoke of mosquitoes. *Baas,*" Jim muttered uncertainly. "But I am no fool, I—"

"No. You are no fool, Jim. That box held rifles and these other boxes—"

"Well then, *Baas,*" Jim interrupted impatiently. "To the meat of the matter and then let us trek."

"What have you heard of this Chief Sami, Jim?"

"Nothing that is good, *Baas.* That is why I say—let us trek before it is too late. He is an evil white man who has made himself the chief of a tribe. He is cruel and glories in torture—'specially in torturing men of his own race."

"And think you, Jim," the Major asked softly, "that we can leave these guns fall into the hands of his warriors?"

Jim's face lighted.

"If that is the work you have in mind, *Baas,* it is soon done. Let us set fire to the wagon and then—trek."

The Major considered this for a moment.

"It is not enough, Jim. The rain might put the fire out before any harm was done. Besides—for work performed there must be pay."

"The pay is death, *Baas,*" Jim grumbled. "The wagon is a good one," the Major said gaily. "And the oxen—what of the oxen, Jim?"

"They are good beasts," Jim's eyes, glowed with admiration. "After I have schooled them a little they will pull a loaded wagon out of thicker mire than this. That bull Biffel—"

The Major laughed.

"What a man you are, Jim! Have you forgotten that our pay is death? Unless—unless our pay should be the wagon and cattle."

"The wagon is already mine, *Baas.* The man Hans gave it to me. As for the cattle— What game do we play, *Baas?*"

"Come, Jim. We must work swiftly. There is no time to waste. As we work, we will talk."

They climbed up into the wagon and pried the lids off the boxes. Some contained rifles; others ammunition; still others parts of a machine-gun which the Major quickly assembled and placed in position at the front of the wagon.

That done, the Major took twenty of the rifles and hid them cleverly in the bushes to the right and left of the wagon, fixing them securely with stakes, loading and cocking the triggers, aiming them so that they would discharge harmlessly into the air. Then he tied stout twine to the triggers and ran the twenty lines to the wagon, arranging everything so that a pull on the lines would fire the rifles.

The rest of the guns he and Jim smashed on the wheel of the wagon.

He and Jim then arranged the interior of the wagon so that a match, quickly applied to a fuse, would blow everything sky-high.

"That will be our last recourse," the Major muttered in English. "If everything else fails—" Then, in the vernacular, "Does the man Hans wear a beard, Jim?"

"No, *Baas.*"

The Major whistled gaily as he searched amongst the debris of the wagon.

"Hot water, Jim," he called as he located a razor. "I will shave and then you can throw a bucket of water over me. I'm filthy."

HALF AN hour later the Major, his face clean shaven, his black hair—Jim had trimmed it expertly—brushed back from his forehead in an immaculate pompadour and dressed in garments which had belonged to the big Boer, Pete, sat on the driver's seat and expounded his plan of campaign to Jim.

He chuckled as a sudden thought struck him.

"I was thinking," he explained to Jim, "of Chief Janva. He is being well paid for his hospitality. We place ourselves between him and the warriors of Chief Sam. If we were not here the people of Janva would be wiped out."

"Ugh!" Jim grunted. "That pig! But the *baas* is always just. He always pays. Chief Janva should—"

He broke off suddenly and going to the rear of the wagon looked back across the veld.

Returning, he said quietly, "Men of Janva's *kraal* are coming, *Baas!*"

The Major whistled thoughtfully. "They will be of use, Jim."

Presently six men, mounted on the long horned racing oxen, rode up to the wagon in single file.

They halted and stared incredulously at the Major.

"What want you?" he asked calmly.

They scowled at him, then their leader, pointing to the broken *dusselboom* of the wagon, said, "Our work is done. You can go no farther."

"You mean?"

"*Au-a!* Why question? From the south drum talk came to us that you were taking guns to Chief Sami and Janva sent us to stop you. Some warriors follow us and a messenger has gone to the white police."

The Major frowned at that.

"And did the drums tell you," he asked, "that Chief Sami is on his way to this place with an armed force? Did the drums say that Chief Sami intends to take the guns and march against Janva?"

The men looked at each other in consternation.

"If this be true," they muttered, "we are lost. Unless," one added hopefully, "Janva's warriors come here before Sami's."

The Major ignored their muttered comments and continued. "Think you that I am on Sami's side? I tell you that the men, whose wagon this is, stole my servant from me and I—as soon as the sickness left me—followed on their trail. But a little while ago I came up with them. And this is what I find. One white man had killed the other—you found his body?"

"Yah, and wondered."

The Major waved his hand.

"The greed of one man made him kill the other. But that is no matter. The man who was left has ridden to Chief Sami, telling him to bring his warriors to the wagon. In a little while they will be here."

"*Wo-we!*" they exclaimed in distress. "And Janva's warriors are a three-hour trek distant. They will come too late. But—" suspiciously—"how do we know you are speaking a true word?"

"Look in the wagon and tell me what you see," the Major said.

One of the men rode 'round to the rear and peered through the tented cover.

"Two of Sami's warriors are there," he announced to the others. "They are bound hand and foot. Gags are in their mouths so that they cannot speak."

"They are Sami's scouts," the Major said swiftly. "Would I treat them so if I were Sami's friend?"

"Maybe not, white man," the leader said doubtfully. "But you are, and the guns—and the drums said—"

"Listen," the Major interrupted, realizing that there was no time for parley; indeed, from the expression on Jim's face he guessed that the Hottentot could already detect sounds of Sami's approaching men. "Here," he patted the machine-gun, "I hold the lives of many warriors. It is the gun of a thousand voices. You have heard of it?"

"Aye."

"Then you know that I have no reason to fear you. If I am on Sami's side there is nothing you can do to stop me. No. Nor Janva's impi could not stop me. But I am not on Sami's side. And Janva's impi will not come in time. Listen!"

He held up his hand for silence and they could hear the chants of warriors hastening toward them.

They surrendered suddenly to the Major's judgment.

"What must we do, white man?" they asked. "If you are not on our side—all our people will be wiped out. How can we stand against Sami's men, and they armed with guns?"

"The white police will save you from that," the Major said.

"There we lied, white man. No messenger has been sent. Janva planned to take the guns for himself."

The Major smiled coldly.

"He will not get them. They will be destroyed when this incident is finished." It did not suit his plans to tell them that the guns were already destroyed. "Now let one of you take the horse and ride back, bidding Janva to make great speed. And you others, tie up your oxen with mine and then hide among the bushes. When I give the word you will show yourselves. The Hottentot shall go with you to give you further orders.

"Is it understood?"

"Aye, *inkosi,*" they answered dutifully and hastened to obey his commands.

Presently the wagon was deserted save that the Major, his steel-gray eyes shining with the joy of adventure, sat by the machine-gun, polishing his monocle—waiting.

The chant of the marching warriors sounded nearer—nearer.

Two horsemen rode into view and at their heels ran some sixty warriors. Crouching down the Major remained unseen, his presence unsuspected.

But when the horsemen and their followers were within a hundred yards of the wagon he rose suddenly to his feet.

"Halt!" he called. "Hands up, Dirty Sam! You, too, Hans!" And, quickly, in the vernacular, "Stand fast, warriors."

They halted, amazed; the warriors talking in high-pitched excited tones; the two white men abusing and cursing each other.

"I tell you," the Major heard Hans say with a voice that had a note of fear in it, "that I have led you into no trap. That man is a white kaffir. I saw him at Janva's *kraal*. He is alone. Come!"

He would have spurred forward but the other—he wore the hideous regalia of a witch doctor—leaned forward and caught hold of Hans' bridle reins, pulling that man's horse back on its haunches with a powerful yank.

"You wait with me," he snarled. "If this is a trap you have led me into—you will not escape. If you have played fair with me, there is no need of haste. We will see."

At his hoarse commands his men quickly scattered, dropped to the ground and started to crawl stealthily toward the wagon.

"Call your dogs to heel," the Major called.

Whipping his revolver from its holster, Hans fired at him.

"A clever miss," the white renegade sneered.

His further words were drowned in the vicious *rat-tat-tat* of the machine-gun and a stream of bullets thudded into the mud almost at his horse's feet.

The warriors halted, looking to their chief for further orders. This affair was not to their liking. To find the weapons with which they had expected to wipe out Janva's people, turned against them, nonplussed them, robbed them of their fighting spirit.

The renegade swore bitterly at Hans, and he shortened his grip on the stabbing *assegai* he held in his hand.

"He is alone, I tell you," Hans protested. "I've played fair with you, Sam. You can trust me."

"Pete trusted you and you've told me what you did to him! But we will see. If he is alone—"

He gave another order to his men, and they crept forward again, taking advantage of every inch of cover.

Assegais began to hurtle through the air. One stuck in the front of the wagon close to the Major's feet; another struck the big bull, Biffel, in the flank, causing it to bellow with pain.

At that Jim rushed forward from the bushes, yelling with rage, flourishing his long whip.

He pulled the *assegai* from the wound, spoke soothingly to the bull and then, at a sharp command from the Major, retreated swiftly to the bushes again, yelling fierce threats.

"Call off your dogs, Sam," the Major drawled again. "I have no desire to kill them, but—"

There was another burst of fire from the machine-gun; yells of pain indicated that some of the bullets had found a chance billet.

"And I am not alone, Sam," the Major shouted, as he pulled, one after the other, the triggers of the hidden guns.

At the same moment Jim and the warriors of Janva yelled loudly, running to and fro, shaking their spears, conveying the impression that the bush was alive with men.

"You swine!" Sam yelled as he drove his *assegai* deep into Hans' side.

As Hans toppled slowly forward and slid from his horse to the ground, the renegade's horse reared and plunged madly, unseated its rider and galloped swiftly away.

Seeing the leader down, Sami's warriors' threw their remaining *assegais* in panic stricken haste, then turned and ran swiftly from the place.

Meanwhile Hans, a vindictive spark of life still left in him was crawling painfully toward the renegade, who, half stunned by his fall was standing up, gazing about him in bewilderment. Then his eyes fell on Hans and with a yell of rage he leaped on the man he believed had betrayed him.

For a little while they struggled, then—before the Major could reach them—there was a muffled report—another. Then both were very still.

TWO HOURS later Janva, with his warriors, arrived on the scene. Instead of the bloody battle they had expected, a very peaceful scene awaited them.

The wagon had been dug from the mire and was now faced around, heading south, the oxen were inspanned ready for trekking, and Janva's scouts—the men who had remained with the Major—were seated about a fire, their bellies filled with vast quantities of food and smoking contentedly.

The Major and Jim, seated at the front of the wagon, watched with amusement the expression on Janva's face as his scouts told him of all that had happened; pointing to the pile of broken rifles, to the metal scraps which once had been a machine-gun, and to the two mounds which hid the bodies of Hans and the renegade white man Chief Sami.

Presently Janva came over to the wagon, removing the tunic coat and the shirt he wore, as he walked.

"I have been a fool, lord" he said humbly. "Will the chieftain take back that which I stole from him?"

"They are yours," the Major said carelessly. "I have no need of them."

"Au-a!" Janva fidgeted uneasily. "It is a great thing you have done for me. But for you my warriors would now be in the land of spirits. What reward—?"

"What I did, I did with no thought of you, Janva; with no thought of reward. Now leave me, for I would sleep."

He rose and made his way into the interior of the wagon where Jim had prepared a bed for him.

Janva groaned miserably. Then his face brightened.

"Lord!" he called. "I shall see to if that there is always a hut kept ready at my *kraal* for you—or for any white man who has need of it. There shall be food in plenty for whoever comes seeking food for him, for his cattle, and those who are with him. And there shall be no thought of payment. What else I can do—I will do."

"You will have done enough, Janva, if you do that much," the Major answered sleepily. "Yet, remember; always, for work done, there must be payment. That is only just. Now, go in peace."

"Aye, lord. May your path always be smooth."

Jim grinned proudly at Janva.

"Said I not that my *baas* was a man amongst men? He is the Major—and I, I am Jim, his servant."

"He is a man indeed," Janva agreed, "and you also—" he grinned—"are no child. Now I go to rejoin my children and hear more of the marvel of this fight. And you?"

"We trek!" said Jim.

His long whip cracked, the oxen strained at their yokes, the wagon moved easily.

"Jim," the Major called.

"Yah, *Baas?*"

"This morning we were beggars; now we possess a wagon and sixteen oxen. For the little we have done—the payment is great. Great, that is, if the oxen are of any use."

"The little we have done," Jim chuckled. Then, indignantly, "They are kings among oxen, these cattle of ours. Now that black bull, Biffel, he—"

He broke off as the Major chuckled softly. His *baas* was making fun of him; poking good humored fun at his inordinate love for cattle.

"*Wo-we!*" he exclaimed as he made his whip slam over the heads of the leaders. "*Trek jou!*"

www.ingramcontent.com/pod-product-compliance
Lightning Source LLC
Chambersburg PA
CBHW020258030726
47499CB00001B/248